THE DEPUTY AND HIS ENFORCER

THE KINCAID PACK BOOK 3

KIKI CLARK

THE DEPUTY AND HIS ENFORCER
The Kincaid Pack Book 3

A deputy bent on finding the truth and the Enforcer whose job it is to stop him...

Nothing is more important to Marcus Rivera than protecting his pack, so he doesn't understand why he has the sudden urge to tell a nosy human deputy things he shouldn't. Marcus follows the rules. Always. But something about Robson's scent has him tempted to break them.

The gorgeous red-head Deputy Robson Medina has been following has a secret. He just knows it, and he won't stop looking until he finds out everything he can about the alluring man. Even if the idea of Marcus being a criminal seems less and less likely the more Robson learns.

As the tension between them continues to grow, it stokes a fire inside Marcus he's never felt before. One that's driving him to trust his wolf's instincts and release the stranglehold Marcus has always had on his control. But when Robson gets a painful glimpse of the magical world Marcus lives in, they have to decide how much they're willing to risk to have it all.

The Deputy and His Enforcer is the third book in the Kincaid Pack series and features a wolf shifter in need of a family, a Puerto Rican human with more than his fair share, furry cuddles, creative mating practices, and a happily ever after.

ACKNOWLEDGEMENTS

As always, this book would probably still be a half-finished file on my computer without my amazing alpha reader, Marina Vivancos. Without her encouragement, enthusiasm, and insight, I would be lost.

When I began writing this book, I quickly realized Robson would need a big family. But naming all his siblings (and aunts and niece) seemed daunting! Thankfully, I had help. :-)

My reader group on Facebook, Kiki's Korner, supplied me with a ton of great suggestions and made it difficult for me to choose but I finally got all the Medinas named.

A special thank you to:

Kai Moncada, Meredith Davidson-King, Mike Van Eimeren, Abby Dixon, Shony Kimi, Cynthia Charron, Lila Perez, Margaret Emme, Jasmine Lingle, Sofia Alvez Perez, Sandy Cooper, Michelle Slagan, Kimberly Beaird Misevich, Lesa Brockwell, Lois Moore, Millie Alice, Crystal Camille, and Eliz Navarro.

And last but certainly not least, an enormous thank you to my two sensitivity readers, Lila Perez and Sandy Cooper. Your willingness to answer my questions about Puerto Rican families, customs, expressions, foods, nicknames—and anything else I thought of—made this book so much better. Robson's family means so much to me and you helped me more than you could ever know to make sure they were real and authentic.

For everyone who has ever felt alone

THE KINCAID PACK SERIES

Prequel: A New Pack for New Year
(Victor & Cole)

The Alpha and His King
(Rick & Kai)

The Second and His Bonded
(Bennett & Kieran)

The Deputy and His Enforcer
(Marcus & Robson)

The Hunter and His Mates
(Drake, Jamie, & Gabriel)

The Enforcer and His Heart
(Nico & Keegan)

The Witch and His Doctor
(Carter & Damien)

CHAPTER ONE

"Ωhat the hell are you doing..."

Robson Medina scooted down in his seat but kept his eyes on the giant ginger slowly exiting the big black SUV a few parking spaces over. *Marcus Rivera.* It had been two weeks since he'd had the misfortune of meeting Rivera and his buddies at a crime scene the Meyerville police chief had kicked Robson out of and covered up.

But the chief had let Rivera and his friends stay.

Robson had hidden his car a little way away from where the dead body had been found. He'd watched and waited, but no ambulance had ever shown up, no more police vehicles, not even the county coroner. Nothing. Only an old beater driven by an extremely attractive Black woman, who'd looked toward where he was hidden but couldn't have been able to see him.

After that night, he'd approached the sheriff about the man the chief had called *Kincaid* and asked to be allowed to do some poking around, telling him that something hadn't felt right. There had been a dead body and an ominous note —yet nothing was even mentioned in the paper or local news. The sheriff had told him, in no uncertain terms, to mind his own fucking business and to stay away from Kincaid and anyone associated with him.

So of course, Robson was risking his job as a deputy to follow Kincaid, Rivera, and the others every spare moment he had.

He watched Rivera's tall, lean frame approach the weird shop on Main Street called *Wicca We Can*, cradling a dead plant in one of his arms, and hold the door open for a couple of people exiting. Rivera exchanged a few words and the smallest smile imaginable with them, but that didn't put the others off, their grins large as they waved goodbye to Rivera.

Robson lost sight of him as he slipped inside the store, but his phone rang before he could decide if he wanted to try and sneak in the back or something insane like that.

Groaning at the name on his cell's screen, he answered with an impatient "What?"

"Wow. Someone's crabby." His brother Hector laughed in his ear, and Robson considered just hanging up. Being the oldest of eight meant he was allowed to do that if he wanted to.

As long as his mom didn't find out. A devout Puerto Rican Catholic and new widow, she would be very disappointed if she found out he was being mean to his siblings.

Sighing, he said, "Just busy. What do you need?"

"Well, I thought I was having a beer with my brother, but that doesn't seem to be happening. So I guess what I need is to find out what's been going on with you. You aren't still following those people, are you?" The teasing tone had fallen away by the time Hector finished speaking, sounding concerned for Robson's mental health more than anything else, his tone delicate.

Finally taking his eyes off the front of *Wicca We Can*, he rubbed at his face and the three days' worth of stubble on his jaw. Fuck. Maybe Hector was right to be worried. Since he'd started following Rivera and the others, he'd let everything else lapse, including spending time with his family. The whole reason he was back in fucking Meyerville, Michigan, to begin with.

"Shit. I forgot we were going to Tommi's for a drink. Sorry." He hesitated, not sure whether he should admit what he was doing or not, but then decided to go for it. Hector was the only one he'd even told about his unsanctioned investigation, needing to vent about his frustrations after his conversation with the sheriff. "I'm... Yeah, I'm in town. I followed one of them to that witch shop. He was cradling a dead plant in his arms, man. Like, what the hell?"

Hector didn't say anything for a moment. "Robito... I know you saw some shit during your tours overseas—"

"I'm not making this up," he said, tone icy. "Something about these people stinks, Hector, and I'm going to figure out what it is."

It was Hector's turn to sigh. "Fine. Just don't... Don't do anything that would require me to bail you out of jail or will get you fired, okay? Mom couldn't handle that right now."

Ouch. A direct hit like only a sibling could give. Their mom had been struggling since their dad died about five months ago. Cancer. The ornery old bastard hadn't told anyone he wasn't feeling so hot until it had been too late. Robson had just been wrapping up his second six-year contract with the army and thinking about sticking it out for a full twenty when he got the news. It had seemed like a good idea until he was needed at home since it wasn't like he knew how to do anything else or had a spouse waiting at home for him.

But his mom had needed him. His dad might have been a driving force in pushing him out of Meyerville and into the arms of the US government, but his mom had always been the most important person in his life.

When he'd heard about his dad being in the hospital with stage four lung cancer, he'd immediately started the process of getting discharged. He was the oldest, and his youngest siblings were still living at home; his baby sister was only thirteen and barely knew him. They needed his help, and it was his responsibility to take care of the family now.

Hector was right though. Following Rivera and the others not only hadn't netted him any good intel—it could cost him his shitty-ass job if he was caught. Despite not liking working part-time as a county deputy, it allowed him to help his mom with bills until a full-time position opened up. His stomach soured at the thought of sitting at a speed trap for the rest of his life.

No, what he needed to do was change tactics.

"I won't, man. I promise."

The door to the shop opened and Marcus stepped out, followed closely by a dark-skinned woman he recognized. Tashmica Torres. She'd been the one who joined the group at the scene of the dead body. He narrowed his eyes as she laughed and raised up onto her tiptoes to kiss Marcus's cheek, his white skin flushing right away.

His hand tightened on his phone as he watched her grin up at Rivera and wipe at his cheek where she'd left a smudge of bright red lipstick. "I gotta go though. Text me to reschedule about the beer."

"Wait! I also called to tell you that Mom and Reesa changed their minds and decided to have the baby shower after all."

Robson bit back a groan. Reesa was the oldest girl, third oldest after him and Hector, and pregnant with her first baby. She was due to pop in like a month and had said she didn't need a baby shower—even though his mom and sister-in-law, Shannon, Hector's wife, had tried to convince her that it was okay to celebrate the baby. But Reesa was sensitive and had confided in Robson that she felt bad forcing people to buy gifts and come to a party so soon after their dad had died.

Robson thought she was being silly—their old man had been an asshole, but he'd had a soft spot for the girls, so maybe Reesa was more broken up about his death than he or Hector or the other boys were.

"Let me guess. They want to hurry and have it before that baby slides out of her?"

Hector laughed and groaned. "Gross, dude. But yeah. So we're all hands on deck to get it done. Shannon and I will be over to the farmhouse Saturday morning to help plan things. Be prepared to at least watch the kids like a good doting uncle even if you don't help organize things for the shower."

"I can help with the shower," he grumbled, eyes zeroing in on the plant Rivera was holding as he headed back toward his SUV, Torres hurrying down the sidewalk in Robson's direction. When he glanced at her, he saw she was looking at him. She winked, and he scooted down farther, tugging at the baseball cap he was wearing.

The plant Rivera now held had to be a different one because it no longer looked dead. It was green and healthy, but the brown-and-blue-glazed pot looked exactly the same.

Robson shifted his car into gear when Rivera started his SUV, preparing to follow him out of town. Not that it would do much good. Every time he'd tried to tail any of them north of town, he'd somehow lose them. It was the craziest thing. He'd have eyes on their vehicle from a bit of a distance, then it was like he would blink and the taillights he was following would vanish. There had to be some sort of hidden turnoff he was missing, but it wasn't like there were a ton of trees or anything near where it always happened.

So most of his stalking happened in town only, which was mostly why he'd failed to garner any real intel. Rivera hadn't even popped up but a handful of times in the couple of weeks Robson had been staking out the town. And he'd only been able to follow him back to a perfectly nondescript two-story house once. When he'd driven past other times to see if Rivera was home, the place had looked empty and dark.

Maybe he's with that woman at night. He gritted his teeth at the idea, the mental image of the two of them entwined together in less clothing than they'd had on when standing on the sidewalk in front of *Wicca We Can* pissing him off for some reason.

Hector was chuckling in his ear. "Just try and be there and be nice to her husband, asshole."

Robson checked for traffic, then pulled out of his spot after a car got between him and Rivera's SUV. "That guy bugs me. He can't keep his hands off Reesa, and he, like, sniffs her hair and shit. It's weird."

"So him adoring her and liking the way she smells is weird to you? You gotta get laid, man. Just give him a chance, okay? You're the big brother, and Reesa will be disappointed if she realizes you don't like him. Then she'll kick your ass."

"She's eight months pregnant," he said, unable to stop himself from laughing at the idea of their tiny sister, who was currently as wide as she was tall, trying to kick his ass. "I think I can take her."

Hector tsked at him. "You've forgotten that she plays dirty. She'll totally knee you in the groin if you aren't careful, just like when we were kids."

He winced at the memory. She'd done just that a couple of times when he and Hector had ganged up on her or been particularly mean. The three of them were the closest in age and had stayed close, but when they were young, he and

Hector could be downright cruel to her at times. They'd totally deserved getting kneed in the nuts.

Frowning, he watched Rivera turn into the parking lot of the community rec center, but he kept going, driving past and circling around the block.

"Fine. I'll be nice. Now I really do need to go." He parked on the street on the opposite side of the rec center and stayed in his car, eyes finding Rivera's tall form and dark red hair easily in the surprisingly crowded parking lot.

"I hope because you have a shift, stalker. Stop doing illegal things."

"It's only illegal if the person being stalked feels threatened," he muttered, watching as Rivera was approached by the same woman who'd been present the night of the dead body—Vanessa Wilkins. She was laughably shorter than the men she'd been with, but his instincts had pinged her as dangerous right away. She held herself like a true fighter just like the men did.

"For fuck's sake," Hector muttered. "Goodbye, Robito. See you Saturday."

"Bye," he said absently, slowly lowering his phone. He watched Rivera and the woman go into the rec center with a few other people, his mind turning fast. He really did need to try a new tactic in gaining information about Rivera and the others.

And he was pretty sure he knew exactly how to do it.

When he'd met Kincaid, Rivera, Young, and Wilkins, he'd noticed that Rivera hadn't been able to take his eyes off him. Smirking, he shifted his car into gear and headed for his parents' house. He could work with Rivera's attraction. Maybe set a little honey trap.

He laughed at himself as he cruised outside of town. The group at the rec center had been pretty large, so whatever Rivera and Wilkins were doing there, he hoped he'd have enough time to run home and change, then be back before he left.

Of course, his mom stopped him as soon as he walked into the house.

"Robito? Can you come here, please?" she called from the living room, her lightly accented voice soft and warm like always.

He turned left into the living room instead of running straight up the stairs to his room, and his eyes widened at the boxes of stuff all over the space. "Whoa. What's all this?"

"Just some things for Reesa's shower. I'd ordered some stuff hoping she'd change her mind, and now everything just needs to be organized." She smiled up at him from where she was sitting in the middle of the couch surrounded by ribbons, votive candles, and… candy? Her tiny frame was practically swallowed up by everything around her. But her dark brown eyes, just like his own, were brighter than he'd seen since he'd been home.

"Yeah, Hector called me and told me the news. I thought we weren't getting together to work on stuff for a few days though?" He carefully tiptoed through the piles of things until he reached the multilevel white stand off to the side, eyeing it carefully. "What's this for?"

"The cupcake display. Now, mi sol, would you be a dear and get the rest of the stuff from the garage?"

"There's more?" He looked around the room, then pegged his mom with a stern look. "Mamá, how much have you spent on this shower already?"

"Don't worry about it. I had some money tucked away for things like this." She pushed herself up and gracefully stepped around everything until she was right next to him, setting a hand on his forearm. "Will you be able to come to the shower?"

"Isn't it usually just for women?"

Snorting, she squeezed his arm and moved past him. "Your sister wants her family there. Who cares what people *usually* do."

He couldn't help but shake his head as he followed her to the large kitchen at the back of the house. That sounded just like Reesa—fuck what anyone else says or thinks. "Yeah, okay. Just get me the day and time and I'll make sure I have it off."

Which wouldn't be a problem. He was lucky if he worked three shifts a week. After his request to follow Kincaid and his people was vehemently denied, he'd run a few searches through the database and gotten some names. And he'd noticed his hours had been cut for that schedule and the next. Even though he'd been promised when he was hired that he'd get at least four shifts a week until a full-time position opened up in a year or so.

If the trend continued, he'd need to get a second job. And somehow hide it from his mom, who would insist she go back to working full-time instead.

Eyeing him, she opened the fridge and pulled out some things. "Are you staying? Or are you running off to see your gentleman again?"

Coughing, he glared at her smirk. "I don't have a gentleman. What are you talking about?"

Walking by him, she reached up and patted his cheek, making a face at his facial hair. "I know, mi sol. You've been disappearing and staying gone for hours at a time. What's his name? When do we get to meet him?"

He groaned as he settled at the kitchen table and rubbed at his eyes. "Mamá, no. I don't have a secret boyfriend…"

At her confused face, he stopped. How else would he explain where he'd been?

"What I mean is… We haven't labeled it or anything." He slid his eyes away at her little shriek of happiness, guilt already pooling in his stomach. He mumbled, "But I do have to head out soon."

She gave his forehead a kiss, then quickly made him a sandwich. "Here, eat this so you have plenty of energy for your man."

"Mamá!"

She laughed like a deranged Tinker Bell as she set the plate with a turkey sandwich in front of him. Luckily for him, the back door opened and his brother Mateo stepped inside, covered in dust and muck.

Mateo eyed their laughing mom with wide eyes and a smile. "I got the skid steer running. But we may need to replace it sooner than we thought."

His mom fussed over the mess Mateo was tracking in as Robson's eyes dropped to his food, appetite gone. He had some money saved from when he was in the military, but he'd been hoping to use it for his own place one day, once his mom didn't need so much help with the house and farm and his siblings. Hell, Mateo had taken over running the farm side of things basically before their dad was even sick, so really Robson had just thought he'd need to stick around in the house and help with bills while Annalisse and Valentina were still in school and living there.

"Robito? Teo is going to get the other boxes so you can get going as soon as you're done eating." His mom threw a wink at him and giggled at his groan.

"Hot date, huh?" Mateo grinned as he stepped into the laundry room off the kitchen and began to strip down to his underwear, throwing the clothes in the wash. He'd been wearing them probably since he'd fed the cows that morning, based on the smell.

"Shut up. Go… clean your room or something."

Mateo laughed as he walked past wearing nylon shorts and pulling a gray T-shirt over his head. "Smooth, dude."

If their mom hadn't been watching with a fond smile, Robson might have done something juvenile like throw a wadded-up piece of bread at Mateo's head. Instead, he finished eating, handed the plate to his mom, and jogged upstairs. He'd come home to change, and he wanted to still try and get back before Rivera left the rec center.

Since he'd showered that morning, he just stripped off his cargo shorts and faded T-shirt and pulled on his tightest jeans and a formfitting black tank top that showed off his tattoos and biceps.

As he headed out, Mateo and his mom were in the living room. She called a "Good luck" to him, and he waved, ignoring Teo's laughter.

By the time he got back to the rec center, it had been almost an hour, and he let out a relieved breath when he saw Rivera's SUV still in the same spot.

He parked his car just behind the SUV and popped the hood. Hurrying while trying not to look like he was, he leaned over the engine and pulled loose a random wire. He glanced around with his head still down, making sure no one was around or paying attention to him, but didn't see anyone. Resting his hands on the front bumper, he looked toward the building but didn't see movement. He let his eyes wander, praying Rivera wouldn't be inside for another hour, and then froze when he noticed the sign next to the front door.

He'd driven past the rec center plenty of times since he'd been home, but he hadn't been this close to the building, and it hadn't been there when he left town. In large letters, the sign read Meyerville Community Recreation Center, but underneath, in much smaller font, it said Sponsored by The Kincaid Group.

"What the fuck? Who are these people?"

Robson had a number of theories on what had happened

the night of the body dump and who Kincaid and the others were, but none of those theories made sense with the fact that Kincaid had apparently paid for the rec center to be built. Especially not his prevailing theory that they were traffickers—human or drugs—and that the local authorities and community leaders were either in on it or being paid off.

Straightening, he took in the center with new eyes. The building was two stories and quite large, holding classes and group activities in the classrooms upstairs—including the birthing class Reesa was taking. The main floor apparently had a pool and a couple of basketball courts. And if that weren't enough, the large section of grass next to the building had a lot of jungle gym equipment, and behind the building was a field used for soccer and football.

Robson had actually been surprised by how large and nice it was the first time he'd seen it. Meyerville wasn't that big, and the school had its own fields and classrooms people could use, so why did the community need their own?

But then he'd started noticing how many more businesses were open downtown and how much foot traffic there was. And a few weeks ago, right when the body was found outside of town, there was a fall festival that was apparently an annual tradition now. He remembered some things when he was a kid but nothing like the town-wide festivities he'd seen. His mom even volunteered to help with something, though she'd told him she'd been unsuccessful in getting onto the actual planning committee two years in a row.

The town Robson had left had been dying, like a lot of small towns in Michigan. But now? Meyerville seemed to be… thriving. And growing. There was talk of a housing development maybe being built just outside of town to provide housing for the influx of people moving to the area.

It was all a little… strange.

"Robson?"

Whipping around, he narrowed his eyes at his sister Reesa, her husband, Patrick, and the tall man standing just behind them. *Rivera.*

"Deputy Medina."

Marcus Rivera's voice was a lot softer than his large frame would imply, but the sound of his voice had Robson's dick twitching in his uncomfortably tight jeans.

Ah shit.

CHAPTER TWO

Marcus Rivera was having a weird day.

First, he'd been basically kicked out of his alpha's home for "working too much" and told to go home and get some rest and not to come back for at least twenty-four hours.

That had been strange in and of itself. He'd been buried up to his eyeballs in old Council archives for weeks, trying to find either an old instance of a situation like theirs or maybe a way to usurp the Council's authority.

His gut clenched at the very idea. His entire life he'd lived and breathed the belief that the shifter Council was to be respected and deferred to at all times. They were an absolute authority.

But recent events had shown him that wasn't the truth.

As soon as he'd gotten home to his neglected house, he'd discovered that one of his plants had died while he'd been holed up in the manor. He'd come home a few times, and his neighbor had said they'd have their son pop over to check things and water his plants, but that obviously hadn't happened. As he'd held the small pot in his large hands, he'd felt an overwhelming urge to try and revive it.

There were very few things Marcus allowed himself to truly care about outside of his pack, but his collection of plants was one of them. The sense of purpose and accomplishment he felt when he helped them not only stay alive but to grow and thrive was something he'd rarely felt.

So he'd taken the dead plant to Tashmica, the head of the pack's coven, to see if she could help him bring the thing back to life. While she mixed up a potion to help him, she'd casually brought up the county deputy that had been following all of them whenever they were in town and mentioned that she thought he might like watching Marcus more than the others.

At his confusion, she'd laughed and patted his hand, telling him to take the next opportunity he found to get to know the other man better.

Then when he'd arrived at the rec center for his and Vanessa's first pack mentorship meeting, he'd been floored by the turnout. Adults, teens, and children had all shown up, some interested in becoming mentors but many hoping to learn more about the pack and themselves. It had been overwhelming for a moment to realize that so many of their kind knew so little about themselves, their abilities... their bodies.

He and V had worked on the fly to come up with a new plan to address the needs of everyone, splitting the group into smaller groups and proposing a schedule of speakers and topics.

Having spent years assisting the Council, Marcus had more knowledge about shifters and the formation of packs and the Council than most, so it was agreed that he'd begin the series the following week and talk about their history.

After all of that, he'd stepped outside alongside a few packmates, with V just behind him in a conversation about starting a sex education class, to find Deputy Robson Medina suddenly right in front of him. The human police officer was blocking Marcus's SUV in its spot, but based on his raised hood, he was having some sort of car problems.

Marcus slowed to a stop as his eyes ran over the deputy's body, taking in the sinfully tight jeans and bare arms on display. Medina's skin was tan in a way Marcus's never could be, his pale whiteness never seeming to absorb any UV rays, though his shifter healing kept him from burning at least.

When Teresa O'Neal stepped forward and called Medina by name, Marcus was jerked out of his lustful thoughts and raised his gaze from Medina's fine backside. He nodded at him and used his title to address him, but Medina barely glanced at him before zeroing in on Teresa.

"Reesa, what the hell are you doing here?" The *with him* was unspoken, but Marcus had learned at a young age to read between the lines and infer what was *not* being said since it was usually even more important than what was.

"Me? What are you doing?" Teresa crossed her arms over her pronounced pregnant stomach and glared at the deputy.

Marcus looked between them and stepped forward since it appeared Teresa's mate, Patrick, wasn't going to step in, too busy listening to V's conversation and offering his own suggestions.

"Is everything alright, Teresa?" he asked, keeping Medina in his line of sight but moving between him and Teresa.

Teresa beamed up at him, and Marcus couldn't help but let the corner of his mouth quirk up as well. "Yes, Marcus. He's my brother. My *annoying* big brother."

Oh. He wondered briefly if Rick knew Patrick's mate was related to the deputy harassing them.

"I see" was all he said, running his eyes over Medina once more, then turning back to Teresa. "I'll see you next week?"

"Definitely!" Teresa surprised him by darting forward and

hugging him tightly, her belly bumping into him first, but she made it work. Her head barely reached his pecs she was so tiny, but her hug was fierce. "Thank you for this. With Patrick's family not speaking to him, we were worried about the baby."

She'd spoken so softly he knew her brother couldn't have heard her. His heart clenched at her words, and he lightly embraced her in return. Traditional shifter families, like Patrick's, often disowned family members who took humans as mates, but he hadn't realized the two of them were anxious about the pup.

"If you have specific questions, you are always welcome to call or email me or any of the other... um." He glanced at Medina as Teresa stepped back and winked at him, letting him know she knew he meant the other pack Enforcers. "Or Dr. Bell."

That seemed to grab Medina's attention from where he was frowning at his car's engine. He stepped forward, eyes a little wide and worry filling his scent, making it a little acidic. "Doctor? Are you and the baby okay?"

"We're fine. Dr. Bell isn't that kind of doctor." She grinned at Marcus, then turned to her brother and threaded her arm through his and led him back to his car. "What seems to be the problem here?"

Medina looked back at Marcus, but he couldn't read the other man's expression. Slowly, he breathed in through his nose, trying to pick apart his scent to get clues as to why the deputy had suddenly decided to abandon his covert tactics.

He closed his eyes and parsed through the many layers of smells surrounding him, trying to ignore the other people around and focus solely on Medina. There was... frustration at the top with hints of arousal and confusion, but underneath... Marcus opened his eyes and met Medina's fierce gaze.

Fear.

Medina was afraid of Marcus for some reason.

"You need help, Robson?" Patrick asked as he moved forward, having finished his discussion with V and the others. He threw a thankful look at Marcus as he passed, pushing up his sleeves as he went. Patrick was a mechanic and worked at the garage where the manor vehicles—SUVs owned by the pack and used by Alpha Kincaid and his Enforcers, and sometimes betas, and his mate, Kai—were taken.

"No, thanks," Medina muttered, barely sparing Patrick a glance. "*Oof.*"

Marcus had to work harder than normal to suppress his laughter as Medina turned a glare on his sister, who'd elbowed him in the gut.

Suddenly, Tash's words from earlier that day came back to him. Her instructions to *get to know* Medina rang in his ears. Stopping himself from clearing his throat, he butted into the family squabble happening at the car's hood.

"Deputy Medina, may I have a word, please?"

Teresa narrowed her eyes and looked between him and her brother. "Wait, how do you even know he's a deputy?"

Marcus remained silent, unsure what her brother would want her to know.

"Marcus, we should head out," V said softly from his elbow.

He nodded but didn't take his eyes off Medina.

"We've… met. In an official capacity," Medina finally said, voice hesitant.

Patrick's head popped up from where he'd been leaning over the engine so fast he hit his head on the hood. Teresa fussed over him, momentarily forgetting her suspicions.

Medina stared him down for several long seconds, and Marcus admitted to himself that he was impressed. Even when humans didn't know about shifters, their primal instincts would warn them against challenging them. Marcus's wolf growled softly, not sure how it felt about Medina trying to assert dominance over them, but Marcus hushed him with practiced ease.

"Yeah, okay. Lead the way." Medina lifted his chin a little, large muscular arms crossing over his chest.

"Marcus…" V was annoyed with him, but she'd get it if he explained about Tashmica. They all took her guidance seriously.

"It's okay. You can go to the manor," he murmured, giving her a brief look. She rolled her eyes, but after brushing her hand down his arm to lightly scent him, she strolled toward where her motorcycle was since she hadn't been to the manor yet to grab a pack vehicle.

He wanted to smile at the way she'd touched his arm but didn't. Scenting was important to shifters—especially canines—but not all packs scented the way the Kincaid Pack did. Generally, and in Marcus's experience before coming to Meyerville, scenting only happened between an alpha and his pack or within an immediate family or between mates. But the Kincaid Enforcers were almost like a pack within the pack or a surrogate family, with close bonds, protective instincts, and scenting to strengthen connections.

Without saying anything else to the deputy, he led the way back into the rec center. There was an office on the first floor where the center's manager worked to make sure things ran smoothly. As soon as Marcus knocked on the ajar door, Brianna looked up from their desk and smiled at him.

"Enforcer Rivera, what can I do for—" They stopped when Medina stepped up behind Marcus, and their eyes went wide.

"I need the room, please." He forced himself to give them a slight smile, letting them know everything was okay.

"S-Sure. Of course. I need to go straighten up the room you all were in upstairs anyway. Take your time." They straightened the top of their desk, nodded once to Marcus, then hurried out of the office.

"Well, that was fucking weird," Medina muttered, slipping past Marcus and stepping into the small room. He stopped at the desk and turned to lean his backside against the edge, arms crossed once more. "You sure scared her out of here."

"Them," Marcus corrected, stepping inside as well and closing the door. "Brianna uses they/them pronouns."

Medina's eyebrows furrowed for a second, and then he shrugged. "Okay. Well, you scared them out of here in a hurry."

"They weren't scared of me," he said, clasping his hands behind his back and taking a relaxed stance.

Medina rolled his eyes. "I heard he—them call you *Enforcer*. So you all are mobbed up, huh? That wasn't the top of my list, but I guess it fits." He looked around the office. "You wash money through the rec center or something?"

Marcus was confused, but he didn't let it show. He wasn't overly familiar with humans and their eccentricities, but it seemed strange that they would wash all of their money before using it. Maybe they were overly worried about germs? They didn't have the healing shifters did after all.

"In the pool?" he finally asked, when he realized that was the only water source at the center other than the bathroom sinks.

"What? No." Medina scrubbed at his face. "As in moving dirty money through the place and giving it back as clean bills."

Marcus narrowed his eyes in thought, then shook his head. "There isn't anything large enough except the pool to clean currency, but that doesn't seem sanitary. People swim in there."

Hand still over his face, Medina peered at him through his fingers. "You can't be serious, but you seem fucking serious."

"I'm generally a serious person, yes." He wasn't sure why they were suddenly talking about his demeanor. He realized he needed to take control of the conversation before it got even more out of hand. "I'd like to ask you to stop following us, Deputy."

His hand slowly lowering, Medina's face went slack with surprise. "You know?"

"We've known since the start. I understand you're suspicious of us, but there's no need. We protect this town and the people in it."

He'd assumed that would be the most reassuring thing he could say to a man like Medina, someone who had a history in the military and now worked in law enforcement, but if anything Marcus's words riled him up more.

"Protect it from what? The only reason it would need protecting is *because* you're here," Medina snarled, pushing off the desk and getting closer to Marcus. He was several inches shorter, but his broad body gave him a looming presence. Marcus had always been tall but lean, so he probably seemed weak to someone as physically strong as Medina.

But even the strongest human was no comparison to a pack Enforcer.

Marcus didn't respond to his accusation, partly because it was true but also because he was distracted by the scent of basil growing in Medina's scent. Inhaling deeply, he felt his brows furrow as he tried to decipher what it meant. It was extremely pleasant whatever it was. Marcus had a large basil plant at his house, and he loved to touch the leaves to release their smell.

"Are you seriously not going to say anything? Not even try and deny it?" Medina stepped back slightly. When

Marcus continued to study his face but still didn't speak, Medina shook his head. "Whatever. Just… I'll stay away from you guys if you stay the fuck away from my sister."

"Teresa?"

"Yes, Teresa! I don't know what you have her mixed up in, but she's pregnant and—"

"Her husband is a friend, and they attended a class on mentoring." Marcus studied Medina's angry brown eyes, fascinated by the way they seemed to sparkle with his ire. "I would never put a pregnant woman or her child in danger. You have my word."

"Your word," Medina muttered, studying Marcus just as intensely as Marcus was him. "I'm not sure how much that's worth, Rivera."

"Marcus." The word popped out of his mouth, and he was momentarily stunned by his lack of control. He couldn't deny that he wanted to hear his name—*his,* not his family's— on the handsome deputy's lips.

Medina rolled his eyes and turned toward the back of the room. He paced away from Marcus and ended up at a large bookcase against the back wall of the office. After staring at the books and knickknacks on the shelves silently, he finally spoke without turning around. "You covered up a murder, didn't you?"

"Covered up?"

Medina glared over his shoulder, like Marcus was being deliberately obtuse. "Yes, covered up. As in it wasn't reported to the proper authorities, wasn't investigated, was made to seem like it never happened."

"I see." Marcus nodded. If that was what Medina thought had happened the night the witch Agnes had been found slain and dumped at the edge of the pack's territory, then it was no wonder he was suspicious of them. "No, we did not 'cover up' a murder."

22

Medina turned fully around and eyed Marcus with a narrowed gaze. "So someone is investigating what happened? Evidence was collected? A case is being built so the person responsible can be arrested?"

Marcus tipped his head slightly as he thought about the questions. "Someone is investigating, yes. What little evidence there was where she was found was gathered and has been preserved, yes. All of the information that is being learned is being compiled to make sure the person responsible answers for her death and any other hateful acts they have committed."

"Meaning you all are handling it yourselves and to butt the fuck out?"

Frustration began to gather at the base of Marcus's skull. Why was this human being so difficult? "Meaning... there are things happening that you could not possibly understand. I can appreciate that answer is frustrating for you, but it's the best I can give you. You can verify that with Chief Baskin or Sheriff Daley."

He knew he was failing to get to know the deputy like Tashmica had instructed, but he didn't know how to do that when he couldn't share large sections of himself or his history and when Medina was so suspicious of him.

Medina snorted. "Both of them are in your pockets. But don't worry, I got the message. Stay out of your shit or something awful will happen to Reesa and the baby."

Horror filled Marcus. "What?"

Medina held up his hands. "Sorry, I meant 'an accident' would befall her. That's how you all operate, right? Cut a brake line or faulty wiring in her house. I got it. I understand and I'll back off. Just leave her alone, okay?"

Marcus could do little more than stare at Medina, unable to believe his attempt at explaining what he could to the man had gone so horribly wrong. Medina seemed to take his silence as an agreement of some sort, so he nodded and slipped past Marcus and was out the door before Marcus could come up with something to do.

Alpha Kincaid was going to be upset when he found out Marcus had made things worse between them and the deputy.

Slowly he followed him out of the office, but there was no sign of Medina in the hallway, the only sound coming from the pool area where kids were splashing and laughing.

"Everything okay, sir?" Brianna spoke from behind him, voice soft.

He turned and gave them a small smile. "Yes, of course. Thank you so much for your hospitality."

Laughing, Brianna moved closer, pausing at the entrance to their office. "Anytime, Enforcer Rivera. I owe Alpha Kincaid everything. The least I can do is give up my office when one of his Enforcers needs it."

Marcus dipped his head in acknowledgment, his heart warming at their words. Many people in the pack felt that way about Alpha Kincaid. Where many packs turned away anyone different—in any sense of the word—Rick opened his territory and his arms to them, welcoming them without question.

Exiting the rec center once more, he breathed deeply to remove the stench of chlorine from his nose. He wasn't surprised that Medina and his car were nowhere in sight, but a part of him had wished he'd get one last glimpse of the man.

The drive to his house didn't take very long, and then he was standing in his empty kitchen, wondering what he was expected to do with himself since he still had over twelve hours before he was "allowed" back at the manor. He placed his revitalized plant back on its shelf next to a handful of others, gently touching leaves and edges of pots.

Turning his head, he eyed his basil plant on the built-in shelf under his large kitchen window. He approached it slowly, like it might attack if he moved too fast, then reached out and gently squeezed a single leaf between his thumb and forefinger. He raised them to his nose and inhaled deeply, his eyes fluttering shut.

Yes, Medina had definitely smelled like that, but why? Marcus had never come across that scent in a human or shifter before.

His phone started ringing in his pocket, and he pulled it out, mind distracted with trying to figure out the meaning of the scent. "Yes?"

"Hey! Heard you got kicked out of the manor." Nico's loud and brash voice battered against the headache forming behind Marcus's eyes. Nico was another Enforcer in the pack, and if Marcus had really thought about it, probably a close friend.

"I was… encouraged to take a break from the archives."

Nico laughed. "Sure, okay. Anyway, want to get dinner in town? I could use a break from the manor too. I'm practically going cross-eyed from all the paperwork I've been going through lately, between the archives and the red-tape shit for the development. Momma's in an hour?"

Marcus hesitated, but one glance in his empty refrigerator made the decision for him. If he didn't meet Nico at the diner, he'd have to go to the grocery store or go without food. "Alright. I'll see you there."

CHAPTER THREE

R obson had handled a lot of weapons in his day, but a hot glue gun might be the death of him.

"I'm just saying, keep an eye out for any of the people I showed you and keep tabs on Reesa. On my way over here this morning, I dropped the folder with all of the information I'd gathered on Rivera's doorstep, so hopefully that'll be the end of it." He shook out his hand, fingers burning and strings of glue hanging from the tips. "Fucking shit. That's hot."

He and Hector were supposed to be using the hot glue to attach fake fall leaves to mason jars, and Hector seemed perfectly fine wielding his, but Robson was struggling. Hector finished the one he was working on—the leaves perfectly layered to cover all of the glass and no random strings of glue hanging off, the bastard. He set everything down and looked around to make sure no one was nearby. Pretty much their whole family was crammed in their mom's house, helping get things situated for the shower that was going to be held in two weeks somehow, but the two of them had been sequestered in the kitchen by themselves. They were sitting at the table with dozens of jars to decorate, and Robson sort of wanted to cry just looking at all of the naked jars still left.

"He actually threatened her?" Hector asked softly.

"It was implied," he muttered, grimacing as he peeled cooled glue from his skin. "He told me they knew I was following them."

"Okay?"

"And he just happened to be with Reesa at the rec center?" Robson scoffed and threw down the stupid leaf he was failing to adhere to the jar and the damn gun.

"Didn't they both say she was there for some mentoring program thing? That sounds just like something she'd volunteer for." Hector's unimpressed face was making Robson want to throw the glue gun at him. "I know the town's grown, but it's not *that* big. The chances of them being in the same place aren't that small really."

Robson grunted in frustration and leaned back in his chair. "What about how when I asked him to stay away from Reesa his response was that her husband was a friend?"

Hector raised his eyebrows. "I'm not following… So now it's suspicious that he's friends with Patrick?"

Rolling his eyes, he leaned forward and whispered harshly, "What if Patrick's in on whatever they're doing and dragging Reesa with him? I told you I got a bad vibe from him."

A throat clearing in the kitchen doorway had Robson sitting up and looking around quickly. Patrick stood awkwardly just in the room, two empty glasses in his hands. "Sorry to interrupt," he said roughly, then headed for the large punch bowl on the kitchen counter.

Robson watched him with narrowed eyes until Hector kicked him under the table, causing him to jerk back and knock his knee into the underside. "Son of a bitch."

Finished with the glasses, Patrick gave them a tight smile, then left the room.

Hector shot a glare at Robson and got to his feet, going to the doorway and peeking into the other room before coming back to the table. "Yeah, the guy who just refilled our mom's and sister's glasses and is now rubbing Reesa's feet is a hardened criminal alright."

"Anyone can pretend to be nice," Robson muttered, but there was no heat behind his words. So accusing Patrick of being involved in something illegal might have been a stretch, but it wasn't like he'd heard Robson whispering to Hector from across the room.

"Yeah, except you apparently." Hector went back to making his half of the leafy jars.

"Cabrón," Robson said, chuckling and throwing a bit of hard glue at Hector's head, hitting his temple.

"Gilipollas."

They both went back to working silently, but Robson's mind was still turning over all the information he'd learned from his short conversation with Marcus Rivera. He shivered when he remembered how cornered he'd felt in the office with Marcus blocking the door, like he was prey to Marcus's predator.

Which was hilarious.

Marcus might have been taller, but Robson would put his money on his training and muscles any day. In comparison, Marcus looked like a weed.

He had learned something valuable about the other man in that room though. While Marcus had remarkable control over his face and body, giving away very little information about his thoughts or feelings, his eyes were a different story. Robson had thought they were light green, but when he had accused Marcus and his friends of covering up a murder, they'd darkened so quickly it had been a little startling.

28

Still waters ran deep indeed.

The part of his brain that had teased and tormented his siblings for their entire childhood wanted to poke and prod at Marcus until he broke his control and got a real reaction. With that red hair and those expressive eyes, Robson bet it would be a beautiful fucking sight.

Wait... what?

His hands froze on a half-finished jar and his glue gun. Where the fuck had that thought come from? Rivera was no doubt part of a criminal organization that had threatened his sister! Robson couldn't be... attracted to him.

Right?

"Fuck," he groaned, head hanging. His dick always had gotten him into trouble, so why would now be any different?

"What's wrong with you?" Hector asked, eyes not leaving the jar he was carefully applying glue to.

"Nothing. Let's just... Let's change the subject."

"Okay." Hector dragged the word out and side-eyed Robson. "How's the job going? You still hate it?"

His hands tightened involuntarily at the question, hot glue oozing out of his gun and hitting the newspaper their mom had insisted on putting down before they started working. "I don't... hate it. I just don't necessarily enjoy it. Which is fine. Not everyone loves their job. As long as it pays the bills, that's all that matters."

Of course, he'd had to take a little money out of his savings the day before because his check had been so pitiful. He'd cashed his check and drawn out the extra before giving his mom the cash like he always did so she was none the wiser. Luckily. She always thanked him and called him her sweet boy when he gave her the money, but he knew she'd scold him in a second if she found out he was using his savings on the bills.

"You served your country for over a decade," Hector was

saying, carefully not looking at Robson as he spoke. "You shouldn't have to be unhappy with your job and your life because you're the oldest. Shannon and I were talking, and we'd like to help more."

Robson stared at the side of Hector's face. "No."

Hector sighed and set his things down, turning to face Robson fully. "You don't get to just say no, Robito. You aren't Dad. It's not your job to take care of everything and everyone. Mom wouldn't want—"

"Stop." Robson's voice was hard. He pointed at Hector as he whispered harshly, "We're not having this conversation. You have two little ones to take care of. Reesa has one on the way. Rafael and Benito are at college. Teo works his ass off on the farm, trying to keep it afloat, and Annalisse and Valentina are in school still. It *is* my job to take care of things because I'm the only one who can."

"Rob—"

"And," he spoke over Hector's protest, "Mom will never find out about any of this. She lost the love of her life a few months ago. She doesn't need to worry about me on top of everything else."

Sighing in frustration, Hector grumbled under his breath as he picked up his glue gun again.

"Hector."

"Fine! I won't fucking say anything. But Shannon and I can chip in a little for groceries and shit, asshole. We both work good jobs, and we can afford it." Hector glanced over his shoulder, then leaned toward Robson. "I know the sheriff cut your hours recently."

Robson scowled at him. "How do you know that?"

"Small-town life, man. Word gets around if you know who to ask." Hector gave him a significant look.

Before he could ask him about it, Reesa was waddling into the kitchen, one hand on her lower back and the other on her distended belly. She grimaced as she lowered herself into a chair across from Robson.

"You okay, mami?" Robson called out, trying to get her to smile.

Her lips were pressed together, but one corner twitched. "This kid is moving like crazy today. I think they're ready to come out."

He and Hector exchanged wide-eyed looks, then both started to rise.

Reesa laughed and waved at them. "Sit down, dumbasses. I didn't mean right this second."

"Oh." Robson dropped back down into his seat and half-heartedly picked up his glue gun again.

"Would one of you do me a favor? There are a few things I'd ordered for the shower that just came in, but I don't feel like wedging myself into my car to go and pick them up."

Robson sprang up out of his seat. "Yes, me. I'll go."

Hector snickered as he precisely laid a line of glue on his jar, but Robson ignored him.

"Awesome, thank you. Tell Tashmica at *Wicca We Can* that you're picking up for me and she'll get you the stuff." Reesa's smile was so sweet and innocent, but he'd known her for her entire life and he scented deception in the air.

Hector wrinkled his nose. "What could you have possibly ordered from there for a baby shower?"

Robson pointed at Hector. "Yes, excellent point. Seems like a very baby-unfriendly place."

"Don't be judgmental. Tash has been very sweet to me." Reesa's smile had dropped off, and she turned her little-sister glare on them. "If it's too much for you, I guess I can just go myself."

"Ay, Dios mío," Robson groaned at her dramatic attitude, rolling his eyes. "I'll go, okay? I just think it's weird."

"Agreed," Hector said, but when Reesa swatted at him, he

quickly added, "but it's your shower and you can have whatever you want."

"Thank you." She leveraged herself out of the chair and moseyed over to where there was still some food out on the counter.

Knowing he should just take the excuse to get out of hot glue gun duty and run, he couldn't stop himself from saying, "I'm surprised Patrick didn't offer to go get the stuff."

Hector shot him a warning look, but Robson ignored it.

Reesa was chuckling as she crunched down on a tostone. "He would have if I'd asked, but he doesn't like to be away from me with the baby so close to coming. Just in case."

Robson curled his lip, not impressed with the weird possessiveness of his brother-in-law. He dodged a slap Hector aimed at his leg and wiped the look from his face before Reesa turned around, eyeing them.

"Sure, sure. Makes sense." He smiled at her to cover the insincerity of his words, then headed for the door. "Be back in a bit. Don't wait for me, Hector. Go ahead and make all of those jar thingies."

He thought he heard Hector call him something, but he was already marching through the house, stepping around boxes and family members.

Pushing open the door of *Wicca We Can* for the first time, Robson froze just inside, instincts bombarded with a sudden urge to getoutgetoutgetout. He gripped the edge of the door to keep from falling to his knees as his heart began to race, his lungs working to fill his chest that suddenly felt like it had a weight pressing into it.

"Fuck!" he gasped out, going down on one knee, the bone striking the floor so hard it reverberated through him.

"Tashmica! Shut it off!"

Robson couldn't even open his eyes to see who was running up to him, but he recognized that deep voice. Then strong hands were holding his jaw and shoulder as a terrifying growl filled the air, causing the hair on the back of his neck to rise up.

From one struggling breath to the next, the air around him eased its assault, and he sucked in a noisy breath, fulling expanding his chest.

"I'm so sorry," a soft feminine voice said to his left. "I set the, um, alarm while we were in the back. It should have prevented anyone from wandering in while we were working. I don't know how he… Deputy Medina, I'm so, so sorry. Are you alright?"

Robson was still trying to get his bearings when he realized Rivera was kneeling in front of him, touching his face gently. His eyes flew open, and he took in the sight of Rivera's intense, concerned eyes and Tashmica Torres standing off to the side, hand over her mouth and tears in her eyes.

"What the fuck?" he croaked out.

A sudden vision of Reesa falling to the ground in pain if she'd been the one to come to the shop had him pushing to his feet, fury lighting his veins and giving him strength. Rivera rose more slowly, hands still raised a little, like he wanted to calm Robson down but wasn't sure how. Tashmica was wincing, her red lips pressed together.

"It was an accident," Rivera finally said, his calm voice the opposite of soothing.

"'An accident'? Really? Because that felt really fucking intentional to me, whatever the hell it was." He looked around the entrance to the store, trying to find what had caused the overloading of his senses like that. He'd never heard of an alarm system that could do that.

"Deputy, please understand…" Tashmica looked at Rivera, who gave a slight shake of his head. Torres sighed and ran her fingers through her curly hair. "It's hard to explain"—she shot a look at Rivera—"but it truly wasn't intentional. I wasn't expecting anyone to come in."

She gave him a sweet smile, her whole demeanor begging him to understand, but he narrowed his eyes as he took a step back, closer to the door. "Except Reesa."

"What?" She seemed genuinely confused, but he'd met his fair share of good liars before.

"Teresa O'Neal. She said you contacted her about an order… Was this trap actually for her?" Robson's blood pressure began to skyrocket again, his protective instincts shooting to the surface. He'd done what Rivera wanted, had even handed over the information he'd gathered—what more did they want from him?

Maybe just to send a message that they would hurt anyone who got too close to them?

"Oh no! She would have been fine!" Torres said, holding a hand out to him, but he jerked back farther, hitting the door with his shoulder blades. "I'd never hurt Teresa or the baby. You have to believe me."

She shot a pleading look at Rivera, who simply clenched his jaw tighter, tendons in his neck standing out as he shook his head again.

"Marcus, this is ridiculous! We should just tell him."

"It's not my decision," Rivera said slowly, eyes never leaving Robson as he reached back and twisted the doorknob pressing into his spine.

"Rick would understand— Wait, Deputy, don't leave. I can get you Teresa's things." Tashmica turned away, but Robson was already throwing the door open and stumbling out.

"Fuck that. Reesa doesn't need whatever voodoo shit you convinced her to buy. Stay away from my family." His voice was little more than a growl as he squared off against Rivera on the sidewalk, locking eyes and refusing to look away.

For the briefest of seconds, it looked like Rivera's eyes lit up, shining with some unknown intent, but they were back to normal so quickly he was sure he'd imagined it.

"You hear me, Rivera?" he called, ignoring the people down the sidewalk who had stopped to watch him.

"Yes, Robson, I hear you." Marcus lowered his chin, but he didn't look away.

"Good. Because next time I won't ask so nicely."

CHAPTER FOUR

"Alpha, with all due respect—"

Alpha Kincaid held up a hand from his spot at the head of the dining room table in the manor. "Enough, Marcus. The discussion is over. As much as it pains me that a member of the community would believe we'd harm a pregnant member of the pack, it is not reason enough to reveal ourselves to him. Teresa herself has said she can't be sure how he would react to the news."

Marcus nodded and dropped his eyes to his half-empty plate, appetite gone. He couldn't get the scent of Robson's terror out of his nose; it followed him everywhere, reminding him of how badly he and Tashmica had fucked up.

"Rick," he heard Rick's mate, Kai, whisper, but Rick cut him off.

"Pup, don't give me those disappointed eyes. The law is clear on when non-knowing humans can be brought into the fold, and this does not count."

Someone snorted, but Marcus kept his eyes down. His alpha was right, and he knew that. He'd known that before he'd even broached the subject, but something in him had made him try, knowing it would probably end in his alpha upset with him. Again.

"But you're considering telling the city council, despite the circumstances not meeting the requirement for them to know? Hell, the fact that the chief and mayor know are technically violations," Bennett Young said. He was the pack's second, the alpha's right hand, and the only one who could get away with pointing that out and *probably* not getting his ass handed to him.

Alpha Kincaid slammed a hand down on the table right on the folder Marcus had found on his porch that morning, silencing all the muttering happening around the table. Marcus didn't flinch—on the outside—but the muscles in his neck tightened automatically, too ingrained *not* to even though he knew down to the marrow in his bones that Rick would never raise a hand to him in anger.

"The fact that this deputy knows so much about us after two weeks is disconcerting enough. Despite him misunderstanding Marcus and his belief his sister was targeted, I truly believe he'll move on if we all stay away from him and his family. Do not approach Teresa and Patrick in public for a while, and his suspicions will die down."

Marcus glanced up without raising his head and found Rick staring right at him. He dropped his eyes back to his half-eaten pork chop. "Yes, Alpha."

There were other murmurs of agreement, and then the conversation shifted, but he couldn't focus on what was being said. Trusting in Rick had saved his life, but his decision about Robson felt... wrong. It was causing a sort of itch between his shoulder blades, the idea that his alpha was making the wrong decision. He knew Garrick Kincaid wasn't a perfect man, but he'd always done the best for his pack and his mate, and Marcus trusted him implicitly.

So why did he feel the urge to argue his point further?

Marcus hadn't argued with his alpha since long before that role was held by Rick. The pack he was born in didn't allow for speaking against the alpha. They'd been a tiny pack on the southern tip of Ohio, barely more than a dozen families, but it was all Marcus knew until he was sixteen and... sent away.

"Hey, wanna go for a run after dinner?" Nico asked, nudging him with his elbow, then shoving more green beans in his mouth.

Despite a lack of any verbal or demonstrable actions on Marcus's part, Nico had decided they would be best friends as soon as Marcus had arrived in Meyerville to join the infamous Kincaid Pack. Nico had also just joined after spending the previous few years as basically a nomadic shifter, visiting different packs but never staying in one place long enough to truly join.

Marcus had been sent—against his wishes—by his mentor on the Council because the councilman had felt it was time for Marcus to "join a real pack."

It was, without question, the best thing to ever happen to him—even if most of the other members of the pack refused to follow tradition and show the deference to Alpha Kincaid that was his due as the leader of such a large and powerful pack. Marcus had given up some time ago in trying to convince the other Enforcers at least to set an example of respect, but since it didn't bother Rick when they bucked traditional shifter norms or mores, the others just ignored him.

"Marcus?" Nico poked him with his elbow again.

"Not tonight, thank you." His wolf was eager to stretch his legs, but Marcus had something else he had to do. An itch to scratch.

Nico just shrugged good-naturedly and went back to his food, chiming in on the conversation happening across from them between V and Fiona about the success of the first mentorship meeting and ideas for future classes.

The original idea for the program had actually been Jamie Foley's. He was now Rick's personal assistant and managed the manor alongside the housekeeper, Beth Wilkins, but before that, he'd come to a pack meeting and suggested starting something that allowed packmates to acquire mentors. It had been a terrific idea, so Marcus and V had run with it.

Jamie probably should have been at the first meeting earlier that week, but he and Marcus weren't... on the best of terms at the moment. When Jamie had first started working for Rick, Marcus had thought he'd finally found an ally, someone who was also from a more traditional pack and would help him convince the others who worked in and around the manor to use Rick's proper title and follow pack and shifter laws more stringently.

He'd been wrong.

It wasn't that Jamie wasn't a traditionalist like Marcus—he was, to an extent. But unlike Marcus, he'd stepped into his job, looked around at what was happening, and then... rolled with it, as Nico had called it. Instead of pushing formalities for pack business, he'd begun offering suggestions on ways to adapt the pack's laws to better suit their forward-thinking alpha.

Things had come to a head when Jamie had changed some of the traditional events the pack held at the Harvest Festival a few weeks ago. When Marcus had found out, he and Jamie had gotten into a heated discussion about it. Rick had, of course, sided with Jamie and then reprimanded Marcus when he'd resisted working with Jamie on the archive project.

After the Council—a group of retired alphas who governed and punished packs when necessary—had failed to condemn another alpha for spying on a Kincaid Pack emissary, Rick had asked Marcus to begin digging into the Council archives, which were accessible to any pack in good standing. Since Bennett and his mate, Kieran, had stormed out of an official Council hearing, they'd all been worried that the Council would retaliate since they obviously had more enemies than friends sitting on the Council.

Not long after that, Kieran's father—the same alpha who had spied on them—attempted to overthrow Rick by attacking the pack. By the end of the encounter, one of McAllister's Enforcers was dead and most of the members had joined the Kincaid Pack, resulting in the McAllister Pack ceasing to exist in any real way and further complicating the Kincaid Pack's relationship with the Council. Even though they had every right to defend themselves from an invading pack, Marcus was worried that the Council would take exception to Rick's lack of diplomacy in addition to his second-in-command storming a hearing and dragging a witness away.

The entire situation was a mess, and Rick wanted to know what the Council *might* do if they decided to make an example of him or the pack. Marcus… didn't like guessing, but he'd given his best answer and then been told to start reviewing the archives. And to use Nico's help.

And Jamie's.

Luckily, since the last hundred years of journals, hearing transcripts, and Council meeting minutes were all digitized, they hadn't had to spend much time *together* as they worked on the project. They'd split up the years, then worked in separate spaces, though Nico often chose to bring his laptop into Marcus's office when he was reviewing his assigned years.

After several weeks, they didn't have much more information than they'd begun with, but there were centuries more of journals, minutes, and transcripts still in hard copy form in Montana within the Council's compound. The question was how to gain access to them.

Within half an hour, everyone had finished eating and begun breaking up to spend the rest of their Saturday evening either relaxing or working on pack business. All of the pack Enforcers were in attendance at dinner. They used to only eat together sometimes, but since Rick's mating, he'd become more insistent about them sharing meals and spending other time together that wasn't work related.

Bennett's mate and Jamie sometimes ate with them too, but lately they'd chosen to eat earlier with the other residents of the manor since the table wasn't large enough for everyone. While Kieran's father had been busy attacking Rick, Kieran had traveled back home and brought back dozens of refugees—members of what used to be the McAllister Pack who'd chosen to join the Kincaid Pack and get away from McAllister and his abusive Enforcers.

Not all of the recent pack additions were staying in the manor, but a large portion were since the pack only had access to so much housing in and around the town. Before Rick had become alpha, the town hadn't seen any real growth in decades, but ever since not only had the pack established new businesses and built community spaces like the recreational center, humans had moved to the area as well, attracted by the expanding town.

Marcus had seen it happen before. When he'd been with the Council, there had been a number of packs that he'd helped observe who had been growing at a fast pace and drawing attention from humans. Even though the humans didn't know why they were truly drawn to the area, it was because of the alphas. Strong alphas with large prosperous packs would exude a type of magic that drew even more individuals into their pack. Sort of like a magnet—the larger the pack grew, the stronger the pull became, and so on and so on.

McAllister's pack might have been outside of Rick's pull, but they'd hated their old alpha so much, many of the new members had agreed to come to Michigan without knowing anything about the pack. Kieran had filled them in on the trip back from New Mexico, but there had still been a lot of apprehension when some of them met Rick for the first time.

It hadn't taken long for the new members to know whether they would stay or not, and most had chosen to become full-fledged pack. But Marcus knew a handful had moved on. He'd heard the reason was usually that they didn't like living so close to humans, but a handful had been too nervous of the pack's powerful coven to stay.

Rick and Kai were still sitting at the table as everyone else began to file out, talking and laughing. Nico was right in front of Marcus, but Rick's voice stopped them before they exited the dining room.

"Hold up, you two."

Turning around, he had to work hard not to blush at the way Kai was leaning over Rick, kissing him, and Rick was squeezing the back of one of Kai's thighs just below his backside. There hadn't been a lot of open affection in his original pack, nor had he seen much of it when he'd been with the Council, but growing up, his alpha had worked hard to rid Marcus of his telling blush or any other outward reaction.

He'd believed that he could… teach Marcus to control his body's reactions to things.

He'd mostly been successful.

Kai smiled sweetly at him and Nico on his way out, and Marcus nodded respectfully as Nico fist-bumped him with a "See ya, Kai."

"Nico," Rick said, not wasting any time. He stood and approached them, crossing his arms over his massive chest.

"Tashmica has three witches coming over the next few months for interviews. She feels they may be a good fit to help rebuild the coven, but we'll see." Rick curled a lip up. "One of them isn't even twenty yet."

Nico laughed. "Damien and Jess are both pretty young and extremely powerful. Age doesn't mean much when it comes to witches."

Rick grunted. Marcus held his tongue since he hadn't been asked his opinion, but he agreed with Nico. He'd once seen a fourteen-year-old girl destroy half a city block after her parents had died in a car accident. Her grief had completely overwhelmed her, and her powers had erupted out of her like a tornado or something. Cleaning up the aftermath had been tricky since a handful of humans had seen her and survived the destruction.

"Either way," Rick continued, "none of them will be allowed inside the pack's territory until they've been thoroughly vetted and approved by you and Tash, and then I come and meet with them."

Marcus jerked his head up, alarm shooting through him. "Alpha, you shouldn't leave the safety of—"

A strong hand landed on his shoulder and gave a squeeze. "We'll take precautions, but I won't hide inside the wards, nor will I let someone into this pack with the power to hurt us."

Nico made a sort of choking noise that Marcus knew meant he was trying not to laugh. Rick sent him a glare.

"The hunter is human and—"

"He's a *hunter*," Nico needlessly pointed out.

"*And* he's retired. I'm not saying we have to trust him, but he saved Kieran's life, and he's kept to himself for the most part since moving here. Leave him be."

Nico held up his hands. "I haven't even been out to that run-down house he bought."

"Mmhmm." Rick's hand was still on Marcus's shoulder, but his stern face was pointed toward Nico. "Get together with Tash and find out when the witches are coming. She doesn't go outside the wards without you and Colt and at least three betas, got it?"

"Yes, Alpha." Nico dipped his chin, tapped Marcus's other shoulder with the side of his fist, then hightailed it out of the dining room, closing the door behind him.

His alpha's reassuring grip was the only thing stopping Marcus from worrying that Rick was really upset with him. Once they were alone, Rick's hand shifted so he was holding the space where Marcus's neck met his shoulder, his other hand coming up to mirror on the other side.

"Jamie mentioned you all have finished with the digitized archives and haven't found anything. Why didn't you tell me that?"

He bit the inside of his cheek to stop from flinching at Rick's words. They weren't said like an accusation, but that was how Marcus heard them. He just kept letting Rick down.

"I'm sorry, Alpha. I didn't mean to hide it from you. I've reached out to a few people I know I can trust in Montana to see if I can get access to the hard copies of older archives." Even though he and Rick were basically the same height, he kept his eyes averted out of respect unless otherwise instructed.

"I didn't think you were hiding it…" Rick sighed and tightened his hold a little more. "Marcus, it's okay if you don't find anything. It was a shot in the dark that the archives would have something useful. I don't want you… You don't need to kill yourself trying to find something that probably isn't there."

Feeling like he couldn't do anything but agree, Marcus nodded.

"Keep looking if you are able to get more files, but I don't want you spiraling because you think you've let me down, okay?"

Marcus sucked in a slow, deep breath, taking Rick's soothing scent into his lungs. "Yes, Alpha."

"Look at me, Marcus."

He raised his eyes and met Rick's gaze, noting the furrows between his brows as he studied Marcus's face, then carefully scented the air.

"Your service to the pack could never be a disappointment, you hear me? But I worry about you. Me and the pack are your whole life. You deserve something for yourself. Is that... Is that why you want to tell that deputy? If you think he's your... If he's special to you, then we can discuss that further."

For the first time in a long time, Marcus couldn't hold back his emotions. His eyes flared in shock as he tried to pull away from Rick's grip but couldn't. "Alpha, no. That's not... I don't have... No." He sucked in a deep breath and tried to slow his racing heart. Once he felt a little more in control, he said, "I don't need anything more than I already have."

Rick didn't look like he believed him, but he just shook his head and released his hold. "Everyone needs something for themselves. I thought since you seemed upset about not being able to bring him into the fold that something more was going on between you two."

"No, I'm just concerned about the situation. He's an unknown entity right now. And yes, he's only human, but he's smart and strong and knows how to use weapons we have no defense against. If he figures things out on his own... I worry he'll assume the worst—again—and attack."

Rick nodded. "I understand your concern, but the likelihood he'll figure out anything of real consequence on his own is pretty slim."

"Maybe," Marcus said softly as he followed Rick out of

the dining room. "But it is a possibility. Humans have done it before, especially when they are living among a large pack with pups and young members who don't have control of their shifts." Rick paused as he neared the bottom of the steps, prepared to ascend and spend time with his family in their private quarters. He looked at Marcus thoughtfully, so Marcus pressed forward. "He said he'd stop his surveillance of us, but now that he believes we attempted to harm his sister…?"

Rubbing at the five-o'clock shadow on his jaw, Rick started up the steps. "Okay. Keep an eye on him for the next few days to make sure he cools off and keeps his word about leaving us alone."

For some reason, Rick's words gave Marcus a weird feeling, goose bumps rising on his arms. He looked around but only saw other residents of the manor going about their evening, no threat that could have caused his instincts to act up.

Shrugging off the feeling, he headed for the back door near the kitchen. There was a lot of noise coming from there as dishes from both dinners had to be cleaned up. Luckily, Beth had gotten more help with the influx of residents, so there were a half dozen people in there helping her.

He slipped outside and stripped, quickly shifting into his wolf and bounding into the trees just behind the manor. His dark coloring would make his wolf harder to spot than his fair skin or red hair, both of which tended to make him stand out anywhere he was.

He'd never been to the home of Robson and Teresa's parents, but he knew where it was and that Robson had been living there since returning from the military, so he carefully but quickly made his way around the edge of town to the small farm.

The cows in the field just south of the house made his

approach tricky. He needed to get close enough to see if Robson was home and keep an eye on him, but if he got too close, the prey animals would go into a frenzy at his nearness, drawing attention outside from anyone in the house.

Carefully, he picked his way past an old shed that leaned precariously to one side and toward where several cars were parked in front of and to the west of the house. He hunkered down between two vehicles and trained his ears toward the two-story farmhouse with fresh white paint and shutters that looked dark blue in the setting sun's light.

He heard a lot of different voices inside, including Teresa's and Patrick's every once in a while, but nothing from Robson. The scent of manure and at least a dozen people overwhelmed his nose.

Crawling a little closer on his belly, he froze when he heard a crunch of stones behind him.

"Hey there, big guy. What are you doing out here?"

Shoot. So much for observing Robson Medina without him knowing.

CHAPTER FIVE

R obson might have made a mistake.

He'd thought the shadowed animal hiding between the cars had been a large dog, but when it rose and turned, he stumbled back at the sight of the enormous dark brown wolf.

"Fuck! Uh, good wolfy."

The beast took a step toward him, and Robson's lizard brain told him to stop moving; he'd never be able to outrun this large creature, so he needed to convince it he wasn't a threat. Holding his breath, he slowly lowered himself to the dirt and stones of his parents' driveway. He didn't want to take his eyes off the wolf, but he could remember hearing somewhere that predators took eye contact as a sign of aggression and might attack to establish their dominance.

On one knee and face tilted toward the ground, he shakily raised an arm toward the unmoving animal. "Easy, boy. I won't hurt you, okay?"

He started to get dizzy and realized he'd stopped breathing as he waited to see what the wolf would do. Sucking in a breath, he tried to see out of the corner of his eyes, but the deepening shadows hid the dark fur of the animal too well. His ears were ringing they were straining so hard to hear the slightest movement or growl.

Finally, after what seemed like an hour, he heard a sort of... huffing sound. Then he felt a wet nose on his fingers, and he flinched so hard he fell on his ass.

"Ouch. Well, that was graceful," he muttered, peering up and smiling at the wolf's cocked head. "Don't tell anyone the big bad infantryman just fell on his ass, okay?"

Tail wagging a little, the wolf crept closer, nose audibly sniffing. Robson held still, the fear from before slowly draining away as the wolf simply smelled him for a few moments, then sat on the gravel waiting for something.

"Um... Are you someone's pet? Jesus, why am I talking to you like you'll answer?" He scrubbed at his face and sighed, suddenly feeling drained. "What a weird fucking day."

After what had happened at the witchy shop in town, Robson had driven around for hours, trying to figure out what he should do. It wasn't like he could go to the sheriff and tell him what had happened, using it as evidence to open a real investigation. There was no way he'd know how to explain the sensation he'd felt walking into the shop, and he knew he'd sound... crazy.

Flopping backward, his upper half at least landed on grass. "Maybe I am crazy."

He heard a huff from the wolf, but he ignored him. If he got mauled for ignoring the thing, it'd still be the second weirdest thing to happen to him that day, and he was suddenly just *done.*

Nothing in his life made sense anymore, not since he'd answered the call about a dead body on the edge of his hometown. He shouldn't have even agreed to go and check it out. The night the call had come in and the sheriff had asked him to swing by because he couldn't get the Meyerville police chief on the phone or radio, Robson had been off duty and already changed out of his uniform. Hell, he'd turned in the keys to his patrol car.

But the sheriff knew Robson lived near where the body reportedly was and that he drove his dad's old car, which had lights in it from when his dad had volunteered with the fire department. Not regulation but close enough for the sheriff to feel comfortable sending him to check things out.

So he'd taken his gun, radio, and handcuffs and driven out to that abandoned house outside of town and found the "missing" police chief standing there.

Annoyed that he'd wasted his time, Robson had been turning to leave when the chief mentioned that he was waiting for help and that they'd "take care of it." The words themselves hadn't been that ominous, but the *way* the chief had said them, the hairs on the back of Robson's neck had stood up, and he knew, without a shadow of a doubt, that the chief and whoever he was waiting for would be sweeping whatever had happened under the rug.

After a decade in infantry, he could smell a bad situation a mile away, so he'd pressed for a few more details, acting like the sheriff would want more information. And then Kincaid and his friends had shown up, and everything had gone to hell.

Spreading his arms out next to him, he ran his palms over the cool grass and took a few deep breaths. That night… things had changed. He hadn't realized it at first, just how much, but after the way Rivera and Torres attacked him at the shop earlier?

The reminder of what had happened and how it could have been Reesa or Patrick walking into the store had Robson's heart beginning to accelerate, his fists clenching at the blades of grass.

He heard a faint whimper over the sound of his blood

rushing in his ears, and then a solid, warm body was lying next to him, pressed all along his right side, a cold, wet nose pushing into his neck.

A gust of air left his mouth as he shivered and jerked away. "Hey, that's not nice."

Chuffing, the wolf just followed his movements and licked at his jaw.

"Gross." Robson laughed as he brought his arm around the big body and buried his fingers in his surprisingly soft fur. He could feel the wolf's tail hitting his leg as he wagged at the petting. "Oh, you like that, huh? Well, no more slobbering on me and I'll keep petting you."

The wolf sighed and flopped half on top of Robson, causing him to cackle. What a drama queen. Using both hands, he wrapped the wolf in his arms and ran his fingers through his fur and rubbed at his ears, shoulders, and back. He instinctively knew not to try and touch the wolf's throat or belly.

After a few minutes, he sort of loosely hugged the wolf and stared up at the bright stars. "This is kind of nice. We had a dog growing up, but my dad wouldn't let us bring him in the house."

The wolf didn't make a noise or move, but when Robson glanced down at his chest, he found the greenish-yellow eyes looking at him curiously.

"Yeah, I know. My dad was a real hard-ass." He looked back up at the sky and sighed. "So why do I miss the ornery son of a bitch?"

Whimpering, the wolf wiggled closer, elbowing Robson in the gut.

"Oof. Easy there, buddy."

Once they settled down again, he focused back on the stars, looking for answers in their twinkling light like he had when he'd been homesick overseas. But just like then, the large expanse of sky and stars left him feeling nothing but small and meaningless.

"How do I tell Reesa that these people she thinks are friends were trying to hurt her?" he whispered to the darkness. Tears burned in the back of his eyes as the wolf licked at his fingers. "What if something had happened to her or the baby?"

His fingers tightened in the furry body now almost completely on top of him, but the wolf didn't seem to mind, his warm, steady weight a comfort to Robson as he realized what he had to do.

He was the threat. He was the reason they were targeting Reesa to begin with.

He needed to take himself out of the equation.

The next morning, Marcus walked slowly up the steps of the manor, mind spinning like it had all night about what he'd learned from Robson. The scent of fear and anxiety had been overpowering when he'd talked about something happening to Reesa or her unborn pup, and then Robson had gone quiet. Marcus had wanted to comfort Robson in a way he never had with another person, but he hadn't known how without revealing himself, so he'd just stayed with him until people had started to leave the farmhouse. He and Robson had both sat up at the sudden noise and watched people stream out the front door, laughing.

Not wanting anyone else to see him, he'd taken off the way he'd come, but not before he'd leaned into Robson once more and licked his sweet, basil-scented neck. He knew he shouldn't do it—Robson had specifically asked him not to "slobber" on him—but his wolf had wanted one more taste before having to leave Robson behind.

That thought was almost as troubling as Robson's fear for his sister.

He nodded at the beta Ericka standing just inside the manor's front door but didn't pause his stride, heading for his office on the first floor. All of the Enforcers except Bennett had offices at the manor, though some chose to work out of the office space they had in town to make themselves more accessible to pack members. Or to get away from the noise. Bennett had previously had a space for his "office" as well, but since he refused to do anything involving paperwork or working at a desk, the space sat unused and was given to Jamie when he came to work for Rick.

The manor used to be nearly silent day and night, but even before the McAllister refugees had moved in, Kai's youngest siblings, Henry and Callie, had brought life and laughter to the quietness.

Sometimes Nico would imply that he was surprised Marcus didn't choose to work in town, away from the chaotic manor, but Marcus would usually simply shrug or say his job was to be available when Rick needed him. But a not-so-small part of him *enjoyed* the ruckus the pups caused. The manor felt lived in in a way it never had before, and he loved it. The vitality and strength of the pack could be felt so clearly from inside the manor that Marcus would sometimes just sit at his desk and soak it up.

Entering his private space, he sent a message to Beth, letting her know he was "in residence" for the day. She liked to know who was around so she knew who to feed, and Marcus never turned down a meal made by Beth Wilkins. She'd been the housekeeper for Rick since he'd built the manor, and she was Vanessa's mom, making her more than an important member of the pack. She was family, and she took care of them like she was all of their mothers.

"Hey, man, you're here early."

Marcus looked up from his black computer screen and found Bennett in his doorway. "You as well."

B shrugged and stepped into Marcus's office, flopping onto the couch with a sigh. "Kieran practically lives here again. If I want to see my mate, so do I." He eyed Marcus's clear desk. "What are you working on so early on a Sunday morning?"

Staring at his dark computer, he struggled with an answer that wouldn't cause Bennett to suspect anything was wrong. Because there wasn't. He was simply… perplexed by his reaction to Robson Medina, but it didn't mean anything. He'd figure out why he was drawn to the human, then solve the problem.

That was it.

He stopped himself from sitting up straight too quickly, then laid both of his hands, palms down, on his desk and gave Bennett a calm look. "Working on a problem, but I think I've finally found the solution."

B raised an eyebrow and turned more toward Marcus's desk, laying an arm over the back of the couch and making a *go on* gesture with his other hand.

"I…" he began, choosing his words carefully out of habit, not because he didn't trust the pack's second, "believe I know why I couldn't let go of the Deputy Medina problem."

The corners of Bennett's lips twitched in amusement, but he covered his mouth with his hand and mumbled, "Oh yeah?"

Marcus's eyes narrowed for just a moment, and then he carefully smoothed out his expression once more. "Yes. I believe my wolf is convinced the deputy is still a threat"—the words were like bile in his throat, but he forced them out—

"and believed the pack would be harmed if that threat wasn't dealt with."

Hand sliding up to prop his head on his fist, Bennett gave Marcus a long look, then a sad smile. "You know, I've never met anyone who can control themselves like you can, but not even you can suppress your scent. Not completely anyway. You and I both know that's bullshit. Talk to me, Marcus."

The panic he felt at Bennett's words was instinctual, but B gave him space to breathe through it until his heart wasn't pounding quite so hard. When he could refocus on the room, he realized Bennett had closed the door at some point, giving them as much privacy as possible in a manor full of shifters.

Bennett's and Marcus's phones both pinged, and they glanced at each other before pulling them out.

Alpha: *Good?*

The lump in his throat made Marcus glad he didn't have to verbally respond. He quickly typed out that he was fine, then almost rolled his eyes when he saw B's response.

Bennett: *No, but I'm taking care of it.*

He carefully swallowed and set his phone facedown on the desk. "I am fine."

Bennett grunted and didn't bother hiding his eye roll. "It's okay that you aren't. I know it's hard for you still to say that, but that's okay too. When you're ready, tell me why you really can't let the Medina thing go."

His wolf wanted that, wanted to trust in his pack second so fully he could spill his guts and fears and hopes and dreams in the quiet space of his office, but his wolf hadn't endured the lessons Marcus had. The ridicule. The taunts.

"I'm not..." He stopped before he lied to the third-highest-ranking member of his pack. Again.

Bennett watched him struggle with sympathetic eyes, and that was what finally gave him the strength to spit out the words. He didn't want to be seen as weak or broken. Especially not by Rick or Bennett.

"I don't know. My wolf… It's almost like he yearns for the deputy. It's… very confusing." He blew out a breath when he finished, oddly proud of himself.

Bennett nodded, eyes wandering around the office as he contemplated Marcus's words. Finally, he said, "What does he smell like?"

Marcus's eyebrows twitched. "What?"

"His scent. Not his emotions or intentions, what does *he* smell like to you?"

"You met him…"

"Humor me," Bennett said, white teeth flashing against his black skin as he grinned.

Fingers twitching where they still lay on the desk's hard surface, he carefully said, "Basil. Fresh basil."

Bennett didn't seem surprised, even though Marcus had never scented anyone with that particular smell before and had struggled to understand what it meant. "Makes sense. Kieran smells like sunshine."

Marcus let his eyebrows rise slightly. "Sunshine doesn't have a scent."

"Well, no, not by itself. But you know how the earth smells when it's been heated by the sun for hours? That's sort of it."

Marcus nodded, though he was still confused. "Okay. That sounds… nice."

Bennett chuckled and sat forward, leaning his forearms on his knees. "It is, but that isn't my point. Rick told me once Kai smelled like his mom's perfume sometimes."

He was extremely confused. Shifters didn't usually wear colognes or perfumes. "What?"

"Not like in a weird way. His mom sometimes wore this subtly scented stuff, I guess, when his dad was on a rampage and she wanted to hide her emotions from him more fully. Anyway," Bennett said, waving a hand like he hadn't just surprised the hell out of Marcus. "What I'm saying is, Rick loved his mom more than anything."

"Okay?"

"And I love the sun…"

Marcus started putting the pieces together finally and shook his head, but Bennett continued before he could articulate how wrong Bennett was. Why did everyone keep assuming Robson was his damn mate?

"And you love your damn plants. I'm guessing fresh basil is your favorite."

It was, but that didn't mean… "He can't be…"

Bennett settled back against the couch and waited him out, knowing Marcus needed to think things through for himself. It wasn't that he didn't believe Bennett. On the contrary, despite his quick dismissal of the idea, his wolf had known from the moment he'd seen the deputy standing angrily in front of Chief Baskin.

But his human side was terrified at the idea. Robson was human. Marcus had only lived among humans since moving to Meyerville, and even then… he barely interacted with them unless they were packmates. Moreover, Robson knew nothing about shifters or witches or anything else that lived among but separate from humans.

And worse yet, Robson didn't trust Marcus and thought he was the kind of person who would attack a pregnant female.

"He can't be," he said again, voice soft and broken.

"Marcus…"

"No." Marcus stood, firming his jaw. Bennett was wrong —his wolf was wrong. No way could a man who despised Marcus be his perfect match. The fates couldn't be so cruel, not after everything else he'd survived. "You're mistaken. I need to make some phone calls."

He didn't say anything else or actually ask Bennett to leave—that would have been extremely disrespectful—so he simply stood there with his gaze downcast and waited for Bennett to slowly climb to his feet. Out of the corner of his eye, he saw Bennett rub at his smooth scalp as he sighed, then headed for the door.

"Alright, man. But when your wolf convinces your stubborn ass to stop fighting the inevitable, let me know." He opened the door but paused in the hall just outside. "I know what it's like to feel like you can't have something, to fight your own instincts until you can't take it anymore."

Marcus thought he was going to say more, but when the pause stretched out, he glanced up and saw Bennett smiling at something down the hall, his whole face lighting up and his scent filling with happiness. Only one thing made Bennett or Rick look like that. Their mates.

"The joy is worth facing the fear, Marcus," Bennett murmured, then strode away, head tilted down and shoulders back, stalking after his mate.

Like a knife to his chest, Marcus realized that he'd never have a mate look at him like that or catch his scent from another room and come and check on him.

No, instead, if he decided to believe Bennett—and his own wolf's instincts—he'd be shackled to a mate that was… human.

CHAPTER SIX

"**H**ave you seen a wolf around the farm?"

His brother Teo froze by the back door where he was pulling his muck boots on. "What? No! Have you? Was it near the cows?"

Robson shoved some more scrambled eggs in his mouth and shook his head. "Uh, no. Saw some tracks that seemed big for a dog. Just thought I'd ask."

He wasn't sure why he was lying about the enormous beast from the night before, but something stopped him before he could tell him. Considering how much Teo cared for those damn cows, Robson should tell him to keep an eye out, but... the wolf hadn't seemed interested in the animals at all. He'd been focused on the house when Robson had found him, and then he'd just... cuddled with Robson on the ground for a while.

He had to have been someone's pet to be so docile. Maybe he'd gotten away from his owner and then couldn't find his house. Hopefully, he made it home okay. Robson felt his chest constrict a little at the thought of the wolf being alone and scared, but shook it off. It was a *wolf*. Even if he was someone's pet, he probably enjoyed his romp through the trees and farmland, scaring unsuspecting deputies and wildlife.

Teo finished pulling on his boots, shooting a suspicious look at Robson. "Well, I'll grab dad's rifle later, just in case. The last thing we need is a wolf or coyote attacking the herd."

"Okay, no. You aren't *shooting* at anything. You'll end up hitting me or something because you think you see something outside."

Teo opened his mouth to argue, but Robson held up a hand and narrowed his eyes.

"I'm serious as shit, man. If I even see that rifle, I'm disassembling it and hiding the pieces."

"Language, Robito," his mom said, bustling into the room in her robe, hair still damp from her shower. She had a shift at the grocery store in a couple hours and liked to be ready early so she could make dinner for them even though Robson was perfectly capable of feeding himself and his siblings.

"Are the girls still in bed?" he asked, ignoring her reprimand and Teo's angry pout. At twenty, Teo thought he was old enough to be the man of the house and take care of their mom and resented Robson coming home after more than a decade and bossing him around. Robson understood that, but he didn't give a shit. He'd do what he needed to even if it caused his baby brother to pout all day about it.

"Valentina is. Annalisse went home with Hector and Shannon last night." His mom shot him a frown as she pulled a roast out of the fridge before going for the Crock-Pot. "Which you'd have known if you hadn't disappeared yesterday. You were supposed to come right back and finish helping, but you didn't come in until after everyone left."

"I know, mamá. I'm sorry. I got pulled into a… work thing." He grimaced at his eggs at the lie.

She tutted but didn't press further, and Teo slipped out the door without saying anything. It was still early, before eight, so it wasn't surprising that Valentina was still in bed. Robson had heard her on her phone when he'd come in the night before.

"Is Val dating someone?" he asked his mom, lip turning up at the thought. She was only fifteen, so he prayed she wasn't, but he barely knew his youngest siblings.

His mom shrugged and continued prepping the roast and vegetables. "Quizás. You know kids these days."

What the hell does that mean? "Umm, not really."

She laughed but didn't say anything else, and he suddenly lost his appetite. He pushed his plate away with the little bit of eggs left on it and leaned back in his chair. He was trying to decide if he should sit outside Reesa's house for the day to make sure she was okay or just tell her the people at *Wicca We Can* had tried to set a trap for her when he realized his mom had stopped moving.

Rising, he moved past the island so he could see her face, unsurprised to see her unfocused gaze and tears on her cheeks. "Mamá?"

She startled and swiped at her face, putting on a wobbly smile. "Yes, Robito?"

"You okay?"

Her smile dropped a little, but she nodded. "Sí. I was just… thinking of papá." Taking a shuddery breath, she went back to chopping carrots. "He would have been horrified at the idea of Valentina dating too. Sometimes you remind me of him so much."

Her voice was soft, but it still felt like a slap across his face. The only people Jesús Medina had been kind to were his wife and daughters; everyone else—including his sons—

only ever got the ornery-as-hell version. Robson couldn't even begin to count the number of times his father had yelled at him for "being a screwup." When he'd turned eighteen and told his dad in no uncertain terms that he wouldn't be taking over running the farm—ever—and was going to go to college instead, it was the one and only time his father struck him though. Robson had still been pretty scrawny at that age, still growing into his limbs and before he knew how to lift weights, so his father's backhand had landed him on the ground, cheek burning and shock stopping him from reacting.

That was also the only time he ever saw his mom raise her voice to his father. When she'd walked in and saw Robson on the floor, she'd laid into him, promising to divorce him, take his kids, and leave if he ever put a hand on any of their children again.

How could she look at Robson and see that man?

Not sure what to say, he awkwardly patted his mom on the shoulder and went into the mudroom, grabbing an extra pair of muck boots. "I'm going to go help Teo with milking and feeding." He started to tell her to send Val out if she got up anytime in the next hour but stopped. Valentina and Annalisse hated farm work almost as much as he had growing up, but how many times had he told them to go and help Teo?

Jesus Christ. He was turning into his father.

His legs felt numb as he muttered a goodbye to his mom and stumbled out the back door. How had that happened? How could he be turning into him?

For two hours, he worked hard on the farm, his body knowing what to do while his mind ran over the last six months furiously. Over and over again he came across instances where he'd ordered his siblings around regardless of their feelings, getting upset if they didn't do as he said.

Sure, part of that was from being a squad sergeant for years. Hell, before he'd decided to leave the army, he'd had his eye on a platoon sergeant position that was going to be opening up soon.

But he'd chosen to come home and help his family, not boss them around or verbally abuse them like their father had. He didn't think he'd crossed the line yet, but he could see the pattern developing and hated it. This wasn't who he wanted to be.

"Teo." His brother had just finished scrubbing the walls of the milk parlor now that all the cows had been milked. Teo shot him a glance but didn't pause in heading for the house.

"Yeah?"

"Can you... wait a second, please?"

Slowing, Teo finally stopped and turned to Robson, arms crossing over his broad chest. "What?"

Irritation flared up at his tone, but Robson took a deep breath. Teo was an adult, and Robson had been treating him like a kid since he got home. He deserved the surly treatment. "I want to apologize."

Teo's eyes widened as his stance relaxed a little. "Yeah?"

"Yes. Mom said... Well, she said something that got me thinking about how I've been treating you and the others since I came home, and I realize it's been pretty shitty." He stepped closer and put a hand on Teo's shoulder, dipping down to meet his eyes, the brown the same exact shade as Robson's, Reesa's, and their mom's. "You've been running things around here for a while, haven't you?"

Teo nodded, his chin jerking to the side but not before Robson saw the wetness in his lashes. "Yeah," he croaked. "Dad wasn't well for a long time. Even before the cancer, his emphysema had gotten too bad for him to do much around here."

Nodding, he didn't say anything for a long moment, just

kept his grip on Teo's shoulder, offering silent support. "What do you want to do?"

Head jerking back around, Teo stared at Robson for a second. "About the farm?"

"Yeah. I never wanted to work on it or be responsible for it, but you've always loved it. So you tell me—what do you want to do?"

Teo took a deep breath and looked around, excitement lighting up his eyes and flushing his cheeks. "I want to get rid of the dairy cows and get into beef."

"Okay. I think we can—"

"And," Teo interrupted like he hadn't even heard Robson, so he snapped his mouth shut and just listened for the first time in too long. "I think we can lease some of the acres we plant cash crops in and focus just on what the cattle need. Without proper irrigation, we've been lucky if we break even on the other crops anyway."

Robson nodded, eyebrows rising slightly. Teo had obviously thought about this a lot.

"Oh, and I know a few other farmers in the area who are looking for someone to wean and vaccinate their calves. That'd be some easy money. We'd just need to set up some hutches and get some proper feed. I bet the girls would even help with them when they're cute and little."

Robson laughed and slung an arm around Teo's shoulders, leading him back toward the house and nodding as he continued to spout ideas. Teo didn't need Robson to take care of things; he definitely seemed to have a better handle on what the farm could become than Robson ever had.

Now he just had to apologize to the rest of his family and figure out what to do about Kincaid and Rivera.

By Wednesday, Marcus hadn't come to any conclusions about Robson or their connection, but he had spent hours each night since Saturday watching the farmhouse. He told himself he was making sure Robson wasn't going to do anything drastic like go after Tashmica or something else ridiculous. But that wasn't why his wolf cried when he caught sight of Robson in a window or why he'd had to stop himself from approaching the man when he'd stepped outside Sunday evening and looked around like he was trying to find something.

The pull he'd felt had been so strong when Robson was outside that Marcus had had to force himself to leave and run home. Last night, Robson had just gotten home from work when Marcus had arrived, and he'd seen him in his uniform for a little while, then seen him in a room on the second floor. He'd told himself not to watch, but when Robson had walked past the window without a shirt on, Marcus hadn't been able to tear his eyes away. The next time he'd caught a glimpse of him, he'd been wearing sweats and a worn T-shirt.

Feeling arousal at Robson's state of undress had left him with a mixture of longing and shame. He promised himself he wouldn't go back to the farmhouse that night. His wolf immediately began to howl in protest.

Groaning at his weakness, he picked up his phone to text Nico to make plans so he wouldn't have a choice but to stay away from Robson. Before he could pull up his messages, the phone began to ring, Teresa O'Neal's name popping up.

Frowning, he swiped to answer the call. "Rivera."

"Marcus? Thank god." Teresa stopped and groaned followed by a whimper.

Marcus shot to his feet. "What's happening? Are you alright?"

"Baby's coming," she panted out. "I can't get ahold of

Patrick. He's at work and they make them turn their phones —" She cut herself off with a yell.

Marcus was already on the move, darting out of his office and into the first occupied one he came to, which happened to be Jamie's. He put his phone on mute and snapped out, "Call Dr. Bell and tell him to meet me at Teresa O'Neal's house. Her baby is coming, and she's alone."

Jamie was nodding and dialing before Marcus even finished.

"Teresa, you still with me?" he asked, keeping his voice low and calm. All he could hear was her panting as he sprinted through the manor and out the front door. There was an SUV parked right out front, and he took it, knowing whoever had left it wouldn't care when they found out why he'd needed it.

"Why the fuck does it have to hurt so much?" she finally said, and he couldn't help but chuckle.

"I don't know, but just focus on how precious that pup of yours is going to be when you finally have them in your arms." Once he was through the gate, he went as fast as he dared on the dirt driveway while only having one hand to steer. As soon as he hit pavement though, he floored it. "I'll be there in just a minute, okay? Doc's coming too. Someone will get ahold of Patrick soon, and he'll be there before you know it."

He hadn't told Jamie to track down her mate, but he knew Jamie would since he'd mentioned she was alone. Despite their differences, Jamie was extremely proficient at his job and at knowing what people needed even before they asked for it.

"Thank you," she gritted out. "I don't… I didn't want to be alone at the hospital in case something happened, but then it was too late to call an ambulance."

"It's going to be fine." He hoped it was anyway. If something happened to her or the pup... He couldn't even finish the thought it was so horrible.

"I guess I could have called Doc myself," she said, almost like she was talking more to herself than to him. "But you've been so nice to us, and I just... I don't know. When I realized I needed help and wouldn't reach Patrick in time, you were the first person I thought of."

He had to slow down a little when he entered the town limits, but he was still technically speeding. "I'm glad you did. Sometimes Doc's in with patients, and that receptionist of his is about useless. Jamie will be able to call his office manager directly. Kieran will get Doc over to your place in a hurry. Don't worry."

She chuckled, then groaned again. "I think... fuck... I think that's the first time I've heard you say something bad about someone."

Laughing softly, he was never more thankful for his enhanced senses and reflexes as he barely slowed at a corner before accelerating once more. "Don't tell anyone, okay? I have a reputation to maintain."

She started to say something back, but a contraction must have hit, and he listened helplessly as she hollered in pain. Once it subsided, he was almost to her house. He turned on to Elm Street and sped past the other cutesy houses decorated for Halloween until he was almost on hers and then slammed on his brakes.

"I'm here. Is the door unlocked?"

"Oh no. I don't think so, but I don't think I can get up." She sounded so sad and scared, Marcus's wolf became even more agitated, clawing to be let out so he could protect her.

"Shh, it's okay." He saw Doc's F-350 truck turning onto the street behind him and let out a silent but relieved breath. "Doc's pulling up too. I'll get us in, and I'll fix the door later, okay? Don't worry about it."

"Okay," she said softly.

"I'm going to hang up now, but I'm right outside, and Doc and I will be inside in just a minute, okay?"

He heard her take a shaky breath. "Yeah, okay. Patrick is coming?"

"Jamie will get ahold of him. Don't worry, Teresa. The pack will take care of you." He knew that she didn't fully understand what that meant since she didn't grow up in a pack and had only been mated to a shifter for a little over a year, but she'd soon know. If Marcus knew Rick and Kai at all, the two of them would be showing up before too long—especially if Jamie mentioned how distraught Teresa was when she called.

"I know. See you soon," she said breathlessly, then hung up, but as Marcus stepped out of his SUV and tucked away his phone, he heard her cries from the street.

Dr. Carter Bell parked right behind Marcus and jumped out of his truck. The man was enormous, like most bear shifters, but Doc always seemed smaller because of his gentle and calm demeanor. He had an old-fashioned doctor's bag in his hand as he approached Marcus where he waited at the back of his SUV.

"What's going on? Kieran didn't give me much information." He shoved his bag into Marcus's gut and reached up to pull his wavy brown hair into a bun.

Marcus filled him in as they hustled up to the front door, Teresa's panting whimpers ringing in his ears. He tried the knob just in case but didn't hesitate when it wouldn't turn to take half a step back, raise a leg, and kick it open. The heavy wood was no match for him, part of it splintering off.

"Wow. That'll need to be replaced," Doc muttered, taking his bag and striding into the house, following the sound of Teresa to the living room.

Marcus barely spared the ruined door a glance but made

a mental note to text Nico to order a new one. He or a couple of pack betas would sit outside until the door could be replaced and secured once more.

Entering the living room, he was horrified to see Teresa on the floor next to the glass coffee table. "Teresa! Why are you on the floor?" He landed on his knees next to her, taking her trembling hand in his own.

Doc was sorting through things in his bag, but he absently said, "Can you carry her up to her bed?"

Marcus looked at Teresa and waited for her to nod an okay, then slipped his arms under her back and legs. He ignored the dampness he felt on her sweats as he easily lifted her into the air.

Cheeks pink, she muttered, "Um, my water broke. I didn't…"

He smiled gently at her. "I know. You don't have to be embarrassed in front of me. This little one will actually be the third pup I've helped bring into the world. I'm practically an expert now."

Doc snorted behind them as they climbed the stairs, but he didn't think Teresa heard it. He was exaggerating, sure, but it was his third time witnessing childbirth. He wanted her to be as relaxed and comfortable around him as possible though.

Entering the bedroom, Doc slipped ahead and peeled the comforter off the bed and untucked the top sheet at the end, turning it down so Marcus could lay her on it. Then he darted across the hall, and Marcus heard the water turn on as he washed up.

"Cover her with the sheet," Doc said as he came back in, then pulled on a pair of gloves from his bag. Once Teresa was covered up, he nodded at her. "If you're comfortable, can you remove your sweats?"

She nodded and reached under the light blue sheet. She

had to stop once as a contraction hit her, but then she pulled the wet pants out from under the sheet and dropped them on the floor, collapsing against the pillows with a groan.

"May I examine you, Teresa? Marcus will stay where he is, and I'll leave you covered as much as possible." Doc was smiling gently, hands at his sides as he waited for her to answer, but she nodded once more.

"Yeah, go ahead." She turned to Marcus with tears in her eyes. "Will you… will you see if there's an update about Patrick?"

He lifted her hand and kissed the back of it as he pulled out his phone with his other hand. "Of course. Do you want me to call anyone else? Your mom?"

"God, no," she said, laughing, then groaning and fisting the sheet in her small hands. Marcus glanced toward her legs and saw Doc arranging her feet flat on the bed and lifting the sheet to her knees. "My mom would freak the fuck out that I wasn't in a hospital. I'll call her when it's over and the baby's here."

He nodded and looked at his phone, seeing he had three texts from Jamie.

Jamie: *Got in touch with Patrick. Apparently he and Teresa only have one vehicle and he left it with her today because she had an appointment. Some neighbor or something drove him to work. We're getting him transportation.*

Jamie: *He called one of his brothers-in-law and they're coming to pick him up and bring him home.*

Jamie: *Rick says to let him know as soon as the baby's born and he can visit or if you need anything else.*

He typed out a quick thank-you and acknowledgment. As he finished, he heard a car pull up outside, then running footsteps.

Smiling at Teresa, he reached down and brushed her light

brown hair back from her sweaty face. "Your mate is here, I believe."

Relief clouded her face as she began to cry. "Oh, thank god!"

He and Doc chuckled, Doc finishing his examination and lowering the sheet once more. They heard Patrick storm into the house, yelling Teresa's name. He sounded frantic, but Marcus caught a hint of excitement as Patrick barreled up the stairs and into the room, smiling widely.

"It's time?" he asked, hurrying over to Teresa's other side, ignoring Marcus and Doc.

Marcus didn't hear her reply, his head swinging back toward the doorway as a snarl ripped from his throat. There was a stranger in the house!

He could hear two more men coming up the stairs and recognized the scent of Robson as one. But Marcus's wolf couldn't let a stranger into Teresa and Patrick's den while she was so vulnerable. Moving without thought, he darted to the end of the bed and prepared to fight off the invading male, fangs and claws extending. His eyesight sharpened as his wolf's eyes surged to the forefront.

When Robson and the stranger appeared in the doorway a moment later, Marcus bent his knees and locked his eyes on the unknown male, prepared to attack. A growl filled the room.

Robson froze, but the other man fell back, eyes wide.

"What the fuck?" his mate whispered, voice full of fear.

CHAPTER SEVEN

R obson couldn't move as he stared at Rivera snarling like an… animal.

Like a wolf, his mind supplied unhelpfully.

The only reason he figured he hadn't turned and run or pissed himself was because Marcus wasn't actually focused on him but on Hector. The enormous man at Reesa's feet whipped around and wrapped his arms around Marcus's chest from behind, whispering into his ear.

From one moment to the next, Marcus's eyes stopped glowing, his teeth retracted into his mouth, and his fingers no longer had claws on them. He took a deep breath, gaze refocusing on Robson.

"That's Teresa's brother Hector," Patrick said absently from where he was sitting next to Teresa and touching her face gently.

Robson narrowed his eyes on his brother-in-law and sister. Neither one seemed at all surprised by Marcus's animalistic display. Sure, Reesa was a touch preoccupied at the moment, but shouldn't they be worried about someone fucking snarling and growling in their damn bedroom?

"What *the fuck* is going on here?" he finally gritted out, eyes bouncing from his sister and Patrick to Marcus and the large man still holding him. And why was that guy still holding on to Marcus? He wasn't glowing or anything anymore, so he could just back the fuck off anytime now.

"Tell you... later, Robito," Reesa panted out, waving her hand at him and Hector to come farther into the room. "Gotta have a baby first."

"Yes, we do," the large man said, voice deep and rumbly. He patted Marcus's chest twice, then released him and turned back to Reesa, quickly stripping off his gloves and putting on new ones. "How are you doing? You're mostly dilated, so things are progressing quickly."

Marcus was still staring at Robson, but he decided to ignore it. He couldn't focus on whatever the hell had just happened at the moment, so he'd simply pretend everything was fine. Reaching back, he grabbed Hector's arm and pulled him forward as he marched into the room.

When he glanced at his brother, he was surprised to find him frowning but unafraid.

"Some things about this town suddenly make a lot more sense," Hector muttered.

Robson raised a brow. "Meaning?"

Hector waved him off and went over to where Patrick was sitting next to Teresa, gripping his shoulder in solidarity. Robson was tempted to drag Hector back out and demand to know what he'd just figured out, but a cry from his sister refocused him.

He sat on the edge of the bed facing Reesa, his back to Marcus where he hovered closer to the door, and took her hand in his. "You alright, mami? Why aren't you in a hospital?"

"I'm okay," she said, squeezing his hand and giving him a shaky smile. "Doc knows what he's doing."

"Doc?" He eyed the man at the end of the bed, who looked like he should be riding a Harley or something instead of smiling gently at his little sister and helping her bring her baby into the world.

"Dr. Carter Bell," the giant said, but he didn't offer a gloved hand.

"Robson Medina," he muttered, eyeing the guy over his shoulder for a minute, then turning back to Reesa.

"Oh, I know," Dr. Bell said with a chuckle that Robson didn't really get, but he refused to say so. He was getting *really* tired of not knowing what the hell was going on around his town and with his family. As soon as Reesa's baby was born and he was sure she was okay, he was getting answers out of Marcus, no matter what it took.

What seemed like only a few minutes later but was actually over an hour, the doctor was reaching under the sheet and coaching Reesa through her pushing. Reesa's screams were going to haunt him for a long time.

At one point, he made Hector switch places with him, and he slipped from the room in search of a wet washcloth, but really he just needed a moment to catch his breath. Watching her in so much pain was killing him. In the bathroom across the hall, he could still hear her, but the sound was muffled once he closed the door.

Hands braced on the sink, he stared at his face in the mirror, telling himself to get his shit together. He'd seen worse things on deployment, so he didn't understand why he couldn't shake off his nerves and just *be there* for Reesa when she needed him.

He didn't hear the door open or Marcus enter the small room, but suddenly he saw him reflected in the mirror, and his breath caught as they locked eyes.

"Are… you okay?" Marcus's voice was quiet, hesitant. Robson had never seen him more unsure before, and a small, petty part of him kind of liked it. He'd been at a disadvantage for weeks trying to figure shit out, so he figured he owed Marcus a little of that.

"Did you turn my little sister into a monster too?" He finally asked the question that had been brewing in the back of his mind since he'd seen Marcus's other side. The fact that Reesa hadn't been surprised or scared by the display worried Robson. He needed to know if she was still the sister he'd known and loved his whole life or if they'd… changed her into something else when he wasn't there to protect her.

Marcus's eyes filled with surprise and hurt, but the rest of his face didn't change. Stoic bastard.

Robson spun around and shoved Marcus's chest, but he didn't even budge, just looked down at where Robson's hands were still on his pecs and made a small noise in the back of his throat.

They were too close. Robson's momentum had brought him right into Marcus's space when he hadn't moved, and they were only inches apart, breathing each other's air and staring into each other's eyes. Marcus was a little taller, so Robson had to look up slightly, but this close together, he felt twice as wide in the chest and shoulders. Even though Marcus looked tall and willowy, he'd just proven he was stronger than Robson could ever be.

So why the fuck wasn't he afraid?

His heart was racing and his breaths shallow, but it wasn't from fear—or at least not all of it was. A tiny instinctual part of his brain was screaming at him to run from the apex predator in the room with him, but the rest of him was transfixed.

Marcus had freckles on his nose and cheeks. How had Robson never noticed that before? And his eyes were a deep emerald green at the moment as he studied Robson's face in return, arms slowly coming up on either side of Robson's body. He knew Marcus was going to put his hands on him, hold his biceps or maybe grip his waist, and he also knew if Marcus did that, Robson was going to do something *insane* like kiss the man.

Just as he felt the heat of Marcus's hands hovering over his hips, Marcus's head swiveled toward the door, ear cocked up like he was listening.

"Doc says the baby's almost here. We should get back in there." Marcus turned back to Robson and inhaled through his nose, eyes fluttering closed. "May I… come see you at the farmhouse tonight?"

"Are you going to finally tell me the truth?" His voice was huskier than normal, and he felt his cheeks heat in embarrassment. Fuck, why was he so attracted to a guy who could probably break him in half with one hand?

Marcus nodded once and stepped back, removing Robson's hands from his chest—which he'd forgotten were even there. Curling his fingers into fists, he lowered his arms with a grimace.

"Then yeah, you can come see me." He stopped himself from saying anything else, grabbing the bathroom door handle and ripping it open. Back in Reesa's bedroom, he focused on her and ignored the silent presence hovering not far behind him.

Not long after that, he heard a baby crying and stared wide-eyed at Dr. Bell as he cleaned off the tiny person his sister had just brought into the world and then carefully passed them to Reesa to hold.

"A girl," the doctor said softly, wiping at his hands and grinning at the proud parents cooing over their new baby. He finished up whatever he needed to do under that sheet, then helped Reesa lower her legs and covered her. "Can you three give us a minute?"

It took him a moment to realize the doctor was talking to

him, Hector, and Marcus. He hesitated, not sure he wanted to leave the big man alone with his sister, Patrick, and his brand-new niece, but Patrick met his eyes and nodded.

Hector led the way out, already on his phone telling their mom the good news as they traipsed down the stairs. Back in the living room, Robson could just see the broken front door and frowned as he turned to Marcus.

"What happened to the door?"

"It was locked when Doc and I got here," Marcus said, not looking up from where he was typing a message on his phone. Apparently, he thought that was enough of an explanation.

Annoyed, Robson huffed and stomped over to it and examined the splintered wood. "This isn't fixable."

"I know," Marcus said from right behind Robson.

He pretended he didn't jump and said, "What are they supposed to do for a fucking door then?"

"I took care of it."

Robson spun around, irritation brewing in his gut once more. "What does that mean? Jesus Christ, it's like pulling teeth trying to get information out of you."

Marcus didn't say anything for a moment, his expressive eyes hidden as he stared at his phone without typing or touching the screen. Finally, he put the phone in his pocket and raised his chin, meeting Robson's annoyed gaze. The intensity in Marcus's eyes drew Robson up short. It was a silent reminder that he wasn't the biggest, baddest asshole in the room if he ever saw one.

"It means that I'm taking care of it. I ordered a new door, and until it's installed in a few days, someone will be outside the house twenty-four seven."

Oh. That... Yeah, that was taking care of it alright. Robson wanted to hang on to his annoyance, wanted to snap at the guy that Robson could take care of his own family, but the sincerity in Marcus's gaze slowly leached the irritation away, leaving him a little jittery.

Clearing his throat, he glanced back at the door. "Why didn't Reesa just unlock it for you? Did she not know you were coming?"

When Marcus didn't respond right away, Robson looked back at him and found he was staring at a spot on the floor of the living room. Taking a deep breath, Marcus quietly said, "She wasn't able to get to the door. It was easier for me to break it."

"Wait." He examined the heavy oak door, then did the same to Marcus's slender frame. "You broke it down? Not that giant dude upstairs?"

One eyebrow rose slightly, but Marcus just shook his head. "No, it was me."

"Jesus," he muttered. He'd known Marcus was strong, had even witnessed it in the bathroom, but seeing the damage he'd done to the door... He shivered and stalked away, ignoring the confused tilt to Marcus's head as he passed him.

He was supposed to work half of a shift that evening, but he texted the sheriff and let him know the news, and Sheriff Daley told him it was okay to take the day to be with his family. Robson pretended that he believed the sheriff actually believed that and it wasn't just another way for him to knock hours off Robson's paycheck. Since he was part-time, his paid time off was pitiful, and he'd been saving it, but he decided to go into the system and put in a couple of hours for the day so it wasn't a complete loss.

The doctor had come down not too long after the three of them and said that Reesa was resting but would be just fine and then headed back to his office or whatever, clapping Marcus on the shoulder on his way past.

Robson expected Marcus to excuse himself and leave as well, but he stayed rooted to the spot near the front door even after more of Robson's family showed up with food and gifts. His mom forced food on Marcus, but otherwise everyone pretty much ignored the giant ginger in the room.

Robson didn't know how they did it since he could barely look away anytime Marcus was within eyeshot of him.

A few hours later, Patrick had carried Reesa down the stairs, ignoring her laughing protests, and gotten her settled on the couch before going back up and bringing the baby down for everyone to meet. Teo had just accepted the little sleeping bundle when the hairs on the back of Robson's neck stood up.

Shooting to his feet, he turned and found Garrick Kincaid, Tashmica Torres, and a smaller, younger man with dark hair and wide green eyes. Kincaid met Robson's gaze, and he and Torres paused just inside the door as if waiting for Robson's okay to come farther in, but the younger man didn't seem to notice, darting forward and kneeling on the floor next to Teresa.

"Teresa, sweetie, are you okay? How do you look amazing after just pushing a baby out of you? Doc said the baby was okay even though she's a little early, but I'm going to need to hold her to be sure, okay?"

Teresa's tinkling laughter eased some of the tension in Robson's back and shoulders. Turning back to Kincaid and Torres, he was surprised to find Marcus had silently moved next to Kincaid and they were speaking quietly. He moved closer, tired of missing out on things.

Kincaid placed one of his big hands on the side of Marcus's neck, and Robson literally stopped in his tracks, narrowed eyes on where they were touching.

"It's okay, Marcus. I understand and I'm not mad," Kincaid was saying, his thumb swiping back and forth a few times.

Robson bit back a growl and stomped forward. "Why

would you be mad? Was your door smashed in? Were you threatened by some guy growling at you?"

Kincaid shot Robson a look that told him to shut up if he knew what was good for him. So of course, he opened his mouth to continue goading him, but Marcus stopped him.

"Because I messed up. Again." He sounded so sad and defeated, Robson forgot about poking at Kincaid and turned to him.

"Hey." He waited until Marcus was looking at him, then smiled reassuringly. "I was just being ornery. It's fine. You said you were taking care of the door."

Marcus didn't say anything and let his gaze fall back to the ground, turning his body more fully toward Kincaid. Robson turned to Kincaid with raised brows.

"Marcus lost control and revealed things to you that he was ordered not to," Kincaid said, voice a little growly, but Robson had a feeling that was just how he normally talked. He didn't seem upset with Marcus or Robson.

"You mean his grr-face?" He held his hands up next to his head like pretend claws and ignored Torres's soft laughter. "Yeah, that was terrifying, but it's not like he's told me what it means yet." Robson crossed his arms over his chest and lifted his chin, daring Kincaid to say Marcus wouldn't be telling him anything.

Kincaid hummed and gestured at Torres to go into the living room. She smiled and winked at Robson, then stepped past him carrying a large gift bag that left the scent of incense behind. He frowned after her, not sure he liked her being so close to his sister or niece after what had happened at her shop.

"Listen, I'll admit I was wrong about the whole mobster slash human trafficking thing," he said, watching Torres pull something out of her bag in a little cloth baggy, "but that woman attacked me at her shop. So why should I not be kicking her out?"

Kincaid chuckled and released his hold on Marcus— finally. "Witchcraft is tricky business."

Robson had been running his eyes over Marcus, trying to decide how to make him look like the arrogant man in the rec center again, when Kincaid's words sunk in and he whipped his head over to him. "I'm sorry, what did you say?"

Slapping a hand on Robson's shoulder, he stepped past him, apparently done with the conversation. Entering the living room, he called to the dark-haired guy still holding Robson's niece. "Mate, give me that pup and no one gets hurt."

"Umm." The guy handed over his niece, then stayed pressed against Kincaid's side, watching the baby. Reesa and Patrick were smiling widely—hell, Patrick looked downright excited to have Kincaid holding his newborn daughter. The rest of his family was either smiling in confusion or not paying attention, talking among themselves.

"I should get back," Marcus said softly behind him, causing Robson to spin around and glare at him.

"What about my explanation?"

Marcus studied Robson's face closely, but he didn't know why. It seemed like he was trying to memorize his features or something. "Tonight," he finally murmured. "I'll meet you at the farmhouse when the sun goes down."

He turned to go, and Robson reached out and grabbed his arm before he got more than a step. "Wait. Where are you going? You didn't even get to hold the baby yet."

His eyes darkening to emerald once more, Marcus eyed Robson's hold on him, following the line of his arm up to his face and cocking his head slightly in confusion. "Back to work."

Fuck, that should not be so adorable now that I know there's some sort of canine instinct behind it.

Robson glanced back at his family, but only Hector was watching them, his gaze on Marcus knowing and a little wary. He knew he'd have to have a conversation with Hector at some point, but he wanted to wait until he knew things for certain, including how much he was supposed to share. Hector had seen the same thing Robson had when they'd entered the bedroom, so he wasn't sure what he'd say if Hector demanded answers. Though his comment about things making sense definitely made it seem like he knew more than Robson did at the moment.

Nodding toward the door, Robson let his hand fall away and followed Marcus out onto the front porch.

"Promise me you'll come tonight." He wasn't sure why he was pushing so hard, but something in him didn't want Marcus to leave without an ironclad assurance Robson would see him again soon.

Marcus's beautiful eyes flashed to their animalistic glow for half of a breath, and then it was gone and he was back to normal. It was enough to make Robson's breath catch in his throat, though, and his pulse to speed up just a little.

Prowling forward, Marcus eyed Robson's chest. "Are you afraid of me?"

The porch wasn't very big, so two steps backward and Robson's ass was pressed against the wrought-iron railing. "You could kill me with less effort than it takes me to lift a pen, couldn't you?"

Marcus stopped with mere inches between them and nodded, his eyes fierce as they studied Robson so closely he could practically feel a physical touch.

"Then why shouldn't I be afraid?"

Marcus's gaze dropped to Robson's mouth, and he couldn't stop himself from licking his bottom lip, inordinately pleased when Marcus sucked in a breath at the sight of his tongue.

"Because," Marcus said slowly, voice barely more than a rumble, "I would do anything to keep you safe and happy. Even if that means staying away from you."

Without another word or waiting for Robson to figure out what the fuck that meant, Marcus leapt over the porch railing and strode toward his SUV, driving away without looking back once.

CHAPTER EIGHT

T he sun was just setting when Marcus shut down his
   office, mind running in circles trying to figure out
what to tell Robson when he saw him in a few minutes.
Explaining he was a shifter would be a complicated conversation all on its own, but should he tell Robson that they
were... mates?

A part of Marcus still rebelled against the idea, but not his
wolf. His wolf had been restless since leaving Robson on the
porch of Teresa's house, the scent of basil lingering in his
nose all day.

Biting his lip, Marcus closed his eyes and remembered
how heavy the scent had been in the bathroom when Robson
had been touching Marcus's chest. Marcus's wolf had been
insistent that they claim their mate right then and there,
audience be damned, but Marcus knew the chances of him
actually being able to convince Robson to be with him
were... not so great. Robson was a big, beautiful, and strong
human—what could he possibly want with an emotionally
damaged shifter?

Sighing, he opened his eyes and glanced around his

darkened office. Maybe he should wait to go and talk to Robson until he had better control of himself. It had been years since he'd lost control like he had earlier, and he was still a little shaken over it. Rick had been extremely gracious in forgiving him, but how many more times could Marcus screw up before he was asked to step down as an Enforcer?

Fists clenching at his sides, he stormed around his desk, heading for the door. He *knew* Rick wouldn't do that, but his stupid brain still automatically assumed the worst whenever anything bad happened.

God, it was exhausting.

He was almost at the end of the hallway where all the offices were when he heard his name. Turning back, he saw Jamie hustling after him, satchel crossing his body and bumping his hip.

"Rick asked me to go with you." Jamie's head only came up to about Marcus's chest, but he stared him down like he was seven feet tall. As the alpha's personal assistant, he held a lot of power and sway in the pack.

But Marcus didn't need a damn chaperone.

"I think I can answer a few questions about shifters, but thanks." He turned to go, but Jamie scoffed and darted ahead of him, drawing him up short.

"Yeah, I wasn't *offering*. I'm telling you that Alpha Kincaid is sending me with you."

Clenching his jaw, Marcus didn't say anything else, just gestured in the general direction of the front door and followed Jamie through the manor. When they reached the entrance hall, he was surprised to see the hunter Gabriel waiting off to the side.

He was even more surprised when Gabriel climbed to his feet at the sight of Jamie and grinned like the fiercest predator in the house. "Hello, gorgeous."

Eyebrows rising a little, he watched Jamie's pale white skin turn a dark pink as he sputtered.

"G-Gabriel. What are you doing here?" Jamie asked, voice a little higher-pitched than it had been a minute ago.

"Looking for you, of course. Seems to be the only place you spend any time nowadays." The hunter's long blond hair was pulled into a bun, his braid tucked out of sight, but Marcus was sure it was still there. All human hunters wore the braids to signify their allegiance to one of the original founding families. Gabriel's had purple beads in it, which meant his family were aligned with the Gunnulf Clan and were more mercenary than ideological. They hunted shifters and other supernatural creatures for money, not because they actually believed they were evil.

As entertaining as it was to watch Jamie fumble over the big hunter's obvious flirting, he had his own human to deal with. Clearing his throat lightly, he stepped toward the front door. "We're expected somewhere."

Gabriel frowned but stepped back, hands up. "Of course. Why don't you give me your number, gorgeous, then I can call you like a proper gentleman," he said, his slight Southern drawl thickening.

"Um." Jamie looked around the entrance hall with wide eyes, his indecision obvious.

Marcus turned toward the door and headed out, throwing a disapproving frown at the smirking beta standing there. The red-haired young man dropped the expression, and his gaze hit the ground. Stepping outside, Marcus inhaled the cool autumn Michigan air. There was just the barest hint of snow hidden in the breeze, but he knew it wouldn't fall for a few more weeks at least. Then it would be months and months of snow and cold until the thaw of spring finally arrived.

Slowly, he made his way to the manor's detached garage

and entered the side door. There was a large metal box mounted on the wall just beside the light switch. He hit the lights, then punched his personal code into the keypad on the box. The front popped open, and he selected a set of keys. The system was synced with Vanessa's phone so she always knew who had a vehicle since she was the Enforcer technically in charge of the manor's security—and Rick and his family's as well.

He was just closing the box when Jamie appeared in the doorway, face still flushed and short blond hair looking more disheveled than it usually did.

Marcus didn't say anything about what had happened, and neither did Jamie, both of them just climbing into the SUV and Marcus backing out of the garage. The ride to the farmhouse wasn't long, but the silence was awkward. He wasn't sure if he should say something or offer some words of reassurance. In the end, he did neither, not because he was judging Jamie for having the hunter flirting with him but because they weren't *friends.*

Not really, not anymore.

Turning onto the short driveway leading to the Medina farm, he spotted Robson on the front porch right away. His large, muscular body was like a beacon to Marcus, instantly drawing his attention and guiding him home. Even though he had a house of his own, he'd never felt like he'd had a *home* before. Not really. Home was about more than a roof over your head in his mind. It was... solace, acceptance, and love.

His chest tightened just at the thought, and he spotted Jamie's sharp gaze on him out of the corner of his eye, probably having caught something in his scent. Marcus worked harder to lock down his emotions. It wasn't the time to wallow in useless things like feeling sorry for himself.

Parking behind a short line of vehicles, Marcus quickly turned the SUV off and exited the car, trying to keep his goal for the visit at the front of his mind and ignore everything else.

Robson stomped heavily down his porch steps, mug of steaming coffee in one of his hands. The light was fading fast, but Marcus could still easily see that Robson was staring at Jamie, and he felt his wolf bristle, wanting their mate's eyes only on them.

"Every time I see you," Robson said as he approached them, "you're with someone new. Who the hell is this guy? Your accountant?"

He felt Jamie stiffen next to him. "Jamie Foley, personal assistant to Alpha Garrick Kincaid. You must be the deputy that has been so… dogged in his pursuit of answers."

Marcus's head whipped around to the bird shifter, lip raised in a snarl. He wouldn't abide Jamie making snide comments to his mate. "Watch yourself."

Eyes wide, Jamie stepped back and nodded quickly. "My apologies, Enforcer Rivera."

Robson noisily slurped at his coffee, scent more amused than annoyed. "See, that right there. What the fuck was that?"

"That was me being rude, Deputy," Jamie said easily, grimacing in apology. "Birds don't always get along with canine or feline shifters, so the 'dogged' comment was a dig at you and your—and Marcus. Apologies." Casting another wary look at Marcus, Jamie stepped forward as he dug in his messenger bag. Robson was staring at him again, but this time he seemed shocked at Jamie's nonchalant way of talking about shifters. "I'm actually here as a representative of Alpha Kincaid. He'd like me to extend an invitation to Kincaid Manor to officially meet him and his mate. This Saturday at six. Dinner will be served promptly at six thirty."

He handed a square envelope to Robson, then stepped back to just behind Marcus and pulled out his phone.

Turning back, Marcus watched Robson set his mug on the trunk of the car next to him and open the envelope carefully.

Robson frowned at the piece of paper he held in his hand. "It's just an address... I was kind of expecting an actual invitation with calligraphy and shit after that spiel."

"You'll be able to find the manor now," Marcus informed him.

"Well, yeah. I figured that was what the address was for." He raised his eyebrows at Marcus, his scent sharpening with impatience. "So I'm supposed to wait until I go see this alpha guy to get some damn answers?"

"No, Robson. I'm going to answer any questions you have now." He took half of a step closer, inhaling deeply to fill his lungs with Robson's scent. "To begin with, the address is spelled so the wards will now allow you to actually see the manor, not just drive past it."

Robson's thick eyebrows scrunched together as he held the paper farther away from his body. "More of that witchcraft shit like what happened to me at the shop?"

Marcus's stomach clenched at the reminder of what had happened, his vision flashing to the sight of Robson dropping to his knees in agony. "That really was an accident," he said carefully. "I'm not an expert on the craft, but I'm sure Tashmica would be happy to answer some questions for you."

The unimpressed look Robson gave him didn't make him or his wolf feel better. Glancing back at the paper, Robson asked, "Why couldn't you just give this to me?"

That was a fair question and one Marcus didn't have an answer for.

Jamie cleared his throat. "Alpha Kincaid has been... forcing us to spend time together."

Robson's head shot up, frown lines etched into his forehead. "He's what now?"

Biting the inside of his cheek to try and suppress the shiver racing down his spine at the growl in Robson's voice, Marcus said slowly, "We had a disagreement."

Eyes narrowing, Robson looked between them, shoving the paper back into the envelope and sticking it into the back pocket of his jeans. "So you two are... what? Together? Little lovers' spat that has Kincaid playing matchmaker to try and smooth it over?"

Face heating, Marcus ignored Jamie's scoffing and shook his head. "No, nothing like that."

"God, no." At Marcus's sharp look, Jamie held up his hands and stepped farther back. "No offense. But no, Deputy. We just both work closely with Alpha Kincaid, and he'd like us to get along better."

Robson crossed his arms over his chest, eyes darting between them once more. "What was the disagreement over then?"

"Wreaths," Jamie said, contempt thick in his voice.

Marcus's spine straightened as he turned to face Jamie. "It was about more than the wreaths, and you know that."

Jamie threw up his hands as he rolled his eyes. "You're stuck in the past, Marcus. The pack needs to move forward and embrace changes."

"Respecting tradition isn't the same as being stuck in the past."

"It is when you throw a damn hissy fit over some damn wreaths."

"It wasn't the wreaths!"

"Guys!" Robson was suddenly between them, raised hands extended toward him and Jamie but not touching either of them. Robson's grin was poorly suppressed, and his eyes were dancing with amusement. Marcus wanted to be annoyed that Robson found his argument with Jamie funny, but he couldn't look away from his gorgeous face long enough to drum up his irritation. "While that was... entertaining, I think we've gotten off track. Now, which one of you wants to explain what the hell an alpha is? Or a pack. Or how my sister is involved. Or why Kincaid showed up at her house today. Or what all of this has to do with the dead body at that abandoned house a few weeks back..."

Jamie sighed. "Marcus will answer your questions as best he can. I'm going home."

A moment later, headlights lit up where they all stood as an old truck bounced down the driveway toward them. The bright light made it impossible for Marcus to see who the driver was. Jamie gave a quick nod to Robson, then turned and hurried toward the passenger side of the truck. When he opened the door, Marcus took half a step forward and inhaled deeply, unsurprised when he caught a whiff of a certain blond hunter.

Robson stepped up next to Marcus as the truck began backing down the driveway once more. "Who the hell was that?"

"Gabriel Morde."

"He's a... shifter too?"

Marcus turned to Robson and studied his strong profile in the dim light of the moon and stars. In the last week or so, Robson had stopped shaving and was instead growing out his stubble. Marcus wondered if he planned on growing it into a beard. He also wondered what the dark hairs would feel like against his fingers... or his lips.

"Marcus?" Robson had turned and was fully facing Marcus, their faces suddenly a little closer than they probably should have been.

Ignoring how the slight uptick to the corner of Robson's mouth made his heart beat just the slightest bit faster, Marcus stepped back to keep his head clear. "Hmm? Oh, no. He's human."

The smile dropped from Robson's face, and he rubbed at the back of his neck, frustration leaking from his pores. "But he's... one of you guys?"

Marcus thought about that for a moment before answering. "Technically... yes, he's part of the Kincaid Pack. But I wouldn't count on his loyalty to the pack in any kind of emergency or if it no longer served his own needs and desires."

Robson grunted and stared at where the truck had disappeared, hand still gripping the back of his neck and brows furrowed.

"Would you... would you like me to start from the beginning and explain things, or would you prefer to ask questions and have me answer them?" Marcus wasn't sure what the best method was to reveal the magical world to a non-knowing human—he'd never had to do it before.

Sighing heavily, Robson turned and met Marcus's eyes, though he wondered how well he could actually see Marcus in the dark. "From the beginning, but not here."

Marcus looked around them, unsure where they could go since Robson's home was full of his family members. And while Hector could be brought into the loop if Robson wanted, Marcus couldn't reveal things to everyone in Robson's family without approval first.

Chuckling, Robson slapped a hand on Marcus's upper arm then headed for the passenger side of the SUV. "Get in, man. I know where we can go."

CHAPTER NINE

"So let me get this straight," Robson said, pointing at Marcus with his fry. They were sitting across from each other in a booth at Momma's Kitchen. Robson was on his second order of fries, and he'd had to switch to water after his second coffee so he didn't start getting jittery, but he was finally starting to see the larger picture of what was behind the scenes of Meyerville, Michigan. "Rick let that bitch-ass Enforcer who beat the shit out of his mate just walk away, and then that Gabriel dude kills him a few weeks ago when he tried to kill Bennett's mate... Kieran, right?"

Marcus nodded. "It's impressive how much information you're retaining."

Robson looked down at his mostly empty plate and bit his lip to stop himself from smiling. That wasn't even a *good* compliment, but from Marcus... it seemed like it was. The more time Robson spent with him, the more he was beginning to see Marcus's odd manners and speech patterns as endearing and less like he was deliberating trying to hide things and mislead Robson.

"Though," Marcus continued, taking a sip of his own

water. He'd declined to order any food, claiming he'd recently eaten dinner, but when Robson had pushed his huge plate of fries into the middle of the table, he hadn't been surprised that Marcus had eaten some. "I feel as if I should point out that Alpha Kincaid didn't simply 'let' the McAllister Enforcer walk away. He was attempting to prevent a larger problem with Alpha McAllister and the Council. Or he was after I... reminded him of that. Or else he probably would have sent the heads of that Enforcer and Alpha McAllister's daughter back to Alpha McAllister in a box for laying their hands on Kai."

Robson froze for a moment, then swallowed the fry in his mouth and took a sip of water. "You're being very cavalier about talking to a cop about murder and assault and almost murder."

Marcus's head tipped to the side a little, and Robson's belly fucking swooped. *What the fuck?* "I am not speaking to you as Deputy Medina. I am speaking to you as my— as Teresa's brother. Teresa and Patrick are members of the pack, and you will more than likely be extended that same privilege should you choose to join now that you are aware of everything."

Narrowing his eyes, Robson tapped the table between them with a finger. "That's twice now one of you started to refer to me as something in reference to you. Explain."

They'd been sitting in their booth talking for hours, and over the course of the conversation, Marcus had relaxed a little, his face actually forming some expressions and even smiling a few times at snarky comments Robson made. But as he watched, Marcus's face completely shut down at Robson's accusation.

"It was a slip of the tongue, nothing more." Marcus took another sip, then raised the nearly empty glass so their server saw it was nearly empty. "What other questions do you have?"

Jabbing a fry into some ketchup, he scowled at Marcus. "The dead body that was reported?"

He waited until the server was finished refilling his glass and checking on them before responding. "Her name was Agnes. She was a witch and was formerly the head of the Kincaid Pack coven."

"Oh, she was the one who orchestrated the attack on Kai, right? Helped his parents try and kill him and his siblings?" Robson had been pretty fucking horrified to hear about some of the awful things that had happened beneath the noses of law enforcement. The attack on Kai had been just months ago, when Robson had been back in Meyerville, but he'd been completely oblivious.

"Yes, her and a couple others. They all fled after blowing up a pack member's house, but Agnes helped Kai's parents sneak past the wards surrounding the territory."

Robson's eyes widened. "Okay, two questions: First, they blew up someone's fucking house? And second, explain the 'ward' thing to me. That's magic, right?"

"You'll meet him Saturday probably. He's an Enforcer now—Drake Hayes." Marcus paused and glanced away for a moment before meeting Robson's gaze once more. "He… lost pieces of himself that day. Including one of his arms."

Robson nodded. "I served for twelve years, man. He won't be the first person I've met missing a limb. He's still on the mend?"

"In some ways. His body is as healed as it will get though. Even with the poison they laced the explosives with, his advanced healing and Dr. Bell's quick intervention saved his life."

"Jesus." Robson could barely wrap his head around something so horrific happening in his own town. "How did no one find out about that? I mean… a house exploded. People notice shit like that."

Marcus shrugged and snagged another fry. "He lived outside of town, so he didn't have close neighbors. Plus, the sheriff and the police chief know."

Of course they did. That was why Robson had been fucking stonewalled every time he turned around. The sheriff hadn't just wanted Robson to forget about Kincaid and the others, he had been actively trying to protect them and their secrets. "Are they… shifters?"

Marcus shook his head. "No, though one of the part-time officers is. When Chief Baskin is ready to retire, she'll probably take over. Though she's a little young."

A part of Robson bristled at the idea of a shifter being the chief of police in his town. It wasn't that he thought they couldn't be trusted, but their loyalty would always be to the pack first. That was the one thing Marcus had made clear from the beginning—everyone in the Kincaid Pack answered to and was loyal to Rick Kincaid over everything and everyone else.

Shouldn't the police chief be loyal to the people in his or her town first and foremost?

"As for wards, they are like magical boundaries," Marcus was saying. "My understanding is that they can be created to keep someone out, keep someone in, or notify the witch who set it when someone crosses it. The strength of the witch determines the strength of the warding and how large the impact is."

"What does that mean?"

"Well… For example, most witches wouldn't have a problem setting a ward around a home to keep a specific person from entering." Marcus waited until Robson nodded his understanding before continuing. "But stronger witches can create larger wards over larger spaces and keep out more people or even more abstract people." Before Robson could complain that the explanation didn't make sense, Marcus hurried to add, "Such as Tashmica. She is extremely powerful in her own right and is able to draw additional strength from the rest of the coven and the pack. She has created warding around the territory that keeps out certain types of people—non-pack shifters or witches from other covens—or warns her when people with certain intentions cross the ward. Does that make more sense?"

Robson nodded, though his head was spinning. Invisible magical boundaries were harder for him to swallow than shifters for some reason. "And that was what I ran into at *Wicca We Can?*"

"Yes. Tash had set a ward to prevent non-pack members from entering, but for some reason it didn't dissuade you from walking in the store. The pain you experienced was the consequence of a crossing a ward you didn't have permission to cross." Marcus's eyes were full of regret as he stared at Robson. "Are you still... upset about that?"

The hopeful way Marcus asked made him want to brush it off and say he was over it, but he had to clarify something first. "So because Reesa is a member of your pack, she really would have been okay entering the shop?"

Marcus nodded. "Yes. She would have been absolutely fine. And maybe her requesting you enter the store was what allowed you to pass the warding... Tash wasn't sure the last I spoke with her. She is very sorry though, and so am I."

"I'm not upset at you for it—you didn't cause it to happen. And I'll probably forgive her eventually, but I want to talk to her myself first. Really get a feel for her."

Marcus's dark red eyebrows scrunched together before quickly smoothing out. "Feel for her? I don't think... I believe she knows who her mates are."

Robson was so confused again. "What?"

"If you want to... feel her, I believe you'll be rejected," Marcus said carefully, eyes on the plate between them. "She has premonitions, and I believe she has seen who her mates are, and you aren't one of them."

The conversation was beginning to remind him of the money laundering discussion, but this time he felt like laughing at Marcus's misunderstanding rather than strangling him over being deliberately obtuse. Leaning forward, he rested his forearms on the table and tried to catch Marcus's gaze but was unsuccessful. "Did she tell you who her *mates* will be?"

"Excuse me?" Marcus glanced up but quickly looked away when he caught Robson's smirk.

"How do you know I'm not one of her *mates*? Did she tell you who each one was?"

He wasn't sure what possessed him to poke at the damn *wolf* sitting across from him, but his breath caught in the back of his throat when Marcus turned hard, glowing eyes on him, and snarled, "You *are not* one of her mates."

His smirk turned into a grin, and he leaned back against the booth cushion, crossing his arms over his chest. "Why not? She couldn't mate a human? That's speciest. She's very attractive and seems extremely intelligent and capable—I'm sure I'd be very happy in her harem."

The growl that filled the space between them sent a shiver down Robson's spine—but it wasn't from fear. *Fuck.* Robson glanced around the diner to make sure no one had noticed the noise while he dropped a hand into his lap and tried to subtly adjust his thickening cock.

The sound cut off abruptly, and when Robson turned back to Marcus, he had to chuckle at the confused head tilt the guy was sporting once more.

"You aren't afraid?" Marcus's green eyes ran over Robson's face and body, a slight furrow between his brows.

"No, Marcus, I'm not afraid." He wasn't exactly prepared to tell him that his dick was suddenly associating the sound of a wolf *growling* with a sexy, possessive Marcus, but he could definitely admit he wasn't frightened.

"Why not?"

He couldn't help but laugh again. He was pretty sure Marcus didn't *want* Robson to be afraid of him; he just didn't understand why he *wasn't*. "I served in the military—I obviously don't have great self-preservation instincts."

He saw the urge to ask about his service in Marcus's eyes, but he didn't want to change the subject just yet. His time in the military had been... less traumatizing than it could have been. He'd come back with his body in one piece and his mind mostly intact, even if he had the occasional nightmare. He knew a lot of men and women weren't as lucky, and it made him feel guilty as hell. Part of him felt like he should have served until he'd sacrificed a bigger piece of himself.

"So what happened with the wreaths that has you and that Jamie guy at each other throats?"

Marcus glanced away. "It wasn't the wreaths... Are you familiar with the Harvest Festival?"

"Sure. We didn't have it as a kid, but I'd heard about it from my family and attended some of it this year. You two were responsible for making wreaths for the festival?"

Shaking his head, Marcus flattened his hands on the table in front of him and kept his gaze turned downward. "No. The Harvest Festival is a pack event that the town is invited to, even though they don't realize the significance of many of the traditions and activities. The committee that organizes everything only includes pack members and is supervised by a high-ranking member so they can report the progress to Alpha Kincaid and deal with any issues that pop up."

"Let me guess—you supervised the committee." Robson could absolutely see Marcus bossing around a group of middle-aged women and making them remake wreaths that weren't up to par.

Marcus grimaced slightly. "I was the supervisor for previous years. This year... I was replaced after I had a disagreement with Jamie regarding certain traditions being included. One of the traditions he wanted to stop using was the one where wreaths made with myrrh were presented to the homes and businesses along the parade route to be hung during the festival. Myrrh is a type of amplifier and is used during a lot of moon rituals, so it's a Wiccan tradition as well as a Kincaid Pack one to use it. Jamie felt it wasn't a good use of time to make the wreaths." Marcus sighed and pressed his fingertips into the tabletop so hard they turned white. "It wasn't the only thing he attempted to change, but it was the final straw that led to our argument."

"Argument? Like, you yelled at each other?"

Marcus nodded. "Yes."

"You, Marcus Rivera, *yelled* at someone?" His teasing tone finally seemed to penetrate, and Marcus rolled his eyes, his hands relaxing once more.

"Yes, I, Marcus Rivera, yelled at someone. I'm capable of losing my temper."

He leaned forward and let his eyes drop to Marcus's lips for a moment. "I think I'd kind of like to see that."

Marcus sucked in a deep breath through his nose, his green eyes deepening and starting to glow just the slightest bit around the outside edge of his irises. "Why?"

Robson bit his lower lip and smiled. "I think seeing you lose control would be a damn fine sight to see."

"Robson..."

Marcus's voice held what sounded like a note of warning, but Robson ignored it. He was still putting all the pieces together of who Marcus was, but one thing he was beginning to realize was that there were vulnerable sides to Marcus that made Robson want to protect him from the world.

Leaning back again, he grinned at the unsteady breath Marcus took. "So is my new niece gonna turn into an animal at some point or what?"

"Marcus!"

They both turned, Robson jolting a little at the reminder that they weren't alone. He'd gotten so wrapped up in Marcus and their conversation that the nearly empty diner had faded into the background. The man striding toward their table was wearing a dirty apron and an enormous smile.

"Hello, Victor. How are you?" Marcus gave his small smile that meant he was pleased, his eyes lighting up with happiness.

"I'm good! It's been too long. How are things at the—" He eyed Robson and gave him a fake smile. "How's the job? Must be staying busy since you haven't stopped by in weeks."

Frown tugging at his mouth, Robson crossed his arms and eyed the younger man a little more closely, wondering if he meant Marcus hadn't stopped by Momma's... or the guy's house. He realized Victor had to be only a little younger than Marcus, who was mid-twenties probably, though his serious demeanor made him seem older and closer to Robson's late thirties.

"Sorry, I've been working on a project for Alpha Kincaid." At Victor's enormous eyes, Marcus's smile stretched just a little wider. He dipped his head in Robson's direction. "Victor, this is Deputy Robson Medina. He's just learning about the pack. Robson, this is my cousin, Victor. He's the mastermind behind the excellent food at this establishment."

Victor grinned, wiped his hand on his apron, and extended it to Robson. "Hey, man. Welcome to the pack."

"Oh, no. I'm..." He stopped himself and just returned

Victor's smile and handshake. "Thank you. It's a pleasure to meet you."

Looking between Robson and Marcus, Victor waggled his eyebrows. "The pleasure is mine. Definitely."

"Victor," Marcus growled.

Victor only laughed. "Cuz, that tone doesn't work on me even if you are a pack Enforcer. I've known you too long."

Marcus grumbled something under his breath as he reached for his glass of water, making Robson and Victor both chuckle.

"I won't interrupt—I just wanted to come say hi and remind you to not be a stranger around here."

Standing, Marcus pulled Victor into a quick embrace, ending with his hand on the side of his cousin's neck. "You're doing okay?" he asked quietly.

"I'm fine. You have to stop worrying about me. It's been three years." Victor gripped Marcus's forearm. "You already saved me, cuz."

CHAPTER TEN

Wendy: *Let me get to my office and I'll call you. Hang on.*

Marcus paced in front of his desk, eyes on his phone as he waited for it to ring. He was pretty sure that if anyone could help him get access to the old archives, it would be Wendy. She'd worked for the Council since before he had and was one of the few people still there that he knew and trusted. She tended to go unnoticed by the powerful former alphas on the Council, but Marcus's old boss had always told him to go to Wendy if he ever needed anything.

Of course, Marcus used to be able to go to his old mentor and boss, Councilman Gregson. His heart squeezed at the thought of him. When he'd been shipped off to "work" for the Council by his pack alpha as a terrified sixteen-year-old, he'd thought it would be the worst thing to ever happen to him. His parents had always been distant, unhappy with his bright red hair and easily flushed skin, but it was his alpha who couldn't stand the sight of him for some reason. Marcus had never fully understood it, but his alpha had singled him out in their small pack and treated him horribly. Verbal and emotional abuse and manipulation had taught him quickly to control himself—the less he reacted, the quicker it would stop.

He froze in his steps as his phone rang in his hand, shaking off his depressing thoughts. "Hello, Wendy. How are you?"

"Marcus, sweetie, I'm fine. How are you? How's your pack? Things have gotten... strained around here, but I've stayed because I had a feeling I'd be getting a call from you." Wendy's voice was soft, and he could barely hear her over the loud music in the background.

"I'm... fine." Even with her precautions, he worried about revealing anything that could be overheard. He trusted Wendy completely, but most of the Council he no longer had much faith in. "Are you sure it's safe to talk?"

"As sure as I can be. I don't think they've bugged my office or anything, but some of the Council members are getting... aggressive in their proposals for dealing with your alpha and pack. They're upset about the disrespect from Bennett Young but..." He only heard the loud music for a moment, then the sounds changed and the background noise faded some. When she spoke again, there was a slight echo like she was in a bathroom. "I overheard Councilman Kincaid saying that it was disappointing Alpha McAllister didn't kill the Council-man's son but that they'd take care of him eventually."

Rick's father was definitely the rotten apple spoiling the rest of the Council from the inside. Rumor had it that he'd been bested by one of his own Enforcers and had handed over his pack rather than die fighting for control. Rick and Bennett—who was also from Rick's father's pack originally—had both been very surprised, but when it had been announced Alistair Kincaid would become a member of the Council, they'd realized he'd seen an opportunity for a different kind of power.

"Who was he talking to?" Marcus asked, stomach souring.

"I don't know. He was on the phone and in another room, so I couldn't make it out. Maybe a woman?"

Marcus rubbed at his forehead. "Is he turning the rest of the Council against us? I was worried after what happened with the McAllister hearing and Bennett's rash decision to storm in and drag Kieran away..."

Wendy sighed. "Garcia and Voight are holding firm against his pushes to retaliate. He keeps trying to convince the Council to make an example of Rick and your pack, says other packs will lose their trust in the Council or will see them as weak."

Sucking in a slow breath, Marcus tried to figure out what to do. He'd been trying to get Wendy on the phone for weeks to try and assess how badly their relationship with the Council had been damaged, but this was the first time they'd been able to speak in private. "What kind of retaliation is he pushing for? A fine or...?"

"No," she croaked, "he wants them to dissolve the Kincaid Pack and... execute Rick and his mate as examples."

"*Fuck.*"

Wendy gasped at his curse, but he couldn't even bring himself to care about his foul language.

"This is even worse than I'd been imagining. He's advocating for the death of his own son? Really?" Marcus stalked around his desk and collapsed into his chair, closing his eyes.

"The others were shocked at first too, but he made it sound like he's trying to be impartial and that he'd propose the same if any other pack had disrespected the Council and shifter law as much as his son had."

Marcus snorted. "Tell me the others aren't buying that garbage. Rick doesn't flout shifter law, and the McAllister hearing was a joke. You know that. Bennett lost his temper because of how horribly Kieran was being treated by Kincaid and some of the others."

"I know, but he's managed to convince a couple of them. Not enough to do anything but… I'm worried, Marcus. He's been meeting in private with his allies, and I'm concerned he'll somehow force Garcia and Voight off the Council. I don't know how, but if anyone could do it…"

"It's him," he finished, stomach revolting at the idea of Kincaid staging some sort of coup and taking over the Council. The man was a sadist and would revel in torturing any pack that tried to stand against him. "My request for some old documents in the archives seems unnecessary now."

She hesitated, almost like she was surprised that had been what he was contacting her about, then she said, "Okay. I have something for you though."

That brought him up short. "You do?"

"Yes, Councilwoman Voight slipped it to me a couple weeks ago, and I've been trying to find a way to get it to you, but I didn't want to risk leaving Mehko to find a place to mail it in a human city." She paused, and his anxiety ratcheted up. "It's… from Councilman Gregson. He tried to mail it to you right before his death, but apparently he was stopped. I'm not sure how Voight got her hands on it."

He squeezed his eyes shut and took a deep breath to try and calm his raging emotions. His office door opened slowly, and Nico's scent calmed him a little. "What is it?"

"A letter, I think. I didn't open it."

He peered at Nico's worried face, then shut his eyes again. "Read it to me, please."

Wendy cleared her throat, and he heard a tearing sound. She quietly read him the last thing Mikel had probably ever written, the back of his mind wondering if it was what had gotten him killed. The Council had declared his death from natural causes, but Marcus and the rest of his pack didn't buy that. Mikel had called Rick right before his death and told him not to trust the Council and that he was coming to see him so he could talk to him freely. They'd never heard anything else from him. Marcus wondered if the letter was written before or after his call to Rick.

When Wendy finished, she said there were some numbers on the bottom of the page.

Marcus croaked out, "What do you mean?"

"Some sort of code. He told me he was being watched. At the time, I thought he was perhaps just being paranoid. You know how eccentric he'd always been."

Marcus grunted in agreement as he slowly sat forward, mind running fast. A code. Holy shit. "I think... Never mind. Can you read the numbers to me? I'm going to copy it down."

"I don't think I should," she whispered, "just in case."

Just in case Kincaid or one of his minions were listening.

"Can you get me the letter?" he asked carefully, guilt souring his stomach at putting her at risk. "I don't want you taking unnecessary risks though."

"I'll do my best." She crinkled the paper a little, then opened and closed some sort of cupboard or drawer. She lowered her voice even further. "I think I may have to bring the letter to you in person."

He sat up straight and met Nico's wide eyes. "Wendy, do not put yourself at risk. It isn't worth your life."

She didn't say anything for a long moment, just quietly breathing into the phone. "If you find something important enough in it," she said softly, "then it just might be. If we don't stop Councilman Kincaid... Marcus, I'll do everything I can. Once I leave Mehko, I'll purchase another phone and contact you. Don't use this number again unless it's an emergency, okay?"

"Wendy..."

"I know what I'm doing," she said, voice a little firmer.

Nico's grim face probably matched Marcus's own. "Okay," he said gruffly. "I won't contact this number again."

She took a shuddery breath. "Thank you. I'll see you in a couple weeks, okay? If you don't hear from me by then... don't wait for me. Come up with a new plan."

She hung up before he could say anything or try and convince her not to put herself in danger for him and his pack. His chest was heavy with guilt and fear.

"What did I just do?" he whispered, looking up at Nico. He thought he might be sick. "She's going to get herself killed playing hero, and it'll be my fault."

"Stop that." Nico stood and came around Marcus's desk, pulling him to his feet and wrapping Marcus's cold body into his warm arms. "She's a grown woman who recognizes the dangers of an out-of-control Council being led by an evil man bent on taking out his own son. Plus, she's smart. Don't count her out just yet."

There was a buzzing in Marcus's ears that he recognized, and he couldn't catch his breath no matter how tightly Nico squeezed him. It had been a long time since he'd felt so out of control, so close to passing out. He needed... he needed...

"Gotta run," he gasped out, dots starting to fill his vision. He felt so weak and useless as Nico quickly grabbed his hand and pulled him through his office and toward the back of the house. It was just after lunch during the week, so a part of Marcus hoped they wouldn't run into anyone near the kitchen, but he knew better.

Kai came skidding out of the kitchen in his socks, eyes wide and worried. "What's wrong?"

Marcus couldn't have responded if he'd wanted to, and he didn't hear what Nico said, but suddenly they were outside and Nico was helping him remove his clothing. As soon as he was naked, he let his wolf out and was able to take a deep breath for the first time since he'd hung up with Wendy.

After taking a few breaths, he noticed the white wolf on the other side of him. *Kai.* His alpha-mate had come with them. His human side wanted to be embarrassed that Kai had seen him having one of his rare panic attacks, but his wolf was just happy to have him there. He nudged his muzzle against the side of Kai's face, scenting himself on his alpha-mate and darting away when Kai playfully snapped his teeth at him.

Turning toward the trees, he ran.

He heard the other two wolves behind him, but he ran as hard and as fast as he could, putting distance between himself and them. It felt like his feet were barely touching the cool grass or colorful leaves as he sprinted through the trees without destination. His breaths were sawing in and out of his chest and he felt alive and invigorated like he hadn't in a long time.

Then he heard it. His alpha's call.

Skidding to a stop, he threw his head back and responded, howling into the sky as loud and long as he could. Before the sound had disappeared into the half-bare trees, he was off again, darting between trunks. No longer running at a breakneck speed, he still followed scents of prey animals and barked at a squirrel before continuing onward, looping back toward the manor so they didn't get too far away.

As he neared a small clearing, his wolf stopped and dropped his chest to the ground at the sight of his alpha standing in the middle of the grassy area, waiting for him. Then he darted forward and feinted to the left before shooting to the right, but Rick had played with him too many times to fall for it. A moment later, he was tumbling to the ground and rolling onto his back, showing his belly to his alpha.

Rick nosed at his exposed throat, then licked his muzzle and lay half on top of Marcus, huffing out a breath as he settled his head on Marcus's chest right over his racing heart.

A moment later, Kai was lying next to him, resting his snout on Marcus's throat, and Nico was sprawled beside him, pressed against his side and also on his back, enjoying the midafternoon sun.

He released a soft cry, and Kai echoed it, lifting his head to lick his face, then settle back down on him. Feeling the weight of his alpha, alpha-mate, and best friend pressing him into the earth and anchoring him finally calmed his panicky thoughts and began to slow his heart and breathing.

He knew he needed to tell Rick about what Wendy had shared and what she planned to do, but his wolf was too comfortable and happy surrounded by most of his favorite scents.

"It's been a while since I've needed that," Marcus said softly several hours later as he let himself and Nico into his small house. He flicked on a few lights as he moved into the kitchen.

"Well, it's been a while since you've let yourself have that. I keep telling you to stop skipping runs and movie nights. Even if your dumb human brain convinces you that needing the reassuring contact of pack is weakness, your wolf knows better. Start listening to him more." Nico plopped down into a seat at the small kitchen table in the corner of the room, crossing his arms over his wide chest and giving Marcus a hard look.

"It's not even that..." Marcus knew he didn't spend enough time scenting and bonding with his packmates, but it wasn't because he didn't see the value in it or thought he didn't need it. He sighed as he grabbed a couple of bottles of water and sat next to Nico at the table. "It's like... if I don't remind myself to do it, I subconsciously fall into old habits and think I'm not... I don't know, welcome or whatever."

It'd been a long time since he'd talked like this with Nico as well. His body and mind were feeling loose after the influx of dopamine the puppy pile had given him, even though he'd had to inform Rick and Kai about his conversation with Wendy when they returned to the manor. Rick had sighed a lot and rubbed his forehead, then sent him and Nico home, telling them he'd see them the next day.

"Sometimes you say shit like that and it makes me really angry at your old pack and family," Nico said, voice a bit growly.

Marcus smiled at him. "It is what it is. Anger won't change who they are or what they did. And it won't change the things they taught me."

Nico grunted and leaned forward, gripping Marcus's forearm tightly. "You're like a brother to me, okay? I'm going to be better about forcing you to go for runs and letting Fi snuggle the shit out of you on the couch while we watch *Moana* for the nine hundredth time."

Marcus chuckled a little, but it died off quickly, his mind slipping to a concern he'd been ruminating on for days. "Do you think..."

"What?"

He took a deep breath. Bennett had told him he could talk to him about mates, but he didn't know if he'd have the guts to bring it up out of the blue with him. "Do you remember when you first learned about mates?"

Nico's eyebrows shot up, and his face split into a grin as he released Marcus's arm and leaned back in his chair. "Sure. The pack I grew up in was pretty open about matings and... mating." He winked at Marcus, chuckling when his face heated in embarrassment. "They didn't have a coven like ours, so they didn't have a lot of the rituals and celebrations incorporated into their pack laws and lifestyle. But on full moons, we'd usually gather as a pack and have a big bonfire, and mated couples would fuck under the moonlight, just outside the light of the flames."

Marcus sucked in a breath, his eyes feeling enormous. "They had sex in the open like that?"

Nodding, Nico sipped some water and adjusted in his seat. Marcus ignored the deepening of Nico's scent, too interested in hearing about such a strange pack ritual.

"Yeah, it was normal to us. I remember as a kid barely even thinking about the fact that most of the adults would slip a few feet away and get naked, but when I went through puberty..." He shook his head and laughed lightly. "I remember there was one couple who didn't even bother leaving their spots by the fire. I guess because it wasn't like we couldn't see the others in the dark anyway, you know? Anyway, this couple would just... she'd drop to all fours right there, and her mate would just go to town behind her."

Swallowing, it was Marcus's turn to shift in his seat. He didn't think he'd ever be comfortable having others watching him during such an intimate act, but the idea of watching others? "Your pack was very..."

"Hedonistic? Yeah. They embraced their wolf sides more than other packs do, but that also meant there were more fights and less opportunity for advancement. We barely had any technology and shunned contact with humans." He shook his head once more, then cleared his throat. "Sorry, I got a little off track there. You wanted to know when I learned about mates?"

"Yeah. Or, well..." Marcus looked away and frowned at the ground. Was he really going to ask Nico about this?

"My parents told me that my mate would be my other half. That they'd make me better and give me anything I needed while I'd do the same for them," Nico said with a shrug when Marcus glanced back at him, his lips pressed together. "I always kind of thought it was bullshit actually."

"Really?"

"Yeah. Then I watched Rick—the biggest, baddest, *grumpiest* asshole I'd ever met—"

Marcus scowled and Nico laughed.

"I watched him fall for Kai so hard and so fast and... I don't know. I watch them sometimes—Bennett and Kieran too—and it's like... they really do balance each other out. And they have a unique connection. I think my parents had that too, but I was so young and anxious to get away from the pack that I couldn't see it for what it was."

"So you think... you think something draws us to our real mates? That we don't just choose someone and fall in love like humans seem to do?"

Nico tipped back in his chair, and Marcus stopped himself from scolding him, wanting to hear what he had to say. He'd tried to convince himself that it wasn't something magical drawing him to Robson, that he'd simply been attracted to him and his wolf had latched on. But the idea had never taken root. Like Nico, he'd seen how the others had seemed to bond quickly and deeply, leaving their bonding bites on each other as well. Not all couples exchanged those, but powerful shifters were more likely to, their animal side especially wanting the visual representation of their mating.

"I think... the stronger the shifter, the stronger the pull, but yes. I think something other than simple attraction draws us to our mates."

The stronger the shifter, the stronger the pull. That made sense actually. He thought about the sweet looks he'd seen Reesa and Patrick exchanging after the birth of their daughter and remembered feeling that they were no doubt mates, but the intensity of their pairing didn't seem to match Rick and Kai or Bennett and Kieran.

"Do you want to talk about him?" Nico asked softly, jolting Marcus out of his thoughts.

He shook his head and ground his teeth together to stop himself from releasing the well of feelings bubbling up inside him. "No," he choked out, "I really don't. It doesn't matter how drawn I feel to him, he can never feel the same way."

"Says who?"

Marcus froze, halfway up from his seat, and then he slowly lowered himself back down. "What do you mean? He's human. There's no way—"

"Says who?" Nico repeated, giving Marcus a look that said he was tired of Marcus being deliberately obtuse.

"Nico, he's not a shifter. He can't feel the pull—"

"Says. Who?" At Marcus's frustrated growl, Nico grinned and stood, stretching his body before pointing at Marcus. "Don't assume shit, man. Two humans may not be able to feel the magical pull of a mating, but who says a human can't feel it for a shifter? We're fucking magical creatures, Marcus." Nico turned and started toward the front door, tossing over his shoulder, "Maybe stop pretending like you have all the answers and go ask someone who knows more about magic than either of us."

CHAPTER ELEVEN

"**H**ere, hold the baby," Reesa muttered, placing a sleeping bundle in Robson's arms before he'd even responded, then shuffling out of the living room.

He stared down at his niece's wrinkly little face and smiled. "Hello, beautiful."

The front door swung open and Patrick strolled in, smiling at Robson. "Hey, man. How's it going?"

"Getting in some quality Maria time, so I can't complain." He hesitated, then said carefully, "That's a nice front door."

Patrick grinned and looked back at it. "Yeah. I told Marcus it was too much, but he waved me off, scented Maria, and left. He's a man of few words but generous to a fault."

Robson hadn't thought he was that quiet, but he took the opening he'd created and ran with it. "Yeah, he seems... nice enough. You guys know him pretty well?"

Opening his mouth, Patrick snapped it shut and looked toward the kitchen. "Hang on one second." He disappeared faster than should have been possible, and Robson sighed.

"Another thing I missed, Maria." He leaned down and

breathed in the new baby smell on Maria's head and groaned softly. "That's the good stuff right there."

"Are you snorting our daughter's scent like a drug?" Reesa asked.

He looked up and had to press his lips together not to laugh as Patrick carried her into the living room bridal-style. She was frowning and had her arms crossed, but Patrick was smiling and had his nose buried in her hair. Which… he was pretty sure she hadn't showered in days, so he wondered how good she could actually smell.

"Oh, is that weird? But your husband smelling you as he carries you around is perfectly fine?"

Patrick chuckled as he settled into the large recliner next to the couch Robson was sitting on, situating Reesa on his lap but not releasing his hold. She sighed and settled in against him, not bothering to fight the inevitable. Robson raised his eyebrows at them and patted Maria's diapered butt when she started to stir a little.

"Teresa knows she's supposed to be taking it easy." Patrick spoke from where he was pressing a kiss to her neck, and Robson couldn't figure out how he felt about their easy affection. A little grossed out because she was his sister but also maybe… a little jealous?

"What were you doing?" he asked his sister.

"Nothing strenuous," she claimed quickly, but Patrick just snorted as he trailed his nose up to behind her ear. "I was just going to make dinner."

Robson shook his head and looked back down at Maria, wondering how he could subtly bring the conversation back around to Marcus.

"So you want to know about Enforcer Rivera, huh?" Reesa asked, grinning when Robson's head shot up in surprise. "Patrick told me you were asking about him as soon as he walked in the door."

He shot a glare at his smirking brother-in-law. "I was just commenting on the door, then asked how well you guys knew him. That's all."

Patrick frowned. "He gave you *the talk*, right?"

"No, but I learned about sex a long time ago," Robson deadpanned.

"Funny. No, I mean the talk about what and who we are and the things we can do."

Robson nodded. "Yeah. I mean, I still have questions, but he gave me the general spiel about shifters, the abridged history of them, and then some details about the Kincaid Pack in general. He even told me he'd leave it up to me about how much I wanted to share with Hector since he'd seen Marcus's partial shift too."

"What did you tell him?" Patrick asked.

"Nothing he hadn't apparently already figured out." At Patrick's and Reesa's surprised faces, he chuckled softly. "Apparently, Hector is a lot smarter and more observant than the rest of us combined. He said he'd heard some rumors and seen some things in the last few years that had him wondering about certain community members—specifically Kincaid and some of the Enforcers—but that he didn't want to know any more."

"Why not?" Teresa said, leaning forward a little like she couldn't understand why anyone wouldn't want to be involved with the Kincaid Pack if given the option.

Robson shrugged with one shoulder, careful not to disturb Maria. "He said anyone who kept themselves secret like that had the potential of resulting in a dangerous situation and he didn't want to get himself or his family involved. I don't blame him, honestly."

Patrick nodded, eyes dropping to Maria and briefly flashing. "He's not wrong," he murmured.

There was a moment where they were all silent, each of

them no doubt contemplating what might be on the horizon and the impact it could have on their loved ones.

Finally, Reesa cleared her throat. "Okay, well, what else do you want to know?" She leaned forward a little, smiling eagerly at Robson. "I don't know everything, obviously, but I've gotten a crash course since mating Patrick. The class at the rec center has been very informative too."

Robson narrowed his eyes and looked between them. "What class? Is that what you were doing there when I ran into you all?"

"Huh." Reesa turned to her husband—er, mate. *Or are they both married and mated?* "I wonder why he didn't tell Robito about the classes and mentoring program."

Patrick shrugged and leaned back in the recliner, finally seeming to have satisfied his urge to sniff Robson's sister. "Maybe he didn't want to brag? Or he didn't think Robson would be interested in attending..."

"Hello? Right here. What classes?" He waved his hand at them to bring their attention back to him.

"Marcus and Vanessa—another pack Enforcer—are hosting... education classes, I guess you could call them, at the rec center once a week and starting a mentorship program," Reesa explained.

"Well, the mentorship program I hear was Jamie's idea," Patrick put in. "Rumor has it that was what got him the job as Alpha Kincaid's assistant."

Robson was so confused. "Wait, wait, wait. Why would shifters need education classes? And why are you basing information on rumors? Can't you just ask one of the Enforcers or that Jamie guy? And also, why do shifters need mentors?"

Reesa and Patrick both laughed at his rapid-fire questions, but Patrick settled down quickly and said, "Maybe in a small pack everyone would know everyone and everything, but the Kincaid Pack is huge. Hundreds of members spread across a really big territory. Some of us live in town, but a lot live in the surrounding area so they aren't so close to humans and can shift more freely. The Enforcers are there if you need them, but it isn't like most pack members are friends with them. They're too busy taking care of the pack."

Robson gaped at him. "Hundreds?"

Reesa nodded eagerly. "Yeah, it's like this whole separate town within the town. Or really, right next to, like a parallel universe."

Robson thought back to Marcus's cousin at the diner Robson had gone to his whole life. "How many businesses are owned by pack members?"

"At least half of the ones in town are either owned by the pack and run by chosen members or are privately owned by pack members. Plus, the factory west of town?" Patrick was grinning again.

"Yeah?" Robson had a feeling he knew where this was going. The factory had been built a few years ago while he was still enlisted, but he'd heard about it. The place employed a few hundred people and had been big news for the area.

Patrick's grin widened. "Pack owned. There were so many new shifters moving to the area to join the pack that Rick was worried about employment for everyone. I mean, if you need anything, the pack will help provide it, but being part of a pack means giving back and taking care of each other, so people want to work."

Robson hummed his response as his mind chewed over that information, an idea starting to form in the back of his mind. "What about the classes?"

"Oh, that's easy. Shifters don't know shit about their own history most of the time," Reesa said, laughing at the sputtering of her husband. "And a lot of them get surprised by... sex things."

Robson made a grossed-out face, and then her words registered. "Wait, what? What do you mean?"

Patrick's face was beet red. "Oh my god, Teresa."

She giggled and pressed a kiss to one of his flushed cheeks. "You should just come to the sexual education class this week. That was the most asked about topic, Marcus said, so they moved it up the list and are going to cover it sooner than they'd planned."

The idea of sweet, awkward Marcus leading a discussion about shifters having sex both amused and aroused Robson. His dick was so confused by the man. "Marcus Rivera is going to talk to a room full of people about sex?"

Patrick laughed, face finally losing some of its color. "Well, no. I think Nico and Bennett are leading the discussion. Nico's a wolf and Bennett a tiger. Since the majority of the pack are canines or felines, the two of them would cover most everyone."

"Jamie's a bird, right? Will he be part of it, you think, or are there not enough bird shifters in the pack?" Robson was definitely going if the class was open to non-shifters.

Reesa shrugged. "He might. Though he doesn't seem the type to talk about sex and sex organs either."

Sex organs. "Good lord, Reesa," he muttered, then refocused on Maria as she began to fuss in his arms. "Uh-oh, someone else was disturbed by her mom's choice in words."

Reesa chuckled as she stood carefully, Patrick's hands on her hips supporting her, and came over to take Maria from him. "I'm going to feed her and lie down."

"Okay," he said, standing and giving her a gentle hug. "Motherhood looks good on you, mami."

"Shut up, I look like hell," she said, kissing his cheek and smiling.

"You do not," Patrick growled.

"Your vision is obviously clouded by mating endorphins

or whatever, but that's okay. I'll take it." She shot Patrick a sweet look, then disappeared up the stairs.

Robson resettled on the couch, glancing at his phone to check the time. He still had about forty-five minutes before he was expected at the manor. Turning back to Patrick, he was surprised by the unfocused look in his eyes and was confused about why his head was tilted at a weird angle.

"What are you doing?"

"Listening to Teresa to make sure she made it upstairs okay," Patrick muttered. A few seconds later, he refocused on Robson with a small smile. "She told me to stop listening to her, that she was fine."

"Could she hear you?" Had her senses changed after… mating with a shifter?

"Oh no," Patrick said, shaking his head. "She just knows me well. Doc and Rick both mentioned my instincts might be more heightened for a while with a vulnerable mate and newborn in the house, and they were definitely right."

Robson nodded absently, then said, "Can you explain more about what that means, 'your instincts'?"

"Oh yeah, sure. So shifters have their human and animal sides, right?" He waited until Robson nodded before continuing. "And while they're separate in that their animal and human halves each have their own needs and desires, there's a lot of overlap. So really they're more like two sides to the same coin, you know?"

His nod was slower but still there. "You almost make it sound like the animal side is a separate entity, but Marcus said shifters are in control even in their shifted form. That it's still them."

"We are, but everything is… extreme when you're your animal."

Robson raised his brows.

"Okay, yeah, that was clear as mud." Patrick rubbed his chin. "So I'm a fox shifter, right?"

"I didn't know that, but okay. Marcus is a wolf, right?" He hadn't had a chance to verify it, but he was positive the wolf he'd met at his house had been Marcus. When he'd thought about bringing it up at the diner, he'd hesitated, wondering how he could ask about the way Marcus had lain on top of him in his wolf form yet barely smiled at him as a human.

"Yes. So for canine shifters like us, scent and pack are everything, no matter what form we're in. But when I shift into my fox, it's like a hundred times more intense. The instincts I have in my human form—to protect my family and pack, to scent mark them, to provide for them—are turned up to a thousand."

"When you're in your human form, how good is your sense of smell compared to a regular human's?"

Patrick tilted his head as he thought about that, reminding Robson of Marcus's confused face. "I'm not sure. I've never been 'regular,' so I can't really compare the two, but full-blooded shifters can smell out scents left by humans and animals up to an hour earlier. Stronger shifters, like alphas and Enforcers, have even stronger senses. I've heard Rick can hear his mate's heart from the other side of the manor despite the noise of other people and the sound-proofing on most of the rooms."

"Whoa. What kind of scents do people give off? Like, body odor?" Should he run home and reapply his deodorant?

Patrick laughed. "You smell fine, don't worry. Most shifters don't pay attention to surface scents like that. We learn from a young age to pay attention to what's beneath that—emotions and intentions."

Robson's mouth dropped open. "I'm sorry, what? You can smell my emotions?"

"Sure. Not as well as stronger shifters, but I can smell

your surprise and that the idea makes you uncomfortable." Patrick inhaled through his nose, eyes closing as he concentrated, and Robson flashed back to every time he'd seen Marcus breathe in like that when he was near Robson. Had he been trying to read Robson's emotions? "Now you're a little angry."

"Stop that," he snapped, then shook his head when Patrick's eyes popped open, hurt clouding his blue eyes. "Sorry. I just... That's kind of invasive."

Patrick's mouth twisted to the side, and he looked away. "Teresa felt the same way at first. We nearly broke up over it."

"What changed her mind?"

Patrick smiled. "I finally convinced her of the advantages of having a mate who could read her so well, know what she needed even if she couldn't voice it, and be completely devoted."

"Completely devoted? What, like you can't cheat on her?" He tried to make a joke even as his hands were clenching and his heart picking up speed at the idea of having someone being that in tune with him. Not being able to have secrets sounded scary at first but... with the right person, why would he want to have any?

Patrick looked horrified. "Of course not! We're mates. It doesn't matter that she's human—my fox knows and is absolutely committed. Shifters mate for life."

Robson sucked in a breath but tried to keep his body from reacting too obviously, hyperaware now of what Patrick might be getting from him. "People keep talking about mates like they're different than spouses."

Chuckling, Patrick kicked back in his recliner and threaded his fingers behind his head, looking completely at ease. "Real mates are. Sometimes shifters will say they're mates, but they aren't really. Usually that happens when packs want to make alliances. But true matings? It's something completely different than just falling in love or choosing to marry someone. For one, you don't choose, your animal side does. Though I've heard they don't actually choose either, they just recognize their mate before the human side does."

"So… magic?" Robson grunted, annoyed with how often that was the answer to things.

"Well, yeah." Patrick tipped his head to look at Robson more fully. "I know you don't feel it the same way we do, but trust me, once you accept him as your mate, you'll be a lot happier."

Robson's stomach dropped out of his body, and he stood so fast he hit his knee on the coffee table. Wincing, he ignored the pain and stared into Patrick's worried eyes as he sat up. "What?"

"Oh, fuck me. I'm so dead."

"Patrick! What did you mean? Is…" He couldn't even say it. How could he be Marcus's… He suddenly felt warmth in his chest as his body remembered the feeling of peace and calm that had enveloped him when wolf-Marcus had lain on him, offering him comfort. He cleared his throat. "Am I Marcus's mate?"

Patrick stood slowly, nodding and hands out in front of him. "Listen, can you please not tell him I told you? Fuck, I messed up. I just… the way you were asking about him and the fact that he told you so much about us… Oh my god."

"Calm down, man. I won't tell him." Robson could barely focus on what Patrick was saying, his mind spinning at what the revelation meant. He raced through his memories, back to the very first one, and clearly recalled how Marcus had stared at him even as Robson had yelled at the chief of police. "Did he know as soon as he met me?"

Patrick's face was buried in his hands, and he muttered something, but Robson couldn't make it out.

"Seriously, will you calm yourself? Marcus isn't going to kill you, for god's sake."

Dropping his hands, Patrick glared at Robson. "You don't know that. You don't mess with another shifter's mating, Robson. That's not just a suggestion—it's literally part of Kincaid Pack law. If he wanted to, Marcus could exile me from the pack for interfering."

Robson rolled his eyes. "Stop being so dramatic. For one thing, I'd never let that happen, okay? For another, I already told you I wouldn't say anything."

"You don't have to, remember? He'll be able to sniff out the truth in two seconds." Patrick collapsed back into the recliner and rubbed at his forehead. "Tell him I'm very sorry and I'll accept any punishment—"

"Oh my god, shut up," Robson growled.

Patrick's mouth snapped shut, his eyes wide as he stared at Robson.

"I know I've been an ass to you, but will you just trust me?"

Nodding, Patrick said, "Yeah, okay. Sorry. Kind of spiraled there for a second. Heightened instincts, remember?"

Robson grumbled under his breath as he headed for the door.

"Where are you going?" Patrick trailed after him.

"I've been formally invited to Kincaid Manor or whatever."

"Whoa, really?"

He paused, hand on the doorknob. "Yeah. Is that not common? Wasn't Reesa invited at some point?"

Patrick shook his head. "No. I mean, I've been there, once. I had to go and formally request permission to tell her about me and the pack, but that's it, and I've been a member for nearly three years."

"Huh." That made it sound like the place was a fortress to keep the pack separate from Kincaid and the others. "Did you feel unwelcome when you were there?"

"Oh no! The opposite. Rick was much nicer than I was expecting, but he's super busy at the same time. He made it clear he and the Enforcers would always be there if Teresa or I needed something though. Which… that's more than a lot of alphas do."

"Really?"

"Oh yeah. My old alpha was pretty high-and-mighty and you better not bother him unless you were dying. My family didn't like that I moved away, but they at least kept in touch. Well, until I mated Teresa." He shrugged like it wasn't a big deal, but Robson could hear the pain in his voice clear as day.

Remembering something else he'd seen Marcus do, he gently placed a hand on the top of Patrick's shoulder where it met his neck. Patrick's eyes widened, but he didn't pull away. "I'm sorry I wasn't more welcoming when I met you, but you're part of the Medina family now. If you need something, you can come to us too."

Patrick grinned. "Thanks, Robito."

Robson nodded once and squeezed his shoulder, then opened the door and slipped outside. He was halfway down the sidewalk when he heard Patrick call his name. Turning, he raised his brows in question.

"Even if he didn't know what it meant right away, Marcus would have felt the pull as soon as he scented you."

CHAPTER TWELVE

Marcus had never considered himself a coward before, but as he sat outside Tashmica's house at the exact same time he knew Robson was arriving at the manor for dinner with Rick and Kai, he decided he needed to reevaluate.

It wasn't that he didn't want to see him—far from it. He spent almost every waking moment thinking about and hoping he'd get to see Robson Medina. But then he'd remember that Robson didn't feel that way about him, that he wasn't yearning for Marcus when they were apart. It wasn't his fault; he couldn't help that he was human, but Marcus also couldn't help how he felt.

He couldn't stop his wolf from wanting to be with his mate.

And every time he remembered that Robson would never feel the way he felt, would never accept all of the things that Marcus wanted or needed from him as a mate, it was like a blow to the solar plexus.

So he was skipping dinner at the manor to try and get some answers from the one witch he knew he could trust.

Exiting the SUV, Marcus trudged up the sidewalk to Tashmica's quaint two-story house. It was covered in ivy with at least a dozen hanging plants on the front porch. He was trying to convince himself that he wasn't doing the wrong thing and avoiding Robson when the front door opened and the blond hunter Gabriel stepped outside.

"Evening, Enforcer Rivera."

Gabriel had a smile on his face, but Marcus didn't trust him—none of the Enforcers did. They couldn't because of some magic the hunter was able to possess that allowed him to be scentless. Anyone who would cover up something so essential to themselves—especially when they wanted to live among shifters—was inherently suspicious.

It was a powerful type of magic, something that even impressed Tashmica and the rest of the coven. When Gabriel had joined the pack, Rick had told him that he would need to break the spell if he ever wanted to be truly trusted. To the surprise of Marcus and everyone else, Gabriel had shrugged and refused to do it. He'd said he wanted the protection and peace living in the Kincaid Pack territory would allow, but he would be okay not ever having their trust.

Bennett had said later that he thought that was bullshit, but so far the hunter had kept to himself mostly—except when he was pestering Jamie.

"What brings you by?" Marcus asked, eyes narrowing slightly when he spotted the small cloth bag in Gabriel's hand. A hex bag. A mixture of ingredients spelled to perform or aid in a magical spell.

"Cup of tea and a chat. You?"

Marcus bared his teeth at the audacity of such a question. Just as he opened his mouth to respond though, Tashmica threw open her door and frowned at both of them.

"I thought I caught a whiff of testosterone out here. Gabriel, are you stirring up trouble?"

Gabriel turned his charming smile toward her. "No, ma'am. I'd never do such a thing."

She hummed her disbelief, but a smile tugged at the corners of her mouth. "Goodbye, Gabriel."

He winked and turned back to Marcus, touching his forehead with two fingers in a sort of salute, then walked off toward the trees until he disappeared.

He turned back to Tash, one eyebrow raised as he walked up the porch steps.

"Don't you give me that look," she said, laughing and leading the way into her house, the scent of plants almost enough to cover the smell of magic in the air. "He might not be a member of the pack, but he's still welcome to come to me for help or advice while he's under our protection."

"What does he need help with?" he asked, rubbing at his tingling nose. The smell of magic was even stronger near the sunroom at the back of her house. They settled around the small table, Tash pouring them each a cup of sweet-smelling tea.

"Marcus, dear, don't make me curse you." She winked, but he had a feeling she was partially serious. "You know better than to ask about what I do for others."

"I apologize," he said, sipping from his cup. "I just don't like the idea of you alone with him. What if he attacked you?"

She laughed loudly. "Please. He knows I could give his testicles gangrene before he even drew his knife."

Marcus choked on his tea, his nose burning as he wiped his face with the back of his hand. "Wow, Tash."

Her dark brown eyes twinkled as she delicately sipped her own tea. "Now, what are you doing here? I heard that delicious deputy of yours was going to dinner at the manor tonight."

Sighing, he set his cup down and leaned back on the plush

chaise he'd chosen. "I'm not sure… Nico suggested you might be able to help clear up something for me."

"You know I will if I can." She set aside her own cup and crossed her legs, leaning forward and bracing an elbow on her knee. "Is this about whoever killed Agnes or mating a human?"

His stomach clenched at the reminder of the unknown foe stalking their pack with the intent of destroying them. He should be focused on protecting the pack instead of mooning over Robson. Fuck, he was a terrible Enforcer. The pack was under threat from multiple directions, and he couldn't stop obsessing over whether or not Robson would ever let Marcus claim him the way his wolf yearned to.

Tash's light laughter broke into his spiraling thoughts. He sucked in a breath and shook his head, trying to dispel his agitation. "Sorry. Lately, I've seemed… I'm not sure. I've gotten so much better about disrupting intrusive thoughts and preventing my panic from spiraling, but lately I feel so… out of control."

Sobering, Tash extended her hand, and he took it, scooting forward on the chaise so he could more easily reach her. "I know that must be scary to someone like yourself who craves control, but that's normal. You have an unclaimed mate running around, and you have… doubts about your mating as well. It's normal to regress when life throws you for a loop."

Her smile was gentle and comforting, something he'd noticed about her as soon as he'd joined the pack. Then, she hadn't been the head of the coven, but she was the one all of them trusted. No matter what your troubles were, a trip to Tash's house—or the shop now that she ran it—usually helped clear things up.

"Is it so obvious?" He knew the other Enforcers knew about Robson being his mate, but it was expected. They all spent a lot of time together, and they had highly developed senses. He wasn't sure if Patrick had figured it out on his own or if he'd heard Carter's words when Marcus had been half-shifted and ready to attack Teresa's brother.

"I suspected, but the way you growled at me when he was injured at the shop confirmed things." She squeezed his hand when he grimaced. "I know you are also worried about the pack and the Council and Drake and…"

She raised her brows but didn't continue, and he chuckled harshly.

"So you're saying having the occasional panic attack is to be expected?" He had to work to keep the scowl off his face, the muscles around his mouth and eyes tightening. "I can't afford to be weak again right now, Tash."

"You were never weak," she said fiercely, standing and tugging on his hand until he was on his feet as well. She wrapped him in a tight hug, her head only reaching his collarbone but still feeling so strong and powerful. "You were injured. There is a difference, sweetie."

He took a shuddery breath and slowly raised his arms, wrapping them around her and embracing the calming feeling enveloping him. Nico was right—what he needed was more of this. He needed to strengthen his bonds with his packmates rather than stay farther away because he was feeling fragile.

"Can humans really understand what it means to mate a shifter?" he whispered into her wild curls.

She snorted but didn't pull back, instinctively knowing he still needed the contact. "You know dozens of humans in this pack who are mated to shifters."

"Yes, but…" He sighed heavily. "They don't carry their mate's bonding bite."

"Oh." She sounded a little surprised, but also like she should have expected the observation. She pulled back a little and reached up to cup his face. "Is that what your wolf wants?"

He made himself hold her gaze as he nodded, reminding himself that claiming his mate wasn't something to be ashamed of.

"That makes sense. You and your wolf are extremely powerful because you're an Enforcer in a large pack. Of course your wolf would be strong in his desires to mate your deputy." She tilted her head and studied his face. "I don't think I've ever seen you blush except when the topic of sex comes up."

"Tashmica!" He pulled back, and she let her hands fall away, a small smile on her face.

Settling back on her chair, she recrossed her legs and waited for him to sit again before continuing. "Other members of the pack don't have as strong of pulls from their animal side, though if they wished to, I'm sure their mates would agree to accepting the bonding bite. Do you doubt your deputy will consent to your bite?"

His face felt like it was on fire, her words painting a picture in his head of a naked Robson beneath him in his bed, head turned to the side and offering his neck while Marcus filled him with his knot. It was his most-visited fantasy when he was alone at night, lying in bed by himself and touching his erection.

"Yes," he choked out. "I have doubts."

"Hmm." She leaned back in her chair and tapped a finger on her mouth, ignoring his discomfort. "Would you feel better if you could offer him the opportunity to bite you as well?"

Breath freezing in his lungs, he stared at her for a long moment. "That's... That's not possible."

She rolled her eyes and pulled her phone out from some hidden pocket in her flowing light pink dress. "Please. With

132

the right combination of words and herbs and a strong enough witch, very few things are impossible. Let me get Damien on it—he actually knows more about mating magic than I do."

That surprised him—not just that the quiet and shy witch Tash had taken under her wing could know about mating magic, but that Tashmica would so readily admit that he knew more. "Really? Why?"

"I never asked, though I suspect he knows his mate will be a shifter," she said absently as she typed into her phone.

"Does he have premonitions as well?" He realized that other than being very powerful—according to Tashmica—they knew very little about the slight man's abilities.

"No, I don't believe so." She tucked away her phone and smiled, letting him know she wouldn't be answering any other questions about Damien.

He picked up his cold tea and swallowed the remaining half a cup. "Thank you, Tashmica. I hope he has some luck. I think... I definitely think Robson would be more open to being claimed by a shifter if he could claim me in return." He shivered at the idea of Robson being able to sink his teeth into Marcus's neck as well and then being able to proudly carry his mate's mark. "Do you have any updates regarding Agnes's murder?"

They knew whoever was orchestrating the attacks against their pack—including the explosion that cost Drake his arm —was the one who killed her, or at least ordered the murder. Whoever they were, they'd been thoughtful enough to include a note with her dumped body, letting Rick know they were coming for him and his pack.

She sighed, her shoulders slumping a little. "Nothing more than I had the last time I spoke with you all. Whatever killed her was powerful magic, and whoever did it was extremely adept at covering their tracks. Which"—she grimaced and shot apologetic eyes at him—"we already knew from the lack of evidence around Drake's home or where Agnes and the others were breaking through the wards before we strengthened them. Whoever it is..."

When she didn't continue, he leaned forward, worry filling him. "What?"

She shook her head to clear her clouded eyes and gave him a small smile. "Whoever it is, they are very powerful, and I think we won't know who they are until they want us to know."

"Is it possible it's a certain Councilmember?" He thought about Wendy's words about how Councilman Kincaid wanted to make an example of Rick and Kai.

She held out a hand and tipped it back and forth, her long nails and bright polish catching the late-day sun. "Not on his own. But I suppose he could be working with a witch—or a coven of witches."

"The Council has a coven that works for them and protects them," he reminded her, but she shook her head again.

"I'm not saying it's impossible, but the Council coven serves the Council because they believe in balance and justice. Maybe one or two could be manipulated or convinced into attacking an innocent pack, but not all of them. And I know those witches, and none of them are strong enough individually to do this kind of magic."

"Could you?" he asked, more curious than anything else as his mind turned over possibilities of who Kincaid could be working with or if it was possible there was another enemy, unconnected to the Council, hiding in the shadows.

Hesitating a moment, she finally nodded. "Probably. I'd have to tap into my connection to Rick and the pack though. I have access to a pack that is extremely powerful and whose bonds are strong—the potential magic in that is pretty much limitless. Though," she added, laughing humorlessly, "tapping into too much would probably kill me."

He reared back. "Well, let's not test that theory."

Her dark brown eyes met his, her face serious and nearly serene. "I have no plans to sacrifice myself, but like you, I would do anything to protect this pack. They are my family, and no one gets away with hurting them."

CHAPTER THIRTEEN

Okay, he understood why they called it *the manor* now. Robson had parked his dad's old Camry off to the side by the detached garage and stood in front of the enormous house, hands on his hips, as he studied it. He didn't understand why he'd never seen the place before—sure, it was back from the road, but he'd never even noticed the *driveway* before. And he'd driven down the road a dozen times at least when he'd been following Marcus or one of the others, trying to figure out where they were always headed.

Now he knew. They were coming to this mansion in the middle of nowhere.

That was apparently protected from snoopy humans by magic.

This pack shit was weird as hell.

The front door opened and a cute blonde with messy curls stuck her head out and grinned at him. "You planning on coming inside, Deputy?"

He tipped his head back as he studied the upper floor of the place, catching sight of a little face in a window before they disappeared and the curtain fluttered back into place.

He vaguely remembered Marcus mentioning Kai had younger siblings, but he hadn't caught their ages.

"Deputy? Alpha Kincaid doesn't like to be kept waiting." She was still smiling, but there was a slight edge to her tone, letting him know she was serious.

Grunting, he headed up the steps, moving past her and into a large entryway. There was a grand staircase just ahead, some seating over to the side, a few doors, and a couple of hallways heading farther into the house. There was what looked like a hostess stand from a restaurant immediately to his right, and he watched as the blonde tapped on a tablet then placed it on the stand. Looking around once more, he caught sight of Kincaid's assistant disappearing down a hallway to the right. Robson hadn't even heard him.

"This place is…" He didn't even know how to describe it. Compared to the old farmhouse he'd grown up in—with too many people and not enough bedrooms—it seemed excessive.

"I know," she said softly, closing the door behind him and then nudging him gently with her elbow. "It took me a little while to get used to this place. Don't think of it as Alpha Kincaid's house, think of it as the pack's headquarters."

When he glanced at her, she was smiling and her eyebrows were arched like she was making a joke that he didn't get. "Um, okay. Thanks."

She snorted and led the way toward the left and down one of the hallways. Stopping at a partially closed door, she knocked and waited for a deep voice to tell her to enter. She pushed the door open and stepped back so he could walk inside, giving him a clap on the shoulder before heading back toward the front door.

Stepping into the room, he was surprised by how large it seemed with only two people inside. There was a large table on one side and a gathering of seating on the other. Rick

Kincaid was sitting in a large chair by the empty fireplace, the small, dark-haired man that Robson remembered from Teresa's house on his lap.

"Um, should I step back out?"

Rick raised a single brow and ran one of his hands down the leg of the man who had to be his mate, Kai. Hip to knee, he caressed his... mate, never taking his eyes off Robson.

Kai's face got a little pink, and he whispered something to Rick that made him smirk, the tip of his fangs showing.

Jesus Christ.

"Come sit down, Deputy," Rick said, nodding at another chair. "There are a few things I'd like to discuss with you before we have dinner."

"Sure, alright." He stepped forward and sank into a wide, comfortable chair. "You can call me Robson if you want. Or Medina if last names are more your thing."

Kai smiled widely and leaned farther into Rick. "Are you sure? We want to respect your position within the community."

He'd never really thought about it like that, but he shrugged. "Going into law enforcement was never my plan and not something I particularly enjoy, so we can be informal." He shot a glance at Rick and added, "If that's okay with you... Alpha Kincaid."

One side of Rick's mouth twitched up. "Pup, will you go find the rest of our family? Beth will be serving dinner soon, and Samantha may still be fighting with Callie to get dressed."

"Sure," Kai said, pressing a kiss to Rick's cheek and moving to stand. Rick's hold on his body stopped him, and Robson was surprised when Rick pulled his mate back into his body, cupped the back of his head, and planted a real kiss on him.

He tried not to stare, turning toward the fireplace and

admiring the decorative screen in front of it, but he still heard the soft gasp and growl from the other side of the room.

He cleared his throat when Kai finally stumbled past him, cheeks bright red but one of his hands unable to fully cover his smile. Turning toward Rick, he couldn't help but grin.

"So was that like a display of possessiveness or something?" Robson smirked a little. "Do you feel the need to establish your territory? Your instincts telling you I'm a threat to your mate?"

Rick tilted his head and examined Robson. He had the distinct feeling that Rick knew that Robson was deliberately trying to push his buttons. He also got the feeling that Rick could rip his throat out without much effort and maybe he should watch himself.

"You know," Rick said, voice gravelly and dangerous, "if Marcus heard you speaking to his alpha like that, he'd have a coronary."

It was Robson's turn to tilt his head, playing at confusion. "Can shifters have coronaries?"

Rick rolled his eyes and stood, crossing his arms as he leaned his shoulders back against the mantel over the fireplace. "Don't be an ass, Deputy. I like you—I do—but when you're in my house, among my pack, you'd better show some goddamn respect."

Standing as well, Robson refused to show any fear to this guy. "Fine, I'll be more respectful. But don't bring Marcus into this discussion. What is it you'd like to say to me?"

Dark eyes narrowed, Rick pushed off the mantel and stepped into Robson's personal space. "First, you've been a real thorn in my side, but the only reason Marcus was allowed to tell you shit about us is because I allowed it. Don't make me regret not having one of our witches wipe your memory."

Robson opened his mouth to interrupt but snapped it shut when Rick full-on snarled in his face.

"Don't ever interrupt me." He waited for Robson to nod, silently, then continued. "Second, my mate is so damn satisfied in our mating that he probably didn't even notice you had a dick. So no, that wasn't about *you*. That was about me and my mate and our not being able to keep our hands off each other."

It took several long moments of glaring into Rick's eyes before Robson noticed something: there was no telltale glow to show Rick was losing control. He'd thought he was pushing Rick's buttons to get a reaction, but he realized Rick was the one manipulating him, playing the big tough asshole of an alpha to see how Robson would react.

Smirking, Robson crossed his arms. "Nice try, but Marcus told me a lot about you, *Alpha Kincaid*. And if what my brother-in-law said was true, then there's no way you'd have actually kept Marcus and me apart." He bared his teeth in a grin. "Though I suppose I do believe the bit about your mate being satisfied. You've got real big dick energy going on."

He could practically hear Rick's teeth grinding together, but before he could try another tack to keep Robson off-balance, the door to the room opened and a glaring Kai stepped in, holding a small child and another one who zipped past him and ran for Rick.

"Alpha!" the little girl screamed, jumping at the last second. Without missing a beat, Rick caught her under her arms and tossed her up into the air to her utter delight.

Eyes wide, Robson turned back to Kai and saw another person standing just behind him, a teenage girl with long, straight brown hair. She was eyeing him warily, then looking at the little girl giggling in Rick's arms. Robson had a feeling it was his being so close to the child that was worrying her, so he took a couple steps back as subtly as he could.

"Samantha's very protective," Rick said, not even looking at Robson. Apparently, you couldn't do anything *subtly* around shifters. "But she'll warm up to you."

"Garrick Kincaid," Kai said, voice stern. "Did you send me out of the room so you could threaten our guest?"

Perching the adorable little blonde on his hip, Rick gave his mate a wink and a smile. "I didn't threaten him. Not really."

Robson raised a finger in the air. "I guess saying you could have had a witch erase my memory isn't technically a threat, though it was *said* very threateningly."

Kai handed the youngest child over to Samantha and stomped across the room. "You said we were just going to get to know Robson."

Rick handed over the little girl when Kai reached for her but then just pulled Kai into his arms anyway, squishing her between them. Her giggle said she was perfectly fine with it. "I am getting to know him. You can tell a lot about someone by how they react to a snarling shifter threatening them."

Rick tried to kiss Kai, but Kai wiggled a hand up between them and put it on Rick's face, pushing him back. "I thought you said you *didn't* threaten him?"

At that point, Robson couldn't help but start chuckling, drawing the attention of both of them. "Oh sorry, go ahead and continue talking about me like I'm not here. It's extremely entertaining for me."

Rick grunted and turned back to Kai. "You see that attitude? Pup, how am I supposed to put up with that?"

Kai cackled.

Robson pounded on the door again. "Open up, Marcus!"

After an entertaining but long dinner at the manor, Robson was simmering at the fact that Marcus had been the only Enforcer not in attendance. When he'd mentioned it to Kai, there'd been an awkward pause, then Kai had delicately said that Marcus had run an errand but hopefully he'd return soon.

Two hours later, Robson had left and there had still been no sign of his supposed mate.

Instead of driving home like he should have, he'd sped toward Marcus's house to demand some answers. Like about why Marcus hadn't been the one to tell him that they were fucking mates.

"Marcus!"

He whipped around when he heard a loud bark and glared at the wolf standing at the bottom of the porch steps. Planting his hands on his hips, he said, "Being cute and fluffy won't save you. We have to talk."

If anything, that seemed to make Marcus happier. He dropped his front to the ground and wagged his tail.

"Marcus, I'm serious."

Barking once more, Marcus darted away, running around the corner of the house. His dark brown fur blended easily with the shadows, so Robson had to hustle to keep up and not lose him in the dark.

"Where are we going?" He wasn't sure why he asked—it wasn't like Marcus could respond—but as they went deeper into the wooded area behind Marcus's house, he felt like he should say *something*. Just in case he was being led to his death or something equally sinister.

After a few minutes, he started to slow down, frustrated at himself and at Marcus. Eventually, he stopped and crossed his arms, waiting to see if Marcus even noticed Robson wasn't following him anymore.

Marcus paused immediately, turning and barking at Robson.

"No. I'm not traipsing through the damn woods any longer. If there is something you want to say to me or show me, then just do it. Otherwise…" He sighed and scrubbed at his stubbled cheeks, wondering why he was bothering. "You know what, whatever. I guess everyone was wrong."

He turned to leave but didn't even get a step before he heard that soft, seductive voice.

"Robson, wait. Please."

Huffing, he whipped back around, prepared to give Marcus a piece of his mind, but froze at the sight before him. Marcus had somehow moved closer without Robson hearing him, so he was only a few feet away… and completely naked.

A long, lean body wrapped in beautiful pale white skin that seemed to glow in the moonlight. His dark red hair looked brown in the dim light, and there was a slight five-o'clock shadow on his jaw that Robson definitely wanted the chance to lick. Head ducked down, Marcus peered up at Robson through his lashes.

"You're naked," Robson finally whispered, trying very, very hard not to notice anything going on with Marcus's lower half and *almost* succeeding.

"Yes, I don't keep clothes in the woods." Marcus took another half a step closer, head tilted as he ran his eyes over Robson's face and noticeably inhaled. "But I didn't want you to leave."

Clearing his throat, Robson eyed the surprisingly firm lines of muscle in Marcus's abs, chest, and arms. He appeared almost thin when dressed in his slacks and button-downs, but he wasn't as skinny as he came across. And Robson knew from experience he was much stronger than his slim build suggested.

"I got tired of following you through the woods," he said,

trying to regain some of his indignation. "Where are we going?"

One shoulder lifted as Marcus dropped his gaze for a moment. "Nowhere," he said softly, "my wolf just wanted to… show you the woods."

Robson raised a brow, not convinced that was the whole story but deciding to let it go so he could focus on the main reason he'd stopped at Marcus's house. "Would you like to know what I found out today while you were avoiding me?"

Marcus's face shuttered, and it was only after that Robson realized how open his expression had been when he'd shifted. "If you'd like to tell me."

Narrowing his eyes, Robson stomped forward until they were barely a foot apart. "You want to explain to me why you've never mentioned us being… mates?"

He hated that he still tripped over the word even though he'd been practicing in his head and with the other couples at the manor for half the day. Marcus's eyes widened slightly, and he jerked like he was going to step back but stopped himself.

"Who told you?" he finally asked, voice strained.

Crossing his arms, Robson rolled his eyes. "It doesn't matter. What matters is that *you* didn't tell me. All the time we spent at the diner the other night and all the things you told me… Why didn't you tell me about this?"

Marcus huffed. "I didn't want to… pressure you."

"Bullshit," Robson spit out, pointing at Marcus. "Even though you're a big bad wolf, you got scared, didn't you?"

Eyes flashing, Marcus stepped into Robson's space so his finger pressed firmly into his warm, smooth skin. "I'm not scared."

Robson realized they were both breathing a little hard for a conversation in the woods—even a heated one. As pissed as he was… the little bit of temper lighting up Marcus's eyes was hot as hell. He hadn't quite snarled the words, but it was close, and it only made Robson want to push harder to see if he could get Marcus to finally lose control. He knew in his bones Marcus wouldn't hurt him, but fuck did he want to see it.

In the past, Robson had always gone for the sweet, submissive guys when he was looking to relieve some stress. And Marcus was sweet, in his own way. But Robson had a feeling that things between them would be a little more... versatile than he was used to.

"Fine, if you aren't scared, then tell me what it means for us to be mates," he asked, lowering his voice and his hand, but he couldn't resist touching more of Marcus's bare skin, so he lightly gripped both of his hips.

Marcus sucked in a breath and looked down at where they were touching. "I-I don't know."

Robson wished it wasn't so dark. He wanted to see the slight flush on Marcus's cheeks that he knew would be there and to be able to tell if his pupils had expanded. Light as a feather, he rubbed his thumbs back and forth over the sexy V between Marcus's hips. He grinned at the way Marcus's whole body shivered.

"Robson..."

"Yes, cariño?"

When Marcus's eyes fluttered shut and he didn't say anything else, Robson couldn't help but lean forward and run the tip of his nose up the side of Marcus's neck, inhaling the scent of his skin and the vegetation around them. When he reached the hinge of Marcus's jaw, he felt him shiver again and pressed a grin into his rough stubble.

"Maybe I should take you on a date. Would that help you figure it out?"

Marcus's head jerked up and down in a shaky nod. Just when Robson was about to step back and give him some space to get his bearings, Marcus leaned into him, burying his nose in Robson's neck and making a sort of whimpery growl that made Robson's balls tingle. Some instinct told him what that sound meant. Without pausing to think, he wrapped his arms around Marcus's slender body, threading the fingers of one hand into the hair on the back of Marcus's head to hold him more securely and let him know he could stay where he was as long as he needed.

CHAPTER FOURTEEN

For three days after their hug in the woods, Marcus's wolf had felt more settled than he had in years. Even Nico commented on how relaxed he seemed.

But by the time the class at the rec center had rolled around on Wednesday, he was feeling restless again. He also couldn't help but be grateful he wasn't the one leading the discussion later that day since all he could focus on was how warm Robson's body had been and how *good* he'd smelled.

Or how he'd been able to feel that Robson had gotten aroused at their contact.

In the moment, his wolf had practically wanted to show Robson his belly, but when he thought about the heated moment later, he'd had the urge to claim again. It was like, in Robson's presence, his wolf wanted to submit, but when they were apart, he wanted to possess and claim him.

It was confusing and arousing, and he wasn't sure what to do.

Luckily, he'd gotten a text from Damien letting him know he had something for him at the shop, so he was just heading out—planning on stopping at *Wicca We Can* before arriving at the rec center—when he heard Kai call his name.

He stopped, almost to the garage, and turned to him with a smile. "Good afternoon, Alpha-mate."

Kai jogged over to him, rolling his eyes. "Good afternoon, Enforcer Rivera."

Marcus's smile threatened to turn into a grin. "Your tone suggests I should be insulted, but I'm honored by my title."

"Ugh, way to make me sound like an asshole." Kai shoved at him, then continued toward the garage.

"I apologize. That wasn't my intention," he quickly said, hurrying after him.

Kai laughed and shot him a grin over his shoulder. "I know. I was just teasing."

Falling into step beside him, Marcus nodded. "As was I."

Skidding to a stop, Kai turned enormous green eyes on him. "You were?"

"Yes?" He was beginning to realize why he rarely joked with the others. Just as he opened his mouth to apologize again, Kai threw himself at Marcus and hugged him around the middle.

"That mate of yours is very good for you," Kai whispered.

Stiffening, he hurried to say, "We haven't—um, we're not… What I meant to say is…"

"Oh my god." Kai leaned back, giggling. "Don't hurt yourself. Let's go. You're going to *Wicca We Can*, right? I'm supposed to meet Jess there in a little bit, so I figured you could drive me."

Nodding numbly, they went into the garage and got into an SUV. They were on the road into town before Marcus could untangle his tongue. "He asked me on a date."

He wasn't sure why he said that—he hadn't even told Nico about Robson asking him out—but when Kai squealed and turned toward him clapping his hands, Marcus was glad he had. Kai had grown up around humans and knew them better than Marcus did—the only humans he normally interacted with were pack members, and even then he didn't spend a lot of time with them. He wasn't the Enforcer most packmates went to for help or advice. When he'd first been promoted, that had saddened him, but he'd gotten used to it for the most part and tried to still serve his alpha and his pack as best he could. The mentorship classes were at least helping him feel more in tune with the pack in general.

"That's great! Where are you going?" Kai asked, cheeks flushed with excitement.

"Um, I'm not sure. He said he'd pick me up on Friday evening at my house." Entering the town limits, he shot a glance at Kai. "Should I not let him pick?"

Kai waved a hand dismissively. "No, that's fine. Have you ever... Have you ever been on a date before?"

Marcus felt heat in his cheeks and cursed himself silently. He'd learned to control his blush a long time ago... except when it came to anything involving flirting or dating or sex. He was glad Kai sounded so nonchalant or else he would have been too embarrassed to answer.

"Not really."

Kai hummed but then didn't say anything else right away. When Marcus glanced at him just as they were turning onto Main Street, he saw Kai's eyes were unfocused, and he was tapping at his mouth with one of his hands, lost in thought.

He was parking the car in front of the shop before Kai responded.

"So I know a lot of shifters are all"—he curled his lip back and gave a fake snarl, pitching his voice lower—"*instincts, mates, sex, sex, sex* when it comes to wooing their other half, but humans aren't quite like that."

Marcus just stopped himself from rolling his eyes. "I already know that much."

Kai huffed and slapped at his shoulder. "I *know*. I'm just saying that you'll have to go slower with Robson than you would if he were a shifter."

Nodding, Marcus opened his door and climbed out. He waited until Kai had joined him at the hood of the SUV, then headed toward the shop's entrance. "That makes sense. How do I know how much time he'll need?"

Kai laughed as he opened the door and stepped inside the cool, dark store. "There's no timetable. You'll just have to keep communicating with him about how he's feeling and what he needs to feel comfortable with your mating."

Marcus had been afraid of that. Sighing, he caught the small smile on Damien's face from where he was standing behind the counter on the opposite side of the long room.

"Damien, you're human," Kai said, strolling forward like he wasn't about to embarrass the hell out of Marcus. It had been hard enough talking to Kai about things—he barely knew Damien. "Do you have any advice for Marcus about how to approach dating his mate?"

Tipping his head back, Marcus stared at the symbols painted on the ceiling of the shop and asked the goddess for patience. He ignored Kai's and Damien's muffled laughter.

"Um, don't rush the deputy," Damien said, voice soft and melodic. "Your instincts will be strong, but you have to be stronger. Wait until he *tells* you he's ready to mate. Don't go off his scent or anything else."

Dropping his head forward, he frowned at the witch. "I understand how consent works."

Damien's light brown skin flushed, and his scent turned sour with embarrassment. "Of course, Enforcer Rivera. I meant no offense."

Kai made a small noise and rushed forward, stopping before he could hug Damien when he flinched. "Oh, Damien."

Marcus tilted his head and inhaled deeper, trying to parse through the overwhelming scents of the shop to dig into Damien's and try and figure out what Kai had picked up on that Marcus had missed. Floating just under the scent of embarrassment was pain and... shame?

Anger flooded through Marcus, and he moved closer. "Someone took your scent for consent? Who?"

Kai gently took one of Damien's hands in both of his and glared at Marcus. Damien saw the look and grimaced, then smiled a little. "It's okay, Kai." He turned to Marcus and straightened his shoulders. "It wasn't anyone in your pack. And they didn't... I ran away before... I ran away."

Nodding slowly, he accepted Damien's words and stepped back to give him some privacy as Kai continued to fuss over him for a few minutes.

He was on the other side of the shop looking at altar candles when he heard Damien approach. Kai had left a few minutes before when his best friend, Jess, came through the place in a whirlwind of laughter and teasing, and then another coven member had popped in to pick up some ingredients for some spell. The woman had smiled at Marcus but left quickly, nodding at him as she swept past, muttering about tarot cards.

"I set the warding for the front door and put the new sign up saying we're temporarily closed," Damien said softly. "Would you like to step in the back and I'll show you what I came up with to help you?"

Nodding, he followed the slender young man past the back counter and through a beaded doorway. The back room was where the coven kept its collection of grimoires, but there were many, many other books stacked in the bookcases lining the walls plus more dangerous ingredients and spell-work implements.

There was a table in the middle of the room with rolled-up maps, stacks of books and loose papers, and a few mortars with ingredient remnants still in them.

"Mating magic is as old as shifters," Damien said, grabbing a small clear jar full of herbs and a... tea infuser? "There isn't a lot written about it, but it's believed that it's only in the past few centuries that shifters began to feel the mating pull toward humans. There are theories that the populations were diminishing or that the shifters were becoming too powerful, but either way the goddess has permitted true matings between shifters and humans."

"Okay," Marcus said, leaning his hip against the table and crossing his arms. Clearing his throat and ignoring the heat in his face, he said, "But how can I fully mate with Robson? We can't exactly exchange bonding bites..."

Damien's smile was small but not mocking. "Most recorded human and shifter matings are with shifters whose animal side is... generally labeled as prey, rather than predator."

Marcus nodded and waited, since that didn't explain Teresa and Patrick or him and Robson.

"The occasional predator shifter who mates a human is usually one with a small pack or no pack at all," Damien added, rolling the jar between his palms, the chain of the infuser taped to the top so the small metal ball dangled over the edge and tapped the side. Keeping his eyes on the jar, Damien added quietly, "Or the human is powerful in a different way."

The last comment gave Marcus pause, but he decided not to focus on it since it didn't apply to their current situation, and he was on a tight schedule to get to the rec center. He mentally noted he should suggest to Kai that he come back and talk to Damien alone. "So their animal sides aren't strong enough to give their mates the bite?"

Damien tipped his head back and forth, eyes still down.

"Sometimes, or they bite their partner and are okay with not wearing a bite mark themselves, or they choose not to because they don't feel the urge to visually mark their mate without many—if any—other shifters around."

"But doesn't..." Sighing, Marcus pushed through his embarrassment. "The bite is more than a visual representation of the mating though, right? I've heard it... connects you and your mate, and doesn't it also change the mated pair's scents too? Rick and Kai... theirs changed to a sort of mixture of both of their original scents." He scratched at the longer stubble on his face. He'd been growing it out a bit since Saturday after he'd noticed the way Robson had stared at his unshaven jaw. "Patrick is a predator shifter and is part of a large, strong pack, so I don't... My wolf wants to bite Robson and be bitten and..." He gritted his teeth, frustrated.

"And it's even worse having to come to someone for answers about your own instincts and mating." Damien glanced up at Marcus and nodded when he grunted his agreement. "I get that, and it's true that Patrick didn't bite Teresa—and I can't say why he didn't without speaking to him about it—but I can tell you what I know for sure: the bonding bite links the shifter's magic to the person they bite. That's why it changes their scent."

Marcus's eyes widened as he considered that information. It made sense. He wondered why he'd never considered that before. "So when both mates are able to provide the bite, the scents mix. But since Robson can't... He'd carry my scent, but I wouldn't carry his."

It wasn't like not being able to trade bonding bites with Robson would be a deal breaker. He already couldn't imagine walking away from his mate, no matter what became of their mating. If Robson decided he only wanted to be friends, then Marcus would be the very best friend he ever had and be there for him any way he could.

"Technically, yes." Damien nodded and held out the jar. "So I made you this."

Accepting the mixture, he sniffed at the lid and wrinkled his nose at the heavy herb scent. "Some sort of tea?"

The tiniest smile curved Damien's lips. "Yes. The mixture will allow your mate to—temporarily—be able to provide you with a bonding bite as well. If you both want that."

He didn't emphasize *both,* but Marcus heard the undercurrent of caution regardless. Deciding not to take offense, he asked, "How does it work?"

"Magic, of course," Damien said with a light laugh. His face sobered quickly though, his dark brown eyes and scent filling with a mix of sadness and joy. "Just remember… Even if you never bite or knot your mate—"

Marcus choked on his spit, face flaming.

"Your mating would still be valid in the eyes of the goddess." Reaching out, Damien clasped Marcus's wrist and gave it a squeeze. "She knows what's in your hearts and souls, and that's all that matters. Your union would be just as strong as any other with or without the bite."

He nodded, too embarrassed to respond.

Giving Marcus one more smile, Damien released his hold and headed back toward the front of the shop, leaving Marcus to his tumultuous thoughts and emotions. Just before he reached the beaded doorway, a terrible thought occurred to Marcus.

"Damien, wait." He held up the jar when the witch turned to face him, face open but eyes guarded as ever. "This stuff won't… force him to be attracted to me, right?"

The horrified expression on Damien's face answered his question immediately, but Damien still waved his hands in front of him and shook his head frantically. "Goddess, *no.* I'd never create something like that. Marcus, I swear to you, all that tea will do is give Robson a temporary infusion of magic so he can bite you back. I swear."

Hurrying forward, Marcus grasped the side of Damien's neck, unable to stop himself with the sound of his racing heart pounding in his ears. "I know, I believe you. I just had to check. It's okay."

Damien sucked in two shuddery breaths, then collapsed against Marcus's chest, his heart rate and scent calming with the additional contact.

"You're okay," Marcus murmured, carefully hugging Damien's small frame. "I believe you. I *trust* you, Damien."

CHAPTER FIFTEEN

With only a few minutes to spare, Robson slipped into the conference room in the rec center and flopped into the empty seat Teresa and Patrick had saved for him in the back. He peered around the nearly full room but didn't see Marcus or the other two Enforcers who'd actually be speaking.

"I didn't miss anything?" he whispered to Teresa where she leaned heavily against Patrick's shoulder, eyes half-closed.

"Uh-uh," she muttered, wrapping her arms around her husband's bicep and settling in like she was going to take a nap.

"Um, what are you doing?"

Patrick's shoulders shook a little, but otherwise he didn't even glance at them, seeming to be paying attention to a conversation happening... at the front of the room. Damn shifter hearing.

"Taking a nap. Your devil niece has been keeping me up at night, and I'm exhausted."

He took in his sister's pale skin and purpling under her eyes and winced. "You didn't have to come…"

She snorted but didn't open her eyes. "If we didn't, you wouldn't have."

That was true. While he wanted to hear what kind of sex ed class shifters needed, he would have felt out of place if he'd come alone or like everyone was looking at him and wondering why the human was there.

"Still…" He felt guilty for apparently dragging his sister out of her house a week after having a baby.

One of Teresa's hands waved at him weakly. "Don't worry. It gave mamá an excuse to babysit, and I can nap here. Patrick is very comfortable."

Patrick leaned down and whispered something to her that made her smile and nod. She leaned back, and within a few minutes she was sitting on his lap, cradled in his arms, and fast asleep. Robson stared, eyes wide, as he slipped over into her unoccupied seat.

Grinning at him, Patrick whispered, "Sometimes I have to remind her it's not my job to take care of her—it's my privilege."

Chest tightening, Robson didn't get a chance to respond, the door closest to the front of the room opening and the three Enforcers filing in. Just before the door closed, it popped back open and Vanessa strode in, hopping onto the table shoved against the wall under the large whiteboard.

Marcus stood near her, arms crossed over his lean chest and the sleeves of his button-down shirt rolled up to his elbows. His brow was creased as his light green eyes quickly searched the room and landed on Robson. Marcus's arms slowly lowered to his sides, his brow smoothing when Robson threw him a grin.

Vanessa said something to him that caused his cheeks to color adorably. Marcus shook his head once and headed down the side of the room, pausing to say hello to a few people on his way. Warmth filled Robson as he watched the way Marcus carefully but genuinely cared for his packmates.

When Marcus slipped into the seat Robson had been in originally, Bennett cleared his throat at the front of the room and got started, his deep voice somehow still easily carrying to the back without him having to raise his voice at all.

Robson leaned over and opened his mouth to ask Marcus what Vanessa had said to him, but Marcus pressed a finger to his own mouth. When Robson pouted and crossed his arms, Marcus smiled at him and tapped his ear, reminding Robson that most of the people in the room would be able to hear everything they said.

Sighing heavily, Robson resigned himself to finding out later and tried to pay attention to what Bennett was saying to the younger people sitting closer to the front. Robson had noticed that the first couple of rows were occupied by mostly teens and men and women in their early twenties, with a wider range of ages filling in the rest of the seats, usually in obvious pairings.

Wait a second.

Robson leaned forward, tuning in and paying closer attention as Bennett talked to the group about listening to their mating instincts.

"Your animal side will know before your human side that you've met your mate." Bennett paused when a hand shot up in the first row, a young brown-haired woman practically dancing in her seat she was so eagerly trying to get his attention. "Yes, Bridget?"

"Enforcer Young, how does our animal side know though?" the young woman asked, her voice a little unsteady but still clear enough to be heard by everyone.

Enormous arms crossed over an impressively wide chest

as Bennett rocked back on his heels in thought. "Well, the best way I can explain it is by scent."

Robson watched as the woman turned to the person next to her, and they both shook their heads, not understanding.

"Did you guys plan this at all, or are you just winging it?" Robson muttered to Marcus, then nearly swallowed his tongue when Bennett pierced him with a glare.

"Deputy Medina, you're welcome to come up here and lead the discussion if it's not meeting your expectations."

The guy behind Bennett, Nico, began to snicker but tried to cover it with a cough. Robson had liked him when he'd met him at the manor on Saturday, but those good feelings were draining away quickly. Feeling his cheeks heat a little at all the eyes on him, Robson refused to back down, standing and meeting Bennett's glare head-on.

"It's not about expectations, *Enforcer Young*." If he wasn't mistaken, it looked like Bennett was about to start laughing, but Robson pushed forward. "I'm guessing the younger people in the front are unmated shifters?"

Everyone was looking at him now, but he kept his eyes on Bennett, pretending he wasn't bothered by the attention.

"That's correct."

"So everyone else is just hoping to maybe learn something they don't already know about their mating but them"—he pointed to the younger people in front, staring at him with wide eyes—"and me don't know jack shit about what it means to find your mate or why shifters seem to have actual, honest-to-god soul mates." He looked around, noting Teresa was still out cold and pointing to her. "Anyone else here a human mated to a shifter—other than Sleeping Beauty?"

Two people raised their hands, a middle-aged woman and a young, buff-looking guy sitting next to a tiny man with bright red hair and face.

Nodding at them, he asked Bennett, "You mind?"

For a long moment, Bennett stared at Robson, face serious, and then he broke into a wide grin and held up both hands before making a sweeping motion to his side. "Please."

Stomach knotting, Robson turned to Marcus, noting his wide eyes and parted mouth, and reached down to grab his hand where it rested on his thigh. "Come on." He looked at the other two humans. "If either of you and your mates would like to join us, I think this will be more helpful."

The small guy next to his buff mate shook his head immediately, face full of terror, but the woman and her mate stood and came to the front. Robson realized he recognized the women from the art supply store on Main Street.

Standing in front of the eager-looking young shifters, Robson grunted and turned to Bennett and Nico. "Can you grab us some chairs? I feel like I'm lecturing new recruits here."

Grumbling, Bennett grabbed a few chairs from the extras stacked in the corner, Nico grinning and following along. Once he and Marcus and the women were seated, he pointed to them. "I'm assuming you've been mated a while?"

They both nodded, the shifter tucking her long hair behind her ears before saying, "Fifteen years."

Pointing at himself, he said, "I'm Robson Medina. I found out Saturday that Marcus and I are mates, but I still don't really understand what that means." He turned to the young people sitting in front of him. "I think it'll be useful for you to hear from humans about being mated to shifters because first, you may mate with a human one day, and you need to understand it's different for them than it is for you, but also because—" He glanced at the human woman. "I'm sorry, what's your name?"

Everyone chuckled as she smiled and extended a hand to him. "Janice."

He shook her hand and turned to her mate. She smiled and leaned forward. "Melissa."

"It's nice to meet you both. I assume you already know tall, silent, and dreamy here?" He jerked a thumb at Marcus, grinning when he heard Marcus huff. When they both nodded, he turned back to the group. "So Janice and I and any other humans mated into the pack come into things without any idea of what it means to be someone's mate. Humans grow up with the concept of soul mates, sure, but it's not the same as what your fearless second-in-command over there was trying to describe to you."

Bennett grunted behind him, but Robson ignored him.

"The closest we have is love at first sight. You all watch movies and shit, right?" When more laughter and nodding happened, he leaned forward on his knees, really getting into the groove. "So that's all we have to go off of. We don't have your instincts or your sense of smell or anything like that, so when we're, let's say, pissed as hell about someone breaking the law and a giant redhead is staring at us in a borderline creepy way, that doesn't instill a sense of true love."

He paused while everyone chuckled, shooting glances at Marcus like they weren't sure if it was okay for them to laugh at his expense. Smiling, Robson leaned back and reached over to snag Marcus's hand, threading their fingers together and winking when Marcus looked at him in surprise.

"But there was still something about him that I couldn't get out of my head," he said softly, not taking his eyes off Marcus's green ones, inexplicably pleased when he spotted the tip of Marcus's tongue peeking out to wet his lush bottom lip. His beautiful mouth was now framed by days' worth of scruff that was quickly becoming a short beard, and Robson wanted to feel it rubbing against his skin more than he'd ever wanted anything before.

"Ahem," Bennett said, stepping up and leaning between Marcus and Robson. "As you can see," he said to the group watching with surprised and amused faces, "there's still mutual attraction even if one of you is human."

Nico cackled behind him as Robson covered his burning face with his free hand. "Ay, Dios mío."

When Bennett stepped back, Robson chanced a glance over at Marcus to check his reaction to being teased by his superior in front of a group of people and was surprised to find Marcus smiling at him gently, though his cheeks were tinged a light pink. Marcus squeezed Robson's fingers and turned to their audience.

"The night I met Robson, I wasn't expecting to find my mate," he said calmly but not like he was hiding his discomfort like he usually did. Robson was beginning to learn the signs and read the subtle cues in Marcus's face and body language, and he was happy to see Marcus actually seemed at ease. "And because he didn't know about the pack—and was very suspicious of us—I convinced myself my wolf was mistaken."

Bennett grunted behind them. "I did that and my mate's a shifter. I think that's a more common reaction than people think."

"Not me," Melissa piped up, smiling widely as she bumped her shoulder into Janice's. "The moment I laid eyes on her, I knew she was meant for me—I just had to convince her. My old pack didn't allow us to tell humans under any circumstances—their way of being prejudiced without explicitly saying we weren't allowed to mate with humans—so I wooed her the human way."

Janice laughed. "It's true. I've never received so many bouquets of flowers and boxes of chocolate as I did when we first started dating. By the time we left Seattle, I still didn't know about shifters, but I knew I loved her more than life itself." She grimaced at Robson. "Though it was still quite the shock when we unloaded our moving truck at our brand-new house in Meyerville and she announced she could turn into a red panda."

Chuckling, Robson raised a fist for her to pound. "Right? Did you freak out?"

"A little, but Bennett was there so he could explain some things while Melissa shifted and showed me her other form. They both explained why she hadn't told me and that we were mates, and by then…" She shrugged. "Like I said, I was already in love, so I got used to sometimes spending Sunday afternoons cuddling with a cute animal instead of my hot wife."

The room erupted in laughter again, but something she said stuck out to Robson, causing him to glance at his own mate. Would Marcus want to spend time together regularly with him in his wolf form? He wasn't sure why the thought hadn't occurred to him considering they'd already spent time like that twice, but it was still an interesting thought. Would it be less fun for Marcus to run through the trees with Robson since he wouldn't be able to keep up?

Marcus raised his eyebrows just a little, asking him if he was okay without being obvious about it. He squeezed Marcus's fingers like he'd done to Robson and refocused back on why he was there.

"Okay, so we've gotten slightly off track," he said, then turned to Bridget. "You wanted to know how your animal side recognizes your mate, right?"

She nodded enthusiastically, then shot a quick look at where Nico was perched on a stack of three chairs, big body loose and relaxed. When Robson pressed his lips together and raised his eyebrows, she blushed and looked at the ground between her feet.

"My understanding—and one of you shifters correct me if

I'm wrong—is that it's an honest-to-god magical connection, right? It's not just being attracted to someone physically."

Marcus nodded. "It was explained to me that the goddess blesses us with a mate and our animal side recognizes them before our human side does because of the stronger senses and instincts."

It was explained to me... Who could have told him something like that? Since Marcus hadn't shared that information, Robson assumed he didn't want to give that detail to everyone, but it made Robson curious.

He looked at Bridget to see if that answer was good enough for her, and she nodded without meeting his eyes. Poor thing. He understood crushing on one of the pack Enforcers, but he was pretty sure that was all it was. It probably happened all the time.

"I guess that makes as much sense as anything else," Robson said, trying not to focus too hard on the idea that some goddess somewhere thought he'd be the perfect match for Marcus. His devout Catholic mother would have a heart attack. As it was, he had to stop himself from making the sign of the cross and asking for forgiveness in believing in another deity. "Does anyone else have questions? Or should we move on to the actual sex part of this sexual education class?"

Marcus sputtered next to him, but Robson ignored him, focusing on the hand that went up in the second row.

A young guy asked, "Since you're human, could you decide to leave your mate one day? Humans divorce all the time..."

He felt Marcus stiffen, but he tightened his hold on his hand and turned to Janice and Melissa. "I think this one is more for you two than us. I'm curious to hear if that happens or not too."

Melissa wrapped an arm around Janice, but it was Janice

who answered. "In theory, yes. But I don't really see that being a possibility. We might not be magically linked through bonding bites, but our relationship is unlike any other I've ever experienced. I can't imagine ever not feeling this way about her and our mating."

"It's extremely rare," Marcus spoke up, body still rigid, like he was worried Robson would take note of the out clause. "Shifter law makes it illegal to force a human to remain in a mating if the human wishes to leave, but I've only ever heard of a handful of cases, and usually there are extenuating circumstances."

When no one else said anything, Robson nodded. "Cool, good to know. But, um, let's back up a second. What the hell is a bonding bite?"

Nico started laughing so hard he almost fell off his stack of chairs. Bennett steadied him with one hand and reached up to the neck of his plain white T-shirt with his other and pulled it aside. Robson shot to his feet and raced over so he could examine the scar more easily. Right at the juncture where B's neck and shoulder met, there was a very distinctive set of teeth marks left in his skin.

"Whoa. Kieran *bit* you?" He'd briefly met Bennett's mate on Saturday and would not have pegged him as the type to get kinky.

"We bit each other," Bennett said, releasing the collar of his shirt. It didn't completely cover the mark, but Robson had never noticed it before on any of the mated pairs he'd met so far. "Shifter mates can bond to one another during sex by exchanging bites."

Returning to his chair, Robson frowned at Bennett. "And this 'magically' links you? So can you hear Kieran's thoughts or something?"

He heard snickering from the crowd, but he ignored

them. These were the kinds of things he came to the class to learn.

Bennett shook his head. "No, but if he's feeling a particularly strong emotion, I can feel it here." He patted his muscular chest right over his heart. "But otherwise, it's just like a warm feeling, letting me know we're connected even if we aren't physically together."

"You can feel that right now?"

"Yeah." He turned to the others and added, "It can be really strong—almost overwhelming—at first, but it fades within a few days so you know it's there but it's not disruptive."

B took over things again, covering topics like the differences in shifter and human puberty. Right when Robson was beginning to wonder if he, Marcus, and the women should head back to the audience, he got sidetracked once more.

"I'm sorry, did you just say a *knot?*"

CHAPTER SIXTEEN

Marcus watched Robson get into his old Camry, Teresa tiredly sinking into the passenger seat, and drive off with barely a glance back at the rec center. When Marcus had tried to hold him back after the class was over, Robson had quickly made an excuse about having to get Teresa home while Patrick went to pick up their pup from the farmhouse. He'd slipped away before Marcus could come up with something to say to stop him.

Sighing, he stepped away from the window, turning back to the empty conference room.

Well, almost empty.

"Soooo. That went well," Nico said, leaning against the opposite wall, arms crossed and grin barely suppressed.

Marcus grunted, not in the mood for his teasing. His mate was freaked-out and alone all because Nico and Bennett had decided it was a good idea to talk about the things their stupid dicks did during the mating process. It wasn't that Marcus didn't see the value in young, unmated shifters knowing how their bodies worked, he just wished that hadn't been how Robson found out.

"Come on, Marcus. It's not like you would have told him yourself."

He jerked his head up from where he was straightening chairs and snarled at Nico. "I would have."

Rolling his eyes, Nico pushed off the wall and approached him, seemingly unconcerned with pissing Marcus off. "Really? You would have sat him down and talked to him about your wolf wanting to knot him if you topped?"

He tried to hold Nico's gaze, but he could feel his face heating just at the words. When he actually tried to think about saying them out loud to Robson? "I wouldn't have... without his permission."

Both of Nico's big hands landed on his shoulders, and he ducked down to catch Marcus's eyes again. "Hey. I'm not trying to be an asshole, okay? But I know stuff like this is hard for you."

That was an understatement. After his childhood of taunting and insults around every turn, Marcus had struggled to talk to *anyone* about personal things. Puberty, sex, and matings definitely weren't things that were talked about in his old pack, and then he'd been shipped off and been surrounded by strangers—most of whom were much older than him. So trying to talk about such personal things now was difficult for him.

But... he would have, for Robson...

Right?

"What if he doesn't come back, Nico?" Marcus flinched at the break in his voice, the raw fear crumbling the wall he kept erected between him and everyone else.

Nico snorted, shifting his hands to cup Marcus's face. "Don't be silly. That man is half in love with you already."

Marcus sucked in a breath, hope trying to combat his terror at losing his mate.

"Just give him some time to wrap his head around things,

then shoot him a text later tonight or tomorrow. Don't let things become awkward."

At Marcus's unimpressed look, Nico laughed in his face and wrapped him in a hug, his warmth and scent filling Marcus with a sense of safety and family that only close packmates could give him.

"Alright, *more* awkward." Slapping his back, Nico leaned away from him and grinned. "At least everything's out in the open now."

Marcus shoved him away with an eye roll and ignored his laughter as he stomped out of the room. He stopped at the office and let Brianna know they were all set and out of the conference room. They smiled and waved as they barely looked up from whatever they were squinting at on their computer.

Nico caught up with him outside, and they climbed into the last SUV in the parking lot. "You hear from Wendy yet?"

The reminder of Wendy and her dangerous mission to smuggle the letter out of the Council's reach soured his mood further, filling his stomach with dread. He shook his head. "Nothing."

Nico clapped a hand on Marcus's shoulder. "It's only been a week. Give her some time. I'm sure she'll get out of there fine. She's smart."

Neither spoke as they drove back to the manor, but the car was filled with the scent of both of their nerves.

For the first time since being discharged, Robson had wished for a longer shift at work. After dropping Reesa off at her house and making sure she was okay, he'd headed to the sheriff's department for the overnight shift he'd been scheduled for. He'd grumbled when he'd seen it—knowing the sheriff had only given him more hours that week because he'd probably gotten a phone call from Alpha Kincaid—but after what he'd learned at the rec center, he could have used the longer distraction.

It was still early when he pulled up to the farmhouse, but he wasn't surprised to see a light in the kitchen was on. His mom had always been an early riser.

Just inside the front door, he left his gun in the lockbox he kept in the credenza in the hall. After hanging up his coat and emptying what he could from his utility belt, he headed toward the kitchen, pausing just outside when he heard his mom talking to someone in Spanish.

Slowly, he stepped into the room, expecting to see one of his sisters half-asleep at the table but found only his mom. She was sitting by herself sipping on a mug of coffee. At his entrance, she glanced over and smiled.

"Buenos días, mi sol."

"Buenos días, mamá," he murmured, looking around once more to make sure they were alone. "Who were you talking to?"

She waved a hand in the air. "Just papá," she said, and then she patted the table in front of another chair. "Come sit."

He lowered into the seat, his chest heavy. "You must miss him a lot." Guilt began to climb in him at the reminder. The whole reason he was living at home was to help her and help take care of his family, but he'd gotten so consumed by Marcus so quickly that he'd barely spoken to her in a week.

"Sí, but I'm so grateful to have you back home, Robito." She ran her eyes over his uniform. "He would be proud of you."

He just barely stopped himself from snorting. Despite what his sweet mother thought, nothing Robson had ever done had been good enough for his dad. Not any promotion in the army, not any of the commendations, not the money he'd sent home on occasion when Hector had told him they were struggling.

And he straight up ignored the way she looked at him when he was in his deputy's uniform. He didn't have the heart to tell her he was unhappy, especially when he didn't know what he would rather be doing. It wasn't that he was against working in a job that served his community... he'd just never seen himself in law enforcement back when he used to daydream about what it would be like to be home when he was on long tours.

"I'm sorry I haven't been around much lately," he finally said, scrubbing at his face to try and drive away the exhaustion creeping up on him.

His mom smiled at him over her coffee mug. "Who is he?"

Groaning, he slumped onto the table. "Mamá."

"Mothers know." She sipped her coffee before placing the mug on the table and reaching over to lightly lay her hand on his wrist, drawing his eyes back to her. "He must be very special to have caught your eye, Robito."

Staring into her soft eyes, he swallowed, fighting back the emotions he'd been pushing down all night. "He is, but... we're so different. I'm not sure it will work out."

Saying the words—even so softly he could barely hear himself—was like a knife to his gut. Was that the magic of the mating, or was that just Marcus being so sweet and beautiful and generous that Robson hadn't stood a chance? Either way... it scared him how deep he was already in it with him.

"Different is good," she said, squeezing his wrist.

He stared at her slender fingers, remembering the way Marcus had done the same thing at the rec center, holding Robson's hand and squeezing it to offer comfort. He'd done it so effortlessly, making it easy for Robson to respond in kind.

"What if we can't get past our differences though?" he whispered harshly, swiping at his tired eyes and pretending there wasn't dampness on his fingers afterward.

"Have you even tried, mi sol?"

No. No, I haven't. I ran away. Marcus had sent Robson a text during his shift, but Robson hadn't responded, not sure what to say to his gentle *Are you alright?*

When he didn't answer, she gave him a knowing look and stood. "If he's special, then he is worth trying for, hm?"

She brushed a hand through his hair on her way out, leaving him alone with his spiraling thoughts and with a decision to make.

The last thing he wanted to do was hurt Marcus, but after everything else he'd learned and had to wrap his head around, he'd for some reason been completely blindsided by the idea of Marcus wanting to bite and... knot him.

During his lunch break, Robson had done some googling to make sure that meant what he thought it did and had been disturbed by some of the websites he'd happened upon. But *Marcus* didn't disturb him. And when he really sat there and thought about it, about Marcus sinking inside Robson's body and then having his cock expand and fill Robson as full as he could get...

Shivering, he shot to his feet. He trudged up the steps to his bedroom, mind going in circles. Basically any thoughts of him and Marcus having sex would turn him on, but did that mean he wouldn't freak out in the middle of them actually having sex?

Fuck, what if his body couldn't take it? He stopped at the end of his bed, shirt unbuttoned and half hanging off his body. What if his body *physically* couldn't take it? No one at the class had said anything about whether shifters were specially equipped to take their partners' magic dicks, but what if they were and it was just a given?

Grumbling to himself, he finished stripping and then climbed into bed with his phone in hand. He'd seen a website with specialty dildos when he'd been researching earlier, and he'd been tempted to express order one so he could try one of the knotting ones out on himself. That way he'd know before he and Marcus got that far whether he'd like it or not.

But the idea of using a toy like that, to test himself out before having sex with Marcus, left him feeling cold and completely unaroused.

No, he was going right to the source.

Robson: *Are you at the manor yet?*

He'd thought he might have to wait a little while for a response. Even if Marcus saw the message right away, Robson wouldn't have been surprised if he'd ignored him for a while after Robson hadn't responded to him all night.

But he should have known his sweet Marcus wasn't like that.

Marcus: *I was just about to leave. Everything okay?*

He couldn't help but smile as he typed.

Robson: *Everything's fine. I just wanted to talk to you, maybe ask some questions about yesterday. Do you have time?*

Jolting at the sudden ringing, he swiped to answer his phone. "Hey."

"I always have time for you, Robson," Marcus said, his voice a little hesitant.

Grinning, Robson settled into his pillow more, tucking his free hand behind his head. "I don't want to make you late. Are you sure?"

He could almost hear Marcus frown through the phone. "Of course. I don't have any scheduled meetings this morning. My work can wait until I arrive."

Something about that struck Robson as odd. "Don't you have to be there by a certain time? Punch in?"

"Punch… in?"

Biting his lip, Robson was reminded of their conversation at the rec center about money laundering. "Have you ever had a real job, Marcus?"

There was silence for a few moments. "I assume you mean a job with humans since my job is very much real."

Chuckling, Robson rolled his eyes at his half-hard dick. Apparently, he found Marcus's confusion over anything not related to pack life arousing. "Yes, that's what I meant."

"No. My first job was to assist Councilman Gregson, and then when I joined the Kincaid Pack, I was brought on as a beta because of my experience with the Council." Marcus cleared his throat softly. "Do you—is this what you wanted to talk about?"

He sighed and adjusted in bed, pulling his blankets up and covering his lower half. "No, sorry. I got distracted."

"Are you in bed?"

For a second, Robson was confused about how Marcus could have possibly known that. It wasn't said in a sultry, *what are you wearing* kind of way; it sounded like Marcus was surprised more than anything.

"Yeah, I just got home from work." He slowly dragged his leg across his mattress, then pulled it back to where it had been. "It's still weird to me that you can hear that so easily."

There was a pause, but Robson waited to see if Marcus would take the opening.

Finally, Marcus haltingly said, "I feel like I should apologize, but I can't change who I am."

The pain in Marcus's voice shot Robson up in bed, making him wish they were face-to-face. "No, cariño, no. That's not what I meant. You... You're amazing and wonderful and..."

"And?" Marcus's voice was so soft it felt more like a caress than a question.

Sinking back onto his bed, he sighed again, suddenly so

tired he wondered why he thought it was a good idea to have this conversation before he got some sleep. "And you deserve better than some washed-up grunt who doesn't know anything about your world."

He heard Marcus suck in a shaky breath. "Why would you say that?"

Slapping his empty hand onto the bed next to him, he had to remember to keep his voice down as frustration shot through him since he could hear his sisters moving around, getting ready for school. "Because it's the truth. I can't give you everything you need or deserve." He swallowed back the emotions building up in his chest and into his throat and croaked out, "I can't *be* what you need. I'm just... me."

"Robson." Marcus sounded upset, and that was the last thing he wanted, but it was like a dam had broken and all the thoughts he'd been ignoring sprang forward, finding all the tiny cracks and *pushing* until he couldn't help but spew it everywhere.

"You can't tell me that when you imagined finding your mate they were human. That they'd be a guy pushing forty with a part-time job that can't actually support his family." He heard Marcus try to interrupt him, but he couldn't stop now that the black sludge of his worst fears was spilling out of him. "I bet you fantasized about mating with someone who could exchange bites with you and take your knot without hesitation and maybe even give you theirs in return. You thought you'd have someone who could listen to you from another room to make sure you were okay and be able to tell how you were feeling without you having to say a goddamn word." He was panting, his words coming fast and hard. "Honestly tell me you wouldn't prefer a mate like that. If you can do that, then you can come over here right now and we can seal the deal on this mate thing."

Nothing but Marcus's own heavy breathing came over

the line, and Robson blinked up at his dark ceiling, spilling the tears filling his eyes down the sides of his face.

"That's what I thought," he whispered, voice ragged and harsh like he was angry. But he wasn't. He understood why Marcus would feel that way. Heart breaking, he murmured, "Goodbye, cariño."

CHAPTER SEVENTEEN

W hat had he just let happen?

Marcus stared at the black screen of his phone as his wolf howled in pain and fear. He'd been expecting to have a conversation about their... anatomical differences.

Instead... Well, he was pretty sure his mate had just broken up with him before they'd even gone on a date. And that was *unacceptable*.

Growling, he ripped off his clothing and sprinted out of his house, shifting as soon as the door was closed behind him. He ran as fast as he could, only slowing when he finally caught sight of the farmhouse in the distance and releasing a howl to let his mate know he was coming. The cows waiting to be milked lowed restlessly, their fear prickling at his wolf's instincts, but the urge to stalk such easy prey was minimal.

No, he was after a bigger prize.

He paused just before exiting the harvested cornfield behind the farm, waiting to be sure the house was empty except for his mate. The machine rumblings and occasional curse let him know Mateo was in the milking parlor doing the morning milking. Straining, he caught the sound of young, female voices bickering in the house and the sound of someone tossing and turning in bed.

Huffing, he lay down in the field, impatient for Robson to be alone so Marcus could slip inside and convince his mate they were meant for each other.

The aching pain he'd felt as his mate had questioned their mating had been nearly unbearable. What was worse was… he'd had those thoughts too, but it had only taken spending a little time with Robson for Marcus to realize that his mate was perfect just the way he was.

And perfect for Marcus.

When everyone else saw an uptight rule follower so set in his ways he'd pick a fight with the alpha's beloved assistant, Robson saw someone who struggled to express himself and loved his pack so much he wanted to always do right by them.

He *saw* Marcus.

Finally, what felt like almost an hour later, the two teen girls exited the house and clambered into an old Chevy truck that looked like it was one pothole away from falling apart. As they maneuvered down the driveway, Marcus slowly approached, eyeing the ancient car Robson drove. Robson's words from earlier came back to him about not being able to support his family with his job.

Were the Medinas struggling financially?

Money wasn't something he'd ever really worried about. He was given a home and a stipend for his work as a pack Enforcer, but most everything else he needed was provided by the pack as well. Most of his meals were cooked by Beth or one of her staff, and she provided him with new clothes when he mentioned he needed them. The SUVs were maintained and kept fully gassed by the betas. If he were ever sick or injured, he could visit Carter.

To the Medinas, he probably seemed spoiled and unable

to care for himself. Did Robson feel like he needed to take care of Marcus too? On top of his mom and his brother and sisters still at home?

That wasn't what Marcus needed from his mate at all.

He had access to those things because he spent every day, all day working and caring for the pack, so the pack cared for him as well. But it wouldn't be Robson's job to make sure Marcus was taken care of.

Unless... He paused at the bottom of the back steps. Maybe Robson *wanted* that. Maybe what Robson wanted from their mating was the ability to take care of and provide for Marcus.

Or maybe Marcus was completely wrong and Robson really just thought they were poorly matched.

Taking a deep breath, he savored the scent of his mate permeating his home. It was mixed with the scents of the rest of the family, but it stood out to Marcus, weaving around his senses and drawing him in. He was halfway up the steps before he remembered to shift back.

He cast one last glance back at where Robson's brother Mateo was, but there were still plenty of cows waiting to have their full udders emptied. Slipping into the house, he didn't hesitate, heading to the front where the staircase began and jogging silently up to the second floor.

The scent of Robson was so strong from the room he was in that Marcus could have found it with a regular human nose, he'd bet.

He didn't bother knocking, simply straightened his spine, squared his shoulders, and turned the knob. The curtains were drawn over the windows, but enough light seeped in that he was easily able to see his mate sprawled on his back in the middle of his bed. His brow was furrowed and jaw tight, like he was maybe having an unpleasant dream or was in pain.

For the first time since the end of their phone call, uncertainty filled him, freezing him in place. What was he supposed to do now that he stood at the end of the large bed and stared at his obviously naked mate?

The sheet and blanket Robson was under were just barely clinging to his waist, leaving his entire upper body for Marcus's ravenous eyes. He soaked in the sight of Robson's large, well-formed muscles and the thick black lines of a tattoo that covered his right pec and shoulder. As he ran his eyes over each gently curved line, blushing at the way his own body reacted to the sight, Robson's frown deepened and his lashes fluttered a few times before slowly opening.

"Marcus?" Robson's voice was rough and gravelly from sleep. He scrubbed at his eyes and the thickening stubble on his chin as he sat up a little, resting on his elbow. "What are you doing here?"

"You…" Now that he was standing in front of Robson, naked and vulnerable in a way he hadn't been since he was a young boy trying and failing to shift for the first time, his words got caught in his throat, choking him until he thought he might suffocate.

Robson's sleepy gaze sharpened at Marcus's continued silence. "Listen, why don't we both throw on some clothes, and we can go downstairs to talk about—"

"*No.*"

The word burst out of him so loudly and with such vehemence that Robson's mouth shut with a clack of teeth, eyes widening. Chest heaving, Marcus took a step forward so his thighs were pressed against the foot of the bed, and even then he leaned forward a little more, wanting to be as close as he could be to his mate without invading his space or making him uncomfortable.

"No," he said again, softer that time, almost on a sigh. He forced himself to hold Robson's gaze as he said, "Having a real mate, one blessed by the goddess herself, isn't something that's guaranteed. But... yes, when I let myself imagine one day finding my mate, I assumed they'd be a shifter like me."

Marcus forced himself to endure the flash of pain that crossed Robson's face, tightening the skin around his dark eyes and firming his lips into a straight line. He didn't try and interrupt though, and he didn't look away from Marcus.

"But you are not a, a... *consolation prize*. Or a burden I'm being forced to carry." When Robson sucked in a breath, Marcus couldn't hold back any longer, placing one knee and then the other onto the mattress. He wanted to crawl forward, to bury himself in his mate's warmth and scent and while away the day. He made himself stop next to Robson's feet, though, even as he greedily inhaled the spike of basil in the room. "I know I'm not very good at expressing myself, but I couldn't let you go on thinking—even for one more minute—that you aren't more perfect for me than any mate I could have dreamed up for myself."

"Cariño," Robson murmured, his eyes softening.

"And if you're not comfortable ta-taking my knot, then we don't ever have to do that." His embarrassment attempted to overwhelm him, but he pushed through, needing to make sure Robson knew how he felt. He was glad the room was so dark, making it less likely Robson could see how red Marcus's face was becoming. "Our mating won't be less amazing or fulfilling without it—because we've been blessed by the goddess. We found each other. And I get to spend the rest of my life showing you my world and working to make you as happy as you could ever possibly be."

For several long moments, nothing but the sound of their heavy breathing filled the room. Marcus's own heart was beating so hard for once he couldn't hear Robson's.

Robson swallowed loudly, then rasped out, "Are you sure?

I don't want you to wake up one day and realize you've been missing out on a real mating—"

"Our mating is real," he snarled, his wolf infuriated at the implication that what they had was less than what other mated pairs experienced. Marcus would die for—would *kill* for—Robson. He would provide him with anything he ever needed and submit to Robson in any way his mate desired. Their mating would be perfect because it would be *theirs.*

Robson's eyes widened a little at his outburst, but he didn't smell like fear. He studied Marcus's face for a moment, then extended an arm. "Come here, cariño."

Diving forward, he scrambled to get his legs under the blankets, then pulled them up and leaned into the warm, smooth skin of his mate for the first time. He couldn't hold back a soft whimper as he plastered himself as close as he could get, tucking his face into the fragrant crook of Robson's neck. He wrapped an arm around Robson's chest, tucking one of his legs between Robson's, his thigh carefully pressed as close to his mate's groin as he could safely get without squishing any of the delicate bits.

One of Robson's arms wrapped around Marcus's shoulders, his other hand trailing slowly up and down the arm draped over Robson's chest. They lay quietly together for so long, Marcus almost fell asleep. He'd never felt so safe or at peace in his entire life—not even when he was with his alpha.

"I'm worried I won't know what you need," Robson whispered eventually.

The hand he'd been using to caress Marcus was resting lightly on his wrist, so he wiggled his arm free and slotted their fingers together, making a happy, satisfied sound when Robson gave him a reassuring squeeze. "All I need is this."

Robson chuckled softly. "I'm serious. I feel like I'm getting pretty good at reading your subtle cues, but what if I miss one? Nico said at the class yesterday—"

Marcus growled. "I should have dragged you out of there as soon as I scented you in the building."

Threading his other fingers into Marcus's hair, Robson gave the strands a light tug. "The class wasn't the problem. The realization that there were things you'd want or need that I had no clue about was."

Huffing, Marcus squirmed closer, rubbing his lips and facial hair against the thin skin of Robson's throat, smiling when Robson shivered. "You worry too much."

"Me?"

"Mmhmm." He inhaled deeply, going a little light-headed at how delicious his mate smelled. "Wolves are social, so we need close contact like this but otherwise... don't worry so much. Nico will make sure my wolf and I are getting—"

There was a stinging tug on his hair as Robson's fingers closed in a fist, but Marcus didn't get a chance to protest before he was flailing as Robson flipped them so Marcus was sprawled on his back with Robson pressed all down the front of him. Robson's grip on Marcus's hair and hand was pinning him as much as the heavy weight of his body.

"Robson, what—"

"I don't care what Nico did for you in the past. That's done. You hear me?" Robson growled into Marcus's face, teeth flashing in the darkened room and making Marcus's breath catch with how beautiful he looked as he staked his claim. "Anything you or your wolf needs comes from me from now on. Do you understand?"

Marcus couldn't help the curve of his lips as he let his body fully relax in Robson's hold, tipping his chin to the side as best he could with the grip Robson had in Marcus's hair. The internal struggle he'd been having with himself over claiming or being claimed ceased as his wolf reveled in his mate's possessive hold. "Yes, mate. I understand."

Robson stared down at him for a long moment, running

his eyes over the exposed skin of Marcus's throat, eyes narrowed in thought. As he slowly lowered his head, Marcus held his breath and let his eyes flutter shut, completely lax on the bed.

Soft lips brushed ever so lightly at the hollow of Marcus's throat, and he couldn't hold in his moan at just that tiny amount of contact. His skin felt like it was electrified, thrumming with life and possibilities in a way he'd never experienced before. Robson's lips moved slowly up to his Adam's apple and then—

"Oh *god*, Robson."

His mate's tongue was so hot and wet as he laved the length of Marcus's throat and hummed like he'd just tasted the most delicious meal of his life. Marcus clutched at their clasped hands, his other one flying up to grip at Robson's upper back as he tried to ground himself.

"Shit, cariño. You're so responsive to me," Robson murmured against Marcus's jugular, pressing a sweet kiss there before he leaned back and met Marcus's gaze. "I'm serious, Marcus. No one else gets to see you like this anymore. If we're doing this, then I'm going to be a greedy, demanding asshole and make sure I'm the only one who gets to make you squirm. I can't do partway, not with you."

Marcus couldn't really think straight, his body arching into Robson's warmth all on its own and his head moving restlessly against the pillow that smelled so much like his mate he wanted to rub it all over his body. "Partway?"

He didn't understand. All he knew was that he wanted Robson to keep touching him, rougher and in more places. Touch him in a way that would soothe his wolf for days and days, knowing his mate had possessed his body like only he could.

Suddenly, both of Robson's hands were on the sides of

Marcus's face, turning him so they were eye to eye. "You with me?"

Working harder than normal to focus, he met Robson's fierce eyes and fell headfirst into their dark depths. "I'm with you," he whispered, hypnotized by the firm hold Robson was using combined with the stern line of his jaw. "I'd go anywhere with you."

The sides of Robson's mouth quirked up, and in that moment, Marcus wanted nothing more than to taste them, to get lost in the feel of his mate's mouth on his own.

"Good to know. But do you understand what I'm asking? I know we have to talk more, but…" Robson's gaze was like an inferno as it swept over Marcus's body. "Fuck, cariño. Things are moving fast here, but I need to hear you say it and then tell me what you need from me right now."

Tipping his head back, Marcus sucked in a breath to try and clear his swirling thoughts, but all he did was inhale more of Robson's scent of sex and want. "Say what? What… what do you need me to say?"

"That it's just us now. No Nico."

"No Nico?" He couldn't be friends with Nico anymore? Nico was… he was Marcus's family. The pain that lanced through him at the very idea of cutting him out cleared his head like nothing else had. "I can't… Robson, I can't lose Nico's friendship." He was crushed that his mate would even ask that of him. How could he suggest—

Robson chuckled and pressed their foreheads together. "I didn't mean don't be friends with him. I just meant I can't… I can't mate with you if you're going to continue to have sex with him."

"What?" Marcus's whole body jerked in shock, bumping their heads together. "Why would you think I'm having… relations with Nico?"

Robson leaned back, then went all the way so he was

kneeling between Marcus's knees, one hand rubbing at his forehead and the other resting absently on Marcus's thigh. "You said that he makes sure you get what you need."

Pushing up onto his elbows, Marcus tried to tear his eyes away from the thick, uncut cock resting against Robson's thigh. Even only semi-hard, Marcus thought his mate *more* than made up for a lack of knot. Licking his lips, he dragged his gaze up the firm lines of muscles in his abdomen and chest, biting his lower lip when he finally found Robson's amused gaze.

"You need to behave yourself until we finish this conversation," Robson said, lips pressed together to suppress a grin.

Swallowing, Marcus nodded and tried to focus. "Um, I didn't mean... sex." At Robson's raised eyebrows, he cleared his throat and continued. "I meant that Nico has always made sure my wolf gets what it needs, dragging me out for runs with packmates, scent marking each other, visiting my house so my den doesn't just smell like me." He shrugged as Robson's shoulders lost their tension. "Stuff like that."

Robson nodded as he studied Marcus. "But he doesn't provide you with the pleasure you need."

It wasn't a question, but Marcus made a face and shook his head anyway. "No. He's like a brother to me."

Nodding once more, Robson leaned forward, planting his fists in the bed on either side of Marcus's shoulders, caging him in. "I know it makes me a dick, but I need to hear it still. That you won't be with anyone else now that we're together."

Marcus cocked his head as he settled back onto the bed. "Why would I be with anyone else?"

Robson's face softened as he slowly lowered himself onto Marcus's body. "That's right. No cheating for mated shifters." He pressed his lips to the hinge of Marcus's jaw and slowly moved forward. "Lucky me. I almost feel bad for anyone you were with before... but not really. Like I said, I'm a greedy bastard. I'm going to enjoy having you all to myself now."

Marcus realized what Robson meant as he reached the tip of Marcus's chin. "You've always had me to yourself," Marcus whispered just as Robson's lips slid up and he was hovering over Marcus's mouth.

Breaths mingling, Robson murmured, "What do you mean?"

"I've never been with anyone before, and I'll never be with anyone but you from now on." Marcus shrugged a little and raised his head just the slightest bit, saying against Robson's lips, "I'm all yours, mate."

CHAPTER EIGHTEEN

I *'ve never been with anyone before.*

The words kept repeating in Robson's head, tantalizing and teasing him as his brain tried to process the fact that the gorgeous man splayed out before him had never been touched or kissed or brought to orgasm by another person. Robson had so many questions, but there was only one he'd ask right now...

"Shifters don't, like, age differently, right? You're not really only sixteen?" He'd lifted his head so he could see Marcus's face more clearly and found the pout on the usually stern mouth adorable as fuck.

"No, I'm not sixteen. I'm twenty-six. Now will you please kiss me?" The breathy way Marcus asked for his kiss undermined the abrupt words, the slight quiver giving away how much Robson's mate needed him.

His mate *needed* him.

The realization lit up a part of Robson's brain that had been dormant, firing up previously untapped instincts that urged him into motion. Dipping down, he licked Marcus's lower lip and hummed at the moan it produced.

"Tell me what you need while I still have a clear head, cariño."

Whimpering and thrashing against the pillow, Marcus wrapped his arms and legs around Robson and clung to him. "You. I need you. When I thought you didn't want this, me, *us* —" Marcus choked on his words, and Robson shushed him, burying his face in his neck and kissing all the skin he could reach.

"I was just scared. I'm sorry, cariño." He licked the tendon running up Marcus's neck, then peppered kisses over his whiskered cheeks and jaw. "I'll make you feel good."

At Marcus's shiver, he pressed a smile into the corner of his mouth. He wondered absently how much of Marcus's reactions—the way he seemed to be almost overwhelmed with sensations and feelings—was due to everything being new and how much was their mating connection. Bennett had seemed pretty cool even though Robson had hijacked his class, so he made a mental note to ask him about shifters' reactions to their mates.

But at the moment, he had something much, much better to focus on.

Gentle as a whisper, he slid his lips across Marcus's, drawing back just enough to separate them when Marcus jerked forward to press their mouths more firmly together. "Ah, ah, ah. Slow down, cariño. We've got all the time in the world."

They were so close he could hear Marcus grind his teeth together. "I'm supposed to be at a meeting this afternoon, and your brother is walking toward the house right now." At Robson's chuckles, Marcus tipped his face away to glare at him, one eyebrow lightly arched. "So maybe go a little faster."

Grunting, he leaned forward and finally gave them both what they wanted, Marcus's soft lips parting on a small gasp at the full contact. Using the opening, he sucked on Marcus's bottom lip until he whimpered, then swept his tongue inside, tasting his mate for the first time. He slid his fingers back into Marcus's thick hair and tilted his head to the side just a little, making the angle so much better and allowing him to kiss him deeper and harder.

Just when he was running the fingertips of his other hand down the side of Marcus's lean body, intent on grabbing his thigh to hitch it up higher around his waist so they could line up better, he heard the kitchen door shut with a bang and felt Marcus jerk beneath him.

Sighing, he slowly pulled away from Marcus's addictive mouth and stared down into his hazy eyes. "Hold that thought."

He groaned in annoyance as he rolled away from Marcus's warmth so he could reach his phone on the bedside table.

Robson: *Can you go occupy yourself somewhere else for a few hours?*

His brother's response came through quickly.

Teo: *Shit. Did I just wake you up with the door? I'm sorry. I'll be quiet. Promise.*

Chuckling, he shot Marcus a heated look, smiling wider when his blush began to spread down to his shoulders and chest.

Robson: *I was awake. But I'm about to have sex with my boyfriend and I can't guarantee how quiet we'll be.*

His brother must have said something out loud when he read the text because Marcus shot upright, eyes wide and horrified. He looked at Robson, mouth gaping slightly.

"What is it? Did he say something offensive?" Robson doubted it, but if needed, he'd go kick his brother's ass.

Ducking his chin, the corners of Marcus's mouth tipped up as he shook his head, then he turned over and tucked himself under Robson's arm. "No," he said softly. "Um, he just laughed and said heaven forbid he be able to take a nap while you, uh, fucked your boyfriend."

Robson frowned at the door, contemplating going down and exchanging words with his brother anyway. He didn't want Marcus feeling uncomfortable in his home or around his family.

Reading Robson's intentions, Marcus pressed a lingering kiss to his pec. "It's alright. He's leaving."

Humming, Robson turned onto his side so they were chest to chest and braced his head on his bent arm. He smiled as Marcus lightly ran his fingers down Robson's chest, tracing his tattoo and the lines of his abdomen. "Do you need to let someone at the manor know you're going to be late?"

"I don't have my phone," Marcus murmured, fingers curling around Robson's side as he leaned forward and licked delicately at one of Robson's nipples.

Robson groaned and threaded his fingers into Marcus's hair, his eyes falling shut. "You could borrow mine."

"Hmm."

Hissing when Marcus sucked on a patch of skin on Robson's pec until it stung in the best way, he tightened his grip. "I'm sure they'll survive without you for a few hours."

After letting Marcus explore his chest a bit, he finally couldn't take the teasing licks and nibbles. He tugged on Marcus's hair to bring his head up and leaned in to press a sensual kiss on his full mouth, groaning at how eagerly Marcus kissed back. It was obvious to Robson that he was inexperienced even in this, his movements a little frantic yet still unsure, but that just made Robson slow things down further. Savor him even more.

He'd teach Marcus how to kiss confidently and then move on to teaching him... other things.

For long, heated minutes, they did nothing but share

languid kisses and lightly caress over each other's bodies. Slowly, Marcus got more sure of himself, his fingers pressing in more firmly and his tongue swiping into Robson's mouth boldly. Before too long, he was gently thrusting his hard cock against Robson's and moaning more and more loudly each time.

Eventually, Robson couldn't handle going slow anymore.

He rolled on top of Marcus again, pressing his back into the mattress, and gave him one more deep, spine-tingling kiss, then started moving down his body with purpose.

Sweeping his tongue across a line of freckles just beneath Marcus's collarbone, Robson groaned. "I love these."

"W-What?" Marcus was panting, his legs moving restlessly against the mattress and his fingers digging bruises into Robson's skin.

And Robson was fucking loving it.

"Your freckles." He propped himself up and pressed a kiss to the bridge of Marcus's nose. The tiny brown dots were mostly on Marcus's shoulders, but the little sprinkling on his nose and cheeks were there if you were close enough to look. "They're so sweet. Just like you."

Cheeks darkening, Marcus averted his gaze as he bit his lip. "Thank you. I… I like your skin too. And your, uh, tattoos."

His voice was so soft and breathy, Robson had to strain to hear him. Grinning, he nipped at Marcus's sexy bottom lip— made even plumper by their kisses—and ducked back down to continue his exploration. He zeroed in on Marcus's nipples next, sucking one into his mouth while lightly pinching the other with one hand. He switched back and forth a couple of times until Marcus was whimpering and thrashing his head back and forth.

"Fuck. When I'm not so tired…" He trailed kisses down Marcus's smooth stomach, nipping playfully at his belly button, then detouring around his weeping cock. "I'm spending *hours* just exploring every inch of your body, cariño."

Marcus's whole form twitched as he sucked in a breath.

Chuckling, Robson leaned forward, pressed a kiss to one of Marcus's hips, then sat up between his legs, gripping Marcus's thighs and eyeing his squirming mate. "You doing okay?"

With a huff and an eye roll, Marcus said, "Yes. You don't have to treat me like a freak because I haven't ever done this before."

Eyes narrowing, he shot forward so fast he surprised Marcus, his body jolting and mouth parting in shock. Hovering over him, Robson said roughly, "Hey. That's not what this is. This is me treating you with respect and care because you are fucking precious to me. You hear me? You are not a freak, and I don't want to hear you say that again."

Marcus was panting, eyes glowing faintly as he ran his tongue over his lower lip, but Robson wouldn't be distracted.

"Do you hear me?" He pressed it because it felt important. Whoever had put that word in Marcus's head could burn in hell for all Robson cared, but he didn't want them taking up space in their bed.

"Yes," Marcus whispered, eyes locked on Robson's. "I hear you."

He held his gaze for a few moments longer, then nodded when all he saw was acceptance in his mate's eyes and ducked back down. Just before his lips met the head of Marcus's erection, soft fingers touched the side of his face and stopped him. Raising his head, he lifted a brow.

"You're precious to me too," Marcus said, voice soft and full of emotion.

Grinning, he turned his head and pressed a kiss to the palm of Marcus's hand. "Good to know, cariño."

Marcus bit his lip shyly and trailed his fingers away, the gentle caress leaving fire in its wake. Robson watched carefully as Marcus leaned back and relaxed against his pillow, looking for any indication that Marcus wasn't one hundred percent on board with things progressing.

All he saw was heat and desire lighting up his mate's eyes so they glowed like shining emeralds.

Slowly, he lowered his head once more but kept his eyes on Marcus's intense gaze. Once his lips met the hot, wet tip of Marcus's cock, he swiped out his tongue, humming at the flavor as it exploded in his mouth.

"Mm. You taste like a summer night under the stars," he murmured as he moved down Marcus's shaft, a plan of action forming in his mind.

Marcus sucked in a breath when Robson brought a hand up to cradle his balls, giving them a light tug as he ran his tongue from the base to the tip of Marcus's dick. "Th-That sounds like a good thing?"

He sucked on Marcus's glans for a second, smiling at the moan it produced, before responding. "One of my favorite things. I can't wait until next summer so we can spend a whole night outside without freezing our asses off."

Marcus chuckled, but the sound was cut off when Robson took the head of his cock back into his mouth, dipping his tongue into the slit. Every whimper and moan that escaped from Marcus's mouth was like a jolt of electricity in Robson's balls, everything made more intense with the knowledge that no one had ever touched Marcus or coaxed such noises from him before.

He found quickly that Marcus really enjoyed when Robson used one hand to squeeze the base of his shaft while taking the rest into his mouth, sucking almost harshly on each upstroke. Robson wished he could take the whole thing in his mouth, but he was out of practice, and Marcus's cock was too long for him to just try and casually deep-throat. Long and slender, just like Marcus, Robson couldn't wait to feel it inside him.

Taking a break so he could catch his breath, Robson carefully guided Marcus legs so his knees were bent and pushed up toward Marcus's chest, grinning when Marcus quickly caught on and grabbed the backs of his knees to hold the position.

"Will I get to pleasure you as well?" Marcus asked just as Robson was positioning himself.

"If you touch me right now, things will end real quick," Robson said, snorting a laugh at the disgruntled look on Marcus's face. How he pulled it off in the position he was in Robson wasn't sure, but it was adorable as hell. "Next time you can touch me as much as you want, okay? This time, I just want to show you how good you can feel."

"What about you?"

Stretching forward, he pressed a kiss to where Marcus's groin met his hip. "Once I make you see the stars, cariño, I'm going to press my cock right here and rub until I come all over you."

He tried to hide his grin at the shudder that shook Marcus's whole body by pressing a few more kisses into Marcus's smooth skin over his hip. When he glanced up once more, it was his turn to shiver as he caught sight of the tips of Marcus's fangs peeking out of his panting mouth.

He was disappointed when Marcus shut his eyes and shook his head a little, his teeth shrinking back to human-sized and his irises no longer glowing when his lashes fluttered open.

"Sorry," Marcus murmured. "My control is usually much better."

"You don't have to be in control here," Robson whispered, his plans changing as he realized how close to the edge

Marcus was. "You won't hurt me. We both know that, so it's okay to just relax and feel."

He didn't wait for Marcus to respond—though based on the furrow between his brows, his mate was confused at the idea of letting go of his tightly held control—and reached up to encourage Marcus to release his hold on his legs. He'd rim the hell out of his mate another time. At that moment, all he wanted was to focus on giving Marcus pleasure without completely overwhelming him.

Once Marcus's heels were back on the mattress and his thighs once more cradling Robson's shoulders, Robson settled in to blow Marcus's mind by blowing his dick. He didn't waste time teasing, simply gripped the base and held his cock up so he could sink down on it again, cleaning the rivulets of precome with his tongue, then sucking as he started working his hand on the bottom half.

Just as Robson was really getting into a rhythm, his ears full of his mate's whimpers and pleas for more, he gave the base of Marcus's cock a squeeze on a downstroke and paused. The very bottom of Marcus's erection, right where it met his groin, was a little wider than it had been a few moments before.

Pulling off with a slurp, Robson bit his lip as he eyed the obvious swelling, heat racing down his spine so fast he nearly came. He must have made a noise or his heart rate changed— something drew Marcus's attention away from where he was thrashing against the pillows.

When their eyes met, Robson grinned and ducked down to tongue the base where Marcus had swelled just a little, the skin more pliant than he was expecting. "Are you going to knot for me, cariño?"

Marcus whimpered, his eyes squeezing shut and heels moving restlessly against the sheets. "I can't. The first time has to be... inside you. My wolf is just excited and close to the surface. Is it... is it weird to you?"

Robson heard the unasked question: *Do you think it's gross?*

"No," he murmured, sucking the engorged skin into his mouth and rolling Marcus's tight balls in his hand as Marcus moaned raggedly. "Nothing about you could ever be weird. It's just different. But different is good. I can't wait to see it and feel it."

Marcus stared down at him with wide eyes, pupils so large Robson could barely see any glowing green anymore. "You'll want that someday?"

Nodding, he ran his tongue back up Marcus's cock and swirled around his head, cleaning off all the precome that had been leaking out. As he dipped the tip of his tongue into the slit to collect more, Marcus jolted, fingers clenching so hard in the sheet beneath him, Robson could have sworn he heard something tear. "Mmhmm. Soon."

"Robson," Marcus cried as Robson snuck a finger down between his cheeks and gently petted his furled hole.

"You want me inside you too, don't you? I might not have a knot, but I think I have enough to keep you happy." He moved his finger against the tight opening and watched the emotions chasing each other across Marcus's face. "Maybe one day we can get a toy that has a built-in knot or..."

He waited to see if Marcus was interested enough to ask what Robson was thinking. After blinking a few times, his eyes cleared enough to meet Robson's gaze. He licked his lower lip and asked huskily, "Or?"

Robson held Marcus's eyes as he released his grip on Marcus's balls, raised his hand, and made a fist. Kissing the tip of Marcus's cock when it jerked, he tilted his head to look at his closed hand. "Think your knot is bigger than that?"

"*Robson!*" Marcus's back bowed off the bed, his head thrown back as his body twitched. He was so close to tipping over the edge, Robson thought for a second he would come just from the idea of Robson's fist inside him.

When he caught sight of Marcus's fangs once more, Robson groaned and lowered his hand, running his palm from Marcus's hip up his abs to his chest. He dug in his fingers as he quickly took Marcus's cock back into his mouth and rode the wave as Marcus's body bucked again. That time, come did start to spurt from the tip as Robson sucked and squeezed the base right over the beginnings of Marcus's knot.

The scream Marcus released made Robson extremely grateful he'd sent his brother out of the house.

It took a few minutes for Marcus's body to relax into the mattress. Robson carefully cleaned his spent cock with his tongue, then raised his head as he licked his lips. Marcus's eyes were barely slits, but he was staring at Robson with an almost predatory gleam.

Grinning, Robson pulled himself up so he was plastered to the front of his sweaty mate and took his lax mouth in a deep kiss as he gently thrust against his relaxed body.

Marcus moaned as he threw one arm around Robson's shoulders and delved his tongue into Robson's mouth, chasing the taste of his own release. Grunting, Robson reached down and coaxed one of Marcus's legs up and over his hip to create a better cradle for him to thrust against.

With his free hand, Robson found Marcus's other one fisted in the sheets and threaded their fingers together, palms meeting as Robson pressed Marcus's hand into the pillow next to his head and started thrusting harder.

"Robson," Marcus moaned when Robson ripped his mouth away to pant against his neck. His heel dug into Robson's ass, driving him to move faster. "Want you to feel good too."

"You make me feel amazing," he grunted into Marcus's

skin, licking up to his ear and nibbling on the lobe. Marcus whimpered and dug his nails into Robson's back, shooting fire down to his dick. "Fuck, I'm gonna come."

Whimpering, Marcus nodded frantically, tightening his leg. "Do it. Please."

"Ungh, cariño." Robson stiffened, grinding his cock into Marcus. He hissed through his clenched jaw as he came between them, the scent of sex filling the room.

He tried to hold himself up from smothering Marcus out of habit, but then he remembered the slender guy under him could bench-press him and let himself settle down on top of him with a sigh. Burying his face behind Marcus's neck and in the ends of his hair, he inhaled deeply.

"Not too heavy?" he murmured, just to be sure. He should move and clean up so they didn't end up stuck together, but now that he was coming down from his orgasm, all he wanted to do was pass out.

"No," Marcus whispered, skimming his free hand up and down Robson's back. "You're perfect."

CHAPTER NINETEEN

P eeling himself away from Robson's warm skin and soft snores had been one of the hardest things Marcus had ever had to do, but he'd forced himself to only press one light kiss against Robson's throat and then carefully crawl away so he didn't wake him. The house had still been empty and quiet, so he hadn't had any problems slipping downstairs without clothes and shifting once he was outside.

Without a lot of time before he was expected at the manor to greet a visiting alpha with Rick and the others, he'd still detoured home, grabbed his phone, dressed, and quickly packed a few things into a bag, leaving it just inside the door. The drive to the manor seemed to only take seconds, his mind full of fanciful thoughts like if he should bring a gift to meet Robson's mom and how to convince Robson to let Marcus get a safer vehicle for his sisters to drive.

He hadn't bothered to shower, not ready to lose the scent of their mating yet, but the looks he'd gotten when he'd slipped in the door had made him feel self-conscious in his skin for the first time since he was a teen. The beta at the door, Todd, lifted his lip in a mocking sneer until Marcus straightened his spine and flashed his eyes at him, reminding the other man where he stood in the pecking order. He wouldn't let anyone make him feel bad for having a human mate or for proudly carrying his scent like any newly mated shifter would.

"Any word on when the Keshena Pack will be arriving?" he asked, already heading toward the offices and making a mental note to let Jamie know Todd's attitude was getting worse, not better. The young man had been a beta for a couple of years but hadn't gained any new responsibilities or moved any closer to becoming an Enforcer. In fact, Marcus would be surprised if the man lasted through the new year.

"A few hours still," Todd said quickly. "Their flight was delayed, so they only just landed in Detroit."

He lifted his hand in acknowledgement but didn't turn around. It was just after noon, and he hoped most everyone else was eating somewhere in the manor or in town. He wanted to close himself in his office without running into anyone else who could potentially sour his mood. The reminder of why he was in a good mood to begin with was enough to lift the corners of his mouth, the ghost of Robson's touch skating over his body and stirring his cock once more.

Until he entered the hallway and saw a large human, blond hair in a messy bun on his head, leaning into Jamie's space near the smaller man's office door. Jamie's back was pressed against the wall, his head tipped back so he could meet Gabriel's eyes as the hunter towered over him.

Marcus opened his mouth, sharp words on the tip of his tongue, when his nose caught up with his eyes and he realized Jamie wasn't *scared*... the hawk was *aroused*.

Freezing, he looked closer and noticed that while, yes, one of Gabriel's hands was braced against the wall next to Jamie's head, partially caging him in, his other was playing with Jamie's fingers down by their sides.

"Marcus!" Jamie gasped, jerking his hand away from Gabriel's touch when he noticed Marcus standing a few yards away. His fair skin erupted in a blush so quickly it might have actually hurt. Jamie dropped his eyes but didn't step away from Gabriel.

For his part, the hunter sighed and rolled his head languidly to the side, giving Marcus an annoyed glare. "Enforcer Rivera."

"Mr. Morde. What an unexpected surprise." Marcus glanced at Jamie, but he was still staring dutifully at the ground. Raising a brow and stepping toward his office door, he said, "I'm surprised Todd let you into this area of the manor. It's generally off-limits to non-pack members."

Gabriel rolled his eyes and turned back to Jamie, running one finger along his flushed cheek before stepping away. The smile he threw Marcus made him appear charming and harmless, but Marcus wasn't fooled. He knew that if he could scent the man, he'd be getting hit with heavy annoyance at the very least, anger more likely. There was definitely a darkness lurking in the hunter's eyes.

"The front door isn't the only way into the manor, Enforcer," Gabriel said, voice laced with just enough of an edge to let Marcus know he thought Marcus was an idiot. Frowning, he didn't get a chance to reply before Gabriel was stepping backward and saying to Jamie, "Think about what I said."

Jamie nodded a little, only lifting his chin high enough to gaze at Gabriel through his lashes. "Goodbye, Gabriel," he murmured.

Grinning, Gabriel said, "I'll see you later, gorgeous," and then disappeared down a side hall that led—indirectly—to where the kitchen and back door were located.

"Jamie—"

"Don't." Jamie's voice had hardened, but his blush was still prominent in his cheeks. Without another word, he turned and stomped to his office, shutting the door firmly behind him.

Sighing softly, Marcus entered his own office, flicking on the lights and heading straight for his desk. It wasn't his place to say anything to Jamie about his… dalliance with the hunter, but it still concerned him. Gabriel didn't trust them enough to reveal his damn scent, so how could he be trusted in return?

Once his computer booted up, he was disappointed to see there still weren't any messages from Wendy about getting away from the Council's territory. The longer she was radio silent, the more his stomach churned. He should have convinced her it wasn't worth the risk or convinced Rick to let him go to Mehko to escort her out or something.

Frustrated at himself, the Council, Gabriel Morde, and the fact that his mood had been completely ruined, Marcus threw himself into work. Even without any more archives to go through, he had emails to answer that had been forwarded from Jamie—generally questions from packmates that Jamie wasn't sure of the answer, so he passed them off to Marcus or one of the other Enforcers, depending on the subject.

Plus, he and Nico monitored the online forums that were popular with shifters, keeping an eye out for anyone who seemed to be in a bad situation and, more recently, grumblings from other packs about the Council overstepping their authority—not that there were many posts about that. The Council was also able to monitor the forums, so they weren't completely safe spaces to complain.

And he was still attempting to set up in-person meetings with other packs to garner alliances in the event they needed support against the Council. It didn't feel like enough and also too much at the same time. A part of Marcus still rebelled at the idea of working against the Council, of not trusting the panel of alphas to be fair and just in their rulings and edicts.

But he only had to remember Kieran's face when he described what had happened to him during the hearing against his father to know that wasn't true. The Council had been completely biased in favor of Alpha McAllister and had asked rude and personal questions of Kieran even though he was simply supposed to be testifying to how he'd overheard his father and sister talking about how they were spying on the Kincaid Pack's emissary.

Something that was very much against shifter law.

The hearing had turned into a joke though, with Kieran being put under scrutiny and his father being found not guilty of the allegations.

And then Alpha McAllister had come for Rick and his son in retribution.

Marcus knew, without a shadow of a doubt, that if Mikel Gregson had still been alive, Councilman Kincaid wouldn't have been able to so easily manipulate the rest of the Council into doing his bidding, and there wouldn't be even a question about whether or not the majority of Council members could be trusted.

An unknown number popped up on the screen of his cell as it began to ring and vibrate on the desk. Frowning, he hesitated before answering.

He knew that area code.

Taking a deep breath, he focused on releasing any tension in his neck and jaw, knowing he couldn't afford to give anything away if the person on the other end was who he thought.

"Marcus Rivera," he answered, his voice devoid of any emotion.

"Enforcer Rivera," a deep but cheerful voice said, setting

Marcus's teeth on edge. He shut his eyes and silently inhaled, exhaling the annoyance. "This is Alistair Kincaid. How are you, son?"

The *son* comment made him flinch. He'd never actually met Alistair Kincaid, who was estranged from his *actual* son. So why was he pretending to be so friendly? "Councilman Kincaid. I'm well, thank you. What can I help you with, sir?"

He grimaced at the chuckle Kincaid released. "I'd heard you were very polite, Marcus, though it does beg the question of why you were conspiring behind the Council's back with our clerk."

Only a decade of experience kept Marcus from reacting to the words said so jovially it was like Kincaid was asking Marcus for his favorite lasagna recipe. Squeezing the fist not holding his cell phone, he concentrated on keeping his heart and breathing steady.

"I'm not sure what you're referring to, sir." He kept his answer short, knowing at least two other people were listening to the conversation on Kincaid's end. He could hear their hearts beating steadily.

"Oh, come now. You're not really going to pretend you haven't been talking to her, are you? We have the phone records and email correspondence."

But they didn't have her—he was almost positive.

Saying a silent thank-you to the goddess, he said, "Wendy? Of course I've spoken to her. I'm working on a project for my alpha and needed her assistance."

Kincaid hummed, and then the line went silent. He pulled the phone from his ear and saw that the call was still connected and realized he must have been muted so Kincaid could confer with whoever was with him.

What an asshole.

"Was there anything else, Councilman?" Marcus wasn't

going to just sit there and act like he didn't have anything better to do but listen to silence.

There was another moment of nothing, and then the phone switched over and he could hear the other end again. Though there was only one heartbeat present now. "No. I think that's it for now. Please give my... regards to my son."

The cold detachment in Kincaid's voice sent a chill down Marcus's spine. "I'll do that, sir."

He didn't wait for a goodbye, simply hanging up the phone and setting it carefully on top of his desk once more, even though what he really wanted to do was throw the device across the room with a roar and then track down Councilman Kincaid and rip him to shreds for his veiled threats against Marcus's pack, his alpha, and Wendy.

There wasn't much doubt left that Kincaid was the sender of the note with Agnes's body, but for the first time, Marcus wondered if the other Council members who had voted against finding Alpha McAllister guilty were the ones Kincaid was working with. There had been something about the way Kincaid had muted the call... like someone more powerful than him had wanted to speak without being overheard.

Sighing, he stood and called out, "You can come in now."

Jamie's tousled blond head poked into his office. "I don't know how you just kept your cool during that call, but that was... impressive."

Marcus waved the words off, organizing the paperwork strewn across his desk from the hour of work he'd managed to get done before the call. "Practice. Is Rick in the library?"

"He and Kai are on their way back from town. They went to Momma's for lunch," Jamie said softly, his voice completely lacking any hostility for the first time in weeks.

"Will you please let him know I'm waiting for him when he gets back?" He glanced over as he put his computer to sleep and shoved his phone in his pocket. When Jamie nodded, he continued. "And can you please contact the secretaries of each of the Council members who voted not guilty during McAllister's hearing and set up a virtual meeting with each, except Kincaid? Make sure they're video calls though. I want to see them, not just hear them."

"Yes, of course." Jamie's light eyebrows were furrowed as he watched Marcus. "What are you thinking?"

Marcus sighed as he headed for the door, Jamie darting out of the way and following him partially down the hall until Marcus answered. "I'm thinking that the Council might be the least of our worries."

Hours later, Marcus was tired and drained in a way he'd never been before, and he had a feeling he knew why: he hadn't heard from or seen his mate since he'd slipped out of bed, and he and his wolf were feeling stressed and worried. All he wanted was to curl up next to Robson and let his strong arms wrap around him and protect him from the outside world.

But his pack needed him to be strong.

So when Rick clapped a hand on his shoulder after hours of discussion and debate between him and the pack Enforcers and asked Marcus if he was good, Marcus firmed his chin, straightened his shoulders, and nodded.

Because he had to be.

Rounding the corner of the hall that led to the kitchen, he was so caught up in going over his orders and worries that he didn't notice the out-of-place scent in the air until he pushed the kitchen door open and stuttered to a halt. Sitting at the booth tucked into the corner of the room and surrounded by Beth, Kai, Jess, Samantha, and Kieran was Marcus's mate.

He thought he was imagining things for a moment until Robson threw his head back in laughter at something Kieran said and spotted Marcus, his face splitting into a wide, intimate smile.

"There you are, cariño." Robson's smile dimmed a little as he took in Marcus's face. "You okay?"

Kai and Kieran exchanged glances, but it was Jess who blurted out, "I doubt it. He got a creepy villain call earlier."

Robson's eyes narrowed, and he laid his palms flat on the table like he was going to push himself up and crawl out of the booth if need be, but Marcus shook his head slightly. "It's fine. I just need something to eat."

Beth popped up and started bustling around, muttering about silly boys not stopping to feed themselves proper meals while they worked. He smiled a little, his head ducking down at her fussing and warmth filling him. Beth might have technically been Vanessa's mom, but she made a point of mothering them all, and Marcus definitely didn't hate it.

Before he could figure out if he wanted to squeeze into the booth or go back to his office and invite Robson to join him when he was done socializing, Samantha was elbowing Kieran next to her and giving her brother and Jess a significant look.

Clearing his throat, Kieran scooted out and stood. "Is Bennett upstairs still?"

Marcus nodded. He'd left his alpha and second-in-command in the library, still discussing tactics for handling the threats they could see… and the ones they couldn't.

Kieran squeezed his wrist as he slipped past, the show of support oddly soothing even though it wasn't something they'd ever done for each other before. Brow furrowed, Marcus stared after him, wondering what he'd meant by it.

"Yes, we need to head off too," Kai said, not bothering to hide his grin as he, Samantha, and Jess stood as well. Once his back was to Robson, Kai met Marcus's eyes and waggled his eyebrows suggestively, causing Jess to cackle and Marcus to blush furiously.

They left, and he shook his head in exasperation when he heard Jess ask Kai if he and Robson had mated yet. Tuning them out, he focused on his mate, who was smirking at him, arms stretched across the back of the booth and showing off his powerful chest perfectly. It was only when Robson's eyes heated and his scent shifted to arousal that Marcus realized he'd licked his lips, then bit his lower one as he ran his gaze over Robson's arms and shoulders.

A throat clearing behind him made Marcus nearly jump out of his skin.

"Here you go, sweetie," Beth said, smiling gently as she handed him a reusable cloth bag. She winked as she added, "I didn't think the two of you would want to stick around to eat dinner with everyone else."

Robson chuckled as he shuffled out of the booth and took the bag from Marcus. "Thank you, Beth."

Eyes twinkling, she nodded and turned back to where she was finishing getting the evening meal ready for everyone else.

Marcus stood there for a moment, unsure what to do until Robson's strong arm came around him, his large hand coming up to rest on the back of his neck.

"Let's get out of here," he murmured against Marcus's jaw, brushing his nose gently along the side of Marcus's face, then pressing a kiss to the corner of his mouth.

Swallowing, Marcus nodded and turned to leave, immediately missing the warmth of Robson's palm on his skin when his hand dropped down, but at least Robson stuck close behind him as Marcus led the way to his office. He was about to push the door open when voices and laughter from the front hall drew his attention.

"That's the Keshena Pack finally arriving," he said softly, opening his door and gesturing Robson inside. "I'll just be a minute. I have to go and say hello to Alpha Okenapowet."

Robson just nodded, not seeming upset at the delay in their departure, and strolled into the tidy space, eyes roaming over the shelves of books and the filing cabinet tucked in the corner. "No problem. Just don't take too long. I don't want dinner to get cold."

The words were mild enough, but the slight growl to Robson's voice sent a shiver down Marcus's spine. He had a feeling it wasn't the food his mate was worried about.

Striding down the hallway, he entered the entry hall and pasted a smile on his face. He liked Alpha Okenapowet; it was her second who he wasn't a fan of. The man reeked of arrogance—though not literally. While his tone when he spoke to Marcus was generally mocking, the few times they'd met in person over the years, his scent had told a different story. One of arousal and frustration.

As soon as he stepped into the bright hall, Alpha Okenapowet paused her conversation with Jamie to turn and smile at him, her perfectly groomed black eyebrows raised slightly as she scented the air.

"Enforcer Rivera," she said, her calming voice and presence filling the entire space and making his smile more natural.

"Alpha Okenapowet. I hope your trip wasn't too arduous." He shook Ava's outstretched hand and leaned in to allow her to brush her lips against his cheek. The greeting was a familiar—and formal—one for shifters, especially high-ranking members of different packs. To a casual human observer, it appeared as if they were old friends, pressing a quick kiss to each other's cheeks, but to a shifter it was a show of trust. It allowed shifters who weren't packmates to closely inhale each other's scents to more clearly read intentions and emotions. But it also showed trust in how close it allowed the other person to get to one of the most vulnerable places on the body—the throat.

Since she was an alpha, he didn't return the gesture, as it would be inappropriate for her to show vulnerability. Instead, he simply turned his face slightly away and allowed her the privilege of scenting him.

"You'll have to tell me about this new mate of yours," she murmured as she pulled back, dark eyes sparkling. Her reddish-brown skin was smooth and beautiful and a clear reference to the Menominee Tribe her pack intermingled with so freely. Last he'd heard, three-quarters of the pack were Native Americans, lineages coming from many different tribes all brought together by Ava Okenapowet.

He inclined his head, ignoring the heat in his cheeks. "Of course." Glancing at Jamie, he received a small nod. "If you'd like, Jamie can show you to the blue salon while your bags are taken up to your rooms. Alpha Kincaid will join you in just a moment."

She smiled, unfazed by Rick's lack of formality in not greeting her himself. Phil, her second-in-command, snorted from where he was just behind her, arms crossed over his wide chest, but she and Marcus ignored him. Phil was the only Enforcer or beta in her pack who wasn't Native American, and Marcus had heard he was a holdover from the previous alpha.

Marcus waited until the small group had disappeared before turning back to his office and his waiting mate. As he got closer, he was unsurprised to hear Nico's laughing voice in there with Robson. When he entered the room, he raised his eyebrows at how the two of them were seated on the small couch together, staring at something on Robson's phone.

"She's beautiful, man," Nico said, and Marcus realized they were looking at pictures of Robson's new niece.

"For a little blob of a person, yeah. She's pretty great," Robson said, grinning. He tucked away his phone, and they both stood, Nico smiling at Marcus in the same knowing way he'd been doing all day. Robson stepped over so he was next to Marcus, one of his hands rising to rest on Marcus's lower back. "Reesa was supposed to have a baby shower next weekend, but I'm not sure if she'll be up for it. It was pretty much just her and my mom throwing things together at the last minute. Is there anyone in the pack that should be invited?" Robson looked between Marcus and Nico. "I don't want to insult anyone by not including them because Reesa and I didn't know better."

Nico chuckled and Marcus smiled, wrapping an arm around Robson's waist and leaning against him slightly.

"I'll touch base with her and Patrick," Nico said, pulling out his phone and beginning to type. "Don't worry about it. I got you."

Marcus started to disagree. Reesa was his mate's sister, so he should be the one to help with her baby shower, but Nico raised his eyes and drilled him with a look.

"You have enough on your plate after today," Nico insisted, brow rising as he dared Marcus to contradict him.

"Does this have to do with the villainous phone call you received?" Robson laughed at the words, but Nico's and Marcus's serious faces sobered him quickly. "Shit, was Jess not joking?"

Marcus shook his head and sighed, scratching at his short beard and collecting his cell from his desk. "Unfortunately, no. Thank you, Nico."

Grunting at the dismissal but not seeming offended, Nico

lifted a hand in goodbye and went back to his phone, probably making a list of things he wanted to do for the shower.

Robson turned Marcus so they were face-to-face, gripping his shoulders. "What happened?"

"Can we talk about it at home? I just need to grab a bag of things from my house on the way." He'd worry about his plants later.

The long pause that followed his statement had his scalp prickling. Frowning, he studied Robson's wide eyes and carefully scented the air. He tilted his head as he tried to figure out why his mate would be shocked about him having a bag of things to bring—

His heart seized in his chest.

"Oh."

CHAPTER TWENTY

"Cariño, wait."

Robson called himself six different kinds of idiot as he tried to hold on to Marcus when he attempted to turn away, his face shutting down so quickly it was like his soul had gotten sucked out of his body. But Robson had seen the hurt in his light green eyes for that brief moment when Marcus realized he hadn't known Marcus would expect to *live* with him already, before the light had gone out and Marcus had tried to hide his feelings from him.

It wasn't until his stoic mask was back in place that Robson realized how much more expressive Marcus had started to become, especially when it was just the two of them. He would probably never be enormously emotive, but Robson had come to love the small quirks in his brows and lips, the tiny wrinkle along the bridge of his nose when he was confused, and the pink blush that flooded his smooth pale skin whenever anything even remotely sexual came up in conversation—

Oh fuck.

Was he *in love* with Marcus already?

Renewed shock flowed through him, and his grip loosened on Marcus's arms. His mate didn't hesitate to bolt toward the door, spine stiff.

He cleared his throat, following after him. "Marcus, I'm sorry. I didn't realize—"

"No apologies are necessary," Marcus said, soft voice clipped and overly formal. "I'm going to have to stay and work late though, so it would probably be best if we said goodbye now. I'll call you tomorrow."

Anger flared to life in his belly, pushing away the lingering shock that had been slowing him down. "Don't do that. Don't just shut me out because I misunderstood." A trickle of fear spread through his veins with each pump of his heart, twisting his gut and speeding up his pulse. This was exactly what he'd been afraid of, why he'd tried to pull away that morning. But he'd pushed his fears aside *for Marcus.* "Let's get out of here and talk about it, okay?"

He was distinctly aware that there were probably at least a dozen people able to listen in on their conversation at that very moment, and it was making him edgy and reluctant to speak openly.

When Marcus pulled open his office door, Robson realized their audience was even closer than he'd thought.

A large white man stood just on the other side of the door, his dark eyes pinned on Marcus and thin lips lifted in a sneer. "This *human* is your new mate? Jesus, Marcus, really scraping the bottom of the barrel, huh?"

"Excuse me?" Robson barked, stepping up next to Marcus so he could intervene if necessary. "Who the fuck are you?"

The guy didn't even look at Robson, just flicked his tongue over his lower lip and let his eyes dip down to run over Marcus's body, his ruddy cheeks getting darker. "Maybe if you hadn't acted like such an uptight bitch all the time you could have found a *real* mate. Hell, all you had to do was ask and I'd have fucked you so good, you never would have—"

Robson knew better—seriously, he did—but he still let his anger get the best of him. Fury ripped through him so hot and fast he was moving before the thought really crystalized in his brain that he needed to shut this guy the fuck up. He heard Marcus yell his name as Robson jumped forward, but it sounded far away thanks to the ringing in his ears.

He knew how to fight—barefisted and with weapons—but he'd never had to fight someone who wasn't just stronger than him but faster as well. Like, really fucking fast.

The guy got several hits in that rang Robson's bell, but each one taught him something about his opponent, and one thing became abundantly clear very quickly: the guy couldn't fight for shit. He depended on his brute strength and shifter speed to win, but he had no tactical skills.

A part of Robson's brain was worried about what that meant for his own mate and his packmates and their ability to win a fight, but mostly he focused on how the guy's shoulders and eyes gave away what he was going to do before he did it. Picking his moment, Robson blocked the next punch the man threw but followed the motion through until he had the guy's extended arm caught under his own. Instead of trying to throw his own punch or stepping away, he moved into the man's space, striking the guy's wide nose with his forehead.

Primal satisfaction filled him at the cry of pain the man tried to bite back, his free hand automatically going to his bleeding nose. Pressing his advantage, it took less than five seconds for Robson to strike the side of the man's knee with his booted foot and follow him to the ground, using the grip he had on his arm to twist it back into a chicken wing hold.

Within sixty seconds of the fight starting, it was over with Robson pressing his weight into his hold to cause maximum pain and prevent the asshole from even thinking about trying to get the fuck up.

Leaning down, Robson growled in his ear, "You ever talk to my mate like that again, and you and I are going to have problems. Understand?"

The guy tried to whimper something about his alpha or maybe Robson's alpha—it was hard to tell with all the sniffling. Raising his head slightly, Robson eyed the regal-looking Native American woman at the end of the hall glaring daggers at the guy under Robson.

Chuckling, he released his hold and quickly moved back, prepared to have to take the guy down again if he tried anything. But the man just lay there like he was too humiliated to even raise his head.

Robson glanced around, wiping at the trickle of blood beneath his bottom lip, and saw Nico and Bennett behind him, both with raised eyebrows. B's mate, Kieran, was just behind them, mouth hanging half-open. Worried he'd just committed a major fucking faux pas, he turned back to the woman. "Listen, I'm not actually a member of the Kincaid Pack, so my actions shouldn't reflect on Rick or his pack. Your man here—"

"Will be dealt with," she said, her voice cold and her flashing eyes still on the man as he slowly pushed up into a sitting position, leaning against the wall with a dazed expression. Finally, she raised her gaze and looked past Robson. "Please give Alpha Kincaid my sincerest apologies. And Marcus"—she turned toward him, a sad smile on her face— "I'm so sorry. All matings are sacred and should be cherished."

Robson finally looked at his mate, having been avoiding it out of fear he'd see anger or pain on Marcus's face, but when his gaze met his mate's... it was like the rest of the world faded away. It was corny and cliché, but it was fucking true.

No one else mattered as Robson stepped closer and Marcus did the same, his chest heaving slightly like he was the one who'd just been in a fight. His luscious lips were flushed a gorgeous red, and his pupils were wide.

A grin began to spread across Robson's face as he took in his aroused mate. *Fuck*. A not-small part of him wanted to bang his chest like a damn caveman and roar his victory. Instead, he snagged one of Marcus's hands, entwining their fingers, and tugged him forward. Marcus came so quickly and easily, he fell against Robson's chest. Which was fine, because that was just where he wanted him.

Lowering his head, he planted a possessive, openmouthed kiss on Marcus's trembling lips, groaning roughly when Marcus submitted easily, taking Robson's tongue into his mouth like it was all he ever wanted for the rest of his life.

Just as Robson's free hand was grabbing a handful of Marcus's ass and his lust-fueled brain was trying to figure out how to get his mate naked, a throat cleared behind him. He would have probably ignored it, but Marcus jumped like he'd been electrocuted and leapt back, one hand covering his kiss-swollen mouth as he stared at whoever was behind Robson with wide eyes.

Peering over his shoulder, Robson grunted in annoyance. "Thanks for showing up, Alpha Kincaid."

Rick's eyes narrowed, and he stepped into Robson's face. "Watch it. You just put a very important alliance in jeopardy over that little stunt, so I'd be *real* careful what I said if I were you."

Veins lighting up immediately, Robson did the opposite of back down. He squared off against the big man, prepared to take him down too if need be. "What I did was defend my mate when that piece of shit—"

He gestured and glanced at the ground where he'd last

seen the guy and saw he was gone. A quick glance showed him everyone but him, Marcus, and Rick had disappeared.

"Which is the only reason I'm not kicking your ass myself," Rick growled, then turned to Marcus, dismissing Robson as a threat completely. "You okay?"

Marcus nodded, the desire draining from his eyes as he dropped his gaze in deference to his alpha. "Yes, sir. I'm fine. Phil has always been... rude, but never so openly hostile before. I'm not sure what changed."

Robson grunted. "I do. He wanted you for himself, but he can't have you, so he lashed out."

A pink flush appeared on Marcus's cheeks, but he didn't deny it, letting Robson know he was right on the money. Huffing in annoyance, he wrapped an arm around Marcus's waist and tugged him into his side, grinning at Rick when his mate turned into him easily.

"Is it okay if I get him out of here? We need to have a conversation about assumptions."

Marcus stiffened but didn't pull away at the reminder of what had transpired in his office just before the fight. "If you need me to stay and smooth things over—"

Rick chuckled as he clapped them both on their shoulders, then stepped back. "No, that's alright. Ava will be here for a few days, so you'll have time to touch base with her. Go talk things out so Robson doesn't get into any more fights."

Robson rolled his eyes at Rick's retreating back. Without turning to Marcus, he slid his hand down from his waist to his ass and gave it a light tap. The quiet gasp in his ear soothed the part of him still worried about losing his mate over something he did or failed to do. Despite what Marcus might have thought, no way in hell would he have just left with Marcus so upset and thinking the worst about Robson.

"Grab the food, cariño," he murmured, giving his ass

another squeeze, then letting him go. "We've got lots to talk about."

Within thirty minutes, he was parking outside Marcus's house, his mate sitting silently in the passenger seat next to him, bag of rapidly cooling food held in his lap. Throwing the car into Park, he dug his phone out of his pocket and quickly pulled up his texts.

Robson: *I won't be home tonight. Let mom know, will you?*

"Um, do you need to get home?" Marcus asked into the quiet car.

When Robson looked over at him, he found Marcus staring into the bag like the answer didn't matter to him one way or the other. "No. I've got nowhere else to be," he whispered. He glanced at his phone screen when it buzzed in his hand.

Teo: *LOL sure thing*

Tucking his cell away, he shut his car off and turned toward Marcus. "I know things got a little… out of hand back at the manor, but let's go inside and talk about the *you moving in with me* thing."

The slightest flinch in the corners of Marcus's eyes was the only outward reaction. Carding his fingers through the hair on the back of Marcus's head and gripping lightly, he gave a slight tug so Marcus tipped toward him, and he leaned forward, pressing his forehead into his temple.

"I'm not saying no, cariño." He nuzzled into the side of Marcus's face, smiling at the way Marcus squirmed when Robson's nose brushed just in front of his ear. "I'm saying let's talk about things."

"Okay."

"Okay?"

Chuckling, Marcus turned and pressed a quick kiss to the corner of Robson's mouth. "Okay, let's talk about things."

Shaking his head but unable to suppress his smile, Robson climbed out of his car and met Marcus on the other side, snagging his hand and leading the way toward the front door. He didn't want to start the conversation until they were seated and he could read Marcus's face more easily than the setting sun would allow.

He frowned at the unlocked front door, but Marcus just lifted one shoulder in a small shrug and slipped past him to enter the dark house. Robson let him go, hovering just inside since he couldn't see for shit, but once the lights came on, his eyes immediately caught on the suitcase sitting next to him.

Keeping his face calm, he shut the door and headed for the small kitchen table he could see. Marcus followed and started unpacking the bag from Beth as soon as Robson sat down. Robson couldn't help but smile as Marcus fussed about the mashed potatoes and chicken being cold, hurrying off to reheat them. Forcing the conversation before Marcus was ready didn't seem like it would end well, so Robson just let him do his thing and dug into one of the side salads Beth had included—and what looked like fresh rolls.

It wasn't his mom's food, but it was damn good. He kept one eye on his flustered mate and the other on the food as Marcus kept putting more in front of him. He was almost finished eating before Marcus sat down with his own plate.

Eating the last few bites, he pushed his plate away and relaxed back into his chair, a smile playing at his lips as he blatantly stared at his fidgeting mate. Marcus had only taken a few bites before he started pushing the food around.

"Did you eat lunch after you left my place?" he asked quietly.

Marcus stilled for a moment, not raising his eyes from his plate. "I didn't get the opportunity."

Humming, he scooted his chair closer but not so close they were touching. "I bet shifting back and forth between your two forms burns a lot of calories."

Slowly, Marcus laid his fork down on the side of his plate, then gripped his hands in his lap. His shoulders were stiff as he spoke to the table. "It does. But no matter how much I eat, I'll always be too skinny."

Whoa. "What? Cariño, you aren't too skinny. You're gorgeous just the way you are." He wasn't sure where this was coming from, but he had a feeling it stemmed from Marcus believing Robson had rejected him before he'd even had a chance to say anything at the manor. "I just want to make sure you're taking care of yourself."

Sucking in a breath, Marcus raised his chin, but he still wasn't looking at Robson. "Thank you for your concern, but I've been taking care of myself my whole life. I've had to. I was always a... a... freak or whatever. With too-red hair, too skinny of a body, and skin that blushed too easily."

There was that word again. Biting back a growl, Robson took a deep breath to calm the anger stirring in his gut at the pieces of shit who raised his sweet Marcus. Leaning over, he clasped the sides of Marcus's face, but he still kept his eyes averted. "Hey."

Nothing.

"Cariño."

Marcus's eyes squeezed shut, a single tear slipping free.

Beginning to panic, Robson's voice took on a harder edge. "Look at me, Marcus."

When his lashes fluttered open and his sad, despair-filled eyes met Robson's, Robson couldn't help himself. Shoving the table back a little, he crawled into Marcus's lap, straddling him, then gripped the sides of his neck as he pressed their foreheads together.

"Mi amor, I don't know who told you such lies, but you are beautiful." He pressed soft kisses to Marcus's wet lashes, the tiny whimpers he released like daggers to Robson's heart. "I love how strong your body is and these adorable freckles on your nose and the fact that you blush when someone flirts or says something suggestive." He peppered kisses across his cheekbones, then rubbed his five-o'clock shadow against Marcus's thicker beard and shuddered. "I fucking love this beard you're growing."

"I'm growing it out for you," Marcus whispered.

Robson didn't know how Marcus had figured out Robson liked it so much, but he was still touched. Sliding his mouth over, he laid a quick, soft kiss on Marcus's mouth. "So sweet. And I absolutely adore your hair. It's so soft and shiny, and when the sun hits it just right... it's like the whole world can see the fire in you. Plus, it's just long enough for me to hold on to if I need to." He threw Marcus a wink and bit back a groan at the pink stain on his pale cheeks. "Fuck. It's so hot that someone as smart, and powerful, and *strong* as you are blushes at a wink. Can you smell how much I want you?"

Marcus whimpered and wrapped his arms around Robson, burying his face into his neck and nodding. "You don't regret what we did this morning?" he mumbled into the thin skin of Robson's throat, making him shiver and groan as his cock twitched.

He wanted to scoff at the very idea of regretting anything that could ever happen between them, but he didn't think that would make Marcus feel better in his vulnerable state. Wrapping one arm around Marcus's shoulders, he used his other hand to thread through the hair on the back of his head and lightly scratch at his scalp. "No, I absolutely do not regret what happened this morning." He paused for a moment, letting Marcus take in how steady his heart was and how truthful or whatever his scent stayed, and then he asked, "Do you?"

Marcus's arms tightened around him. "Of course not."

"I'm glad," he murmured, scratching a little more at Marcus's head, then just slowly carding his fingers through his hair for a few minutes and letting Marcus take all the comfort he needed from him. When Marcus's hold loosened a little, he continued the conversation. "But you were hurt by me not knowing you'd want to move in together."

He stated it like a fact but wasn't surprised when Marcus stiffened in his hold, then slowly nodded into his neck. "I realized…"

When he didn't continue, Robson pressed him a little. "What, cariño?"

A slight tremble shook Marcus's body, but Robson wasn't sure if it was because of what he was about to say or because he liked the endearment. It took a minute, but Marcus finally said, "I realized that I'd done what everyone had warned me not to do."

Robson frowned at the plant sitting by the window across the room but kept running his fingers through Marcus's hair. "I don't understand. What did you do?"

"Tried to rush you," Marcus said so softly Robson almost couldn't hear him. "Everyone warned me that you'd need more time, and I thought I understood that, but I still did it."

Oh.

CHAPTER TWENTY-ONE

As Marcus leaned his trembling body into his mate's strong chest, he realized it had been over a decade since he'd allowed anyone to see him so vulnerable. Longer, really, since it had been years before he left his parents' pack that he'd last sought real comfort from another person. Everyone in that pack had been about being strong and never showing weakness. Marcus couldn't even remember the last time he'd been held by his mother, though he assumed he had been when he was young.

But Robson was different.

Of course, the entire Kincaid Pack was different than his old one had been, but he'd still never felt quite comfortable enough to let down his walls with Rick or the other Enforcers. But in the safety of his mate's arms... he didn't have to be Enforcer Rivera.

He was just Marcus.

A little neurotic, a lot insecure, and one hundred percent Robson's.

Even though he'd tried to ruin things because of his fear of Robson rejecting him or their mating. He'd felt so small and humiliated when he'd realized Robson wasn't expecting them to move in together and was in fact quite shocked by the assumption. He'd instinctively wanted to hide until he could face Robson again without bleeding his feelings all over the place.

His mate was too smart for that though.

And when he'd attacked Phil for insulting Marcus? Nico and Bennett had come running, both staring at Marcus like they were worried he'd be upset, but he'd barely been able to take his eyes off the sight of Robson fighting for him—and winning. His human mate had taken down the second-in-command of a shifter pack in less than a minute.

It had been the hottest thing Marcus had ever seen.

Others might have worried that their mate didn't see them as able to take care of themselves or insulted that as an Enforcer he should have defended himself on his own, but not Marcus. While he didn't doubt his ability to win a fight against an opponent of equal strength, he also knew that wasn't where his biggest strengths lay.

Once the tremors began to fade, he raised his head and pressed a kiss to Robson's swollen lip and bruised cheek. Robson hummed at the small touches, his fingers tightening just a little in Marcus's hair and sending a shiver down his spine at the slight burn.

"You know," Robson murmured as Marcus continued to lay kisses across his face, silently thanking him for standing up for him. "It's not that I don't want to live with you eventually."

Eventually. He refused to let the word take the wind out of his sails again, pressing a kiss to Robson's mouth, then leaning back. "But you aren't ready."

Robson tilted his head back and forth. "Debatable. I shouldn't be since we haven't known each other that long, but that actually isn't the biggest reason."

"What is?"

"My family," Robson said with a sigh. "They need me, so I can't just up and move out on them, and—"

"I understand that," Marcus said quickly, hope flaring to life in his chest despite his best efforts to keep it under control. "I'd never expect you to leave your family. I could come live with you there."

Robson smiled fondly at him. "Don't you think maybe you should meet them once or twice before we move you into the farmhouse?"

Idiot. He dropped his gaze and nodded. "Of course. Yes. They wouldn't want a stranger living with them."

"Cariño." Robson tipped his chin back up and kissed him. "They will love you, but yes, it might be too much to ask them to live with the man I've only mentioned once or twice that I was seeing. We'll introduce you to everyone and bring you around for some family dinners, and then I'll break the news to them."

Smiling weakly, he nodded. "Okay."

After nuzzling Marcus's face a little, Robson asked softly, "Do you want to talk about that phone call you got right now, or have you had enough heavy stuff for a while? We can talk about it in the morning if you want."

Marcus shook his head. "Later. Can we... can we just lie together for a little bit?"

"Yeah, cariño, we can do that." Robson pressed a soft, lingering kiss to his mouth, then scooted back off Marcus's lap. "Eat a little more food first though."

That was a good idea—Marcus's body was starving suddenly, the lack of meals all day catching up to him. Robson cleaned up the containers Beth had sent the food over in, washing everything and setting them to dry on the rack. Just as Marcus was finishing, Robson came over and stepped up behind him. He leaned forward and wrapped his arms around Marcus, his face pressed next to Marcus's.

"You want to snuggle as your wolf or like this, sweetheart?"

He tipped his head back to look up at Robson, surprised but pleased that Robson would even think to suggest that. Warmth filled him at the small smile on his mate's face and the kiss Robson laid on him upside down.

"You wouldn't mind if I shifted?"

"Not at all. Whatever you need." Robson stepped back so Marcus could stand, then led the way to his living room, already stripping out of his button-down shirt.

Standing at the end of the couch, he paused with his hands on his belt when Robson started chuckling behind him. Turning, he raised a brow. "What's so funny?"

"There's no way we'll both fit on that." Robson gestured at the couch.

He turned back to look at the brown sofa more critically. It was a hand-me-down from Beth and her husband when they'd bought new things a few years ago. Marcus didn't spend a lot of downtime at his house, so he'd never really considered the cuddling ability of it, but Robson might have a point. It wasn't very long or very wide, so a full-grown man of Robson's size would have enough issue getting comfortable on it. Add his wolf?

"Um, probably not." He turned in a circle, his brain feeling sluggish after the emotionally wrought afternoon and evening.

"Where's your bedroom?"

Oh, right. He pretended to scowl at Robson's grin, but he snagged Robson's hand where it hung at his side and linked their fingers before heading up the stairs. His house was pretty small compared to some of the others the pack owned, but it was plenty of space for just him. Of the two bedrooms upstairs, one had a desk and computer that he rarely used, but he turned toward the other room.

His large bed with a navy blue comforter took up most of the space. There were bedside tables on either side and three bookcases stuffed full against two walls, with a comfortable chair by the window that he liked to sit in when he read in the evenings. On the other side of the room were two doors, one leading to a small walk-in closet and the other to the bathroom.

"This is nice, cariño," Robson murmured, pressing up against Marcus's back and kissing the nape of his neck.

He'd been scenting Robson's arousal since they were sitting at the table, but he didn't feel any pressure to do anything about it. Robson coasted his hands down Marcus's chest, bringing them to rest at the top of his pants, fingers working to undo his belt then his button and zipper.

Marcus hummed in contentment and closed his eyes as Robson slowly knelt behind him and stripped his pants and briefs down his legs. He stepped out carefully, then laughed softly when Robson lifted each foot and peeled off his socks as well.

Standing once more, Robson wrapped his arms around Marcus again and hugged him firmly. No words were needed; Marcus was simply basking in Robson's warmth and soothing scent. He couldn't stop a small, sad noise from escaping him when Robson stepped back.

"Let your wolf out," Robson said with a chuckle.

Marcus threw a look over his shoulder—not a pout, no. He was a pack Enforcer; he'd never do something like that—and caught his breath at the sight of Robson pulling his T-shirt off over his head, muscles rippling with the smooth motion.

At Robson's throat clearing and pointed look, he blushed and shifted, sinking into his wolf and letting himself embrace that part of him. It only took a moment, but by the time he turned around, Robson was pushing his jeans past his knees.

Winking, Robson straightened and stepped out of the bundle on the ground, left standing in a pair of black boxer briefs. "You don't mind if we get under the covers, do you? You won't get too warm?"

Marcus cocked his head as he thought about it, then shook it with a bark.

"Oh, okay," Robson said, laughing and stepping over to the head of the bed. When he bent over to pull the comforter and sheet back, Marcus couldn't stop himself from darting forward and bumping his head into his underwear-clad ass, sending Robson tumbling onto the bed. Chuckling, Robson stood back up and swatted at him. "None of that, cariño. We aren't playing right now; we're resting."

Huffing, Marcus sat and waited for him to finish with the bedding.

Robson laughed again. "I feel like you should be scarier than you are to me. But you just seem like a big puppy."

Marcus bared his teeth and growled, indignant, but that only made Robson laugh harder.

"Get in," Robson said, gesturing at the turned-down bed.

Snapping his teeth at his mate, Marcus leapt onto the bed and moved to the other side. Once Robson climbed in and started pulling the covers back up, Marcus turned and settled down next to him, resting his muzzle on Robson's toned stomach, his instincts driving him to protect his mate's most vulnerable spot while they slept.

Robson settled the sheet and comforter over them, then lifted them to look at Marcus with raised eyebrows. "You going to be okay down there?"

He chuffed and shut his eyes.

Thick fingers speared into the fur on his neck and

scratched lightly. "Okay, cariño. Let me know if you need anything else."

Even though he was tired, Robson lay in bed with a cuddly wolf for nearly an hour just staring at the ceiling and thinking about how much his life had changed in a matter of weeks. He wanted to laugh when he thought about how wrong he had been about Marcus and his friends and the insane theories he'd come up with about them.

Well, he hadn't been *completely* wrong. Technically, he'd been right that they hadn't notified the proper authorities about the murder of the witch... Agnes, he was pretty sure Marcus had said her name was. And while part of him still wanted to urge them to follow the law, it was a small part that was shrinking every day. The more he saw of the pack and learned about their laws and magic, the more he knew the human criminal justice system wouldn't be able to deal with murdered witches sent as messages to alpha wolf shifters.

Seriously, his life was so weird now.

Marcus huffed and rearranged himself, digging his chin into Robson's stomach in the process, but didn't wake up. Robson peeked at him under the blankets but couldn't make out much with the sun having set outside and no lights on in the room.

His poor, sweet Marcus. Robson didn't know what a "villainous call" was, but whatever had happened today combined with his little bit of a meltdown in the kitchen had completely drained him.

Robson wondered if he'd always be on the outside

looking in with the pack, only useful in comforting Marcus after the fact.

Sighing, he reached down and carded his fingers through the thick but soft fur on Marcus's head and neck, smiling when he wiggled closer at the gentle touches. He supposed there were worse things in life.

He was just beginning to wonder if he should get up and find something to do since sleep was eluding him when he heard a loud vibration that had him sitting partially upright. He stared at where he'd left his pants halfway across the room, phone still tucked in the pocket. He thought about letting it go, but between work and his family, he was paranoid he'd miss something important.

As gently as he could, he eased out from underneath Marcus and slipped from the bed. By the time he'd pulled his phone out, the vibrations had stopped, but he realized quickly it hadn't been his phone ringing. He had a couple of missed texts from his brother Rafael but no missed calls.

When he dug out Marcus's, he saw there was a missed call and voicemail from Bennett Young. Glancing at the bed where his mate was nothing more than a lump under the covers, he decided not to bother him.

He stepped out of the bedroom and jogged down the steps, heading for the kitchen to grab a drink. He called B back on his own phone, not surprised when he answered right away.

"Robson? Is everything okay? I was trying to reach Marcus."

"He's sleeping. When I saw you left a message, I thought I should call and make sure you didn't need him for some kind of emergency," he said, making sure to keep his voice low so it hopefully wouldn't disturb Marcus.

"No, nothing like that," Bennett quickly said. "I was just… checking in, I guess. Making sure he was okay after today."

Robson grunted as he filled a glass with water from the tap and took a drink. "Because of the phone call he got or because of that d-bag I taught a lesson to?"

B's deep chuckle practically vibrated the phone in Robson's hand. "Both, I suppose. Though Marcus seemed more than okay with how you handled that confrontation."

Robson grinned. "Yeah, he did."

Laughing again, Robson could just see the big guy shaking his head in exasperation. "Anyway. Did Marcus talk to you about the call he got from Councilman Kincaid?"

Kincaid? As in Rick Kincaid? "Not yet. We talked about some other things, then he needed some furry time, so we got in bed and he fell asleep."

There was silence for a long moment from the other end of the line, and then Bennett cleared his throat. "Furry time?"

"Yeah." He realized that could mean something *totally* different and started laughing, covering his mouth to try and muffle it. "As in his wolf form, dude."

"Just checking," B said, voice dry, making Robson laugh harder. "Well, I'm glad he's doing okay."

"Yeah, I got him," Robson said absently, suddenly remembering he'd wanted to talk to Bennett. "Hey, can I ask you something?"

"Of course." No hesitation, no joke. It was subtle, but in that moment, Robson could completely understand why Bennett was second-in-command of the pack. Robson wasn't even technically a member and the man was already there for him, no questions asked.

"The way shifters react to their mates... is it like extra intense?" It wasn't exactly what he wanted to ask, but he also didn't want to embarrass Marcus if he found out about the conversation.

"What do you mean?"

"Well..." Sighing, he set his glass down and rubbed at his

face. So much for subtlety. "Okay, so when Marcus and I are… *together*, it seems like he's almost overwhelmed sometimes. Is that because of his inexperience or because I'm his mate?"

Bennett didn't say anything for a minute, then asked, "Does it matter?"

He stilled, then lowered his hand, squinting at the counter in front of him. "I mean… I guess not. I just… I feel things for him I've never felt before, right? But it seems even more intense for him. And don't get me wrong, I like it. I love how he reacts to me, but sometimes I wonder… is it *me*, or is it his instincts reacting to me being his mate."

B chuckled softly. "Those are the same thing. *You* are what his instincts are reacting to."

"But would he feel the same way if some random goddess or whatever hadn't decided we'd be a good fit?" He was getting almost frustrated, and he wasn't sure why. He knew how he'd ended up with Marcus wasn't as important as the fact that he did and they were destined for each other.

"Would you have given him a second glance if the universe hadn't kept throwing you together?"

He wanted to say yes, but Marcus wasn't his usual type, so would he really have? The idea of maybe missing out on something as beautiful as their mating had his stomach dropping and his feet moving for the stairs. "I don't know," he finally whispered hoarsely.

B made a sort of agreeing noise but didn't say anything else as Robson climbed the stairs, intent on putting eyes on his mate for some reason.

As he reached the doorway and saw that Marcus had shifted back to human and was snuggling with a pillow with a frown on his face, Bennett said, "I will say the intensity of feelings I have for Kieran drastically outweighs anything I've ever felt before. To me, it doesn't matter that some higher power chose him for me. All I know is that I'm damned grateful every day that they did."

CHAPTER TWENTY-TWO

M arcus hadn't actually thought he'd fall asleep, but the warmth and darkness under the blankets combined with his mate's comforting scent had lulled him into unconsciousness rather quickly. By the time he woke up, he'd shifted back into his human form and twisted around so his head was up by Robson's, sharing his pillow. They were pressed so close together, Robson's front to his back, that Marcus could feel a trickle of sweat rolling across the small of his back from all the heat they were generating.

Grumbling but not opening his eyes, he shoved at the covers to get some cool air flowing over them. Robson murmured something and tightened his arms around Marcus's chest, but Marcus didn't think he was awake yet. Which wasn't too surprising considering how little sleep he'd gotten that morning.

Marcus knew he should feel bad for disrupting his mate's sleep, but he couldn't help but smile and wiggle in happiness at the memory. His movement seemed to help wake up a certain part of Robson's body, his erection nestling between Marcus's cheeks.

Holding his breath, he arched just a little, pressing his ass more firmly against his mate, and bit his lower lip when Robson thrust against him in return, his hand sliding down Marcus's body to settle on his hip.

He listened more closely, but it sounded like Robson was breathing deeply and evenly enough to still be asleep.

He was conflicted. On the one hand, he knew his mate needed his sleep. Peering over, he caught sight of the alarm clock and was surprised to find it was only just after ten, so he'd only been asleep a few hours. Sighing, he slowly turned over in Robson's arms and stared at his sleeping mate in the dark of the room.

On the other hand, his wolf was still pretty close to the surface and he... wanted. All day, Marcus had been doing his best to focus on his work, but he'd suddenly see Robson's hand in his mind and remember his words. He'd never considered the fact that they could use an alternative to the typical knot so Robson could claim his body like Marcus could his.

And he definitely hadn't been able to stop thinking about the *toys* Robson had mentioned. If there were knotting ones, were there others? Would Robson be open to... playing with other toys?

Just thinking about it had Marcus's cock leaking in excitement. A tiny voice in his head whispered that he should be embarrassed about thinking about such things, but he silenced it. Robson was his mate; anything they did together would be beautiful because it was between *them.*

Oh so slowly, he placed his hands on Robson's body and guided him onto his back, grinning when Robson went easily without waking. One of his thick, muscular thighs was cocked out to the side, and Marcus took the space it created between Robson's legs as an invitation, climbing over Robson's body and settling against him.

He hadn't gotten much of a chance to explore his mate's body that morning, so he took his chance then, starting at the hollow of Robson's throat and working his way down, kissing and licking as he went. He paid special attention to his mate's nipples, smirking at the groans Robson let out when he nipped lightly at them.

By the time he was licking the ridges of Robson's abs, he was certain his mate was awake even though his breathing had barely changed and his eyes were still closed. He wasn't sure why Robson was pretending to stay asleep, but he'd play along for a while longer. Moving lower, he steered clear of Robson's cock and detoured to one of his hips, kissing and then sucking a hickey into the thin skin over the bone.

When Robson's thighs twitched, Marcus glanced up and saw that Robson had a fist in his mouth to stop himself from making any sounds. "That's cheating," he whispered right against the spot where Robson's groin met his thigh, the scent of his mate so thick there that it was making him light-headed.

"Didn't want to disturb your fun," Robson said, lowering his hand and raising his head a little.

Marcus smiled as he darted his tongue out to lick one of Robson's testicles, pride filling him at the sharp breath Robson sucked in. "It's much more fun now because I can actually touch the parts of you I really wanted to."

Chuckling, Robson folded an arm behind his head and raised a brow. "Oh, what parts are those?"

He could feel a blush growing on his face but held his mate's gaze. "I want to suck you. Is that okay?"

Robson's face softened and his other hand came up to cup Marcus's cheek. "Of course. We're mates—that pretty much gives you carte blanche to my dick, I think."

Marcus knew he meant it as a joke, but he shook his head anyway. He'd had the lesson of consent drilled into him since he was old enough to know what arousal smelled like. "Consent can't be given with scent or assumptions; it has to be verbalized."

The grin Robson gave him was so wide it resplit his puffy lip, a drop of blood welling up. The reminder of how well his mate had defended him caused a shiver to rush down Marcus's spine.

"This is me verbally consenting to you touching my dick whenever you want."

Marcus crawled up his body and licked at the blood, humming at the sharp coppery taste. "What about when you're sleeping?" he murmured against Robson's lips.

"As long as you wake me before the finale, I'm all good with you getting the party started while I'm still asleep, cariño."

Shuddering at the idea of spending the rest of his life waking Robson with soft kisses and blow jobs, he sealed their mouths together, licking inside with a moan. When he pulled away, Robson was kneading one of his ass cheeks.

"My kinky puppy," Robson panted, pressing his wet lips against Marcus's throat under his beard.

Groaning, he tipped his head farther back even as he swatted at Robson's chest. "'M not a puppy."

"Tell that to your cuddly wolf," Robson said, nipping at Marcus's throat hard enough to make him keen. "Good spot, huh?"

"I want... I want to suck you, but then will you claim me?" He could barely focus as Robson continued to assault his neck and jaw.

"Mmm, whatever you want. Just tell me how to do it."

Scrambling, he fumbled to grab one of Robson's large hands and bring it up between them. Robson raised a brow, then groaned when Marcus kissed his palm before sucking one of his long fingers into his mouth.

"Fuck, cariño."

"Will you… use your hand? Like you said this morning? I want to feel how you'll… knot me with it." He pressed kisses all over Robson's hand but kept an eye on him through his lashes, nervous when it seemed like Robson was frozen, though the scent of his arousal was still thick in the air. Then Robson used the hand Marcus was kissing to grip the back of his neck and bring their faces close together.

"Are you sure? I'm not saying I don't want to," he rushed to add when Marcus started to answer. "But that'll be intense for your first time, mi amor. We don't have to jump right to fisting."

Fisting. Marcus shuddered at the word on his mate's tongue. He still preferred to think of it as Robson knotting him in his own way, but the naughty word sent electricity shooting through his whole body.

Swallowing, he nodded slowly. "I know. I just… I have these herbs from Damien, so we can bite each other if you want, but it feels important to me and my wolf to give my whole body to you this way. To trust you and… submit to you. To give myself completely to you and our mating."

Eyes narrowing, Robson studied his face closely, then nodded. "Okay. We're going to have a conversation about what the hell you mean by 'herbs,' but it can wait."

"Later," Marcus murmured, pressing a sweet, wet kiss to Robson's mouth. Pulling away, he scooted back down, planting a kiss here and there on Robson's body but mostly focused on getting back to his destination.

Robson hummed and spread his legs wider. "Yeah, later. After you suck my cock and I use my hand to knot your ass, right, cariño?"

Marcus shuddered but didn't bother responding verbally. Instead, he dove right in, sucking first one then the other ball into his mouth, running his tongue over them and gripping his mate's hairy thighs tightly.

He spent several long minutes sucking and licking until his spit was running down into the crack of Robson's ass and his hips were twitching sporadically, muscles tense under Marcus's hands.

"Unless you want this to end a lot quicker than either of us planned, you better move things along," Robson said, voice tight and growly.

Grinning up at his flushed mate, he scooted up just a little so he could more easily reach the head of his cock, grabbing the wide base with one hand and using his other to prop himself up. Robson's foreskin was pulled nearly all the way back, revealing the wet, red tip to Marcus's watering mouth.

"Cariño," Robson rasped when Marcus got transfixed, trying to figure out what he wanted to do first.

He smiled, shooting his mate an apologetic look, then leaned down, took the whole head into his mouth, and sucked. The tangy taste of his mate's precome exploded on his tongue, and he moaned, knowing immediately he'd never be able to get enough of the addictive flavor.

When he started using his fist to stroke up and down on the shaft and his tongue to play with the edge of Robson's foreskin, his mate shouted out a couple words in Spanish that Marcus was pretty sure his mom would wash his mouth out with soap for if she ever heard.

He was just starting to find his rhythm, bobbing his head up and down as he took in a little more and giving the base of Robson's dick a squeeze on his downstrokes, when his mate released an impressive growl and grabbed his biceps, pulling him up his body until they were face-to-face.

"I think I was getting the hang of—mnph!" He melted against Robson's body as his mate devoured his mouth, his hold on Marcus possessive and a little frantic.

"On your back, cariño," he murmured when they parted, both breathing heavily. "And please tell me you actually have lube in one of these nightstands."

Nodding, he pointed at the one he'd stashed the bottles he'd bought the other day in as he slipped off his mate and rolled onto his back, shivering more at the wave of excitement coursing through him than the loss of contact.

Robson dug around in the drawer for a moment, then settled between Marcus's thighs holding both bottles, face lined with confusion. "You have two types of lube but no condoms?"

Face heating, he gave a half shrug. "I wasn't sure which kind would be better and... um, we don't need condoms. Parahuman, remember?"

"Parahuman. Right. Sure." Robson nodded, eyes on the bottles as he ran his tongue over his bottom lip. Finally, he set aside one and opened the other, coating his fingers. "We'll start with the water-based, then use the silicone for the fisting."

Sucking in a breath, Marcus nodded, trusting that Robson knew what he was talking about. Leaning over him, Robson planted one more kiss on Marcus's mouth, then knelt between his legs and cupped the back of one of Marcus's thighs, raising his leg up and to the side.

"Yeah, hold it right there," Robson murmured when Marcus grabbed the back of his knee and pulled up his other leg too.

Being so exposed to his mate's eyes tightened his stomach but also filled him with a sense of pride as Robson groaned and squeezed one of his butt cheeks. A shiver wracked his body as Robson circled his hole with wet fingers.

"Now, if I remember correctly from the class yesterday," Robson murmured as he gently eased one of his fingers inside Marcus's body. Throwing his head back and moaning, he had to focus to hear what Robson was saying. "The knot forms when you come, right?"

Biting his lip, Marcus nodded, his breathing already picking up speed as Robson pumped his finger in and out.

"So what I'm going to do," Robson said, sounding like they were having a reasonable conversation around the kitchen table and not like he was easing a second finger inside Marcus's ass, "is get you nice and stretched out for my cock, then after I finish inside you, I'll work my... *knot* in. Sound good, cariño?"

Dear goddess, did it ever. Marcus could barely breathe as jolts of pleasure shot through him every time Robson twisted or spread his fingers. "Y-Yes. Sounds good."

Humming, Robson leaned forward and licked up Marcus's painfully hard erection. "But you can't come until my fist is inside you."

"Robson..." he whined, thrashing his head back and forth as his mate stroked his prostate. "I can't... I don't know if I can wait..."

The chuckle Robson let out was pure sex as he sat up and grabbed the lubricant again, rewetting his fingers and easing three inside. The burn was more intense at first, but Marcus held Robson's heated gaze and breathed through it. Before too long, he was moaning uncontrollably as Robson plunged his fingers in and out of him, his other hand planted on Marcus's chest to hold him steady.

"Fuck. You're so beautiful, cariño," Robson said as he eased out and quickly coated his thick cock in lube, the sight of his foreskin moving with each stroke of Robson's hand mesmerizing Marcus.

Panting and more aroused than he'd ever been before, he held his shaking legs up nearly to his chest as Robson pressed slowly inside him. The stretch and burn made him gasp, but the sense of fullness and *rightness* was what made his heart trip in his chest as Robson leaned over him, planting his fists in the mattress next to Marcus's shoulders, and worked his cock back and forth until he finally was all the way in.

Robson's lips were suddenly on his as he kissed Marcus almost frantically, one of his hands moving to sink into Marcus's hair and Robson's hips starting to move. He was being so careful it brought tears to Marcus's eyes, but he blinked them away, not wanting his mate to worry if he saw.

Wrapping his legs around Robson's waist and his arms around his torso, Marcus held on as tight as he dared. Robson ripped his mouth away to catch his breath, peering down at Marcus with a wide smile on his parted lips.

"Not gonna last," he whispered as his hips started moving faster and losing rhythm.

Marcus shook his head, sliding one hand down to dig into Robson's firm ass. "Don't care."

"That's good." Robson chuckled and started laying sweet, lingering kisses down the side of Marcus's neck, pausing when he met the junction where his neck met his shoulder.

Marcus groaned loudly when Robson lightly bit down and sucked at the skin between his teeth. The pseudo-bite stirred Marcus's wolf. Whining, he exposed his throat more fully to his mate, chin tipped up and to the side.

Robson released his mouthful and carefully moved to the hollow of Marcus's throat. Just as his tongue started to slide up the thin skin, Robson tightened his grip on Marcus's hair and drove his hips forward hard.

The feeling of possessiveness—of *claiming*—filled Marcus so fully and quickly, he cried out, hips jerking upward as he worked hard to hold back his climax even as Robson's cock released his seed deep inside Marcus's body.

Marking him as clearly as any bonding bite would.

Marcus was so close to the edge that the moist breaths Robson was panting against his neck as he recovered were driving him crazy. He arched his back and moaned as Robson gave another weak thrust.

"Easy, cariño," he murmured into his skin.

"Need you" was all he could gasp out as his fingers dug into Robson's skin, his body feeling like all the nerve cells were lighting up at once.

"You have me." Robson pressed a kiss to Marcus's throat, then lifted his head and took Marcus's mouth in a claiming nearly as fierce as their mating.

Moaning around Robson's thrusting tongue, he wiggled on his softening cock and pressed his own erection up against Robson's firm abs, seeking some sort of relief from the ache growing in his testicles. When Marcus became more focused on humping into Robson's body than kissing him, Robson pulled away with a chuckle, peeling his sweaty torso off Marcus's.

"You still want my knot, cariño?" Robson growled.

"Yes!" His fingers twisted in his hair, hips rising off the mattress as his back arched. The need inside him was growing to a size his body couldn't contain, and he knew he'd soon explode with it. "Hurry, Robson."

"Shhh. Flip over for me."

Based on the noise Robson made when Marcus flung himself over onto his stomach, he might have accidentally kicked his mate. His whole body felt uncoordinated and shaky in a way that nearly frightened him.

But Robson was there, and he knew he was safe with him.

"Raise your hips a second. Good, perfect." Robson slipped a couple of pillows under him, raising his backside for easy access. Marcus whimpered just at the thought, pressing his face into the sheets that smelled like both of their arousals. "Try and relax a little."

Marcus barked out a laugh, the noise so sudden and loud

it stilled Robson for a moment. Then he chuckled as well and kneaded Marcus's cheeks.

"I know. But it'll be easier for you if you're aroused but relaxed."

A thought slipped into the back of Marcus's head, dampening his enjoyment of the moment. "Have you... done this before?"

"No," Robson said easily as his hands left Marcus, but the sound of the lube opening immediately followed. "But I've done some research before and double-checked a couple things after how you reacted this morning. Figured it'd come up sooner rather than later."

Marcus pulled another pillow over and buried his grinning face into it.

"Ready?" Robson asked, the fingers from his dry hand trailing down Marcus's back and up onto his ass. When Marcus nodded and took a deep breath, trying to relax into the bed, Robson gripped one of his cheeks and spread him, pushing multiple fingers inside him right away.

Robson was more careful not to tease his prostate very much, but it didn't matter. The sound and smell and feel of Robson slowly working him more and more open was enough to drive Marcus's arousal higher still.

His hips kept twitching, rubbing his cock in the now damp pillows beneath him, but Robson eventually gripped his hip with his free hand to slow the movements. Closing his eyes, he concentrated on breathing and staying relaxed. He found a sort of calm place in his head where he could experience how amazing Robson was making him feel without having that *right on the edge of coming* sensation crawling under his skin. Every once in a while, Robson would twist his fingers or stretch them in such a way it'd sent a jolt up Marcus's spine, lighting up stars behind his closed lids.

Somehow, he was still surprised when Robson murmured, "Keep breathing, cariño," and suddenly his knuckles were *right there*.

He realized he had stopped breathing when Robson growled out his name and stopped pressing forward. Sucking in a breath, he tried to bear down as best he could.

For a moment, it felt like he wouldn't be able to take it, that his body simply wouldn't expand far enough, and a sob caught in the back of his throat. He wanted this so much, wanted to feel like his body had been so thoroughly claimed by his mate that he could never question their mating ever again.

And then Robson's knuckles pushed past his rim, and the rest of his hand slid in so much easier.

Marcus couldn't catch his breath. It felt amazing and terrifying at the same time, and he was worried he'd never get to feel this way again.

"You okay, cariño?" Robson's voice was soft and husky, full of... something. He pressed a soft kiss to one of Marcus's ass cheeks, then nipped playfully when Marcus didn't respond right away.

Jolting at the sting, he released a hoarse cry, tears slipping from behind his squeezed-shut eyes. It wasn't from pain; everything just felt so big, so intimate. "*Yes.* It feels... It's so..."

"It's good, huh? How's it feel when I move it?" Robson turned his hand slowly, and Marcus bit back a scream, that one small movement somehow lighting up his whole body. "Oh yeah, that's good too."

"Robson," Marcus panted out, fingers scrambling for purchase on the sheets. "Please."

"Right here. I've got you."

And then Robson slowly made a fist inside Marcus, and that was it, that was all his body could handle. Crying out, he came all over the pillow beneath him, his body contracting so hard on Robson's hand that it became a little painful.

He must have blacked out after he orgasmed but only for a few moments. When he came to, Robson was whispering to him how gorgeous he was and how proud Robson was that Marcus could take his whole fist. As Robson continued lavishing praise on him, he slowly and carefully started pulling back out.

The sensations were overwhelming for Marcus's spun-out body, riding the edge of pain by the time Robson was done. He zoned out afterward, marveling at how he felt like he was gaping open and wondering how often they could do that.

The water ran in the bathroom for a little while, and then Robson came back and gently cleaned Marcus's backside before easing him over and wiping down his front. Boneless and nearly asleep, Marcus barely heard Robson stripping the pillowcases off the ones Marcus had covered in semen, but he hummed happily when he was pulled into a warm, firm chest.

"Feel okay?" Robson whispered, running a hand up and down Marcus's back.

"Amazing. Can we do that every day?"

Robson chuckled softly. "Kind of a lot of work for every day, but I could be convinced to pencil in fisting once or twice a week."

When Marcus giggled, he realized he was more out of it than he'd thought. He sort of felt like someone had popped a bottle of champagne inside his belly and it was bubbling up into his chest. Nuzzling into the little bit of hair on Robson's chest, Marcus let sleep take him, feeling like nothing bad could ever happen as long as he was with his mate.

CHAPTER TWENTY-THREE

"This was a terrible idea," Marcus muttered out of the corner of his mouth, thumb tapping on his thigh but face impassive as ever.

Robson caught his brother Teo trying to suppress a smile on the other side of Marcus as he sipped from a plastic cup. Narrowing his eyes, Robson said, "That better not be beer. You aren't—"

The rest of the table erupted in laughter, but Robson ignored them and kept his eyes on his brother, who just rolled his own and took another sip.

Marcus looked absently between them, his gaze only briefly leaving the front of the room where Robson's mom, tias, and baby sisters were finishing setting up. Robson's mouth had been watering for days with the amazing smells permeating the farmhouse. He couldn't wait to get up there and fill a plate full of food. He knew there were roasters of pasteles, platters of crunchy tostones served with his Tia Priscilla's famous garlic sauce, and two huge bowls full of arroz con gandules.

Marcus inhaled toward Teo before returning his focus to the women currently terrifying him. "It's Coke."

Teo threw him a weird look, then looked at Robson. "Sometimes I forget under all that big brother bossiness is an honest-to-god cop."

Grunting, Robson took a sip of his beer but didn't answer. His hours had been slowly increasing now that the sheriff had apparently gotten the go-ahead from Kincaid. Which… was good. Really. It was just that he was bored and the other deputies were annoying and he wanted to spend more time with Marcus, not less.

Sliding a hand over Marcus's fidgeting one, he gave his mate a reassuring smile. "She's going to love you, cariño."

Marcus's Adam's apple bob as he swallowed, his green gaze shooting over to where Robson's mom was laughing at something one of her sisters said. Robson wasn't sure how Nico had pulled off getting his mom's sisters there for the shower on such short notice, but he owed the man. None of them had known until Nico was knocking on the farmhouse door, loaded down with suitcases. Tia Mya had practically shoved the poor guy out of the way to get in the door and wrap Robson's mom in a hug.

There had been a lot of tears and a lot of smiles. Reesa had been beside herself with the amount of attention she and the baby were getting. All of it filled Robson with such a sense of peace and gratitude it was almost more than he could handle.

And then there was his anxiety-ridden mate.

Smirking, Robson squeezed Marcus's hand and threaded their fingers together. Leaning closer, he whispered in his mate's ear, "Wanna slip away for a blow job? I bet that would relax you."

There were choking noises from at least two people at the table, but Robson couldn't take his eyes off the delightful pink filling Marcus's cheeks as he turned to stare at him in horror. "Robson, they can hear you."

Robson tore his eyes away to give a charming smile to the rest of the table. "I know."

Everyone but Teo had super hearing at their table, and the one just behind Marcus had another three or four people, but Robson was getting used to being around folks with enhanced abilities. In fact, he was finding it ridiculously charming how adorably frustrated Marcus got when he was turned on by Robson's suggestions and embarrassed that others could hear them. It was a fun game Robson had started playing to get his mate to actually leave his office at the end of the day or to take a real lunch break.

Nothing got Marcus to leap to his feet faster than when he needed to sprint around his desk to slap a hand over Robson's mouth.

Nico, Vanessa, and Fiona were grinning at him and Marcus, Colt looked amused but wasn't staring because he was a nice guy like that, and Patrick was laughing, but his head was down to try and hide it. Robson had gotten to know the other Enforcers pretty well in the last week and a half. He'd made a point to visit Marcus at least once every day at the manor—either to eat lunch together or to drag him away at night, depending on his own work schedule—and had spent quite a bit of time with the others as well.

He could see why Nico was Marcus's best friend—the man was hilarious and always willing to lend a helping hand. But Robson was secretly on a mission to befriend the two female Enforcers. There was just something about them that screamed how deadly they really were, and Robson found he liked that. He rarely missed his time in the military, but he sometimes missed the men and women he'd served with, and Fi and V reminded him of his fellow infantry soldiers: tough with a dash of crazy.

"Offer stands, cariño. You let me know if you change your mind." He winked, pressing a quick kiss to the corner of Marcus's stern mouth.

Marcus was saved from answering by Robson's mom stepping up onto the raised platform Nico had brought in and set up at one end of the large conference room they were using in the rec center for the party. There was a throne-like chair on top with a small table next to it. The tables of food were along the wall to the right of the platform, and a table overflowing with gifts was on the left.

"Thank you, everyone, for joining us today," his mom said, the room quieting without her having to even raise her voice. "Please fill your plates. Reesa will begin opening gifts once she eats and feeds little Maria."

There were only about a half dozen tables set up for people to sit at, and it was mostly Robson's family, the few friends Reesa still had from school, or packmates filling them, but there were a few people he didn't know from Teresa's and Patrick's jobs. Everyone began to file up to the tables loaded down with food, conversation and laughter filling the air. Marcus stuck close behind Robson, like that would make him blend in even though he was a couple of inches taller with red hair. Of course, he balked when Robson detoured to the table closest to the front to kiss his mom and tias on their cheeks and thank them for the meal once they had plates full of food. Marcus offered a weak smile, though, and thanked them as well.

Robson's mom knew exactly who Marcus was, having heard all about him over the last couple of weeks, but his Tia Priscilla asked who he was in Spanish.

"That's my Robito's new boyfriend, Marcus Rivera," his mom said, smiling proudly at her sisters, who all tittered like that was the best news they'd heard the whole trip.

Marcus's eyes were a little wide, and he looked a little like a deer caught in the headlights—which was *hilarious* to Robson—but he smiled more naturally and said, "It's a pleasure to meet you all."

Deciding that was enough for now—but knowing his mom would track them down later for a longer discussion—Robson snagged Marcus's hand and entwined their fingers, giving him an encouraging tug back toward their table.

"Buenos días," Marcus blurted as he stumbled away after Robson.

"Cariño… did you mean to just tell them good morning?" Robson asked as they threaded through the tables and tried not to laugh when Marcus groaned behind him.

"No! I *know* adiós is goodbye, I promise. I just…" He sighed as they reached their table and set his plate down. "I don't know. Now they probably think I'm an idiot."

Fiona's head jerked up from where she was inhaling tostones off her plate. "Who thinks you're an idiot?"

Robson recognized the look in her eyes as she scanned the room for a threat. "Easy, Fi. No one." He pulled out Marcus's chair and waited for him to sit before taking his own seat. "They don't think that. I'm sure they thought it was adorable just like me."

Groaning again, Marcus pinched the bridge of his nose just as the others rejoined their table—except for Patrick, who'd disappeared with Reesa to help with Maria.

Nico raised his brows as he took in Marcus. "What happened?"

"I made a fool of myself in front of Robson's mom and aunts," Marcus spit out before Robson could say anything.

Teo laughed as he dug into his food. "I'm sure it's not that bad."

"I told them good morning in Spanish instead of goodbye," Marcus snapped.

Choking on his bite of food, Teo had to be slapped on the

back by Colt—though based on his grimace, it was a little hard, but at least he was able to breathe normally again. "I'm sure it wasn't… They probably didn't even notice."

Robson had to bite his lip to stop from laughing at how testy Marcus was getting, but at least that meant his mate was feeling comfortable enough to show his annoyance with Robson's brother. They continued to squabble back and forth, with Teo giving more and more ridiculous suggestions of things Marcus could start saying instead of goodbye. Robson had finished his plate of food and was contemplating seconds by the time they were both snorting with laughter, something Robson had never heard from his mate. Based on the raised brows of the other Enforcers, it was new to them too.

About an hour later, Reesa was halfway through opening her gifts—there were definitely more gifts than people in attendance, and Robson kept sending fake annoyed glances at his mate when she was handed another "with no tag"—and Robson was half listening to Teo and Nico talking about dairy cows versus beef, laws about raw milk and processing in Michigan, and estimated costs for improving operations at the Medina's farm.

Annalisse and Valentina were darting around the platform handing Reesa gifts, keeping track of who gave what for thank-you cards, and collecting the discarded wrapping paper. Robson smiled as he noticed Val carefully collecting the ribbons and wrapping them into a crown for Reesa to wear the rest of the day.

Fiona, Vanessa, and Colt had moved closer to the front so they could see what Teresa and Patrick had gotten, and he'd lost track of who was holding his niece, who was being passed around like a football. Robson had one arm around Marcus and was just contemplating getting a piece of cake when Marcus turned to him with fear-filled eyes.

His adrenaline spiked for a moment until he heard his mom next to him say, "May I sit with you?"

Smiling up at her, he slid his hand up to the back of Marcus's neck and gave him an encouraging squeeze. "Of course, mamá."

Settling, she peered around Robson and gave Marcus a sweet smile. "So, Marcus, you're the reason I haven't seen very much of my eldest son the last couple of weeks?"

Robson knew his mom was just teasing, but the horrified look on Marcus's face had him swooping in to clarify. "She's joking, cariño. Take a breath."

"Sure, yes, I knew that," Marcus rambled, his hand coming down onto Robson's thigh, nails digging in almost painfully.

"Es hasta más dulce que tú," his mom said, smiling at Marcus before giving Robson a proud look.

Hiding his grimace of pain, he laid his hand over Marcus's, hoping it would get him to loosen his hold, and turned to his mom. "Definitely sweeter, but Marcus had a... different kind of childhood, so some social things are hard for him."

Marcus's grip tightened further, but Robson kept his focus on his mom. She gave him a questioning look, obviously picking up that by *different* he'd meant *terrible*. When he nodded in confirmation, she stood, tutting about sweet boys needing coddling, and moved around the table so she could sit next to Marcus. Of course, she had to move Teo to do it, but he just rolled his eyes good-naturedly as he moved to Nico's other side so they could keep talking about... the Kincaids building a dairy processing plant?

What the hell had he missed?

He tried to stay focused on his mate and mom in case Marcus needed rescuing, but his curiosity was piqued, and he kept getting distracted. After about fifteen minutes—by which time his mom had Marcus confiding that he'd never had a great relationship with his family and really wanted things to go well with the Medinas—Robson completely tuned into the other conversation at the table but kept his hand on Marcus's neck so he'd know he was still there if he needed him.

"You two are just talking hypothetically, right?" he butted in after a moment of listening to Nico rattling off different spots the plant could go.

"Maybe or maybe not," Nico said, pulling out his phone and typing something. "There are quite a few people who are new to the area and looking for work. A processing plant could provide good jobs, and it would be good for the local economy."

Robson stared. "How would you convince a company to come to town to build a plant here?"

Teo jumped in. "He wouldn't! You know that super-rich guy who moved to town a few years ago—Kincaid? His foundation or whatever built this place?"

Eyes straying to where Rick was grinning at them from the next table over, Robson cleared his throat. "Yeah?"

"Well, Nico works for him and said he thinks the guy would be interested in investing in a plant." Teo was practically vibrating he was so excited.

"I thought you wanted to get out of dairy?" He didn't want Teo to agree to something because Nico was pressuring him or because he'd gotten caught up in the moment.

When Teo glared at him and he heard his mom chuckle, he realized he'd garnered the attention of her and Marcus too.

"I do–did–I don't know, maybe. It's not that I don't like the dairy cows," Teo quickly added to Nico. "They're just so much work and our parlor is kind of falling apart."

Nico nodded, making more notes on his phone. "That's

fine. I'm sure Rick would be willing to pay for some upgrades so we can even expand your herd."

Teo turned to Robson with huge eyes.

"We're not looking for a handout—"

"It wouldn't be one," Rick said, stepping up behind Teo and Nico, giving Robson a hard look. "We'd be business partners. You'd provide the farm and labor, and I'd provide capital for improvements."

Staring up at Rick like he was some sort of genius, Teo said, "Are you... Mr. Kincaid?"

Extending a hand and smiling, Rick said, "Yeah, but you can call me Rick." He turned to Robson's mom. "Mrs. Medina, thank you so much for allowing me and Kai to come, but we have to be headed home."

He extended an envelope to her, smiled, and walked away. Robson spotted Kai up by Reesa and Patrick, getting one last snuggle in with Maria. When his mom gasped, he refocused on her.

"What's wrong?" Marcus asked, tentatively placing his hand on her arm.

"He... he gave me a check," she whispered, tears in her eyes. "And gave me back the one I paid to rent the room."

Eyebrows raised, he leaned over to take the check from her trembling fingers, adding absently, "I told you I'd take care of the fee." When he'd tried to ask Marcus how much it would be, his mate had laughed and said the pack wouldn't be charging them when it was a shower for two of their own members.

Staring at the number on the check, he turned to Marcus. "That's too much."

"It's a gift from Al—Mr. Kincaid. You can't give it back," Marcus said, humor threading through his voice.

"Five grand isn't a gift," Robson whispered harshly. "You wonder why I thought you all were doing shady shit..."

"Robito," his mom muttered, taking back the check and staring at it, "watch your language, por favor."

He tried to hold on to his frown when Marcus downright *giggled* at him getting scolded by his mom. "Yeah, Robito, behave yourself."

Leaning in, he pressed his lips to Marcus's ear. "Careful, cariño. Don't make me tell her how we can't stay at the farmhouse at night because you'd keep the whole house awake."

He ignored Nico's snort of laughter, nuzzling into Marcus's hairline as he gasped in horror. "You wouldn't."

"Try me, cariño."

"I can't believe you kept saying things knowing the others could hear you," Marcus mumbled as Robson kissed down his neck later that night as they lay pressed together in Marcus's bed.

Robson just laughed as he sucked on a particularly sensitive spot until Marcus was arching beneath him, leaking dick smearing precome over his skin. "I can't believe you haven't gotten used to it yet."

Marcus hummed and ran his fingers through Robson's hair, then gave his head a gentle nudge to get him to move farther down his body.

Chuckling, Robson let himself be maneuvered until he was propped up between Marcus's legs, his erection right in front of his face. "Did you want something, cariño?"

"Please, Robson. You said at the shower…"

"That I'd blow you?" Robson smirked, moving his mouth closer and blowing on the tip of his cock until Marcus squirmed. "Pretty sure there was a time limit on that offer."

When he glanced up, he caught the cutest little pout on Marcus's mouth. "What if I wanted to talk?"

Sucking in his lower lip, Marcus nodded and propped himself up onto his elbows. "Of course. What was it—unf!"

Marcus flopped back onto the bed and grunted as Robson swallowed half his cock in one go. It wasn't that he didn't have something to talk about with Marcus—he did—but he couldn't resist a turned-on Marcus with a pouty lip.

Ten minutes later, he was heaving on top of Marcus, straddling his chest and rubbing his come into his mate's skin like he knew he liked. He was pretty sure if he could, Marcus would be purring as he relaxed into the bed. Once his breathing was under control and he was spooned up behind Marcus, he clasped their hands together and brought them to Marcus's chest, kissing the crook of his neck.

"What did you want to talk about?" Marcus whispered, sounding half-asleep already.

Smiling softly, he nosed up into Marcus's thick, soft hair and pressed a kiss to the back of his head.

He thought about saying he didn't think he wanted to be a deputy anymore.

He thought about saying he was worried about how stressed Marcus was getting over the Council and that woman Wendy, who he still hadn't heard from.

He thought about saying he didn't know where he'd fit into the pack if he officially joined, even though he was starting to really become attached to all of the hooligans at the manor.

He thought about saying that he was in love with Marcus and was ready to tell his mom they were going to move into his bedroom until Teo had the farm either expanded to handle more dairy production or switched over to the beef cattle and Robson's paychecks weren't necessary anymore.

He thought about saying he wanted to drink that weird

voodoo tea so they could exchange bonding bites while Marcus knotted him.

But in the end, as he held Marcus as he fell asleep, he decided none of those things were important enough to keep his mate awake when he was clearly exhausted.

He'd talk to him about all of it in the morning. Sunday mornings in bed were made for soul-baring discussions.

Right?

CHAPTER TWENTY-FOUR

Marcus was pissed.

And for the first time in over a decade, he didn't care who knew.

Drumming his fingers on the steering wheel, he sped toward the location Rick had texted out to the Enforcers at 5:00 a.m., Nico in the seat next to him. The only other information in the text were the words *Get here now.*

The flurry of responses from everyone asking what was happening and that they were on their way had gone unanswered. Marcus swore that if this was a weird training thing, he was going to have a few choice words with his alpha.

As they neared the turnoff where they'd have to park and walk the rest of the way into the woods that bordered the southern edge of the territory, Marcus's anger began to drain away, trepidation taking its place. He slowed as he carefully drove down the short dirt road that ended in a makeshift parking lot. The area was sometimes used by pack members who lived in the southern half of the territory for group runs.

There were too many vehicles already there, and one of them was definitely Tashmica's hunk of junk.

"This isn't some new training thing, is it?" he whispered as he parked the SUV and glanced at Nico. His best friend's face was set in a serious expression, a wrinkle between his brows.

"I don't think so." He nodded at a dusty Benz on the end. "Pretty sure that's Damien's and"—he flipped around in his seat when a pair of headlights turned onto the road behind them—"that's Doc's truck. What the fuck?"

They hurried out of the SUV just as Doc parked haphazardly behind them, not bothering to turn off his truck before he grabbed his bag and jumped out, flying past them without a word. Hurrying after him, Marcus carefully scented the air, but the wind was blowing the wrong way. When they caught the sound of yelling, all three of them started running without saying a word to each other.

Breaking into a small clearing, it took Marcus a moment to figure out what he was seeing. There was a stranger standing just inside where Marcus could feel the warding along the border was. They had both hands up, head tilted down. With the oversized hoody and jean vest that they were wearing, hood pulled up over their head, Marcus couldn't get a clear view of them. But the air was heavy with magic, so he knew they were a witch, whoever they were.

But after a quick glance and sniff, he turned his attention to where most of the commotion was coming from, trusting that Tashmica and Damien—who were standing between the stranger and the others, muttering a spell and creating a shimmery barrier—would protect them. About twenty feet from the stranger, Doc skidded to a stop on his knees next to a bruised and bloody—

"Wendy!" He tried to rush forward, but Nico and Colt were suddenly on either side of him, holding him back. He struggled for a moment, running his eyes over her bruised-and dirt-covered form, then sagged against his friends. "Is she going to be okay?"

"Let Doc work," Colt said, his low voice extra rumbly with worry.

Rick was ordering Fiona and Vanessa to check the perimeter of the territory for any other breaches and Bennett to bring Gabriel Morde to him. Bennett pulled out his phone and turned away, speaking to Drake a moment later and telling him to find the hunter and bring him to the location. With so many pups and the alpha-mate in the manor, it had become common for one of the Enforcers to stay behind just in case.

Marcus knew at least part of the reason was because of the hunter with free rein of their territory. Especially since Gabriel had found his way into restricted areas of the manor more than once.

He watched Fi and V strip and shift, V sprinting in her wolf form along the edge of the border, heading left, and Fi's hawk taking to the air and going to the right.

Marcus turned to Colt in confusion. "Why does he want Gabriel here?"

The hunter hadn't been around as much the last week, and Drake and Jamie had been weirdly stiff around each other during meetings and meals. Marcus hadn't asked about it since it wasn't his business, but if the hunter had something to do with Wendy's injuries...

"Witch said he knew him and that was how he knew Wendy was in trouble," Colt said, turning hard eyes on the stranger.

Marcus turned to look just as the witch grabbed the edges of his hood and slowly lowered it, revealing dark brown skin with a curved scar on the left side of the man's jaw and dark, messy curls. White teeth flashed as the man smiled.

"The barrier is unnecessary. I don't mean your pack any harm, Alpha Kincaid," the witch cajoled, not sounding the least bit worried about the number of hostile people glaring at him.

His voice had a distinctive Louisiana accent that Marcus had heard from a few witches before, giving him a clue as to which coven the man came from. If this was the witch who'd spelled Gabriel so he had no scent, it meant he was extremely powerful and adept at blood magic.

Which meant he was probably a La Fleur coven member.

"Since when does the La Fleur coven work with mercenary hunters?" Marcus spat, striding toward Tashmica and Damien but being careful to stay behind them. His fear and anger for Wendy turned to the only outlet available. "Does Beatrice know what you're doing for him?"

The head of the coven was one powerful witch, but she also followed a strict code of ethics. The coven didn't take sides, didn't align with any packs, and was strong enough to stand against the Council if they ever decided they needed to.

Their edict was to protect the human world from the supernatural one.

And they were damn good at it.

The witch's smile took on a hard edge as he took half a step forward. Marcus scented Damien's nerves at the movement, but his outward appearance stayed calm, his hands and voice steady as he and Tashmica repeated the spell holding the shield in place over and over again.

"You don't know anything about my coven, wolf." His dark eyes narrowed on Marcus, taking in his hair and then running the length of his body. "You Rivera?"

Marcus hid his shock as he felt Rick stalk up next to him, his wolf very clearly just beneath the surface as he flashed his eyes and used his deep alpha voice to question the man. "Why?"

The witch rolled his eyes and reached for something at the small of his back. Marcus and Rick both tensed, prepared to pull their witches back if he produced a weapon, but it was a dirty envelope with writing on the front. The man threw it onto the ground and took a step back, hands back in the air.

"She had that for you. Told me to make sure Marcus Rivera—and only Marcus Rivera—got it." He hesitated, then sighed and lowered his arms. "Look, she told me to take the letter and to leave her behind. That's how important it was to her."

Exchanging a glance with Rick, Marcus still hesitated to step forward even though the envelope had settled on his side of the barrier, not the witch's. It wasn't so much that he didn't believe him as much as he was... scared to read what Mikel had written to him in that letter. What was so important it probably resulted in his death? And that Wendy nearly died to bring him.

Whatever the message was, it was going to be a game changer.

"Easy, hot stuff. Don't bruise the goods."

Everyone but Tashmica turned at the voice, watching as Drake marched Gabriel into the clearing, cheeks flushed and scent going crazy. The smirk on Gabriel's face was even more self-satisfied than normal as he winked at Drake over his shoulder, then shook off his hold on his arm and approached the witch.

"He says he knows you," Rick said, voice hard, "and that you told him to find Wendy."

If Marcus hadn't been watching so closely, he would have missed the slight falter in Gabriel's stride. Shrugging, he walked right up to the man and embraced him, slapping his back hard enough that dirt floated into the air. He coughed and stepped back, holding the witch by the shoulders and eyeing him carefully.

"You good? If you'd have given me some notice, I could have met you before you crossed the border." Gabriel sounded almost… concerned?

The witch ducked his head, and Marcus suddenly realized that despite how powerful he was, the man was probably only in his early twenties. "I had to ditch my phone after I found her, just in case." He flicked his eyes to Marcus and Rick and said, "She made it to about three hours from here. I found her starving and dehydrated and covered in claw marks that were healing really slowly for some reason."

Swallowing, his eyes traveled past them to where Marcus could still hear Doc working on assessing and treating her most serious wounds so he could then move her to the clinic without causing more damage. Marcus glanced back and saw that Drake was kneeling next to Doc, offering his assistance, and Colt stood between her and the stranger so Marcus still couldn't get a good look at her. The scent of her pain and blood filled the air so heavily, though, he wasn't sure he wanted to.

Turning back, he saw that the witch's dark eyes were unfocused and haunted as he recalled what he'd seen. "Whatever they sent after her… Let's just say they didn't bother looking for the letter on her. Just attacked and maimed with the intent to kill. She was lucky to get away alive, but on foot, she never would have made it all the way here."

No one spoke for several long minutes, the only sounds coming from Doc, Damien, and Tashmica. Finally, Marcus chanced a glance at Rick and saw he was staring at Gabriel and the witch, arms crossed over his chest.

"How did you even know about her, Morde?" Rick finally spoke, voice edged with anger.

Gabriel sighed and ran a hand through his loose blond hair. "Look, he didn't mean to tell me."

Marcus stiffened as he realized who Gabriel meant, and Rick's sharp growl filling the air meant he'd come to the same conclusion too.

"Meaning what? You tortured the information out of my assistant?"

Releasing his hold on the witch, Gabriel turned to fully face Rick, jaw set and shoulders back. "I'd never hurt him. You know that."

"I don't know jack shit about you, hunter," Rick said, storming forward and right through the barrier.

"Rick—!" Bennett's harsh cry cut off as he stopped himself from rushing forward, instead taking Rick's place next to Marcus and behind Tashmica.

"But I chose to give you the benefit of the fucking doubt, so tell me why I shouldn't kill you both and make your bodies disappear." Rick snarled into Gabriel's face, pointing between him and the witch. "I feel like it would make my night a whole lot fucking *better* if I just ordered my witches and Enforcers to take care of you and went back to cuddling the hell out of my mate."

"Alpha Kincaid—" Gabriel was cut off by the witch putting a hand on his arm.

"Gabriel saved my life two years ago," the man said, raising his chin when Rick turned his snarling face toward him. "And he called in the debt I owed him to have me find that woman for you."

Between the magical barrier, all the people and noise around him, and his own heartbeat thumping erratically in his ears, Marcus couldn't get a clear enough reading on the witch to judge his truthfulness, but judging by the tilt of Rick's head as he studied the man, he could.

"You're the one who spelled him to hide his scent?" Rick asked suddenly.

The witch glanced at Gabriel, then looked back at Rick. "Uh, yes, sir. A spell of my own creation."

Grunting, Rick crossed his arms and nodded at Gabriel but continued to speak to the witch. "Break it."

"What?"

"Break. The. Spell."

There was a tense second where Rick and the witch just stared at each other, then the witch matched his stance with his arms crossed as well and shook his head. "No."

Some sort of silent acknowledgement passed between them, then Rick nodded and lowered his arms. "I can respect your loyalty to your friend, but I don't trust him, so his word isn't enough to vouch for you to stay in my territory or join my pack's coven."

The guy's eyes widened. "Oh, no, I can't stay. Like I said, I was doing Gabe a favor. And now we're square, right?"

Nodding, Gabriel extended a hand and the two shook and embraced once more. "Thank you, Keegan."

When they separated, the witch—Keegan—tried to take a step back toward the barrier, but Rick held up a hand, stopping him. "Hang on. I can't let you go yet."

Keegan's brows lowered. "You can't keep me here. My coven will—"

"I'm not *keeping you here,*" Rick said, turning and walking back to the other side of the barrier, not seeming bothered at all about turning his back to Gabriel or Keegan. "I just can't let you leave until V and Fiona confirm for me that this wasn't a distraction."

Marcus turned around when he heard Doc stand, having had one ear on him the whole time just in case. "Is she going to be okay?"

Doc nodded, clapping him briefly on the shoulder. "She will. But she'll heal faster with a little help from magic." He glanced at Rick. "Can you spare a witch? You seem to have more than enough at the moment."

Rick rolled his eyes. "Take Damien if you need the help, and Drake can—"

"Sir," Marcus interrupted, braced for Rick's anger, but all he got was a sigh. "Um, I'd like to go with them to the clinic. If that's okay with you."

"Yeah," Rick said on a slow exhale, "okay. You two"—he turned to Damien and Tashmica—"go ahead and lower the barrier. Damien, you're with Doc, and Tashmica… if either the hunter or his friend move, blast 'em."

The shimmery barrier immediately began to dissipate as soon as they stopped their chanting, Damien bending and picking up the envelope at his feet and Tash summoning a fireball to hold in her hand as she kept her eyes on Gabriel and Keegan.

Damien held the envelope out to Marcus, smiling gently. "Here you go."

As soon as he took it, Damien hurried over to kneel by Wendy, asking softly how he could help. Marcus was absently aware of them making a plan to lift and move her carefully to Doc's truck, but he couldn't take his eyes off the dirt-smeared envelope in his hand. His name was written in Mikel's strong, thick lettering right in the middle.

"Marcus?" Doc was talking to him. Glancing up, he refocused on what was happening around him just as Doc said, "We're ready."

"Right. Okay." He glanced down once more, then folded the envelope and shoved it in his back pocket. "Let's go."

Just as they were leaving, he heard Fiona's screech as she returned first to the clearing, but V's answering howl wasn't too far in the distance. He hesitated just long enough to hear Fi give the all clear, then hurried after Doc and Damien.

Praying to the goddess that his friend would be alright.

CHAPTER TWENTY-FIVE

Waking up the morning after Wendy arrived and finding his mate gone from their bed had been pretty shitty for Robson. But a week later?

He was sadly getting used to it.

Each night he did his best to tire out his increasingly stressed-out mate in an attempt to get him to sleep through the night, but each morning when he woke, Marcus's side of the bed was freezing cold. There would be a note on his nightstand or a text on his phone letting Robson know where he was if he was out of the house. As grateful as Robson had been that Wendy was going to be okay, he'd been scared and then pissed when he'd woken up and not known where Marcus was or what was happening. Thankfully, Marcus hadn't fought him on keeping him in the loop and had even apologized for upsetting Robson.

But they were both at their breaking point.

Sometimes Marcus would just be downstairs, staring at the letter from his old boss with a forgotten mug of coffee next to him, but some days it was worse. Some days, Robson would wake up at six and Marcus would already be gone to the manor and locked in his office. It wasn't healthy, and it wasn't helping Marcus figure out the coded message at the bottom of the letter.

Robson had considered asking Nico what he should do to help Marcus, but he'd hesitated. It wasn't that he thought Nico wouldn't help him or would make fun of Robson for seeking his advice, but Robson needed to prove to himself, his mate, and their pack that Robson could take care of Marcus on his own.

Fuck. When did it become *their* pack?

Throwing back the covers, Robson sat up and swung his legs over the edge of the bed, mind spinning. As much as he'd held back, worried about not having a place in the pack beyond being Marcus's mate, he'd somehow managed to get sucked into the vortex of crazy and protective that made up Rick Kincaid's pack. When Robson had discovered the gym in the basement and started working out with Fi and Vanessa, showing them tips to take down bigger or stronger opponents, he'd felt a rush of accomplishment. But he'd still felt like he didn't have enough to give to be a proper pack member.

But maybe that was just his own bullshit? Leftovers of never feeling good enough for his dad and like it was his job to do everything and take care of everyone. He'd thought he was doing better—and spending more time out of the farmhouse than in it definitely helped, allowing him to get to know his siblings again without stepping on each other's toes. He'd been better about listening to what Teo, Annalisse, and Valentina *needed* rather than just ordering them around.

Maybe being a friend to Fiona and V was enough, and taking care of Marcus so he could take care of the pack better was enough, and protecting the pack as best as he could as a deputy—even though he was bored out of his mind with his job—was enough.

Okay, that last one he might have to keep working on.

Nodding to himself, he pulled out his phone and sent a text, then went to shower. There hadn't been a note on Marcus's side of the bed or a text from him, so his mate was somewhere in the house, probably wallowing in self-recriminations about how he couldn't figure out Gregson's letter.

It was time to protect his mate from himself.

Thirty minutes later, he was showered, dressed, and had set a plan in motion to help pull Marcus out of his downward spiral. He descended the stairs two at a time and bounded into the kitchen, not surprised to see Marcus slouched over that damn letter at the table. Even though the scent of coffee was pulling at him, his mate's pull was harder and more immediate.

"Good morning, cariño," he murmured, stepping up next to Marcus and running a hand over his tense shoulders. He was a little surprised when Marcus immediately turned and pressed his face into Robson's stomach, wrapping his arms around his hips tightly, body trembling. "Oh, sweetheart, it's okay."

Marcus shook his head, pressing even closer, and Robson was alarmed at the dampness he felt seeping into his T-shirt. "I can't do it," he whispered hoarsely, voice full of anguish. "I'm not smart enough."

"Hey!" Threading his fingers into Marcus's hair, he jerked his head back and glared down at his tear-streaked face. "Don't you fucking say that. You're brilliant, cariño. You just need to give yourself a break and let the answer come to you."

Marcus scoffed as he swiped at his face, pulling out of Robson's hold. "Mikel *died* and Wendy almost did too to get this letter, this message, to me. I can't just sit back and twiddle my thumbs, waiting for inspiration to strike."

Robson's mouth dropped open a little, shocked not just

by the words but by the tone Marcus used. He'd never spoken to Robson like that before, and Robson wasn't a fan of it. Taking a breath, he tried to rein in his temper, knowing Marcus was just tired and stressed. "Okay, but you can't keep going like this, Marcus. I can't either."

It was Marcus's turn to look surprised and hurt. "You… What are you saying? You're done with me?"

"*What?*"

"Because I thought you understood that sometimes the pack would have to come first and that it was my job to protect them any way I can. I thought you—"

Darting forward, Robson gripped the sides of Marcus's face and forced him to look at Robson, their noses nearly touching. "Stop, cariño, stop. That's not what I meant. You know that. Take a few deep breaths for me."

He got two breaths sucked in before he broke, collapsing into Robson's arms and sobbing uncontrollably. Carefully, Robson led them into the living room and lowered onto the couch, Marcus falling on top of him and crying just as hard. The pain wracking his mate was killing Robson, but it had been for days now. Marcus needed this, needed to grieve Gregson and be grateful for Wendy and let go of the idea that everything was on his shoulders.

Arms wrapped around Marcus as tightly as they could get, Robson slowly rocked him and whispered over and over, "It's okay, cariño," "I love you so much, and nothing can change that," and "You always have and you always will protect our pack. You're so good at it, sweetheart."

By the time Marcus's sobs had slowed to just shuddery breaths and the occasional whimper, the shoulder of Robson's shirt was completely soaked, but he could feel a lightness in his mate that hadn't been there for weeks. The weight of responsibility had been slowly crushing him, so slowly not even Marcus had realized it was happening apparently.

Marcus cleared his throat, but Robson spoke before he could. "If you even think about apologizing, I swear I'll... I'll... I want to say spank you, but I feel like that would be fun and a terrible punishment."

Giving a gasping hiccup, Marcus peeled his face off Robson's shirt and leaned back, glaring playfully at him. His gorgeous pale skin was so red and blotchy it looked painful, but the tepid smile on his mate's face seemed genuine for the first time in a week. "You can't say things like that," he croaked.

"Sure I can," Robson said, shifting Marcus onto the couch and standing. He hurried into the kitchen and got a glass of water. Reentering the living room, he handed it over and resettled on the couch, pulling Marcus back onto his lap. He waited until Marcus had drunk most of the glass, then said, "You're my mate and the man I adore above all else—there isn't anything I can't say to you."

Face softening, Marcus set aside the glass and wrapped his arms around Robson's neck. "I suppose that is true."

"Mmhmm." Leaning forward, he nuzzled at Marcus's soft beard before pressing a sweet kiss to his salty lips. "And it means that it's my job to make sure you're taking care of yourself, and you haven't been, have you, cariño?"

Biting his lip, Marcus's eyes drifted toward the kitchen and that damn letter. "No, but—"

"So," Robson interrupted, pretending like Marcus hadn't even spoken, "you and I are going to go for a run in the woods. You furry, me human."

Marcus chuckled. "Is there another option for you?"

"Don't be sassy," Robson said, not meaning a word of it. "We've got to get going." When Marcus squirmed in Robson's lap, he couldn't help but laugh at the pretty pout Marcus was giving him. "We don't have time for sexy times, cariño, so suck that lip back in."

Sighing, Marcus climbed off Robson's lap and trailed into the kitchen, face already starting to cloud again as he stared at the paper still sitting on the table. "Maybe we should just—"

"Nope." Robson wrapped himself around Marcus's back, kissing the side of his neck. "The stupid letter can wait. Strip and then outside." He felt Marcus shiver at the order and pressed a smirk into his hair before pulling away. With a light tap to Marcus's ass as he slipped past him, Robson said, "Come on. We're already running late."

He saw Marcus's body jerk at the slap but didn't let himself get sidetracked again, striding toward the front door and smiling when Marcus followed. On the small porch, he waited patiently as Marcus stripped, eyeing him suspiciously.

"How can we be late for a run?" Marcus finally asked, slipping his briefs off.

Grinning at his mate's half-hard dick, he made a *please continue* motion with his hand. "Better keep going or you'll get cold in a hurry standing out here naked."

Grumbling, Marcus sent him one last half-hearted glare, then shifted into his wolf, sidestepping in his excitement as soon as he was changed.

"There's my fluffy buddy," Robson said, grinning as he knelt and rubbed at Marcus's neck and shoulders. He laughed when Marcus bumped into his chest with his head, nearly knocking him over, but Robson was learning that was his favorite trick to pull, so he was braced for it. "I've got a surprise for you. Come on."

Marcus tipped his head in question, then bounded off the porch, apparently satisfied with just going with the flow in this form. Jogging down after him, Robson set their direction and pace but didn't worry about Marcus darting all around him, sniffing and barking in excitement. Marcus had needed this, badly, and Robson was beginning to realize that reminding him to take a break and embrace his furry side was going to become just another way he took care of his mate.

He was watching Marcus closely, so he saw the exact moment the others came into range of his nose or ears. Skidding to a halt, Marcus lifted his head and focused on something ahead and just to the right, then suddenly threw his head back and howled so loudly it startled Robson.

Laughing, he had to sprint to keep Marcus in sight as he took off running, howls and roars and a screech answering his call. Panting but grinning, he finally caught up to his mate in the large clearing where the others were waiting. There were a lot of wolves, but Bennett's tiger was present as well and a screeching red-tailed hawk who came to land on his shoulder that he was pretty sure was Fiona.

Hissing, he turned and gave her a look. "Easy with the talons, Fi. We don't all heal instantly."

She nipped at his ear, then made a sort of sharp cheeping noise as she rubbed her head against his.

"Yeah, okay, you're forgiven." He glanced back at where Marcus was jumping and running around like a puppy with a couple of other wolves. It was hard for him to tell who was who since he hadn't spent a ton of time with them in their shifted forms, but he thought it was probably Nico and Kai playing with him. There was a huge black wolf overlooking the play off to the side, Bennett's tiger sitting not far from them, and Robson was pretty positive that was Rick.

This was way more than he'd anticipated when he'd texted Nico after he'd woken up.

"This is exactly what he needed," he murmured to Fi, reaching up to gently stroke her soft feathers.

He moseyed closer after the playing seemed to die down,

sidling up next to Rick. "So do we actually run at some point or just keep watching them play?"

The black wolf turned and eyed Robson, his gaze flicking to where Fi was still perched. His head cocked to the side like he was confused. Finally, he turned back to the others and loosed a howl that shook Robson's bones.

He swore Rick tossed him a wolfy grin before he took off toward the trees, the others bounding after him. Chuckling, Robson followed, knowing he'd never keep up but also knowing, as much fun as Marcus was having, his mate wouldn't let him get left behind.

Fiona took off into the air, releasing a screech as she swooped around his head, then flew toward the front of their group.

A feeling of connection seeped beneath his skin, filling his heart and soul with happiness and hope. Putting on a rush of speed, Robson whooped into the air and laughed when the wolves in front of him barked in response.

Then, he simply ran with his pack.

CHAPTER TWENTY-SIX

Sleeping in a pile of shifters while they were in their animal forms wasn't something he'd ever thought he'd do. It actually had been pretty nice too. Though at one point someone had pinned his leg to the ground so he couldn't move, and he was pretty sure it was Bennett secretly getting back at him for the sex ed class thing or possibly their slightly awkward phone conversation about feelings.

It was late afternoon by the time he and Marcus trekked back into the house, Robson feeling exhausted but Marcus looking peaceful and ready to take on the world.

"Thank you for today, Robito," Marcus murmured, plastering his front to Robson's and kissing his throat. He loved that Marcus had started using his family's nickname for him sometimes. Marcus was still terrified Robson's mom wouldn't like the idea of him moving into Robson's room, though, and bent over backward to be overly polite to her whenever Robson managed to drag him to the farmhouse for a meal.

But she did like it. And he knew that because he'd already

talked to her about it. At first she'd tried to tell him that they needed their own space as a new couple, but he'd told her that he wasn't comfortable with that while Annalisse and Valentina were still in school and Teo was just getting the farm turned around.

He just needed to get his skittish mate on board.

"You're welcome, cariño." He wrapped his arms around Marcus and gave him a squeeze. They stood quietly like that for a few moments, and then Robson murmured, "I love you. You know that, right?"

Marcus's arms tightened, but he didn't look up from where his face was buried in Robson's neck. "You said that earlier when I was upset… I wasn't sure if you really meant to say it or not."

"Of course I did." Robson pressed kisses into Marcus's hair. "I love you and I'll always take care of you, no matter what you need."

Slipping his hands up the back of Robson's T-shirt, Marcus whispered, "I love you too and want to take care of you as well."

"You do, cariño. I was lost and miserable before I met you. You give me purpose and make me laugh and have brought so much love and light into my life."

Sucking in a breath, Marcus pulled back and stared up at him. "Robson…"

"And I'm ready for us to finish our mating," Robson continued, smiling gently as Marcus's pupils dilated and his irises began to glow. "Fuck, I love when your eyes do that."

Marcus bit his lip but couldn't hide his smile. "I used to have much better control, you know."

"I know. That's what makes it so hot." Robson gave him a slow, sweet kiss, sucking lightly on his bottom lip before pulling away. "I love that you can't control yourself when it comes to me."

"I couldn't from the beginning."

"I remember. You stared at me so hard at that crime scene I thought you were the one who dumped the body." At Marcus's flat look, Robson had to press his lips together to hold back his laugh. "I'm kidding. Sort of."

Marcus tried to hold his unimpressed look but ended up smiling and digging his fingers into the small of Robson's back. "When you say 'finish our mating'…"

Grinning, Robson slipped from Marcus's hold and dragged him into the kitchen. "I mean, where's that tea so we can exchange bites while you knot me?" The soft thump and curse from Marcus had him chuckling. "Did my shifter mate just trip over his own feet?"

There was a pause, and then he whispered, "Maybe."

"So adorable," he muttered, stopping and scanning the counters but not seeing the jar. He threw a raised eyebrow at his mate, who managed to still blush as he scooted past Robson and dug into a cupboard. Even after weeks of Robson saying and doing dirty, delicious things to his mate, that blush kept coming back.

Robson hoped it never went away.

Marcus cleared his throat as he filled his kettle and set it on the stove. "Damien said we could steep the herbs in warm water from the tap, but that it'd be more… potent if we used boiling water and let it sit for at least ten minutes before you drink it."

Nodding, Robson stepped back and pulled his shirt off over his head, pretending not to notice the sharpening of his mate's stare on his exposed chest. "Okay, I'm going to go get the shower ready. Once you get the tea steeping, come join me."

He winked and turned away, hustling up the stairs as his mate called after him that he was being a tease. And maybe he was, a little, but he also really needed to shower after spending hours galivanting through the woods and napping on the ground with a bunch of mud-splattered animals.

By the time Marcus was slipping into the shower stall behind him, Robson was nearly done, giving his body one final rinse. He smiled, though, when Marcus wrapped his arms around him from behind and peppered kisses across Robson's shoulders.

"What took you so long?" he murmured, leaning back and letting Marcus support most of his weight.

Body vibrating with silent laughter, Marcus's arms tightened. "Water takes a few minutes to start boiling."

"Hm." They stood there for several long minutes, letting the hot water rain down on them. The silent, peaceful moments they managed to carve out together were some of Robson's favorites, filling a space in his chest that had been aching for connection, for family since he'd shipped off to the army. As much as he loved his mom and siblings, having someone that was just for him, his perfect match, gave him purpose and filled his life with meaning.

Just as he was considering suggesting they move things into the bedroom, Marcus shifted behind him. Robson sucked in a breath as one of Marcus's hands skimmed down his front, sparking electricity in its wake. Robson's cock was only just starting to take interest, but as soon as Marcus's fingers wrapped around him, he groaned and tipped his head back onto Marcus's shoulder. His mate's long, talented fingers could drive him crazy so easily.

"Are you sure about this?" Marcus whispered, squeezing and stroking Robson's cock and pressing a sweet kiss to the junction of his neck and shoulder.

Shivering, Robson stretched his head to the side, offering more fully that sweet spot he knew his mate wanted. "One hundred percent positive."

Marcus's hand tightened on the base of Robson's erection, and he let out a soft growl that made Robson's balls tingle. "Let's dry off then. The tea's probably ready."

Twisting around, Robson threaded his fingers into Marcus's hair and took his mouth in a quick, hard kiss. "Let's do this."

He turned the water off, and they tumbled out of the shower stall, hindering more than helping each other with the drying-off process. Laughing, he finally ended up getting most of the excess water off and then flicked the end of the towel he held at Marcus's hip.

His mate was not impressed, his hand slapping down onto the spot like it had actually hurt him.

"I can't believe you did that," Marcus said, sounding like the uptight guy the rest of the pack saw.

Snorting in his face, Robson reached around and palmed Marcus's ass and kissed his stern mouth, darting his tongue inside when Marcus melted against him right away. He slowly moved them out of the bathroom, unwilling to release his hold or move away from his mate's sweet lips.

When they fell onto the bed, naked bodies entwined, Marcus pulled away and looked around, confusion furrowing his brow.

"What's wrong?" Robson ran a hand down Marcus's smooth back and fondled his ass. He couldn't help but grin as Marcus shivered against him.

"The tea…"

"Oh, right." A quick glance around helped him locate the steaming mug on the table on his side of the bed. After giving Marcus another quick kiss and ass squeeze, he wiggled out from under him and knee-walked over, sitting cross-legged up by the pillows. He caught a whiff of the tea when he picked up the mug and made a face. "He couldn't have made it smell better?"

"Maybe it won't taste as bad," Marcus murmured as he

twisted around then crawled over next to Robson, settling on his side by Robson's legs and caressing his thigh comfortingly.

"How much do I have to drink?" He knew the answer, but he was hoping he was wrong.

"The whole thing."

Robson grimaced and raised the mug to his lips, metal chain from the diffuser rattling around until he secured it with his finger. "You could at least sound sorry about that."

He would have liked to say the soft smile Marcus gave him that always managed to warm his chest was enough to cover the horrid taste of the tea.

It wasn't.

"Fuck!" He coughed and sputtered on the bitterness, eyes watering a little.

Face concerned, Marcus pushed up and peered in the mug, frowning at the amount of liquid death left inside. "We don't have to—"

Robson didn't bother responding. He wasn't letting some foul-tasting water stop him from bonding with his mate. Hell no. He'd been through way worse for way less.

Deciding it was best to just chug the rest, he lifted the mug and tried to swallow as fast as he could, hoping the tea would bypass his taste buds if he was quick enough.

It didn't.

"Blegh!" Shuddering and shaking his head, he set aside the empty cup.

"Are you okay?" Marcus asked finally, barely concealed laughter at the edge of his voice.

"I'm fine and really glad I don't have to do that again." He scooted down and turned onto his side so he was face-to-face with Marcus. Tracing the smile tugging at Marcus's lips with his pointer finger, Robson pretended to scowl. "You could have a little more sympathy for me, cariño."

Marcus pressed his lips together and nodded solemnly. "I'm so sorry that was so awful for you."

"Hmm." He couldn't hold back his laughter as he leaned forward and laid a soft, lingering kiss on his mouth. Even after Marcus parted his lips and tried to deepen it, Robson kept it light. When Marcus pulled away with a huff, Robson chuckled and flipped onto his back, gesturing at his body. "What are you waiting for?"

They'd asked Damien after they'd first talked about the tea how long the effects would last, so Robson knew they technically had hours, but neither of them would be able to wait that long. After Robson's teasing kisses and challenging tone, Marcus's eyes were already flashing, his wolf still close to the surface after spending so much time in his furry form.

Sure enough, as Marcus moved over Robson's body, settling between his legs, his movements were smooth and predatory. Robson's usually sweet and compliant mate appeared more than ready to take possession of Robson's body, and he was ready for it.

Marcus wouldn't be rushed though. Robson realized quickly—as his mate was slowly driving him insane as he kissed and licked his way across Robson's chest and over his abs—that Marcus was going to fucking savor the moment no matter how much Robson wanted to hurry things along.

"Mierda!" Robson's back arched sharply, and he fisted the sheets as Marcus kissed the spot under Robson's belly button where he'd just bitten him. The tiny pain had shot right to his balls, causing them to draw up close to his body and precome to leak from his cock.

Humming, Marcus swiped his tongue over the small puddle of precome pooling under the head of his dick, and then he prowled forward until he was right above Robson's head. When he leaned down and slotted their mouths together, Robson wasn't surprised that Marcus was more aggressive than usual, pushing his tongue into Robson's mouth almost violently and nibbling on Robson's lips. The part of Robson that usually liked to take control during sex was quiet as his instincts drove him to submit to his mate and give himself completely. They needed Marcus's magic to ignite the spell in the herbs, and the only way that would happen was if Marcus's wolf laid claim to his mate completely.

When Marcus lifted his head, he was somehow holding the bottle of lube from the nightstand, but Robson wasn't sure how he'd gotten it without him noticing. Everything was getting deliciously hazy around the edges, and he grinned, feeling almost loopy.

"Herbs are working," he murmured, throwing his arms around Marcus's shoulders and nuzzling into his beard, groaning at the feeling of the coarse hairs abrading his lips and cheeks. "So good."

Marcus chuckled. "We may have let the tea steep too long if you're feeling this relaxed."

Oh, yeah. He remembered that part now. Damien had included some magic voodoo stuff so Robson would stay calm when Marcus knotted and bit him. Like he was some kind of punk-ass new recruit who couldn't handle intense situations.

"Psh. We got this," he said, nibbling on Marcus's earlobe for a moment before releasing his hold and falling back to the bed, arms outstretched. "Make me yours, cariño."

Glowing eyes were Marcus's only response for a minute, and then he grabbed a pillow, shoved it under Robson's hips hurriedly and spread his thighs. Robson chuckled at Marcus's eagerness, but the sounded was choked off by a moan as Marcus sank a finger inside him.

Body undulating against the sheets, he slapped a hand on

the mattress and growled. "Don't go slow, Marcus. You know I can take it."

Marcus had gotten *very* good at fingering Robson while he sucked his brains out through his dick, and Robson loved it. But the careful stretching Marcus was trying to do wasn't what they both knew he could handle—it was how Robson treated Marcus's prep. Robson would cut off his own dick before hurting Marcus, but he liked that slight edge of pain, and Marcus was well aware of that.

Thankfully, Marcus just grinned at him and added a second finger, roughly pegging Robson's prostate in retaliation. Heat flowed through him, racing just under his skin and warming his whole body. Gasping, Robson spread his legs a little wider, wanting his mate closer, closer, closer.

Marcus was studying him intently, noting every twitch of his hands and catch of his breath. When their eyes connected, it was like a bolt of lightning down Robson's spine. He could see Marcus's wolf right there in his glowing gaze, and he realized it wasn't just Marcus watching Robson's reactions so closely.

Marcus's wolf wanted to know how to please him; he could see it in his steady gaze.

Spotting the tips of Marcus's fangs as he pressed a third finger into Robson's hole, they both moaned and Robson threw his head back, fully exposing his throat, hoping it would be enough to tempt his mate's wolf to speed things up.

With a snarl, Marcus was pressing Robson's body into the bed and licking up the side of his neck. "Don't rush me, mate."

"Who me?" he asked breathlessly. "I didn't say a word."

Sharp teeth nipped at his skin, and he cried out, wrapping his legs around Marcus's waist. Marcus hadn't drawn blood, but they were on the edge of control, and Robson wanted to tip them over, to see his mate lose his hold completely and take from Robson everything he was willing to give and then some.

He wanted to be Marcus's entire focus, his whole world.

Maybe it was greedy or selfish, but in that moment, they were alone in a way they never had been. There was no pack or looming threat. No family members they were responsible for or pups to watch out for. There definitely wasn't any fucking letter standing between them.

There was only them. Their mating, their *bond*, practically shivered in the air around them as Marcus sank his long cock inside Robson's body for the first time.

"Cariño," he murmured, holding on as tight as he could, urging Marcus not to hesitate, to take what he needed. What they both wanted. Moving his lips up to Marcus's ear, he pressed a kiss to the shell before breathing out, "Claim what's yours."

The hard thrust Marcus gave him after that made his eyes roll back in his head. He dug his nails into Marcus's back and nodded, lifting his hips to meet the next one.

"Fuck, yes, just like that."

Marcus's face was buried in Robson's neck, but his whimpers and panting breath let Robson know it felt just as good to him. It wasn't too long either before he felt a slight sting as the base of Marcus's dick caught on the edge of his rim.

"There it is," he murmured, arching his back and moaning. "Come on, cariño. Knot me."

Crying out, Marcus drove forward, one strong hand creating bruises on Robson's hip as he held his lower half up from the bed with one hand. Robson moaned at the slight burn as Marcus grew inside him, tying them together. He could feel the heat of Marcus's come filling him, and it was…

Amazing.

All of the sensations flooding him were almost enough to

tip him over, but as Marcus's grip on his hip relaxed and he lowered back down onto the pillow, Marcus lifted his head and frowned down at Robson's still-hard cock. He cocked his head in a completely wolfish manner that made Robson bite his lip, so he didn't comment on it.

"Bite me," he whispered, satisfied when Marcus's head snapped up, eyes and fangs still on display. "I can't do it until you do."

The magic from Marcus's bite was the last ingredient Damien had said. Like a match to kindling, it would ignite the spell inside Robson. He could feel it buzzing in his veins, wanting out but stuck until Marcus released it.

He could still see a tiny bit of worry in Marcus's eyes though. A part of his mate still thought that binding them together with the bites was something Robson wasn't ready for or would grow to regret.

Robson knew the truth.

Grabbing one of Marcus's hands, he raised it first to his mouth and kissed the palm, then laid it on his chest right over his heart. "You feel that? How steady it is? I want this. I want you. I want to be your mate in every way imaginable and then some. Nothing could change how much I love you." Marcus's face softened, but there was still something there, something Robson was missing. Suddenly, he realized what it was. "Cariño, I'll never get tired of you. If you ever get sent away again, then I'll be right there beside you. You'll never be alone again. I promise you."

Tears filled his poor, sweet mate's eyes, but those were the magic words. Despite how much he loved Rick and the pack, a part of Marcus was still worried about not being enough and getting kicked out of the family he'd struggled to make.

Opening his mouth, Marcus leaned forward and licked the spot between Robson's neck and shoulder. Reaching up,

Robson threaded his fingers through his hair just as the first pricks of pain lit up his whole body.

It wasn't like anything he'd ever felt before.

It was almost like there really was a fire in his veins, burning him up from the inside. It was painful but also the most intensely erotic thing he'd ever experienced. Screaming, he tightened his hold in Marcus's hair and shot his load between them, completely untouched, but he barely noticed.

Gums aching, he sliced open his own lip as his canines extended into fangs abruptly. Hissing, he didn't hesitate to strike at the lovely pale skin in front of him. His instincts were so strong and urgent he didn't think he could stop himself if he wanted to.

Marcus grunted against Robson's neck and released his hold when Robson bit him, raising his head a little to rub their cheeks together. As soon as Marcus's blood hit his tongue and throat, the flames burning him up began to lessen, effectively extinguished.

Moaning, he released his teeth and collapsed back onto the bed, his entire body feeling wrung out yet also energized. He had to force his eyes open, but when he saw the healing bite mark on Marcus, he couldn't help but grin smugly.

He'd done that.

There was a warmth in his chest that he instinctively knew was the bonding connection Bennett had talked about, but it was already fading as the magic began to fade, his teeth shrinking back to normal.

Marcus gently touched Robson's cut lip, brows furrowed. "It's healing."

"Is it?" He ran his tongue over the spot, but the memory of slicing it on his fang was a little hazy, so he couldn't remember how bad it had been. "I can still feel your magic in me a little bit."

"Must be helping," Marcus murmured, leaning down and

gently kissing the spot. "Your bite mark doesn't look too bad either."

"That's good," he said, then yawned. He shifted, his back starting to hurt from the slightly arched position the pillow was causing, but the stinging tug at his hole reminded him that wasn't a great idea. "Not sure how I would have explained why my neck looked like someone had gone all Edward on me."

"Who's Edward?"

Chuckling turned to groaning when it tightened his body too much. "Never mind. That reference isn't worth explaining."

Marcus bit his lip, trying not to look pleased with himself since his knot was causing some discomfort. "Sorry. This isn't a great position to be tied in."

Robson grunted his agreement, but he wouldn't have changed a single thing about the experience. "It's fine. Though next time we're doing it from behind so I can go to sleep in a more comfortable position afterward."

Marcus's cheeks were still a little flushed from exertion, but they noticeably darkened at Robson's words, and he carefully lowered himself onto Robson's chest so he could hide his face in his neck. "You want to do it again?"

"Oh, my sweet puppy," Robson said, laughing gently when Marcus growled at him. "Of course I do. Though Nico mentioned that you can learn to control your knot, right?"

Marcus nodded slowly, and Robson thought he might be tired too, but then he realized his worrywart of a mate was thinking about things again. "You... You'd really come with me if I had to move again?"

His voice was soft and full of emotion, and it broke Robson's heart. "Cariño... I can't think of a single thing I wouldn't do for you. There aren't any conditions on my love or our mating. This is it. You're stuck with me for the rest of our lives."

Steady, even breaths fell on Robson's skin as Marcus considered his words, his arms tightening around Robson a little though. By the time he responded, Robson was nearly asleep and Marcus's knot was starting to shrink, but he still clearly heard him.

"I believe you, Robito."

CHAPTER TWENTY-SEVEN

"You seem... less tense," Tashmica said, sipping her tea and recrossing her legs where she had made herself at home on the couch in Marcus's office.

He snorted, finished typing a response to an email from a pack member, then closed out of his computer to take a break. Settling next to her, he picked up the other mug, his cheeks heating at the reminder of the tea Robson had drunk last night, his neck tingling where he knew the scar from his mate's teeth was.

Tash smirked as she held her cup in front of her mouth. "Ah, now I know why."

"It's not... that," he said, ignoring her soft laugh. "Or not only that. Running with the others yesterday helped a lot too. When I get so focused and stressed, I tend to ignore my wolf, but Robson helped us get back on the same page."

Setting aside her mug, she reached over and gripped his arm, purple nails catching his eyes. "I'm so happy that things worked out between the two of you, sweetie."

Chuckling, he laid his own hand over hers. "Thank you for helping me get to a place where I could let myself be happy with him. I don't know what I would have done if I'd ruined things before they'd even started."

"None of us would have let that happen." She winked and they went back to their tea, the silence between them speaking of years of friendship and trust. Finally, once their cups were empty and he was eyeing his desk once more, she said carefully, "Any luck with the letter?"

He sighed and sagged back against the couch, rubbing at his face, then scratching his beard. "No. I know the numbers are a cipher—Mikel was obsessed with books and poetry. His office was so full of them it was claustrophobic. But without knowing the *exact* book or poem and the edition he used as a reference…"

"Seems difficult but not impossible," she said, pulling him out of a familiar spiral. "He wouldn't have made it so you couldn't figure out what he used."

Groaning, he sat forward, cupping his head in his hands, elbows braced on his knees. "I know. I know the damn answer has to be right in front of my face, but I can't find it."

Humming, she stood and meandered over to his desk where the letter was sitting on the front corner. "No clues in the message he wrote you?"

"None that I could see."

She was quiet as she read it, then pointed at something on the page. "What does this mean? 'My squire'?"

Marcus shrugged, not looking up. "He called me his squire when I worked for him. It became like a term of endearment and an inside joke because it…"

When he trailed off and raised his head, squinting at the wall across from him as his brain churned furiously, Tash-mica hurried back over, sitting on the table in front of him. "What is it?"

"I'm an idiot," he whispered. The clue was so subtle he'd completely missed it for the last week. Shaking his head, he climbed to his feet, stopping only to kiss the top of her head. "You're a genius, Tash!"

"Um, okay?"

Not answering, he raced toward the door and threw it open, calling back at her, "Grab the letter and meet me up in the library!" Then he was gone. He repeated a prayer to the goddess that the book was there and not at his house somewhere, but he was almost positive he'd stored it in Rick's library when he'd first arrived in Michigan, before he'd had a place of his own.

Then he'd forgotten about it.

Tearing into the library, he ignored the questions Bennett and Rick threw at him as he ran from one bookcase to the next, scanning them quickly. "It has to be here," he muttered, stumbling to the one in the farthest corner, vaguely remembering thinking that no one would notice or be bothered if he stored a single book there.

He dropped to his knees when he spotted the worn spine, tears springing to his eyes for some reason. "I found it."

Tashmica was hurrying into the room just as he carefully pulled the tattered volume of Henry Wadsworth Longfellow's *Tales of a Wayside Inn* from the bottom shelf and cradled it in his hands.

"Is that it?" she asked, pausing by the table where Rick and Bennett had been working. They were both half standing like they weren't sure if they should be worried about Marcus's behavior or not.

"I think so." He stood and carried the book over to the table, laying it down so they could see. "Mikel gave this to me right before I came here. Longfellow was one of his favorite poets, though he preferred to read his translation of *The Divine Comedy* more than most of his original work." Marcus chuckled wetly, swiping at his eyes before carefully opening the book and thumbing to the page that had been earmarked years ago by Mikel. "'The Poet's Tale—The Birds of Killing-worth' made an inn in Massachusetts famous."

Rick slowly stood and circled around to stand next to Marcus. "This book is the cipher?"

Marcus shook his head and tapped the page. "This poem is. The inn is in Mikel's hometown. He used to be so proud of that and would brag about how he'd stay there when he went home to visit his old pack and family." Clearing his throat, he looked up at Rick's wide eyes. "Do you have a piece of paper I can use?"

There was a scramble to find a notebook, and then they all sat around the table as Tashmica carefully read out each set of numbers—line, word, letter—and Marcus painstakingly copied out the coded message Mikel had gone to so much effort to get to him. A part of him worried it would be a warning about Rick's dad wanting to remove him as alpha or something else they'd already figured out. It wasn't that he thought the letter needed to be *worth* him dying for—nothing was worth that in Marcus's opinion—but if it wasn't at least something new, it'd be a devastating blow.

It was definitely something new.

As the message became clear, Marcus's adrenaline started to rise, his heart beating faster.

"Jesus, Marcus, what does it say?" Rick finally growled.

"Hang on. I want to get the whole thing before starting to read it." They were almost done. The list of numbers was really long because they denoted letters instead of words, but the message itself wasn't more than a few lines. There was a sting in his left arm like he'd been stung by a wasp, but when he felt his bicep, he couldn't find anything wrong. Shaking off the weird sensation, he refocused on the poem.

Finally, they were done.

Marcus took a deep breath and read Mikel's final message to the room. "*I found the original Council charter, and your pack needs to see it. In case this is broken, I won't share more, but this is huge. You'll find it at the Red Horse Inn."*

There was silence for several long moments, then Bennett broke it by saying, "That's it? All this secrecy over the Council charter? How in the hell will that help us?"

Tashmica was tapping at her phone and started cursing. "There are a ton of results for Red Horse Inn. How are we supposed to know which one to go to?"

He opened his mouth to reassure her, but Jamie piped up from the doorway. How he'd managed to sneak up on *all* of them, Marcus had no idea. "It's called Longfellow's Wayside Inn now."

"Yes, it is. How did you—"

The others started questioning Jamie, but Marcus ignored them as he realized his gut was churning. Something was wrong. Something was *very* wrong.

And then it hit him: Robson was scared.

Robson was *hurt.*

It took him a moment to realize the room had quieted and everyone was looking at him.

"What's wrong?" Rick asked, already standing and coming closer.

"It's... Robson," Marcus gasped out, stumbling to his feet and patting at his pockets. Where was his phone? Had he left it in his office in his haste to get to the library? "I have to go. I have to find him."

"Hold on a second." Rick clapped a hand on the side of his neck, but for once it did nothing to calm Marcus. Instead, it cranked his anxiety higher. His mate was hurt, and Marcus needed to get to him *right now.*

Jamie stepped farther into the room, phone pressed to his ear. "Yes, sir. Thank you. We'll be there as soon as we can."

Who was he talking to? Why couldn't Marcus hear who it was? *Oh.* His ears were ringing so loudly he couldn't hear anything beyond the library. He took a couple of deep breaths, trying to calm himself down before he passed out. Robson needed him calm, not in the middle of a panic attack.

Tucking his phone away, Jamie gave him a grim look. "He's okay. The sheriff said he was taken to the hospital in Dunport and will be fine. We can go and see him, and we'll be able to bring him home as soon as he's discharged in a couple hours."

"What h-happened?" Marcus had to sit back down, one hand rubbing at the spot where he'd felt the sting even though there wasn't any pain anymore. That must have been where Robson had been hurt.

"Um." Jamie looked at Rick, his hesitation sending Marcus's heart rate through the roof once more.

"What happened?" he asked more insistently.

"He was shot," Rick said finally, his voice calm, but it wasn't enough to stop Marcus from going light-headed. "A graze really, according to Craig."

Craig? Oh, right, the sheriff. Marcus's brain definitely wasn't getting enough oxygen because it was taking forever for things to process.

Pushing to his feet, he swallowed the bile back down that was trying to crawl up his esophagus. "I need to get to the hospital. Excuse me."

Dunport was twenty minutes away and the county seat. Robson drove there for every shift to pick up his deputy's car, and it had never seemed that far.

Now it felt like he was on the other side of the country.

Rick was saying something behind him, but Marcus couldn't focus beyond putting one foot in front of the other and getting to his mate.

He was shot kept circling in his brain over and over and producing worst-case scenarios of Robson lying in a pool of blood, of Robson gasping for breath, of Robson *dying* while Marcus was safe in the manor.

Suddenly Rick and Nico were on either side of him, bracing him as they went down the stairs. Their voices buzzed around him, but he couldn't hear them, couldn't hear anything. He wasn't quite sure how, but from one moment to the next, he was on the steps and then in the back seat of an SUV.

Shaking his head, he tried to get his brain to engage. Nico was next to him, hand on his shoulder, Rick was driving, and Tashmica was in the front passenger seat, though she was twisted around to keep her eyes on him.

"I think he's coming back around," she murmured. "Sweetie, can you hear me?"

"Yes, sorry. I'm not sure what... Are we going to the hospital?" He was panting for some reason, and his muscles were so tense they were sore. Trying to relax, he focused on breathing, nearly swallowing his tongue when Nico slipped him his phone and he saw he had six missed calls from different Medinas. "Oh no."

"It's going to be okay," Nico said, rubbing a small circle on Marcus's back. "Once you see him and hear him ordering around the nurses, you'll feel better."

But would his mate's family ever trust him again? He'd been unreachable when Robson had needed him most. As he stared at his phone, a text came through from Patrick, and he was almost too scared to open it.

Patrick: *I stayed at the house with Maria but Teresa should be almost to the hospital. Don't let his family keep you out of things. You're his mate, even if they don't know that. Teresa will help. Give him my best.*

He stared at the screen for another minute, expecting another message asking why he hadn't answered or why he wasn't already there, even though it had probably been less than thirty minutes since he'd felt the initial pain in his arm.

When nothing else came through, he thumbed back to the rest of his texts and sucked in a breath when he saw one from Robson.

Robson: *I gotta head to the hospital—I'M FINE—but will you come please? I need you to keep my family from smothering me. Love you.*

Swallowing, he quickly typed out a response, though he wasn't sure if Robson would even still have his phone on him.

Marcus: *I'm so sorry I didn't see this right away. I'm on my way right now. I love you too. I'm so sorry.*

Despite how badly he'd fucked up with his phone, Marcus felt better knowing Robson had been well enough to send him a text. He leaned back against the seat and closed his eyes, trying to concentrate on breathing.

The drive seemed to take three times as long as normal, but they were finally pulling into the hospital's parking lot. Unfortunately, the woman at the desk was less than helpful.

"He already has two visitors in with him," she said, barely glancing up from her computer. "You're welcome to wait with the others in the waiting room."

Sighing, he stepped back from the counter and headed into the small area off to the side where he immediately saw Teo pacing, then spotted Teresa sitting between Annalisse and Valentina, both of whom were leaning on their big sister and crying.

As soon as Teo saw him and the others, he stalked over. "Do you know anything? Mom and Hector went back, but we haven't gotten an update yet."

Marcus opened and closed his mouth, not sure what to say, but Rick stepped forward and put a comforting hand on

Teo's shoulder, leading him away. "We don't know much, just that it isn't serious…"

Teresa gave him a tired smile from behind her sisters. "You know, all those years serving and he barely got hurt. But less than a year as a deputy and we're all in the hospital waiting for news. How messed up is that?"

"I'm sorry I didn't answer when you called," he croaked out after falling into the chair across from her. "I accidentally left it in my office. I… I'm so sorry."

"Hey."

Her firm voice brought his head up from where he'd dropped his gaze to the scuffed laminate tiles beneath his feet. "Yes?"

"You don't need to be beating yourself up because you didn't answer when we called. If it had been more serious, we'd have tracked you down. You got here like ten minutes after we did." She smiled at him, waiting for him to respond.

He finally nodded, not sure he should let himself off the hook so easily. He'd never fully appreciated how dangerous his mate's job could be. Robson had always seemed larger-than-life and unstoppable. His fragility as a human had never really crossed Marcus's mind.

He jerked his head to the side when he caught Robson's voice coming from the other side of the ER. "*This is fucking ridiculous. I need like two stitches.*"

The relief that coursed through him at his mate's ornery voice made his knees weak and would have sent him to the ground if he wasn't already sitting. He caught Teresa's eye and tapped his ear, then gave her a thumbs-up.

She smiled like she'd known he was fine, but the relief was in the way she loosened her hold on her sisters. "You should go see him."

His lip lifted in a snarl. "That woman at the desk wouldn't let me. Said he already had two people back there with him."

"That's dumb." She rolled her eyes and tapped Annalisse's side. "Can you sit up for a second, mija? I need to get my phone." After she dug it out of her pocket, Annalisse settled back against her and Teresa awkwardly typed out a message with one hand. "There. That should help."

He wasn't sure what she meant until he heard Robson's voice get louder. "*Of course I want him back here!*" There was some grumbling from Hector about Robson being an asshole that made their mom scold him, and then he heard Hector moving. A minute later, he stepped into the waiting room and gave Marcus a sheepish look.

"You can head back, Marcus. He's the third on the left— though you could probably just follow the cursing."

He ducked his head to hide his laugh as he stood, threw Teresa a grateful smile, then headed back toward the triage bays. The woman at the desk gave him a look but didn't stop him, so he followed Robson's voice to where he was telling his mom that he wouldn't quit his job without another one lined up, no matter how much she wanted him to now.

Did he want to find another job? Marcus paused outside the drawn curtain and tried to remember Robson saying something to him about not liking his job. Even though Robson had started working more in the last couple weeks, Marcus couldn't remember him saying anything about being a deputy one way or the other.

Had he really been unhappy and not told Marcus? Why wouldn't he confide in him? They were mates. They should be able to tell each other anything. Did he not feel—

"I can hear you overthinking out there, cariño."

Embarrassed at getting caught, he tried to hide it as he pulled back the curtain to reveal his mate lying propped on a narrow hospital bed, but the moment his eyes landed on him, they zeroed in on the stark white bandage around his bicep with red seeping through in the middle. The contrast against his beautiful tan skin and the black lines of his tattoo made Marcus light-headed again.

He couldn't take his eyes off the saturated bandage even as Robson quietly asked his mom to give them a minute alone. On her way past, Mrs. Medina gave him a quick hug and whispered that she'd be over with her brood to collect his things the following weekend.

That got him to tear his eyes away as he watched her walk toward the waiting room. "What?"

"She's done waiting for you to be ready to move into the farmhouse," Robson said, laughter in his voice. "Close the curtain, cariño, then get over here and give me a kiss. I was shot, you know."

Robson making light of what had happened had the opposite effect on Marcus than he'd probably intended. Tears filled his eyes as he whipped the blue curtain shut, then flew across the small space and threw his arms around his mate.

"Hey, hey, hey. It's okay." He tried to wrap his arms around Marcus and hissed a little, making Marcus cry harder that he'd hurt Robson more. "Oh, my sweet, sweet mate. I'm fine, I promise."

"You could have *died*," Marcus rasped out, burying his face in Robson's throat and climbing all the way into the bed, careful to stay on Robson's uninjured side. "And I couldn't even answer my phone."

Robson was still in his scratchy uniform pants, but his shirt had been removed, and Marcus couldn't stop running his hand over his smooth, warm skin.

"Marcus, stop. Look at me." Robson's growly voice was like a caress down Marcus's spine. Once their eyes were on each other, Robson gave him a soft smile. "Not having your phone attached to your hand isn't a crime. You getting here ten minutes earlier wouldn't have changed anything even if I had been more seriously hurt."

Wincing just at the suggestion of a worse injury, Marcus refocused on his hurt arm, raising his hand to lay it gently just under the bandage. "What happened?"

Robson grunted and rolled his eyes. "A bunch of wannabe SWAT officers getting overly eager during a warrant execution."

"Another officer shot you?"

"No, it was the suspect. But the whole thing was sloppy as hell. My old infantry unit could have done a better job with blindfolds on."

Marcus stared at his mate for a long moment. "You really don't like your job, do you? Why didn't you ever tell me?"

Robson cupped his face and pulled him close for a kiss. "Because you've had enough on your plate without me complaining when I don't even know what I want to do instead."

"Robito," he murmured, pressing another lingering kiss to his lips. "That's not how being mates works. You have to tell me your stuff, not just listen to mine."

"You're right. I'm sorry, cariño." He tugged Marcus back down to his throat, letting him burrow close for comfort.

They lay together quietly for several moments, then Marcus heard Rick approaching the curtained bay, so he forced himself to sit up a little. Though he couldn't make himself completely leave the reassuring warmth of his mate's arms.

"May I come in?" Rick asked from just outside the curtain.

He waited until Robson nodded okay before giving Rick permission to enter. Slipping in, Rick quickly ran his eyes over Robson's injured arm, jaw tight.

"I spoke with one of the pack nurses on duty, and she said

she'd come do your stitches shortly, then get you discharged." Rick waved off Robson's thanks and just kept going. "Tomorrow, I'd like you to put in your notice with the sheriff's department."

Marcus jerked in surprise and felt Robson tense too. They exchanged glances, and then Robson said, "Listen, Rick, I appreciate what you did to get me out of here quicker, but I can't just—"

"I'm going to hire you."

Robson's mouth snapped shut with a clack.

"What do you mean?" Marcus asked.

"I mean," Rick said slowly, "that my father will gather as many allies as he can, and then he'll come after us."

Marcus looked between them as Robson met Rick's stare head-on, face grim. "You think the pack is going to be going to war with the Council."

Nodding once, Rick turned to leave, pausing at the curtain and glancing back at them, eyes glowing. "I think it very well might be inevitable. And if I'm right, I want someone with your tactical experience by my side."

Robson dipped his chin in acknowledgement, jaw set and arm tightening around Marcus. An understanding passed between them, one that not even Marcus could fully grasp.

One thing he knew for certain—both his mate and his alpha would do whatever it took to protect their pack.

Goddess help anyone who stood in their way.

CHAPTER TWENTY-EIGHT

Turned out, being bonded to a shifter had some additional perks.

"I've never seen anything like it," Doc said as he finished removing Robson's stitches two days after his injury. Two. Days. "The graze was deep enough to require stitches, yet it's already healed. Did you know this would happen?"

That question was aimed at the slim man standing in the corner of the exam room, seeming like he hoped he'd disappear into the drywall if he pressed back hard enough. Which... Robson wasn't a hundred percent sure the man couldn't do it. Magic was weird.

"Um, no. Well," Damien quickly added when Doc raised his brows at him as he sat back from where he'd been studying Robson's mostly healed skin. "I had several theories about additional benefits or side effects the bonding herbs could have. Hypothetically."

"And you didn't think those were relevant to share with the guys you gave them to?" Robson asked, slipping his T-shirt back on.

"I honestly didn't think it was likely you'd receive enough

magic from Marcus during your bonding bites for it to really make a difference," Damien said, holding his hands up like he was pleading his case, hoping not to get the shit beat out of him. "Really. They were untested hypotheses. More fanciful ideas than anything else."

Rolling his eyes, Robson hopped down from the exam table. "Any other side effects I should know about?" He shot Doc a worried look. "Am I going to start flashing my eyes when I get mad or... anything?"

Or grow a knot suddenly.

Doc smirked and crossed his arms over his huge chest, rolling his stool back and forth a little like he knew exactly what Robson *wasn't* asking. "Your bloodwork came back fine. I doubt you'll have any physiological changes beyond the advanced healing, and that might fade over time."

Relieved, he nodded in thanks and headed for the door, shooting Damien an annoyed look. It wasn't that he was mad about being able to heal faster than before—he just didn't get why the young guy was so damn close-lipped about so many things.

"I'm sorry," Damien whispered, dropping his eyes to the floor.

Sighing, he rubbed at his face, then hesitated with the door partially open. "It's... Well, it's not fine, but whatever. I'm over it. Do you want to come to the farmhouse tonight for the fake housewarming party?"

Damien looked confused but nodded slowly. "I'd like that."

"Cool." He shot a look at Doc. "You too, Bell."

Doc gave him a sarcastic salute, so Robson laughed and flipped him the bird before heading out of the clinic. Robson had joked about having a housewarming for Marcus—who his mom had seriously moved in against his mate's lackluster protests—and his sisters and mom had latched onto the idea.

Teo had just laughed and wandered outside to gaze adoringly at his cows or whatever.

He'd refused to let them plan a huge thing or spend days cooking, but there would probably still be thirty to forty people coming in and out throughout the evening.

As instructed, Robson had handed in his notice to the sheriff, then explained that he'd be working for the pack in a sort of advisory and training capacity so the man understood why. He still wasn't sure it was a great idea to work so closely with Rick, but for the first time since moving home, he felt like he had a true purpose beyond his family or Marcus.

This would be his way of giving back to the pack that had become like a family to him.

Well, some of them. There were hundreds of members he'd never even met, but that would change. One of the things he planned on undertaking—with Rick's okay—was assessing all the pack members who could potentially be called to fight in any coming battles. Then he'd have to train them.

One thing he was a little worried to bring up to Rick, though, was utilizing the hunter Gabriel. Robson had heard about him from Marcus and the others, even seen him creeping around the manor a couple of times, but hadn't thought much about him until he'd seen him the other day during their run through the woods. They'd apparently come close to where the hunter was living, and he'd been outside training with a wooden dummy right at the edge of the woods. Robson had been seriously impressed with the man's speed and skill and thought he could be very valuable to the pack... if certain shifters could get their heads out of their asses about him not having a scent.

Robson's life was seriously weird now.

Driving past *Wicca We Can* on his way through town, he grinned, remembering the conversation he'd had with Tashmica while the others had packed up Marcus's things. He'd been under strict orders from his mom, mate, and sisters to not lift anything, but he hadn't been bored. Tash had popped in and sat down at the kitchen table with him and said she'd heard he had questions about magic. After talking for hours, he still didn't get the whole magic and witches thing, but he didn't feel apprehensive about her or the rest of the coven being part of the pack or about Reesa popping into the shop.

Sailing out of town, he relaxed into his seat, stretching his healed arm out to the side and tensing the muscles. It was insane that his wound was healed already but also awesome. Plus, it would give Marcus a little peace of mind about Robson's breakable human body. His mate had been a little clingy the last couple of days, but Robson got it. He'd be the same way if Marcus were ever hurt, no matter how minor the injury.

When he pulled up to the farmhouse, the sun starting to sink lower in the sky, he couldn't help but shut off the old Camry and smile up at the lit-up windows. Warmth filled him knowing his mate and his family were inside, happy and safe and waiting for him.

A pale, smiling face topped with red hair peered out at him through the front door window. Stepping out of his car, he met his mate on the front porch and wrapped his arms around him.

"How were things while I was gone?" Marcus had been nervous about being alone in the house with Robson's family, and Robson had done his best to hide how hilarious he found that.

Sighing, Marcus pressed a kiss to his bite mark on Robson's neck, then stepped back. "It was fine, obviously. You don't have to be so smug about it."

"Would I do that?" He laughed as Marcus rolled his eyes

and turned back toward the house. "I invited Damien, by the way."

That caught Marcus's attention, causing him to swing back around. "So he was at the clinic? What did he say? Were you rude to him?"

If Robson wasn't one hundred percent confident in his mating, he would have been worried about how concerned Marcus was about the attractive young man. "Barely. He said that he didn't think I'd get enough magic from your bite for anything to happen, though apparently sped-up healing was one of the 'hypothetical' ideas he'd come up with of what *could* happen." He rolled his eyes, reaching around Marcus to open the door. "He seemed worried about me being pissed, but I think he was okay once I told him he could come to the house tonight."

They slipped inside but hurried upstairs to their room before anyone noticed Robson was back. He'd forgotten to have Doc rewrap his arm so his family wouldn't see his healed scar. Once they were in their room, Marcus snuck into the bathroom across the hall and grabbed the bandages. When he came back, Robson was sitting on the end of their bed, shirt off, arms braced behind him.

Marcus paused just inside, eyes running over Robson's chest and shoulders. "We should get back downstairs and help your mom."

"Okay," he said, smiling when Marcus didn't move other than to close the door behind him.

Their gazes held for a long, heated moment, Marcus biting his lip. Finally, he took a step forward, holding up the roll of bandages. "Should I?"

His mate was the cutest when he was trying to be serious but his erection was tenting his slacks. "Please. It's hard for me to do... certain things myself." He winked as he sat forward, delighting in the blush climbing into Marcus's cheeks.

He behaved himself as Marcus carefully wrapped his arm over the fresh scar, then tugged him between his legs, planting his hands on Marcus's slim hips. "Did you talk to Rick today? When are we going to Massachusetts?"

Marcus had made a half-hearted effort to say he'd go by himself to retrieve the charter Gregson had hidden after telling Robson about deciphering the code, but Robson had squashed that idea immediately. Even though they didn't know for sure that Councilman Kincaid was having them watched, it was a safe bet as far as Robson was concerned.

Scowling, Marcus set his hands on Robson's shoulders and leaned into him. "We aren't. Rick thinks it'll be too obvious if I go anywhere right now."

He grunted. "I hate to admit it, but he might be right. His evil father knows Wendy was bringing you something, so all eyes would be on you as soon as you stepped outside the territory."

"Fine, but guess who he wants to go instead."

Robson almost said Bennett. As the pack's second-in-command, he was the most logical choice, but that wouldn't explain Marcus's attitude about the whole thing.

Oh.

"Jamie?"

"Yes! Because he's from the same pack Mikel used to be alpha of, so it won't look suspicious if he visits his family back there."

While that made sense, Robson had questions. "Rick's sending his tiny little assistant—who looks like he couldn't throw a punch, let alone fight off possible attackers—all by himself on a dangerous mission to retrieve valuable intel?"

"Not by himself, no. Also, no shifter is completely helpless. You know that."

Robson scoffed, pulling Marcus even closer and wrapping his arms around his hips. He had to tip his head all the way back to see Marcus's face. "A shifter who manages a schedule for a living would be no match for whoever went after Wendy. She barely survived."

Shuddering, Marcus ran his fingers through Robson's hair. "You might have a point."

"Who's he sending with him?"

"Drake, I think." At Robson's surprised face, Marcus smiled. "He's got a lot of experience in diplomacy, which will be needed with the coastal birds. They can be *particular* about who comes into their territory. Even though he'll be with Jamie, since Jamie isn't technically a member of their pack anymore it could get dicey. Plus, Drake is smart and deadly. Don't let the missing limb fool you."

Robson rolled his eyes and pretended to gnaw on Marcus's side until he was giggling and struggling to get away. He knew Marcus wasn't really trying to get free since he could break Robson's hold in a second. "So sassy. Drake isn't the first amputee badass I've known, remember? Is Gabriel going too?"

Marcus froze, then gripped Robson's face and tipped his head back to see his eyes. "Why? What do you know?"

Laughing, he shrugged. "Nothing. I just… I don't see Gabriel being any more willing to let Jamie go off into danger than I was for you."

Eyes narrowing, Marcus looked off to the side, gaze becoming unfocused like he was trying to figure something out. Robson let him think for a few moments, then decided he might need to distract Marcus from coming to any disturbing conclusions about the three men. As far as Robson was concerned, the hunter had gotten lucky that most of the shifters he hung around depended so much on their enhanced senses that they didn't notice what was right in front of them sometimes.

Cupping the back of Marcus's thighs, Robson gave him a tug until he was settled on his lap, straddling him. "When do they leave?"

Marcus hummed, nuzzling into the side of Robson's face. "Probably pretty soon. They should be able to get in and out quickly and get back to the safety of our territory."

Uh-huh. Sure, because sensitive missions always went exactly to plan.

"Your mom sounds like she's getting annoyed with your sisters for being on their phones instead of helping her, and Teresa and Patrick just pulled up. We should probably go downstairs," Marcus said softly, making no move to pull away as he settled his head on Robson's shoulder, moist breath heating the skin of Robson's neck.

He held Marcus tightly, enjoying the moment and hoping for thousands more just like it in the future. And he knew he'd get them. Sure, things were tight in the house at the moment with some of Marcus's things getting stored in a unit in town, and they'd have to share their bathroom with Teo, but Robson was kind of looking forward to getting to know his younger siblings better and for Marcus to have the chance too. He couldn't wait for the holidays when Benito and Rafael would be home as well.

Sighing happily, he pressed a kiss to Marcus's cheek and eased him up. "Alright, let's go, cariño. We have to go save my mom before guests start arriving."

Marcus's soft smile lit up the room and Robson's chest. "Okay. Let's go."

Hours after he talked to Robson in their bedroom, the last of the pack had finally headed out and he, Robson, Teo, and Patrick were finishing cleaning the kitchen. Robson's mom, Annalisse, Valentina, and Teresa were all asleep—the first three in their beds, the last on the couch with little Maria next to her in some sort of portable sleeping thing.

Placing the last of the leftovers in the fridge, Marcus turned and scanned the rest of the room, but almost everything else was taken care of. Robson was drying the last of the dishes, laughing with Patrick over something Callie had done the last time Robson was at the manor. He walked over and kissed the back of Robson's neck, whispering in his ear that he was going to bed and not to keep his brother-in-law too late.

As he and Teo silently climbed the stairs together, he was surprised at how *normal* it felt to be surrounded by so many people. He'd been on his own for so long, he'd been worried he'd feel suffocated living with Robson's family. But it was the opposite.

The constant noise soothed a piece of him that had been aching for that sense of connection since he was a kid, shunned and ridiculed for his differences by his family and pack.

It was funny, Marcus realized as he waved good night to Teo and entered his bedroom, that he'd ended up mated to someone who would have fit in to his family's pack so much better than he ever had. Robson's dark hair and unflappable nature were exactly the kind of traits they'd valued. Whoever Marcus's red hair and freckles had come from, they'd sure as hell cursed him to an agonizing childhood.

Taking a deep breath, Marcus held it in his chest and closed his eyes, focusing on clearing his mind. Thinking about his old pack and family tended to suck him into a downward spiral he would struggle to extract himself from afterward.

His past might always be a part of him, but he was done giving his time and energy to thinking about it.

"You okay, cariño?" Robson asked as he stepped up behind Marcus, wrapping his arms around him.

He nodded and turned around, lightly kissing Robson's mouth as he rested his arms on his shoulders. "I'm more than okay. I've never had this before, you know. Not really."

Robson cocked his head and looked around them. "To share a room?"

Marcus chuckled and pressed even closer, letting his mate's heat and scent sink into him and soothe the last of his worries away. "Well, not that either. But I meant a family like this."

"I know," Robson whispered, eyes filling with sympathy. "They can be a lot sometimes, but I think you'll grow to love them."

Shaking his head fiercely, he quickly said, "I already do. How can I not? They've welcomed me into their home without a second thought and gone out of their way to be kind without making me feel out of place... They are the best gift you could have ever given me."

Robson snickered as his hands began to tug the edge of Marcus's shirt out of his pants, then slipped underneath and pressed into the skin of his back. "I can't decide if you're setting the bar for gifts incredibly low or high."

He tried to give his mate a stern look, but the light scratching Robson started doing to the skin on his low back was terribly distracting. "I'm being serious."

"I know," Robson whispered, leaning forward and pressing a kiss to his mouth. "You're welcome."

"I'll never be able to get you anything as nice in return," he said absently, a lot of his focus transferring to where

Robson was starting to dip his fingers into the back of Marcus's pants.

"Are you kidding me? You gave me a whole pack and a world of magic. I'd say we're square."

Nodding, Marcus gasped out, "Square," just as Robson slid a finger between his cheeks. Eyes fluttering shut, he arched his back just a little to give his mate better access.

Chuckling, Robson whispered into his ear, "No regrets so far?"

Marcus knew he meant not just moving in with Robson's family but mating with a human and all the things that had come with it. Robson didn't sound worried though; if anything, his mate was a little smug.

Marcus couldn't blame him. He tightened his arms around him. "Never. I love you, Robito."

Grinning, Robson ducked down and pressed a kiss to the crook of Marcus's neck, right over where he'd left his mark. Just like every other time he did it, it sent a shiver through Marcus. He prayed that would never change.

Lips brushing against the sensitive skin, Robson murmured, "I love you too, cariño."

He sighed happily. "Let's go to bed."

Robson raised his head and met his eyes, gaze more serious than it had been a moment before. "Lead the way. Wherever you go, I go."

Together. Forever.

Marcus could definitely live with that.

Interested in Marcus's cousin, Victor, and how he ended up working at the diner? You can now get his delicious novella on Amazon or FREE through my newsletter!

A NOTE FROM KIKI

Thank you. Thank you. Thank you.

Thank you for reading Marcus and Robson's book! If you enjoyed their story, please considering leaving a review to help other readers find them.

Wanna never miss a release or sale?
Follow me on BookBub or on Amazon!

To always make sure you know what I'm working on, have the opportunity to read early copies of my books, and get freebies, subscribe to my newsletter!

SNEAK PEEK!

THE HUNTER AND HIS MATES

As personal assistant to a powerful alpha of a large pack, there are certain rules Jamie has for himself to make sure he's successful at his job.

First, nothing and no one gets to the alpha without his say so.

Second, schedules will be enforced for everyone. At all costs.

Third, a certain Enforcer with an enticing scent and scarred face is *not* to be stared at, drooled over, and/or daydreamed about.

And fourth, human hunters are never, *ever* mate material —no matter what their smiles or Southern drawls do to him.

But what if his own rules are preventing Jamie from finding something unique and magical and hotter than he could ever imagine? Because being caught between a grumpy cougar and a dangerous hunter was the last place Jamie thought he should be... but it might just be exactly where he needs to be to find *both* of his fated mates.

The Hunter and His Mates is the fourth book in the bestselling Kincaid Pack series, which is most enjoyable when read in order.

This installment is an MMM romance featuring a scentless human trying to make a home in a pack of shifters, an Enforcer with mild PTSD and a possessive streak a mile wide, and the sweet little hawk who adores them both.

Available on eBook, Paperback, Audio, & KU!

READ AN EXCERPT FROM *THE HUNTER AND HIS MATES* BELOW!

His little bird worked way too much.

Tracking him down at the manor had been a risk, but one he hoped would pan out in securing him a date with the gorgeous creature who haunted his days and nights. The way Jamie had called him out on his silly pickup line had made his fucking dick hard. As sweet and innocent as he came off, there was some real spunk hiding under the surface, and Gabriel couldn't wait to find out what else Jamie was keeping tucked out of sight.

When he heard the front door close, he turned and faced the opposite direction, leaning his shoulders against the wall and crossing his arms. "It's rude to eavesdrop, cat."

The back of his neck had started tingling as soon as he'd stepped out of the room decorated in varying shades of blue, an indication that he was being watched by a predator. After living all of his three and a half decades as a human among shifters, he'd developed the sixth sense out of survival.

Though he was only guessing at who it was spying on him and Jamie from a darkened doorway.

Sure enough, the grumpy cougar stepped from out of the shadows, his fist clenched in clear annoyance.

Gabriel's blood heated at the sight of his other obsession

since New Mexico: Drake Hayes. Pack Enforcer, former emissary, and one ornery SOB.

He was also disturbingly sexy with his stubbled cheeks, intense eyes, and well-muscled body.

Scars or not, Gabriel was always grateful for the spell that concealed his scent when the cougar was nearby, knowing he'd lose a testicle if the man ever found out.

"What are you doing here, hunter?" Drake asked, a low growl clear in his voice.

"What you're too chickenshit to do," Gabriel said with a smug smile, pushing off the wall but not invading the other man's space. He wasn't completely insane.

Drake hissed at him. "Watch yourself. You may have proven useful to the pack in the past, but one wrong move and I'll personally see to your banishment."

While he didn't doubt Drake would do his damnedest to make sure that happened whether Gabriel stepped out of line or not, he and Rick Kincaid had an understanding. It would take *a lot* for Rick to go back on his word, Gabriel was sure of that, and he was also sure he wouldn't ever come anywhere near breaking his end of the bargain.

Smiling widely just to annoy Drake further, he took one more step forward. "Is that what you're doing out in the woods behind my house every morning? Waiting for me to… make a move?"

Drake reared back at the suggestive tone, his brows furrowing in confusion. Shaking it off, he snarled, "Someone needs to keep an eye on you."

Biting his lip, he whispered loudly, "Oh, kitty cat, you can keep two on me."

The loud snarl and flash of Drake's eyes should have sent Gabriel on his way like a boot to the ass.

So why were his balls tingling like Drake had just whispered something dirty in his ear?

"You should stay away from him," Drake said, and Gabriel grinned.

"Who? Rick? As a member of the pack, I have every right to visit my al—"

A hard shove had his back against the wall again, two hundred pounds of pissed-off cougar all up in his face. "You know that's not who I meant."

Baring his teeth in return, Gabriel didn't fight the hand fisted in his shirt, holding him in place, but he did meet his gaze, refusing to submit. Even though, as an Enforcer, Gabriel technically should have, there was no way he'd bare his neck in that moment. "Yeah, I do. But as long as no one else has the balls to go after the sweet little bird, I don't give a shit what you think."

"You can't give him what he needs," Drake spit out, fangs lengthening.

"Wanna bet?" Gabriel drawled as he reached down and rearranged his half-hard dick in an obscene way. "I'll keep him so satisfied, you'll never see him walk straight ag—"

There was an ear-splitting roar right in his face and a flash of teeth. The self-preservation part of his brain was ringing the alarm, urging him to duck and cover, but he'd always been a little too quick to ignore those instincts.

Pounding footsteps were drawing close as Drake snarled, "Stay away from him."

Just as the enormous second-in-command rounded the corner, Gabriel raised his chin and said an inch from Drake's razor-sharp fangs, "Make me."

CONTINUE THE SERIES NOW TO FIND OUT WHAT HAPPENS NEXT!

Scan the QR code with your phone to go straight to Amazon

ALSO BY KIKI CLARK

Kincaid Pack Series

A New Pack for New Year

The Alpha and His King (Rick & Kai)

The Second and His Bonded (Kieran & Bennett)

The Deputy and His Enforcer (Robson & Marcus)

The Hunter and His Mates (Drake, Jamie, & Gabriel)

The Enforcer and His Heart (Nico & Keegan)

The Witch and His Doctor (Carter & Damien)

Kincaid Pack Coloring Book

Kincaid Pack Universe

The Mobster's Mate (Quinten & Caden)

Silver Oak Pack Series
(a Kincaid Pack Series Spin-Off)

Tempest (Cash & Ore)

Trident Agency (co-written with E.M. Lindsey)

Sunshine

Priest

Blue Collar Hearts Series
Out In the Cold (Beau & Coop)
Laying Pipe (John & Lukas)
Banger (Hank & Kevin)

Leather & Chrome Series
Reckless (Tank & CJ)
Temptation (Six & Ollie)
Yearning (Houston & Kenneth)
Joyful (Rooster & Emmett)
Possession (Tomas, Mason, & Vinnie)

Forever Family Trilogy
Favor (Declan & Jeremy)
Easy (Simon & Jackson)
Faker (Samuel & Will)
Collected Works—*Best Deal!*

Most of my books are also available in audio! Be sure to check out
my website or Audible.com.

ABOUT THE AUTHOR

A small-town Michigan girl, Kiki has enjoyed reading since she first picked up a YA fantasy as a child. After that, she devoured everything she could get her hands on and dreamed of one day writing her own books that touched people's hearts.

In 2020, she proudly joined the ranks of authors releasing character-driven, emotionally satisfying books showcasing that everyone deserves to find love.

To keep up-to-date with Kiki, sign up for her newsletter: http://www.kikiclark.com/newsletter.

Keep in touch by following her on any of these platforms:

facebook.com/kikiclarkauthor
instagram.com/kikiclark2017
bookbub.com/authors/kiki-clark
goodreads.com/kikiclark
amazon.com/author/kikiclark